A NOVEL

A. MEREDITH WALTERS

Copyright ©2012 by A. Meredith Walters

Cover design © 2013 Sarah Hansen, Okay Creations

Editing services by Tanya Keetch/The Word Maid

Paperback formatting by E.M. Tippetts Book Designs

ISBN-10: 1490412727

ISBN-13: 978-1490412726

For my girlfriends:
Because you weren't a bunch of b**ches!

CHAPTER
1

"**D**amn it!" I yelled after opening the very business- like white envelope that now lay in a crumpled heap on my apartment floor. My roommate, Riley, poked her head in from the hallway, her brown hair rumpled from her two hour nap.

"Everything alright, Mays?" Riley asked, frowning. I rubbed my hand over my face, pushing my bangs back from my forehead in an agonized gesture.

"Yeah, everything is just peachy. Except that I'm now going to have to get a second job," I bit out sarcastically. Throwing the piece of paper onto the coffee table and leaning backwards on the horribly ugly yellow and green couch that came cheap, courtesy of the local good will.

Riley Walker, my best friend since our freshman year at Rinard College in Bakersville, Virginia and recently acquired roomie, picked up the discarded letter and read it quickly. Her eyebrows shot up and she looked at me in shock.

"3500 dollars! Maysie Ardin, are you freaking crazy? Did you take a trip to Vegas without me knowing?" My answering scowl was the only reply given. Okay, so I had been a little excessive in the shopping area. But I had really thought the new clothes and that adorable Vitamin A bikini had been essential for my weekend trip to Virginia Beach with two of my sorority sisters.

I just hadn't realized how trigger-happy my swiping hand

had become. But the monthly credit card statement screamed at me that I had been way too lax on the whole self- control thing during the last thirty days.

My Visa was supposed to be used "in emergencies only." My parents had given me a 5,000 dollar limit, stressing that I was NEVER to even think about using it, unless I was broken down on the side of a deserted highway with a serial killer hot on my heels.

Not even I could explain how I justified my Manolo Blahnik heeled sandals as an emergency. But damn, they had looked amazing with my fitted red sundress. Too bad I had broken the heel the same night I wore them for the first time. I cringed inwardly at the memory.

The parentals had received last month's bill and had forwarded it to me with a very nasty letter attached. They were not happy. Not that they were ever happy with anything that I did. But this time they were thermal nuclear. They expected *me* to pay for it. And every month after that until I could prove fiscal responsibility.

The obnoxious thing was that for once, I understood why my parents were pissed at me. And I could see how making me pay the bill was reasonable. And that just irritated me even more.

It was probably because this kind of spending wasn't the norm. Yeah, I love designer shoes and handbags as much as the next twenty year old, soon to be college junior. But I had spinelessly allowed myself to be talked into one too many shopping trips with my new sisters at the Chi Delta sorority. And those girls didn't spend lightly. I hadn't been making the best choices lately; that had become very apparent.

I groaned. "No, if I had been to Vegas, I wouldn't feel like such shit." I lifted my foot to admire another pair of my insanely expensive pieces of footwear. Which I hated to admit didn't look as amazing as they had the first time I had put them on my feet. In truth, I now felt like a Grade A moron.

Riley rolled her eyes. "You did not buy yourself those obnoxiously overpriced shoes did you? I mean really, Mays... they're probably made by tiny little child laborers in the South

Pacific somewhere. You could feed a family of four for a month with how much those things cost. You have caved to the man, my friend." I threw a pillow at Riley, who caught it and tossed it back. I was used to Riley's never ending rants about the evil caste/Greek system at our school and how disappointed she was that I had been lured into their succubus-like hold. I would never admit to her how much her biting criticism hurt my feelings. So instead I tried to blow it off.

"I know, alright. Enough with the soapbox rant. I just have to figure out how the hell I'm going to make enough money to pay this off and still have some sort of a life this summer." I tugged my dark hair out of its ponytail and got to my feet.

Everything would make sense after a shower. "Can't you get more hours at Bibi's?" Riley suggested, following me into the kitchen. I shook my head as I opened the refrigerator looking for my bottle of Fanta.

"Shit Ri! Did you drink all of my Fanta again?" I asked; feeling irrationally pissed about the fact that my best friend continued to eat and drink my stuff, even though she had her own food in the cabinet.

Riley shrugged, not letting me change the subject.

"So, you gonna ask your manager for more hours? That seems the most logical thing to do," Riley suggested, reaching around me to grab the bag of grapes on the top shelf.

I took one of Riley's sodas and popped the tab, daring her to remark about it. Riley wisely stayed quiet. "I've maxed my hours there already to pay for my fall sorority dues. There's no way Layne will give me anymore and let me stay part time. And I can't go full time and juggle my summer school classes. The shop is only open until six."

I loved my job at Bibi's, a vintage clothing boutique in downtown Bakersville. My boss, Layne, who was also a part owner, was easy to work for. But there was no way I could pinch any more time there without bailing on my classes. And I needed to take those classes and do well.

I had stupidly gotten D's in biology and statistics last spring during rush and I was in danger of losing my scholarship. My parents were threatening to yank me out of school all together and make me attend the local community college back home in Morganstown, South Carolina.

And that was something I would avoid at all costs. Aside from the mortification of having to move back home, I'd be forced to share a space with my conservative, always disapproving parents. And that was a fate worse than death.

So I sucked it up and decided to retake the classes over the summer. I was trying desperately to prove to my parents that I could handle my independence. That they weren't wasting their money on a college education and that I wasn't going to flush my opportunities down the proverbial toilet.

Even if what I really wanted to do was spend my days hanging out by the pool and making out with Eli Bray, my new townie hook-up, who kissed so well it made my toes curl.

No, I would try and do the right thing. The grown up thing. The mind numbingly boring thing.

So, getting another job was the only course of action. "I need to find something that will let me work evenings, after class and that won't interfere with my job at Bibi's," I explained, tossing the empty can into the recycling bin.

Riley propped herself up on the stool at the tiny island in the middle of the kitchen. She folded her long legs awkwardly underneath her and looked thoughtful. I tapped my foot impatiently. I loved Riley. We had become fast friends during freshman orientation two years ago. Riley was the out-spoken and passionate hippie who had lived three doors down from me in our all girl dormitory. Even as I made new friends and we began to move in different social circles, we always stayed loyal to each other.

I couldn't be as relaxed with anyone else the way I could be with Riley. We just got each other. Even finishing each other's sentences at times. We clicked. But it didn't change the fact that there were definite things about my friend that annoyed the crap out of me. One being how calm and unconcerned Riley could be when I was seconds away from freaking out.

"So, any ideas?" I finally asked impatiently. Riley tapped her finger over her mouth.

4

"Well, I was going to head down to Barton's in a bit to put in an application. They're hiring wait staff for their evening rush. Might be an idea for you to come with me. Put in an application for yourself. It's a bar, so you could work evening shifts and it wouldn't mess with your classes and shifts at Bibi's," Riley offered.

I smiled and reached over to hug her. "Riley, you're a God send. That's a perfect idea."

Riley pulled back, always somewhat uncomfortable with any kind of physical affection. "Well, I'm about to hop in the shower and then we'll head down there."

I nodded and felt a little bit better about the impossible situation I had found myself in when I had opened my mail that morning.

My phone beeped in my pocket. I pulled it out and saw I had a missed call from Eli. I grabbed my pack of cigarettes from the counter and went out the sliding doors onto the small balcony.

I loved the tiny apartment that I shared with Riley. I had hated living in the dorms, with the paper-thin walls and communal showers. So, when Riley suggested we look for a place to live together for our last two years of school, I had jumped at the chance. I was also happy to be able to tell my parents that it was cheaper to live off campus than to pay the room and board through the school.

My academic scholarship only covered tuition and books, leaving my already cash strapped folks to cough up the rest. I pitched in by getting a job to cover food and other living expenses. I had felt really good with how mature I was being, well until the credit card statement made me realize my maturity still had a long way to go.

I sat down in one of the two white lawn chairs that Riley had gotten and tapped out a cigarette. I lit it and took a drag, feeling my nerves a little less jangly with every puff. It was a nasty habit and I had every intention of quitting. Just not right now.

I put the phone to my ear and listened to it ring. "Hey baby," Eli's slow drawl came through on the other end. I couldn't help but grin and exhale a lung full of smoke.

"Hey, sorry I missed your call. What's up?" I could hear Eli lighting his own cigarette, or maybe something else, on the other end and take a long inhale.

"Nothin'. Just wanted to see what you had going on today. I was thinking of going to Randall's to hang for a bit, you wanna meet me over there?" I stubbed out my smoke and stretched out my legs. I had only been dating Eli for a few weeks. It wasn't anything serious. Eli's cousin Randall lived down the hall and that's how we had met.

Riley and I had been coming in from getting breakfast and I had seen this guy lugging a guitar case up the stairs and into the hallway. He had a nice, easy smile and hooded blue eyes. I was instantly entranced.

Later that same day, as I was leaving for work, I had come out into the hallway to find the same guy playing on that same guitar on the steps leading outside. He had been playing the melody from *Under the Bridge* by Red Hot Chili Peppers and I couldn't help myself from stopping to listen. He wasn't that great or anything, mediocre at best. But I used it as an excuse to stop and sit down beside him.

He was good looking, in that slacker, grungy kind of way, with messy blond hair that always hung in his face and bedroom eyes. I had ended up calling in sick to work in favor of hanging out listening to this guy play his guitar. Afterward I sat with him in his cousin's apartment while he smoked a joint and talked about the fate of modern music ad nauseum.

I found out the guitar guy, Eli Bray, lived in town and worked at a local garage. He had no plans to go to college and barely made it through high school. He smoked pot like crazy and did little more than hang out with his cousin Randall and his cousin's girlfriend, Cicely and play his guitar.

When I really thought about it, I was slightly mortified to be attracted to someone like that. I was the complete opposite of Eli in every possible way. But considering my recent descent into slackerdom, perhaps that explained the inexplicable attraction.

Riley hated him and made that clear on the few times I had invited Eli over. Riley had barely spoken to him and often opted to pretend he wasn't there at all. So I started waiting for my roommate to leave before asking Eli to come over, which annoyed me because it felt too reminiscent of living at home with my folks again.

Despite the fact that Eli was motivationally challenged, he was pretty fun to hang out with. And shit, to be totally honest, he turned me on like crazy. We hadn't slept together yet, but there were plenty of other lust-fueled activities to spend our time on. And truthfully, that was the sole basis for the relationship.

So when Eli suggested that I hang with him at Randall's, I had a hard time resisting the offer. Considering I knew we would put in an obligatory show for about twenty minutes before Eli would drag me into the spare bedroom. It made my toes tingle to think of spending an afternoon like that.

But I had other priorities just then. Ones that unfortunately, didn't involve hot guitar boy's tongue.

"Can't, I have to go find a second job. Had the heart attack surprise of an overly inflated credit card bill this month." I picked up my pack of cigarettes and headed inside.

The beautiful thing about Eli is that he didn't immediately chastise me like Riley had. He didn't question what I had spent the money on. It could have been he was being respectful, or more likely, he just didn't care. He simply took my word that I had other plans and didn't push me for more. But on the other hand, it made me feel like he really could have cared less about what was going on in my life. Which is the very reason I could never contemplate taking this *thing* we had going on to any sort of other level. Eli Bray and boyfriend didn't belong in the same sentence. And for now, I could live with that.

"Okay, babe. Well, I'll be at Randall's this afternoon. Come by if you can. I'll catch up with you later." No assurance of when I'd hear from him again, just a vague 'see ya.'

Before I could reply, the line went dead. Okay then. Riley emerged from the bathroom, a waft of steam following her into the hallway. "You didn't use up all the hot water again, did you?" I complained, grabbing my robe from the back of my bedroom door.

Riley shrugged. "Should be a bit left, no promises." I groaned and closed the door to the bathroom.

I took out the tweezers and spent a few minutes plucking the crazy bushes I called eyebrows into some semblance of shape. I pulled the skin at the corner of my eyes and stuck out my tongue. I was pretty, even I could admit that. With dark brown hair that stopped just below my shoulders and even darker eyes. I was slender without being skinny and was pleased with the way I had curves in all the right places. Despite my attractive appearance, I had gone largely unnoticed in high school when it came to the opposite sex. So it had been quite a shock when I came to Rinard College and discovered that guys actually liked me. Desired me even.

As a result of this new self-realization, I discovered that I liked to date, and date often. I had had a string of sort of serious boyfriends on and off since I was a freshman. None of them lasted longer than a month or two. Now that I was entering my junior year, I had every intention of continuing on my semi-monogamous path.

I was by no means a delusional romantic. I was 100% into every guy that I dated, but I had never experienced real "love." Sure, I had lost my virginity mid-way through my first year of college to a guy I swore was the cutest boy I had ever seen. But two months later, I found myself being dumped for a hot sophomore with double D breasts in his biology class. Sure it had hurt, but I got over it. I always did. That's how I knew the love bug hadn't bit me yet. Maybe I was a bit behind the curve in that department. I thought about Eli and almost laughed at the thought of him being my "one."

No way in hell.

I rushed through my shower, finding that the water turned frigid after about four minutes. Damn Riley! I hurriedly got ready, forgoing blow-drying my hair in favor of a quick and sloppy bun at the back of my head.

I threw on a knee length black cotton skirt and teal tank top. Dabbing a bit of lip-gloss on and I was ready to go. Grabbing my brown leather handbag, I followed Riley out of the apartment.

We ran into Eli's cousin Randall as we were making our way to Riley's beat up Volvo. He was lugging a huge guitar amp out of his trunk.

"Hey, Maysie. You comin' by later?" Randall asked in that stoner way of his. His eyes were bloodshot and a little unfocused, making it obvious a wake and bake had been part of his morning routine.

Riley rolled her eyes and got into her car without greeting our neighbor. I smiled politely and shook my head. "Can't. Have to find another mode of gainful employment. But I'll try and stop by this evening. Will you guys be around?" I asked, glaring at Riley as she gave the car horn a quick toot.

Randall started rolling the amp toward the apartment building. "We're heading out to the lake for a party tonight, should be killer. Swing by if you want." I tried not to growl in frustration. Eli hadn't mentioned anything about a party. Reinforcing that a serious relationship is not what we had.

I plastered a fake smile on my face. "Yeah, maybe. See ya around." And with that I got in the car. Riley gave me a look as she pulled out of the parking lot. "What?" I asked defensively. Riley pulled a face.

"Why do you insist on hanging out with those losers? They look diseased." I groaned.

"Jeesh, judge much? They're nice, all right? And have you looked at Eli lately?" I muttered, picturing his cut abs as I turned on the radio. Riley just shook her head as she pulled out into traffic, heading toward downtown Bakersville, where Barton's Bar and Grill was located.

"You can do so much better than that mouth breather. It's bordering on gross," Riley quipped, turning the radio station from the pop I had chosen, to a band that sounded more like screaming than actual music.

"Look, can we not talk about Eli? I know how you feel about him, but the last time I checked, it was my life," I said with irritation. God, I loved her Riley, I really did. But her moral superiority was a little hard to swallow at times.

Thankfully we pulled up to Barton's and further discussion

about the matter was essentially brought to an end. I got out of the car and looked up at the building. Barton's was a favorite with the Rinard crowd. I had spent many a night procuring underage booze and getting wasted within its four walls. The establishment was more liberal than most bars in their carding system, so it was very popular with the younger college set.

Riley and I pushed open the door and walked inside. The smell of stale beer hit me in the face as we made our way inside. During the day, Barton's was a run of the mill restaurant but it couldn't hide its seedier watering hole side.

We approached the hostess stand and waited. "Maysie! Riley! What the hell are you doing here?" a girl squealed from behind us. I turned around to see my friend Jaz Digby, decked out in her official Barton's polo shirt and short black skirt.

I had completely forgotten that Jaz was a part-time waitress here. Jaz had lived on the same floor as Riley and me freshman year and I had remained friends with her despite not having hung out socially in a long time. Riley thought she was obnoxious. Though, the truth was Riley found most people to be obnoxious, so her feelings about Jaz weren't surprising.

Jaz was beautiful in an exotic way. Her mom was Japanese and her dad, American so she inherited the best parts of both heritages. "Hey, girl! We're here to fill out applications," I said, giving her a quick hug. Jaz beamed at me.

"That's awesome! We've been shorthanded for weeks! I'll go get Moore," Jaz said, going toward the back of the restaurant. Riley sat down on the bench by the front door and I followed suit, crossing my legs and bouncing my foot.

Jaz came back out a few minutes later and sat down beside us. "Moore will be out in a minute. It would so cool if you guys worked here. The tips are fantastic."

"That's what I need to hear," I said, smiling with the promise of fiscal relief.

"I thought you were working at that shop in town," Jaz commented, turning to me. I shrugged.

"Needed a heavier cash flow, so a second job it is." Riley snorted beside me and I ignored it.

"Well, whatever, I hope you get the job. I'll put in a good word for you," Jaz promised, squeezing my hand. Jaz suddenly started straightening her shirt, pulling the neck down so that her cleavage was more pronounced. She discreetly smoothed her straight black hair and rubbed her finger across her teeth.

I looked at her in confusion. What was with all the preening? Then a deep voice caught my attention. It was one of those voices that you imagine hearing in a darkened bedroom. After naughty sex. The kind of voice that was a combination of the most decadent chocolate and outright sin. "Are you the ones wanting applications?" I looked up and swallowed. Damn, who the hell was this?

A guy stood there, holding out two sheets of paper. I sat there, staring like an idiot. Because sweet lord was he cute. No, cute didn't even begin to cover what he was. The guy standing in front of us had short-cropped dark hair and beautiful blue eyes. He had a tiny dimple in his chin and his nose was slightly crooked, like it had been broken it before. He was tall and lean, but I could see the muscles of his arms beneath the fitted Barton's T-shirt. He sported an eyebrow ring and I caught the glimpse of metal in his tongue when he spoke. I could also see the upper edges of a tattoo along the side of his neck. Holy bad boy Batman! He oozed sex appeal. And from his arrogant stance, he knew it.

Jaz jumped to her feet and gave the boy a hug. "Jordan! I didn't know you had gotten back?" she squealed. I looked at Riley who only rolled her eyes. Jordan hugged Jaz back before disengaging himself from her clingy arms.

"Yeah, just walked in two seconds ago. Moore is still on the phone, so he asked me to bring out the applications." Jordan looked at me and my stomach flipped over. I opened my mouth but no words came out. God, I must look like an idiot. But I couldn't stop staring at him. The longer I looked at him, the more I realized there was something familiar about him. I just couldn't quite place what.

Jaz plastered herself to his side, making a point to press her ample breasts against his arm. Riley snickered and I was finally able to break the intense staring contest we seemed to be engaging in.

"My friends here want to apply for the wait staff positions. Jordan, this is Maysie Ardin and Riley Walker. Guys, this is Jordan Levitt."

"Charmed." Riley deadpanned before taking the paper from his hand. Jordan smirked then handed the other one to me.

"Here ya go, Maysie," he said, his eyes twinkling; as though he knew how much it turned me on to hear him say my name.

I cleared my throat a few times before answering with a shaky, "thanks."

He looked at me a few more seconds and I felt my cheeks start to flush. I always seemed to blush at the most inopportune moments. My face was hot and I knew I had turned a bright red.

"Jordan! Are you going to start tending bar tonight?" Jaz asked and I suddenly found my friend's voice grating. I finally understood why Riley found her so annoying. Jordan stopped looking at me and turned to Jaz.

"Yeah, Moore put me on the schedule from seven until close. I'm pretty stoked." Jaz squealed again. I had to suppress my eye roll, which took significant effort.

Jaz turned to Riley and me as we started filling out the applications. "Jordan just got bumped up to bartender. He's going to be great!" she gushed, pressing herself close to him again.

"Jeesh, is she going to start dry humping him next?" Riley whispered under her breath, shooting a look in their direction. I laughed quietly.

"It's starting to feel like a low budget porno in here. Just cue the cheesy 70's background music. Bow chick-a-wow-wow," I whispered back, trying to discreetly watch the pair as they talked.

Okay, Jordan was hot. Like, ridiculously hot. He had a delicious edge about him that was hard to ignore. He was this weird mixture of tatted up bad boy and gorgeous guy next door. But I felt embarrassed for Jaz, watching the other girl as she flirted shamelessly. No guy was worth shredding your self-respect like that. Even if he did have an amazing smile and the most kissable lips I had ever seen. And I couldn't stop myself from fantasizing about running my tongue over his eyebrow ring.

"Bartender, huh? I bet you'll make some serious scratch," I

commented, handing my completed application back to him. He tossed his perfect smile in my direction and I felt my panties getting wet. Dear lord, the flash of his gleaming white teeth was like a hot button to my nether regions. Down vagina! Down, girl.

Jordan scanned my application for a minute. I frowned, not knowing why he was looking at it. Wasn't that stuff confidential or something? "You live over on Ox Hill Drive?" he asked, glancing up at me again.

Riley shoved her application at him. "Yeah, we do. So when will we hear whether we got the job or not?" she asked, cutting him off. I had to chuckle as Jordan blinked at Riley in surprise. He seemed taken aback by her hostility. He just didn't know that Riley's hostility was her way of saying howdy.

"Um, well, let me take these back to Moore. Don't go anywhere." He shot me another quick smile before disappearing into the back of the restaurant.

Jaz sighed heavily and dropped back down onto the bench. "Fuck, what I wouldn't give to have him bend me over one of those tables and..." Riley coughed loudly, stopping her from finishing the thought.

Jaz fanned herself with a menu. I laughed. "Got it bad?' I asked, watching as the other girl pulled her shirt back into place, effectively covering her boobs again. Jaz closed her eyes dreamily.

"Who doesn't? Jordan Levitt is like a Rinard deity. Don't tell me you've never heard of him before?" Jaz looked at Riley and me like we had just touched down from outer space.

I shrugged. "Nope. Who is he?"

Jaz rolled her eyes. "Oh, he's only the hottest, most unattainable piece of ass on campus. He's a senior and lives over at the Pi-Sig house. He also plays in the band Generation Rejects. He's the most amazing drummer ever."

Ah. That must be where I knew him. He was a Pi Sig and I was a Chi Delta. We must have crossed paths at a mixer or something. Though, it still bothered me that I felt I should be able to place him.

"Yeah, I'm sure he's right up there with Keith Moon," Riley snarked. Jaz frowned at her.

"Have you ever heard them play?" Jaz shot at her. Riley looked at me, I shrugged again.

"Nope, can't say I've had that particular pleasure," Riley replied, crossing her arms over her chest. I recognized the signs of my best friend's ire rearing its ugly head.

"Well, listen to them sometime and then you can get all judgmental. They're freaking fantastic. If you guys work here, you'll see them. They play here every once in a while, though they usually play at the some of the other bars around town and the next town over. Which, I guess is why you've never heard of them, seeing as you don't do much outside of saving the planet, or whatever it is you do." Wow, Jaz was being really bitchy. Riley looked as though she wanted to pull the other girl's hair out.

I immediately intervened. "Well, that sounds cool. I look forward to hearing them sometime." I was saved from playing bouncer between my two friends by the arrival of Jordan and another guy who looked to be in his late thirties, with a receding hairline.

Mr. Baldy held our applications in his hands and gave us a genuine smile. "Hi, I'm Moore Pruitt, General Manager. Are you Maysie and Riley?" We both got to our feet and held out our hands to shake his.

"Yep, that's us," I responded, smiling pleasantly.

"You're hired," he said simply. My eyes widened in shock.

"That's it? You don't want to interview us or anything?" I asked, feeling confused. I looked at Riley, who seemed as taken aback as I was.

"Nope, we are seriously under staffed right now and I could use the people. Can you come in this evening for training?" he asked, going behind the hostess stand and pulling out two black polo shirts with the Barton name emblazoned on the front.

"Um, sure," I stuttered, taking the shirt. Riley took hers and nodded.

"What time do you want us here?" she asked.

Moore looked down at a clipboard in his hands. "Evian comes on at 5:00 and Damien is in at 5:30. What time are you done today, Jaz?" he asked.

"My shift is over at 4:00," Jaz said, giving her boss an apologetic smile.

"I can train them. My shift starts at 7:00, but I'll come in early. No worries," Jordan piped up from behind Moore. I looked at him and he gave me a toothy grin and then winked. Fucking hell, he had actually just winked at me.

I couldn't help but notice Jaz glower at me as she watched our exchange. Moore looked relieved with Jordan's suggestion. "That would be great Jordan. Girls, come in around 4:30 and Jordan will show you the ropes. I'd like to have you shadow tonight and then we can put you on the schedule for next week. Does that work for you?"

Riley and I nodded. "Don't we have paperwork to fill out?" Riley asked as she stuffed the shirt into her bag.

"Jordan will have you do all of that this evening. Welcome to the Barton family," Moore enthused, giving us a huge smile before smacking Jordan on the shoulder and heading back toward the kitchen.

"Well, I guess we should get going. See you this evening," I said, turning around to leave, clutching my new Barton's shirt in my hands.

"Bye girls. See ya later," Jaz called out, less friendly than she was before.

"See you this evening," Jordan called back and I had to suppress the urge to skip out of the restaurant.

CHAPTER 2

I straightened my form fitting black polo shirt and pulled down on my black short shorts. I felt a little exposed. I knew I looked good. The shorts were tiny and showed off my long legs, but I still felt a bit under-dressed. I had pulled my brown hair back in a high ponytail and toned down the makeup, opting for a more natural look. I figured I'd be covered in bar grease by the end of the night anyway, so what was the point?

Riley came out of her room, sporting her own version of the Barton attire. Her polo shirt was less tight, making me wonder if I was given the wrong size. Riley wore black trousers instead of shorts, but they were cute with a nice little flare at the bottom. Riley wasn't one to show of her...um...assets. But she still looked pretty.

"Ready?" Riley asked, picking up her messenger bag from the couch.

"As I'll ever be," I responded, locking our apartment door as we stepped outside. A commotion at the end of the hallway grabbed my attention as we walked toward the car lot.

Randall and his girlfriend Cicely were heading out of their apartment. Eli and two other girls were behind them. A redhead with too much make up and a shirt that barely covered her ginormous tits was hanging on Eli's arm and he was laughing as she whispered something in his ear.

I glared at him as we made our way toward the group. "Hey

17

guys," I said, staring at the guy who took off my underwear on a regular basis, as the skank ran her nails up Eli's arm. Riley groaned from beside me and continued out to the car.

Eli looked up and smiled lazily, not concerned that he appeared less than innocent with some bitch snaked up against him like that. But the truth was, he probably didn't care. "Hey, babe! You coming to the party with us?" The redhead gave me a once over and then leveled a glare my way as Eli came toward me. I knew I looked good. A hell of a lot better than that crabbed out hoe. Humpf!

"No, I'm heading into work. I got a job at Barton's," I told him, my breath catching as he wrapped his arms around my waist and pushed me against the wall. I heard Cicely snicker behind us as Eli's hand slithered up my bare thigh. See! This is why I kept the boy around! His fingers were something akin to the touch of God!

I couldn't help but tremble at the feel of his fingers playing with the hem of my shorts. "You look hot," Eli breathed, as his tongue tasted the side of my neck.

"You guys going to the party?" I asked a little breathlessly as he pressed himself against me. I could feel his hard on through his jeans and I had to wonder if that was for bimbo or me Barbie back there.

I also couldn't help but notice his group of friends was still standing in the hallway waiting for him. Um, embarrassing much? I knew Eli was already drunk. I could smell the Jack Daniels on his breath as he moved to nibble my ear.

"Yeah. We'll probably be down there all night. You sure you can't come? I'd like to see what you've got going on underneath here." Eli pulled at my collar, looking down my shirt. I smacked his arm and pushed him back.

Eli laughed and stepped away. "No can do, I've got to do the whole responsible thing." I hated how wobbly my voice sounded, but Eli brought out the bitch-in-heat side of me like nobody else. Eli smirked.

"Well, I'll miss you. I'll call you tomorrow," he said lazily.

I would have smiled at the fact that he actually said he'd miss me except that the fucking red head had a hold of his arm again and was pulling him out toward Randall's car. I put a hand to my flushed face. It was crazy how he could make me go from zero to sex starved in point two seconds.

"Um, okay. Have fun," I called out, but Eli didn't hear me, having already gotten in the back of the car, with slut one and slut two.

I got into Riley's car. "Don't say a word," I warned, shooting her a look.

Riley lifted her hands. "What? I wouldn't dream of telling you he's a douche bag. Considering that you actually allow him to stick that filthy tongue down your throat. And I definitely wouldn't tell you that he clearly has a standing appointment with gonorrhea. That would be just too mean. I just really hope you guys are safe, if you know what I mean."

I sighed and didn't comment. Riley was right of course. My run in with Eli left me with a sick taste in my mouth. Yeah, I wasn't so sure about our pseudo relationship anymore. As good looking as he was and as much as I loved the way his tongue made me wet, I thought more of myself than that.

Refusing to think too much about my floundering love life, I focused on the night ahead of me. I was excited to be working at Barton's. I was looking forward to the tips and the increase in cash. The number $3,500 kept flashing through my mind like a neon sign and I knew I had to get my shit sorted and fast.

I had talked to a couple of my sorority sisters and knew they were planning on coming in tonight to give their support. So, I was looking forward to my evening. And though I hated to admit it, I was looking forward to seeing Jordan again.

My stomach fluttered as I thought about his blue eyes and tongue ring. I had heard that tongue rings could feel amazing. You know, when they were doing things...ah, hell. I could admit I had fantasized about his tongue underneath my panties ever since I had laid eyes on him that afternoon.

What was wrong with me? I had just got hopelessly turned on by the guy I was sort of seeing and now I'm getting even more turned on thinking about my new co-worker! My hormones were seriously out of whack!

And damn if the blush didn't start. By the time we pulled up outside of Barton's and parked in the employee area around back, my cheeks were scarlet. Riley arched an eyebrow at her. "Why are you all red? You all right?" she asked.

I rubbed at my face. "I'm fine. Let's go inside," I replied airily, getting out the car. Barton's was pretty dead. It was only 4:30, so we had some time before the dinner rush hit and then the later drinking crowd. I followed Riley through to the kitchen toward the small manager's office. We poked our heads inside, seeing Moore sitting at a desk and Jordan in a chair, his feet propped up on the table in front of him.

Jordan looked up when we arrived and gave us a huge grin, his eyes immediately finding mine. Moore looked at us over his shoulder. "Hiya girls. Good to see you. Thanks for jumping in with both feet today. I hope you'll enjoy working here," the manager said, swinging his chair around to face us.

I couldn't help but smile at him. He seemed like a really nice guy. Moore grabbed a stack of papers on his desk and handed them to Riley and me. "You'll need to fill these out and then Jordan will start walking you through our computer system, how to punch in at the start of your shift, give you a tour...the whole shebang. Jordan has been here for three years, so he knows about as much as I do when it comes to how this place ticks."

I gripped the forms in my hand and felt suddenly stressed. I had never waited tables in my life. I imagined the worst-case scenarios. You know the ones where I drop someone's food in their laps or make an ass of myself by tripping with a tray loaded down with glasses.

What had I gotten myself into?

Jordan must have noticed my suddenly pale face because he got to his feet and slung an arm around my shoulders companionably. "Don't fret, my pet. You'll be golden. You've got me looking out for you." He smiled down at me and I noticed he was quite a bit taller than I was. But instead of making me feel better, I felt like I was going to barf.

"You'll have to excuse our girl, Maysie. Stress is her middle name," Riley commented, shooting me a smirk. I stuck my tongue out and wiggled out from underneath Jordan's arm, not feeling comfortable being that close to him. Especially since the smell of his aftershave was doing strange things to my insides.

"You'll be fine. And if you have any questions or concerns, don't hesitate to ask me. We're one big family here at Barton's," Moore said kindly.

Jordan chuckled. "Yeah, a big dysfunctional family," he added. Moore ignored his comment and shooed him out of his office, saying he needed to make some phone calls.

Jordan walked us out of the office and into the kitchen. There were two older guys scrubbing dishes and I could see a few other people out back smoking. "It's a good thing I never saw the kitchen when I ate here," Riley muttered under her breath, taking in the grease stained surfaces and wafts of cigarette smoke coming in from the open door.

I shot her a look but Jordan just laughed. "I swear it's all perfectly hygienic. No cockroaches or pissing in people's food. We're a civilized bunch here." One of the guys washing dishes looked over at them.

"Civilized, huh? Don't start speaking that fancy college talk. Otherwise, Pocco and I'll take you out back and kick some street into your ass," one of the guys called out.

The man grabbed Jordan's arm and put him in a headlock. Riley and I exchanged horrified looks as Jordan slugged his captor in the stomach, forcing him to release his hold. "Watch the hair, Fed. This takes hours," Jordan put his hands over his short hair. Fed (who the hell has a name like Fed?) swatted him with a grimy dishtowel.

"Fucking pansy," he mocked, though he said it with a smile.

"You're gonna chase them off before they even get started, man," Jordan joked, pulling me by the arm over to the two dishwashers. Pocco and Fed were easily in their forties and the looks they gave me and Riley was more than a little skeevie.

"Pocco and Fed, this is Maysie and Riley, the new waitresses." Pocco gave Riley the once over and actually licked his lips. Really? He licked his flipping lips! He was short and overweight with a goatee.

"Nice to meet you ladies. Welcome to Barton's," Pocco said, his voice tinged with an accent as his eyes roamed over our bodies.

"Um, thanks," I said, feeling uncomfortable.

Riley put her hand on her hip and stared both men down. "Maybe if you can stop eye fucking me for more than two seconds, I could say the same." My jaw dropped but the dishwashers barked out a laugh. Jordan gaped at Riley, then grinned.

Fed, the taller of the two with more hair, hit Jordan's arm. "This bitch's crazy. I like her. She'll fit in just fine."

I looked at Riley, who shrugged. The men were still howling with laughter as we moved on to tour the rest of the kitchen. Jordan leaned in close to me and whispered loud enough for both Riley and I to hear. "Those two are a sexual harassment lawsuit waiting to happen. But they're all talk. I don't think either of them has gotten laid since the original line up of Guns and Roses were together."

I tried not to sigh as I felt him lean against my arm. My skin tingled where he touched me and I gave myself a mental shake. I had enough romantic drama with Eli. I did not need to be lusting after this hot bartender.

Jordan led us around, introducing us to the rest of the kitchen staff. Rozzi was the head cook and Jordan let us know that he was going through a nasty divorce after his wife caught him screwing Lyla, the other bartender.

Cal and Tito, the two line cooks were, according to Jordan, an item, though they tried to keep their relationship on the down low. Jordan told me that he had caught them making out in the freezer after hours, a couple of times.

"You weren't kidding when you said this was a dysfunctional family. This is like Melrose Place," Riley said, after meeting Dina, another waitress who had a second job as a topless dancer the next town over at a club called Badlands.

"Yeah, these people are a little nuts. But they're cool. You'll see," Jordan assured as he led us to a table to fill out our tax forms and the other paperwork for Moore. "Riley you'll be shadowing Damien tonight. Mays, you'll be following Evian and just so you know, I want to offer my condolences in advance."

I almost crowed over the way he shortened my name. I couldn't help but smile brightly at him. "Oh, yeah? Is Evian that bad?" I asked. Jordan grimaced.

"Let's just say, the kitchen crew doesn't call her Evian the Terrible for nothing." Oh great. Just what I needed. To be trained by a sadistic dictator bitch.

"Do you guys want something to drink before I head over to the bar? I have to do inventory before my shift," Jordan said.

"I'll have a Coke," I answered, looking up at him through my lashes. I glanced at Riley, who was giving me *the look.* "What?" I mouthed to her. Riley shook her head and turned to Jordan.

"Yeah, I'll have a Coke too, thanks," she told him blandly.

"Two Cokes it is. Be right back." Jordan gave me a wink before heading over to the server station to fill up two glasses with soda. Riley smacked my in the arm.

"Stop it!" she hissed. I frowned and rubbed my arm.

"What are you talking about?" I whispered back.

Riley pointed at me, waggling her finger. "I know that look on your face! You're picturing him naked with *you naked.* Just stop it! Give your libido a rest, woman! Or did you forget about Eli? Wait, maybe I shouldn't be complaining about *that.* But seriously, you just met the guy!"

I rolled my eyes. "I'm not thinking about him in any way, Riley. Chill out. And even if I was, who cares?" I picked up a pen and started filling in the blanks on one of the forms.

"Because if you date him and it ends badly, it'll be weird and awkward working here and you'll end up quitting. Then you'll be back at square one. Haven't you ever heard you should never date someone you work with? I mean, that's common sense." Riley huffed out an exasperated breath. I shrugged, which I knew annoyed the crap out of her.

"I'm not going to date him. I doubt he even notices me. I mean, have you looked at him? I'm sure he has girls falling at his feet every time he blinks. Besides, he's got that bad boy, player thing written all over him. I have my hands full with one player already." I didn't mean it to sound as depressing as it did.

23

But what I had said was true. I knew Jordan's type. And I was attracted to them like bees to tasty, hormone soaked honey.

He was gorgeous, he played in a band, he was a freaking frat boy and he had the whole tattoo, piercing thing going on. I was very aware of what he was, without knowing any more than that. I knew I was as susceptible to those twisted charms as the next girl. But it didn't mean that I would necessarily do anything about it.

Riley gave me a look of disbelief. "Oh, he notices you all right. His eyes have been glued to your ass every time you turn around." At that moment, Jordan reappeared with two glasses of Coke. I almost choked and knew that I was turning an unhealthy shade of red. I desperately hoped he hadn't heard anything.

If he had, he played dumb. Jordan slipped into the booth across from us and leaned against the wall, putting his feet up. "So, you gals feel ready?" he asked, reaching across the table and snagging my Coke. He drank from the straw and handed it back to me with a smile.

I gave him a mocking glare and moved my drink out of his reach. "Yeah, we'll see. If I can make it through the night without dropping something or making an idiot of myself, then we can call it a success. Until then, the jury's still out," I commented, sucking on my straw. I couldn't help but feel gooey over the fact that my lips were touching the same piece of plastic that Jordan's had a few seconds before.

Hell, I was as bad as Jaz. Maybe worse.

Jordan clicked his tongue ring over his teeth. "Nah. You'll be fine. There's no way you could suck at anything you tried to do," he commented, looking at me intensely. I raised my eyebrow.

"How would you know that? You don't even know me." I remarked archly. Jordan rubbed the back of his neck and I could see the dark curves of his tattoo. I wondered what it was. Then I thought about taking his shirt off to get a better look.

Then I thought about taking his pants off and rubbing my tongue down his...

Christ, get your mind out of the gutter! I told myself harshly. "I can just tell. Call it a hunch," Jordan answered, pulling my thoughts away from the X-rated turn they had taken. Riley snorted and she elbowed my side discreetly under the table.

Jordan blinked, seeming a bit surprised by his forwardness and pulled his feet under the table, sitting up. "Well, sorry to leave you lovely ladies, but I have to get behind the bar and do my inventory. It's my first night on as a bartender. Can't give Moore a reason to fire my ass." He scooted out of the booth and stood at my elbow.

I looked up at him and gave him a small smile. "Well, thanks for training us," I said lamely. Why couldn't I ever think of something clever and witty to say? I hated to admit that Jordan made me tongue-tied. Since when do boys make me tongue-tied?

Jordan squeezed my shoulder and I swore his fingers lingered there. "If you need anything, come find me. You know where I'll be." His mouth quirked up in a grin as he jerked his thumb in the direction of the bar. My mouth quirked up as well as I grinned back.

"Yeah, you can't hide, I know where you work," I joked and wanted to slap myself in the forehead. I sounded like an idiot. Ugh!

Jordan just laughed and looked at Riley. "Same goes for you too, Riley," he added. Riley gave him a knowing look.

"Yeah, sure," she said, looking between the two of us. Jordan cleared his throat.

"Okay, well then. See ya later," he looked at me one last time and then headed off toward the bar.

"Good God, the sexual tension is giving me hives," Riley griped. I pulled on her ponytail.

"Will you just shut up already," I sighed, looking over at the bar. As though he could sense me staring at him, Jordan looked up from wiping down the counter. I quickly looked down at the paper in front of me, knowing that if people could die from embarrassment, someone had better start digging my grave.

CHAPTER
3

I tried to finish up the paper work but it was difficult considering I could feel eyes burning into my skin. But I was proud of myself that not once did I look up to watch him. Not once did I cave to the masochistic need to ogle his fine ass. Nope, I played non-nonchalant. Someone give me a friggin' Oscar, because that kind of acting deserves some sort of award.

"You Maysie?" a gruff voice barked from beside me. I looked up, startled. A petite girl, not much older than me stood beside the booth, hands on her hips, looking annoyed.

"Uh, yeah?" I said more as a question than a statement. Something about this girl's vibe completely intimidated me and I wasn't even sure of my name at that point.

"You need to follow me. I'm not gonna be slowed down because of you and if my tips suck, I will kick your ass. Do we understand each other?" Ah. This must be the delightful Evian. I looked at Riley who was biting down on her bottom lip to stop herself from laughing.

I gave her a look of death and slid out of the seat, following Evian the Terrible into the kitchen, where she clocked in. Evian clearly had a case of little man syndrome. She was tiny. Like seriously tiny. The top of her head came up to my chin and I wasn't an Amazon woman by any stretch. Her dark brown hair was styled in a pixie cut and her arms were covered in tattoos. All in all she was one badass mama. And not someone I wanted to piss off.

"Hey, Ev. Get over here and let me see those fine tits of yours!" Pocco called from the back. Evian whipped around and pointed her finger in his direction.

"You so much as look at my boobs, Pocco, and I will gnaw off your testicles and have them for dinner," she growled. I swallowed audibly. This chick was scary. Pocco only laughed.

"Ah, chica. You know you want to ride Pocco's bone coaster." Evian looked like she was about to go over there and carry through on her threat but was distracted by Moore calling to us from his office.

Thank God. I didn't want to see Evian gnawing anything off of anyone's body. I shuddered. Moore gave Evian the run down. I was to shadow her this evening. Evian was to let me watch for a while then let me handle a few tables on my own. We were to split the tips 50/50. Evian looked like she wanted to spit nails.

I gave Moore a weak smile and followed a thunderous Evian back out into the restaurant. She was mumbling under her breath and then came up short. Her tiny face was dark. "If you think I'm splitting my tips with you, you're fucking mental." Okay, well so much for any cash ending up in my pockets tonight. I knew better than to argue with Evian. I wanted to keep my appendages, thank you very much.

Evian stormed off and I leaned against the bar, already exhausted and the night had just begun. "Don't let her bully you." Jordan appeared at my shoulder and leaned in, his elbows propped on the counter. I tightened my ponytail and straightened my shirt.

"Easy for you to say. That chick is gonna eat me alive," I groaned, sitting on a stool and laying my head down on the bar.

Jordan rubbed my shoulder and I tried not to tremble as he touched me. I looked up at him and he gave me a smirk as though he knew the affect he had on me. He leaned in closer and dropped his voice to a whisper. "Well, just so you know. Evian has her boyfriend dress up in her bra and panties and likes to whip him with a riding crop."

My eyes widened. "You're making that up," I scoffed, shooting a look over my shoulder at Evian, who was hounding one of the high school bus boys about how to set the tables in her section. Jordan shook his head.

"No, trust me. Ev has a serious dominatrix side. Her boyfriend, Greg, is this uptight accountant. I think he's forty or something. But yeah, they're into some serious kink." Jordan chuckled.

I shook my head. "How the hell do you know all of this stuff?" I asked him. Jordan tapped his ear with his finger.

"I keep my ear to the ground, my friend. It's amazing what you can learn when no one thinks you're listening." I frowned at Jordan and got up from the stool, knowing I should go over to Evian before she tracked me down.

"Remind me to keep my deep dark secrets close to the chest then," I joked.

Jordan's eyes smoldered at me suddenly and I found it hard to breathe. "Ah, but Maysie, I want to know all of your deep, dark secrets. I look forward to figuring them out." His voice was husky and I couldn't tear my eyes away from him. Shit. He was going to be difficult to stay away from.

But who says I even wanted to? We had chemistry and he was fucking hot. I was a hot-blooded college girl, why shouldn't I indulge? So I shot him a saucy look before turning around to leave. "Well, you'll have to work for it then," I told him over my shoulder. I could hear him laughing as I walked away with a little extra sway in my hips and I knew he was watching me as I did.

Once the evening shift started, we were slammed. Barton's was hugely popular and there was a 45-minute wait by 5:30. I was running around like crazy. It was official; I was Evian's bitch. Sure she took the orders and greeted the tables. And it was more than a little fascinating to watch how seamlessly she transformed her militant persona into a people pleasing, syrupy sweet, good ol' gal. Once she had played up the people at her tables, I was expected to punch the orders in, expedite the plates and take them to the tables. I had to handle the drink refills and getting orders from the bar. And that nasty bitch-face kept all of the tips.

Riley on the other hand lucked out and was paired with Damien. He was a cute guy who was also a junior at Rinard. They seemed to hit it off and she had already earned a wad of cash. I tried not to hate on the fact that my feet hurt and I had nothing to show for it.

The noise in the place was deafening and I could barely hear myself think. My calves ached and I was getting a headache because I had forgotten to eat before the shift started. My mood was going straight to the toilet.

I hollered out a beer order to Jordan and Lyla, who were slinging drinks like they were in Cocktail or something. They had a crowd three people deep all the way around the bar. They knew how to work the room that was for sure. I watched them while I waited for my order. Lyla had turned up the volume on the speakers and was gyrating to a Bon Jovi song. The guys were hooting as she turned around to shake her ass.

I couldn't help but start to move myself. I loved to dance. Most weekends, I'd drag Riley or a few of my sorority sisters into the city to find a club. And I was pretty damn good at it, if I do say so myself. So, I started to move my hips in time with the pounding base.

"Damn, that's hot," Jordan called out, watching me. I flushed red and stopped dancing. Jordan came out from around the bar and put his hands on my hips. "No, don't stop," he whispered in my ear and started to move behind me.

There were a bunch of catcalls as I caved and started dancing with him in time to the music. My ass swirled back against his hips. We rubbed against each other and Jordan snaked his arms around my waist to hold me and pull me back against his chest. We swayed together, our bodies moving in a perfect rhythm. The hot press of his hands mixed with the musky sweet scent of his sweat was intoxicating. I felt his lips brush the bare skin at the back of my neck and we both trembled with a need that threatened to consume us. I could feel the hammering of his heart against my back, as I pressed even closer to him. I lost all sense of time and place and for a moment I forgot that we were in Barton's, and we were *supposed* to be working.

All I could feel, all I could think about was Jordan Levitt, with his arms around me, pressed against my back like he couldn't tear himself away. "What the hell are you doing?" My head whipped up at the sound of Evian's terse question. She looked murderous. I moved away from Jordan instantly.

Jordan cleared his throat. "Aw, give her a break, Ev. You've been running her ass off." I noticed his voice was ragged and I chanced a peek at him. He met my eyes and winked at me. I looked away, feeling suddenly embarrassed for dancing with him like that. In front of a room full of people. Shit, what had come over me? This was my work place! Not a damn club!

I was feeling flustered when Lyla brought the drinks to me that I had needed for one of Evian's tables. She gave me a knowing grin, looking between Jordan and me. I grabbed the order and practically ran from the bar. After delivering the drinks to the table, I went up to the hostess stand to grab a mint. And to catch my breath. Wow.

Riley came up beside me. "What was that? I think I got pregnant just watching you two," she snarked.

I laughed it off but was quietly mortified that everyone in the place had been witness to our lascivious spectacle. "Great, just the kind of first impression I wanted to make," I muttered. Riley snorted.

"Yeah, well, apparently that's Jordan. Damien says he's a notorious flirt. So I wouldn't worry about it too much," she commented, sending my stomach to the floor. Good to know that Jordan wasn't acting any differently toward me than he had with anyone else. Nothing like feeling like the next in a long line of girls with glazed over eyes, flirting with him to make this gal feel all warm and fuzzy.

"Yeah. I guess it was nothing," I agreed, going off to find Evian.

"Mays..." Riley called out but I waved her off. I didn't want her to see how much her words had bothered me.

I spent the next couple of hours staunchly ignoring Jordan. He tried to catch my eye a few times, but I would quickly look away. My pride was hurt and I felt like nursing my wounds secretly. Around 8:00 I finally had fifteen minutes to kill. So I scavenged some bread sticks, nearly inhaling them. Grabbed my cigarettes out of my purse in Moore's office, and headed out back.

I sat down heavily on an overturned milk crate and lit up. The first drag provided instant relief. Thank you nicotine. Jordan had knocked me off balance and I didn't like the feeling. I pulled out my phone and frowned when I realized Eli still hadn't texted me. Hell, he was probably balls deep in another girl by now. I really needed to reevaluate this so called relationship of ours.

I heard the kitchen door open behind me and turned to find Jordan taking a seat on the stoop. He took the cigarette from behind his ear and put it to his lips. I tried not to stare as he inhaled. How did he make smoking look so sexy?

"How's it going?" he asked after we had sat in silence for a few minutes. I leaned over and put out my smoke.

"My feet are on fire, but other than that, I'm doing fine," I replied, looking at him as he stared off in front of him.

He finally glanced over at me and smiled. "Let me help you out there," he said, pulling my foot into his lap.

"What are you doing?" I gasped as he slipped off my black sneakers and started kneading the soles of my feet with deft fingers.

I couldn't help the groan that escaped my lips. Jordan raised his eyebrows at my response and then grinned as he moved his hands up my legs and started rubbing my calves. "You're so tense," he murmured as he rubbed me.

"Damn, you're good. I'm gonna have to take you home with me." I moaned as he worked the kinks out of my feet and lower legs.

Jordan chuckled and I realized what I had said. I blushed, yet again. "I think I might have to take you up on that," he mused after letting me pull my feet away. I slipped my shoes back on and got to my feet.

"Yeah, uh, well thanks," I said quickly, picking up my lighter from the ground.

Jordan grabbed by arm before I was able to escape back into the kitchen. "Mays," he said quietly and I looked down at him. He was playing with the barbell in his tongue and I was mesmerized by the way he flicked it back and forth across his teeth.

"Yeah?" I asked a little breathlessly. My earlier annoyance

with him was instantly gone. Jordan rubbed his hand up my arm and goose bumps broke out along the trail of his fingers. Jordan looked at me, his eyes sparkling.

"I'd really like to take you out sometime. I want to get to know you better," he said, not breaking eye contact.

My heart sped up, I felt lightheaded, and I thought I might pass out. Thoughts of Eli or not having a thing with a guy I worked with all went out the window. All I could think about was that this gorgeous man who wanted to spend time with me.

But I had to play it cool. I smiled slightly and cocked my head to the side as if considering his offer. When what I really wanted to do was scream, 'HELL, YEAH!' I tapped my finger on my chin, as though I were deep in thought and Jordan's lips quirked in a smile. "I guess that would be alright," I admitted coyly.

Jordan grinned. "Why don't you wait for me until after my shift is over? We can go and do something," he suggested, pulling me closer, his hand brushing the back of my knee. Oh crap. My stomach knotted up and I could feel my palms start to sweat. But I nodded and I was proud when my voice didn't shake.

"Sounds good. See ya then," I said, pulling away. Jordan let his hand drop and got to his feet, following me into the kitchen.

The rest of the night became almost unbearable. All I could think about was getting done so I could hang out with Jordan. I felt his eyes on me as I ran food. He made a point to brush my hand with his when he handed me drinks.

I felt exhilarated. High on the euphoria of anticipation. I was going to go out with the most fantastically gorgeous guy I had ever laid eyes on! And he seemed to like me! Me! Miss Morganstown, South Carolina herself. I was so lost in my own little bubble that I didn't notice three of my sorority sisters show up.

"Maysie!" I heard someone call out. I looked over at the door of the restaurant and saw Gracie Cook, one of my pledge sisters.

"Hey girl!" I said, coming over to give her a hug. Gracie was easily my closest friend within the sorority. We had clicked right away. She was adorable in a waifish sort of way and I loved hanging out with her.

I looked over at the other sisters who came with her. Vivian

Baily and Milla Wood stood behind her. I went down the row, giving each a hug. I loved Vivian, she was bubbly and fun. Milla on the other hand, I hadn't figured out quite yet. She had this air about her that was kind of off putting. She seemed to have this calculated look on her face. As though she were plotting ways to take over the world, the room, whatever.

"We're heading over to the bar. Come see us when you have a sec," Gracie called as they made their way through the crowd.

At around 10:30, Moore came out and said Riley and I had been cut. He told us to come back tomorrow to get our schedules for the week. He patted us both on the back and let us know he thought we had done really well. I glowed at the compliment, feeling good that I hadn't dropped anything all night.

"I'm gonna go hang with the girls. You want to join?" I asked Riley as we gathered our things from the back.

Riley rolled her eyes. "I'll pass on sorority bonding for the night. I'll meet you at home, I'm wrecked." I wasn't surprised by her answer. I had not as of yet, convinced her to hang out with my new sisters. And I knew better than to push her about it.

"Well, don't wait up, because I'm supposed to hang with Jordan after his shift." Riley's mouth set in a grim line.

"Didn't we talk about this Mays?" she asked.

I looked away from her. "It's just hanging out."

"And denial is just a river in Egypt. You ain't foolin' nobody," she quipped and I just shook my head.

"Well, I'll talk to you tomorrow." And with that, I walked away, not wanting to hear any more of my friend's caring but annoying warnings.

I took my hair out of the ponytail and let it fall over my shoulders. I figured I could hang out with my friends while I waited for Jordan to get off of work. He was on the clock until 12:00. That gave me time to have a few drinks and try not to obsess about how nervous I was to spend time with him.

Coming out to the bar I was surprised to see Jordan chatting it up with Vivian and Milla. Though, he *was* a Pi Sig, so it made sense that they knew each other. Gracie had saved me a spot beside her and I hopped onto the barstool. Jordan was still talking to Milla, so Lyla took my drink order. She knew I was only twenty, but she hooked me up with a Jack and Coke anyway.

Working here was definitely going to have its perks.

I could tell Gracie was already a little drunk as she leaned over to give me a beer scented hug. "How was your shift?" she asked me. I looked over at Jordan, but he seemed to be engrossed in whatever Milla was telling him. I felt a twinge of jealousy at seeing him talking to another girl. But I reined that in quickly.

"It was pretty good. Though I had to shadow this chick named Evian and she was a complete slave driver. I'll be lucky if I can feel my feet in the morning." I sipped on my drink, wishing Jordan would look at me.

Vivian leaned passed Gracie and kissed my cheek. "We've missed you at the house this week! You need to get your ass over there so we can start planning Fall Rush," she enthused. Vivian and I were Rush chairs and we were expected to plan the parties for the fall. I was excited to have some responsibility in the sorority. I loved the girls and I couldn't wait to meet some new people.

I realized Jordan had finished his conversation with Milla and was watching my exchange with Vivian with a strange look on his face. I gave him a smile. "Hey, Jordan," I said. Jordan glanced from me to the other girls and he looked as though he had swallowed glass. What the hell was his problem?

"So, you get to work with the infamous Jordan Levitt," Milla commented, looking between Jordan and me. I turned to Milla and smirked.

"Infamous, huh? Do tell," I joked, drinking some more of my cocktail. I was starting to feel a little lightheaded. I was a cheap date, that's for sure.

"Uh, there's nothing to tell," Jordan interjected, looking suddenly nervous. Milla grinned at him. Though even I could see how predatory that smile was. Damn, she wanted to jump his bones too! Was there not a girl within a sixty-mile radius that was immune to Jordan Levitt's irresistible charm?

"That's not what Olivia tells me," Milla said coyly. Olivia? Did she mean Olivia Peer, our president? Did she know Jordan? I looked at Milla questioningly.

"I'd better get back to it," Jordan said quickly, moving away without looking at me again. Milla drank her beer.

"Don't tell me you don't realize who he is," she said, looking over at Jordan who was putting glasses away behind the bar. I frowned.

"Um, that's Jordan Levitt. He's a Pi-Sig right?" I didn't get what she was trying to say.

Vivian sighed. "He's not just any Pi-Sig, he's the president. And he's dating our president. Together they're going to have little president babies. They've been going out since our freshman year. How did you not recognize him? He's over at the house all the time." Vivian looked at me like I was an idiot.

It felt like the floor had just opened up underneath me. He was dating someone? And not just anyone. He was dating Olivia fucking Peer. The most beautiful and perfect human being I had ever met. Everyone loved Olivia. Including, apparently, the guy I had just spent the entire evening lusting after.

What the hell? And he had been shamelessly flirting with me the whole time while he had a girlfriend! I downed the rest of my drink, feeling the sudden need to get very, very drunk. Milla was watching me closely. My discomfort with Milla intensified. She was a huge gossip and was forever circulating rumors about people. So far I had stayed out of her line of fire and I didn't need to give her any reason to look at me at all.

I smiled painfully. "No, I didn't recognize him. But I don't think I've ever met him before," I choked out, waving a hand at Lyla to get me another drink. Gracie grabbed a handful of peanuts and tossed them into her mouth.

"They're only like Rinard royalty for Christ's sake. They are the most perfect couple. It's almost sickening," she remarked.

Sickening is right. I felt like a moron. And more than that I wanted to punch Jordan in his stupidly gorgeous face. He had been totally leading me on and that did not sit well with me. I noticed that Jordan was making a point to stay on the other side of the bar.

He asked me out and he had a girlfriend! One of my sisters to be precise and now he was avoiding *me?* Lyla brought me another

Jack and Coke and I drank half of it in one gulp. Gracie looked at me with a frown.

"You alright?" she whispered. I gave her a weak smile and nodded.

"Fine, just tired." I could hear my words starting to slur together and my head felt fuzzy from the alcohol.

I wanted to get out of there. But as I continued to drink and continued to get more wasted, I found that I wanted to confront Jordan fucking Levitt and set him straight. How dare he make look like a fool?

The bar was heaving and after a while, Vivian and Milla joined a group of Kappa Taus at a table near the back. Gracie sat with me while I threw back drink after drink. "Girl, you'd better take it easy. You're going to feel like shit in the morning."

"Yeah, yea," I replied, finishing my fourth drink. "I've gotta pee. I'll be back," I said, getting to my now very wobbly feet.

"Do you need help?" Gracie asked, laughing as I braced against the bar to steady myself.

"Nah. I got this," I hiccupped and headed to the bathroom. After finishing up, I left the bathroom and found myself face to face with none other than Jordan fucking Levitt himself.

"Hey. I think we need to talk," he said, his face unreadable. Damn if I didn't still want to stick my tongue down his throat. He was too yummy for his own good. And that pissed me off even more. I tried to move around him and he grabbed my arm. "Maysie. Please, just hear me out," he pleaded, but I yanked my arm away, almost falling over in the process.

"Get your hands off of me," I bit out. Jordan ran his hands over his face in frustration.

"I had no idea you were a Chi Delta," he said. I rolled my eyes.

"Makes it a little inconvenient I guess," I mumbled, crossing my arms over my chest.

I hated how hurt I felt. But I had really started to like him. And now he was hands off. Life sucked. "Inconvenient? What are you talking about?" Jordan asked, frowning.

I barked out a laugh. "You know, the fact that I'm in the same sorority as your *girlfriend*. Makes it hard to tap my ass," I spat out hatefully.

Jordan flinched at my words. "Shit, Maysie. That's not at all what I was trying to do." I felt like I was swaying on my feet and had to lean back against the wall so I wouldn't fall over. That would just be perfect. You know, make more of a jerk of myself.

"Then what were you *trying* to do Jordan? Because *you* asked *me* out. When you had a girlfriend. That's skeevy," I said coldly. Jordan sighed.

"I would have told you about Olivia." I snorted. Like I believed that. Jordan glared at me. "Will you just stop it already? I'm telling you the truth. Yeah, Olivia and I have been together for a while. But I feel drawn to you..."

"Drawn to my tits and ass, I'm sure," I scoffed crudely.

Jordan smirked and that annoyed me even more. "Well, you do have mighty fine tits and ass, Mays."

I drew myself upright. "You do not get to talk about my body in any way shape or form," I hissed.

Jordan's smirk dropped and he looked contrite. "I'm sorry. Really." I huffed and looked away from him. This conversation was over as far as I was concerned. I really wanted to knee him in the balls, but I held myself back.

"Maysie. Listen. I really like you. Of course I'm insanely attracted to you. I mean, look at you." His eyes roved over my body in a way that made me throb between my legs. Stupid vagina! "But, I also like talking to you. I wasn't really thinking about Olivia when I asked you out. I was only thinking that there was this beautiful, amazing girl that I wanted to get to know better. And look, things with Olivia have been strained for a while. I mean she's off partying in North Carolina all summer..."

Okay, that was it. I didn't want to talk about his relationship with my sorority sister. I wanted to get the hell out of there. I put my hand up to stop him. "Just shut up, alright. I don't care what your reasons were for asking me out. All I know is that you have a girlfriend. Not just any girlfriend, but the president of my freaking sorority. And right now, what I think is that you're some two timing douche bag who wants to get a piece of something on the side while his girlfriend is away. And I have no interest in being that girl." I pushed off of the wall and walked around him.

I heard him let out frustrated breath. "You're not just a piece of anything. Don't ever think that. I really like you, Maysie," he said softly, stopping me in my tracks. Damned if I didn't want to believe him. Damned if I didn't still want to turn around and launch myself into his arms. But I had more pride than that.

"Whatever," I threw back at him and walked away. I should have felt good for putting him in his place. But I didn't.

I felt horrible.

CHAPTER
4

I woke up the next morning with a horrible taste in my mouth and my head feeling like it had been run over by a Mack truck. I groaned and rolled over in my bed, startling when I touched a hard body lying next to me. I sat up, the blanket falling to my waist and gasped at the fact that I was naked.

Then it all came flooding back to me. Jordan. Jordan asking me out. Finding out Jordan was dating Olivia too-perfect-to-be-real Peer. I had gotten completely tanked and taken a cab back to the apartment. Then around three in the morning there had been a knock at my door.

Eli had shown up, completely stoned. Of course I had let him in. I was drunk; I was depressed over the whole Jordan fiasco. And more importantly I was extremely horny. So I had allowed him to maul my body with his hands while he trailed slobbery kisses across my face and neck. I tried not to imagine that it was Jordan as Eli took my clothes off and proceeded to give me some of the most awkward oral sex of my life.

Maybe it was the fact that he could barely stay awake while his tongue slid over me. Or perhaps it was the fact that I was dangerously close to calling out another guy's name. Whatever it was, the mood left about as fast as it had arrived. So I had pulled Eli up rather forcibly by his hair and made him stop with the God-awful tongue tango he was attempting to perform on my nether regions.

He had protested and tried to keep going at it. But I had hauled him up by his shoulders and made him lay down on the other side of my queen sized bed. I hated cuddling while I slept, which was the reason I very rarely let guys stay the night. I liked my space. There was nothing more annoying than waking up with someone's arm over your face and hot morning breath in your ear. Yuck. No thank you. The morning after was just not my thing.

And of course, Eli was all up in my personal space and I really had to pee. So I, not too carefully, heaved him onto his other side. He grunted but didn't wake up. I threw on a pair of shorts and an old Rinard College T-shirt and opened the door to my room.

Riley was coming out of hers at the same time. "Morning," she said and then looked around me into my room where Eli was snoring like a freight train in my bed. She snorted. "Niiice..."she said slowly. I closed my door a little louder than I meant to and moved past her to the bathroom.

"He showed up here early this morning. He was wasted, I couldn't let him drive home," I explained. Though it annoyed me that I felt the need to explain anything. I was an adult. If I wanted to have a guy over, that was my business. I had to check myself. I was feeling overly touchy and I knew Riley really didn't mean anything by it.

"Whatever, I wasn't going to say anything," she commented, heading to the kitchen.

"Wow, there's a first," I said sarcastically, going into the bathroom. I closed the door on Riley's laugh. When I was done I padded into the kitchen to find Riley had made coffee.

She held out a steaming cup. I took it and cradled it to my chest. "Oh, sweet nectar of the Gods," I moaned as I took my first fortifying sip. Riley pulled out the bread and popped two pieces into the toaster.

"Want any?" she asked and I shook my head, feeling queasy to my stomach. She slathered her toast with peanut butter and my nausea intensified.

"God, that's disgusting," I groaned, looking away as she took her first bite.

"That's what you get for tipping the scales toward alcohol poisoning last night. You're lucky a hangover is all you ended up with. You were loaded. What the hell brought that on?" Riley asked, looking at me questioningly.

I rooted around in the cabinet for the bottle of ibuprofen and shook out three capsules in my hand and swallowed them without water. I drank another sip of coffee and looked at her. "I was just hanging out with Gracie and the girls. Things got a little crazy is all," I evaded.

"So, you didn't meet up with Jordan after work? I thought you said that's what you were planning to do." I stiffened at her question. The mention of Jordan made my already upset stomach roll over painfully. The night was a bit fuzzy but one thing was crystal freaking clear. He had a girlfriend. And that made him completely untouchable. Because as much as I wanted something to happen with him, I just wasn't that girl. Never had been, never would be.

My silence piqued Riley's curiosity. "What happened? Did you not end up *hanging out*?" She used air quotes and I felt an irrational urge to slap her. I was used to Riley's snarky commentary but for once it touched a raw nerve. I felt like an idiot for being made a fool of. Jordan had led me on and I didn't take that very well. What's worse is I had felt something for Jordan in the 24 hours I had known him that I had never experienced before. It was more than lust, more than attraction. It was this crazy connection that would be near impossible to ignore.

But ignore it I would. Because he was a dick and that's all there was to it.

"Yeah, that's just not gonna happen," I muttered, dumping the rest of my coffee into the sink and putting my mug in the dishwasher. Riley dropped her plate on the counter and I gave her a look of death until she shrugged and put it in the dishwasher as well.

"Why? What happened?" she asked innocently. The lack of jaded sarcasm in her voice made my hackles drop a bit. I sighed and perched up on the stool at the island.

"He has a girlfriend," I admitted, dropping my head into my palm.

Riley's face darkened. "That asshole," she hissed, coming immediately to my defense. And that was why I loved her. She had my back no matter what.

"I know, right?" I said, grabbing my cigarettes from the wooden bowl on the counter where we kept our keys. Riley followed me out onto the balcony. She must have sensed how upset I was because for once I didn't hear a word about the cancer stick I was lighting up.

I leaned back in the chair and let out a drag. "He was coming onto you really strong last night and the whole time the nut sack had a fucking girlfriend? You should castrate him!" Riley's voice was filled with self-righteous anger and I gave a weak laugh.

"Yeah, I contemplated serious bodily harm once I found out, trust me." I took another drag from my cigarette and exhaled, watching the smoke plume out in a thick cloud. "And you don't even know the worst part," I continued. Riley watched me, waiting.

"His girlfriend is Olivia Peer," I told her. Riley's eyebrows drew together as she tried to place the name. "You know, the president of Chi Delta?" Recognition registered and her eyes widened in surprise.

"You are shitting me?" she breathed out.

I shook my head as I leaned over to stub out my cigarette. I flicked the butt over the banister of the balcony. I propped my feet on the wrought iron and leaned back in the chair. "Yeah, I couldn't have been more surprised than if he had told me he was gay." Riley, who had been leaning back in her own chair on two legs, slammed back down onto the ground.

"So he at least came clean, right? I mean he told you he had a girlfriend?" she asked.

"Nope." I let my mouth pop around the word. "I found out from one of my sisters. Vivian told me he and Liv have been dating for like three years or something. I *knew* he looked familiar, but I just assumed it was because he was a Pi Sig and I had seen him at parties or something. But now that I think about it, I have heard his name mentioned a lot. I can't believe I was such an idiot. Of course a guy like Jordan Levitt would be with a girl like Olivia

Peer. They're both beautiful, popular, and fucking perfect. They make sense," I said a little depressed.

Riley swatted my arm. "Stop with the self-hating bullshit. You aren't some fugly social reject. You're hot and popular and all that other trite crap as well. Olivia ain't got nothin' on you, babe." I grinned at my best friend, appreciating her efforts to perk me up.

"Love you, Riley," I said, blowing her a kiss.

"Back at ya, chica. But seriously, I want to kick his ass. That was a total dick move. Asking you out while he was taken. What a dog. But do you see why I told you to stay away from guys you work with? Because now it'll be weird."

I stood up and opened the sliding door. Riley followed me inside. "No it won't. Because I barely know the guy. There's no sense in getting all worked up over someone I just met. At least I know it's not going anywhere. Now we can just be friends. No drama."

"Who can you just be friends with?" Eli asked from the hallway, his voice husky from sleep. I whipped around to see him ambling into the living room, pulling his shirt over his head.

Riley smirked and went back to her room, leaving me with a barely functioning Eli. He sat on the couch and pulled on his Doc Martens, tucking the laces inside. Which for some reason I found really annoying all of the sudden. I mean, how lazy do you have to be to not put forth the extra two seconds it takes to tie them?

I found myself glaring at his shoes and had to snap myself out of it. "Uh, nothing. No one. Just some guy at work," I replied in what I hoped was a blasé attitude. Eli zipped up his jeans and left the button undone and I could see the dark hair trailing from his belly button and disappearing into his pants. Normally I would have found that hot. This morning I found that he just looked sloppy and unkempt. Nothing like the sexy deliciousness of Jordan Levitt.

Crap. Snap out of it! Eli pulled on my hand and I ended up in his lap on the couch. He wrapped his arms around my waist and started sucking on the skin at my neck. I pulled away.

"If you give me a hickey, I'll kill you," I warned and Eli chuckled.

45

"You've never minded it before," he said as he tugged the collar of my shirt down so he could lick the cleft between my breasts.

I felt the familiar stirring between my legs and then just as suddenly as it came, Jordan's face flashed in my mind and it was like throwing a bucket of cold water on my libido. I slithered off of Eli's lap and plopped down beside him. Eli reached over and tucked a piece of hair behind my ear.

"Sorry for my less than stellar performance last night. I was fucking wasted. I didn't even make you come. That's unforgivable," Eli murmured as he worked his fingers under the elastic of my shorts.

Normally, I loved Eli's sexual candor. But now, with another boy on my mind, it just made me feel uncomfortable.

I barked out a fake sounding laugh and wiggled out from underneath his hand. "That's okay, baby. You needed to sleep."

Eli looked at me strangely but didn't comment on the way I kept trying to dodge his touch. We both knew it was unusual for me to stop him once he got started. But I just wasn't in the mood and he'd have to deal with it.

"Yeah, thanks for letting me stay the night. I enjoyed sleeping next to you." His heavy lidded eyes smoldered at me and I had to blink in surprise. Eli was anything but a romantic. So his sweet sentiment threw me.

Eli leaned over and kissed me softly on the lips. "You're beautiful first thing in the morning. I think I could get used to that," he whispered as he attempted to deepen the kiss. This is what I had wanted him to say since we had started hooking up. But now it just left me feeling cold.

But then I got angry. Angry at myself for letting stupid Jordan Levitt interfere with whatever Eli and I had. He and his two-timing ass were definitely not worth it. So I forced myself to give into Eli's mouth as his tongue swept against mine, his teeth nibbling on my lower lip. He groaned in the back of his throat and pulled me against him as we sank into the couch.

"Sorry to interrupt but Maysie, we've got to head into Barton's and get our schedules," Riley said, suddenly appearing in the living room. I pulled away from Eli abruptly but he continued to tease the underside of my breast with his fingers, not feeling in the least bit self- conscious about the fact that my roommate was standing less than five feet away.

He looked up and gave Riley a lazy smile, his fingers squeezing my nipple as I squirmed. "Why don't you join us over here, Riley. It would be hot to have us all together, ya know. What do you say?" Normally I would have laughed at Eli's efforts to make Riley uncomfortable. He loved to say outlandish crap just to piss her off. He knew she didn't like him so he used that against her...a lot.

But this time, his words just bugged me. I shoved his hand away from me and pulled my shirt down. "Shut up, Eli. That's messed up," I told him sharply. Eli looked at me and for once I didn't see the stoned, could give a shit demeanor he typically wore. In fact, he looked almost hurt by my tone. Well, that was just ridiculous, considering he had never expressed an interest in how I felt about anything before.

"In your dreams loser. Now, get the hell out of our apartment so we can get ready," Riley retorted, turning on her heel and heading into the kitchen.

Eli got to his feet and I followed him to the front door. I held it open for him as he walked out into the hallway. He turned around and took my face into his hands. He cradled me as he gave me the sweetest, most gentle kiss he had ever given me. What the heck was going on?

"I'd like to see you tonight. Are you free?" he asked me. I chewed on my lip, unsure as to what had suddenly changed between us. This was not the Eli I was accustomed to.

"Uh, I'm not sure. I'll have to see if I'm on the schedule at Barton's for the night," I told him.

Eli ran his fingers up into my hair and pulled me toward him again, giving me another kiss. This one hungrier than the last. "I'd like to take you out. Just the two of us. I don't think we've done that yet."

I shook my head. Dates hadn't been high on his priority list. Getting both of us naked had always been number one in both of our minds. So Eli asking me out had me flustered. And for the first time, I was feeling a little guilty about my interactions with Jordan the night before.

"I'll call you," Eli said softly, kissing my forehead before making his way down the hallway. I closed the door to the apartment softly and leaned my back against it. I closed my eyes and ran my hand over my face. Eli had left me feeling very confused.

"Lover boy gone?" Riley asked, poking her head around the door to the living room. I nodded as I headed to my room. "I want to leave in fifteen minutes. I've got to head to the library today to start my independent study proposals. Will you be ready?" Riley asked.

"Yeah, just let me jump into the shower. I'll come with you to the library. I have a mountain of work before class on Monday," I said, grabbing a pair of jeans and a tank top before disappearing into the bathroom.

I took the quickest shower in history and pulled my still dripping hair into a bun at the back of my head. I didn't bother with makeup, so I was ready in seven minutes flat. "Impressive," Riley remarked as we headed out.

We chatted about nothing in particular as we headed to Barton's. Riley parked around back and we made our way in through the employee entrance in the kitchen. The day staff was on. We hadn't met any of these people, so I had no idea who anyone was.

We stopped at Moore's office and I wasn't surprised to see him sitting at his desk, click clacking on his computer. I could tell he was the type to take his job as general manager very seriously.

He looked up when we arrived and gave us a smile. "Good morning, Maysie, Riley. Nice to see you. The schedule is tacked up on the board by the expediting station. Maysie, I put you on for this evening. Riley, you have the lunch shift tomorrow. I tried to work around the schedules you guys gave me but if there are any conflicts, let me know and I'll sort it out."

We both said our thanks and went to find the schedule. Once we found it, we looked for our names and started writing down our shifts. I was working three nights through the upcoming week, which didn't conflict with my classes or my shifts at Bibi's. It seemed Riley and I had opposite schedules and I was bummed we wouldn't be working together.

I couldn't help but look for Jordan's name and my stomach dropped when I saw that we pretty much had the same schedule. Just great. Clearly avoidance wouldn't work.

"Looks like I'm being thrown in the deep end this evening. Let's get back to the apartment so we can grab our stuff and head to the library. I've got to be here at 4:00," I said, trying not to show how freaked out I was at the prospect of working with Jordan tonight.

Riley tucked her handwritten schedule into her pocket and we headed back through the kitchen, calling out our goodbyes to Moore as we walked by.

We spent most of the morning in the campus library. It was dead since most students were away for the summer. I was able to finish the rest of my statistics homework and got a good head start on my biology research paper on natural selection. We went to a deli around the block to get lunch and I sent a text to Eli, letting him know I had to work.

I didn't hear back from him, which wasn't surprising. I guess whatever had been up with his behavior that morning was fleeting. We finally headed back to the apartment around 3:15. That gave me enough time to eat something and get changed for my shift. I went ahead and laid out clothes for tomorrow. I had to open Bibi's in the morning and knew that I would be wrecked from having to help close tonight.

Riley was heading to a movie that night with some of her friends, so she let me borrow her car. My little VW Bug was in the shop with a dodgy alternator. I'd have to use some cash to pay for that now that my parents had closed their wallets. I tried not to panic over how fast I was accruing debt.

I pulled into Barton's and hurried inside. I clocked in and went to Moore's office to let him know I was there. It looked as though he hadn't moved. He was still sitting behind his desk, pecking away at his keyboard. Did this guy ever go home? He gave me a shift checklist and instructed me to go through it. I was to use this as my guide until I got into the swing of things.

Pocco and Fed were manning the industrial dishwasher. Fed tried to squirt me with the hose as I walked by, making a suggestive comment about my nipples through the wet shirt. I chose to ignore them and headed out to the dining room.

Damien was working again and I was happy to see Jaz as well. She squealed and ran up to me. "Yay! I'm so happy you're working tonight!" she said in that perky way of hers. She was sitting at the bar. I was relieved to see Jordan hadn't come on yet and it was only Lyla.

"Hey, Maysie. You ready for tonight? It'll be absolutely crazy," Lyla said, handing me the soda I asked for.

"You're lucky to be on the schedule. Servers kill to be on Saturdays," Damien said, sitting on the stool beside me.

Barton's usually had a band on Saturdays so I hoped to make good tips. "Yeah, Devil's Stone is playing at 8:00. But Generation Rejects has the stage at 11:00!" Jaz enthused. My heart plummeted. Jordan would not only be working the bar tonight but his band would be playing.

"Oh, yeah?" I asked weakly, drinking the rest of my soda so I could get started with my shift checklist.

"They haven't played here in almost six weeks. So I'm sure the place will be packed! Wait until you hear Jordan sing! He's unbelievable!" Jaz gushed.

"I thought he played the drums," I said, intrigued despite myself.

"Oh, he does. But he does some of the singing too. What I wouldn't give to have that guy's moves. He's usually knee deep in pussy by the end of the night," Damien commented crudely. Jaz leaned over and smacked his arm. I frowned.

"But he has a girlfriend," I pointed out. God, this guy was a complete player! I was so thankful I had wised up before being sucked into his rock god pants.

"Don't listen to Damien. Jordan isn't like that. Sure he's a flirt and everything, but he has never cheated on Olivia. He likes to give off the bad boy vibe and lord knows he plays the part. Unfortunately, he has remained faithful," Jaz sighed, clearly disappointed by that fact.

I wanted to shout, *faithful my ass*! Lyla was counting the bottles of tequila behind the bar and she looked up at Jaz's statement. "Well, he always has been before...but things change," she gave me a look and I flushed, staring down into my empty glass.

Jaz huffed. "No, he's whipped. He's had more than enough opportunity to hook up. Especially since Olivia's out of town. But there's nothing that would make that boy stray. I mean, who can compare to Olivia Peer? She's gorgeous!" Jaz said. I swallowed around the lump in my throat. I was officially over this conversation.

I handed my glass to Lyla who looked at me a little too perceptively. I gave her my best I-don't-care-about-anything grin and headed over to what would be my section for the night. The rest of Barton's evening staff clocked in over the next forty-five minutes. Aside from Jaz, Damien and me, a girl named Ginny, who I recognized from my biology class this summer and an older guy named Leo also clocked in.

Then, around a quarter to five, Jordan came in through the kitchen doors. I almost dropped the bottles of ketchup I was holding. He looked amazing. Of course he looked amazing! I bet there wasn't a day in his life he didn't look like sex on a stick. His dark hair was freshly buzzed and I could see the gleam of his eyebrow piercing. I hated that I noticed he had replaced the ring with a silver barbell. His polo shirt was snug over his muscles and his cargo pants hung low on his hips.

Lyla gave him a quick hug and he called out a greeting to Jaz and Damien, whose sections were closest to the bar. I tried really hard not to watch him as he scanned the rest of the dining room. But I felt the moment his eyes found me. It was like my entire body thrummed with it.

"Hey, Maysie," he called out. I grudgingly looked up and our eyes met. And just like that first time I saw him, the air hummed with electricity. The chemistry between us was palpable. I jerked my eyes away from him and lifted a hand in greeting, not trusting my voice at that moment.

I felt him watch me for a few seconds longer and then turn

away. I snuck another look in his direction but he was talking to Lyla and pulling the rack of glasses off the counter to put them away. I busied myself with finishing up my prep work.

By the time I was done, it was 5:15 and I had my first table. And then another one and another one until all five of my tables were full. I ran around like crazy. But at least tonight I got to keep the tips. And so far they were fat. By 7:30, I had $60. I was glowing, I was so happy.

I had just scooped up a 20-dollar tip left by some older business guys who I had flirted shamelessly with while they checked out my chest. I practically skipped to the back to have a quick smoke before my next table was sat.

I pushed open the outside door and almost collided with Jordan, who was coming inside. "Sorry," I mumbled, my good mood evaporating instantly. It sucked that when I looked at him, lust warred with embarrassment in my mind. Embarrassment over what might have been had I not found out how close I came to being "the other woman."

"Hey, Mays. How's it goin'?" he asked, holding the door open for me so I could step out. I really needed the nicotine, so I ignored my discomfort and stepped around him to get to the milk crate and have a seat.

"It's going good," I replied shortly.

I could see Jordan out of my peripheral as he hesitated. He still held the door open, as if unsure whether to go inside or not. *Go inside. Please, just go inside.* I pleaded silently. My Jedi mind trick clearly wasn't working, because Jordan let the door close and sat down on the stoop beside me.

He watched me as I smoked my cigarette. Finally I looked at him and arched my eyebrow. "Can I help you with something?" I asked snidely. Jordan smirked, as if amused by my bitchiness.

"Is this how it's going to be between us now?" he asked. I looked at him, refusing to drop my eyes. No sense in him seeing how much he had screwed with my head in the short time I had known him.

"Well, how do you expect me to act? I mean, it's not every day the guy you *may or may not be* interested in, asks you out, but conveniently forgets to inform you that he has a girlfriend. It puts a bit of damper on things, don't you think?"

Jordan raised his eyebrows at me and smiled. "*May or may not be interested in, huh?*" he teased and I could smack myself for my monumental slip up.

"It doesn't matter how I feel. This..." I gestured between us with my hand, "is off limits." I finished, not liking how this conversation was going. Jordan looked down at the ground and kicked a rock.

"Why does it have to be off limits?" he asked quietly.

It was my turn to smirk. "Do you even need to ask?' I questioned in disbelief. How could he be so dense?

Jordan cleared his throat. "What if it wasn't? Off limits, I mean. What if..." The kitchen door opening cut him off and Jaz and Leo came out, immediately lighting up their cigarettes.

"Maysie, you just got sat," Leo told me, taking my seat as I stood up.

Jordan got to his feet as well and he was still watching me as I picked up my lighter. It annoyed me that I was curious by what he had been about to say. What did he mean about not being off limits? I met Jordan's eyes again but dropped his gaze a second later. Without another word, I turned and went back to my section.

CHAPTER
5

I successfully avoided any further contact with Jordan for the rest of the night. I was proud of the fact that I had resisted the urge to check him out behind the bar. Which, was a feat unto itself because I wasn't sure I was capable of such self-restraint.

The crowd in Barton's started to thicken as the night wore on. Devil's Stone started playing at 8:00. They were clearly a local favorite, though I didn't really enjoy their screaming rock. The noise volume was deafening and I was fighting a killer headache but my tips had been stellar! Jaz and I did a little happy dance as we stood waiting for drinks at the bar.

"I've made $250 already! And I still have another two hours on the clock!" Jaz yelled over the music. I grinned at her, pushing back my sweaty bangs.

"I know! I've made almost $300! It's insane!" Jaz gave me a pout.

"That's not fair. The new girl should not be getting more tips than me!" She tried to come across like she was teasing, but I knew her well enough to see the irritation on her face.

"Well, when you look like Maysie, guys will throw money at you," Jordan said as he brought our drinks over to us. He smiled at me but I quickly looked away. Jaz did not like his comment at all. She huffed.

"Well, thanks Jordan. You sure do know how to make a girl feel good," she sulked.

Jordan reached over the bar and squeezed her arm. "You know I think you're pretty, Jaz." He grinned at her and Jaz instantly melted. She wore a goofy smile as she turned back to her tables. I rolled my eyes to try and cover the flash of jealousy I felt at the compliment Jordan had given her.

I yanked my tray off of the bar, my annoyance obvious. "Hey, Mays," Jordan yelled from behind me. I grudgingly turned back around, my back straight and my face blank.

"Yeah?"

Jordan cocked his head to the side, his eyes burning into mine. "Jaz may be pretty, but you're fucking gorgeous," he called out loud enough for me to hear over the thumping base of the band. He grinned at me and then he freaking winked. I *hated* and *loved it* when he did that.

I couldn't help but blush at his flirting. We held searing hot eye contact for what seemed like an eternity until someone called out Jordan's name and he turned away from me. Damn, he was going to be the death of me! How the hell was I going to stay disinterested and unaffected by him when he said shit like that? The obnoxious thing was he *knew* he got to me. Just like he knew he got to every girl he came into contact with. I hated like hell that I was just another chick in a long line of flirtations. It hurt and it sucked that it hurt.

I had to rein in the anger that reared up. I painted a happy smile on my face as I continued to tend to my tables. Things stayed steady while Devil's Stone played. I was able to forget about Jordan Levitt and his endless mind fucks, as I was lost in the Barton madness. And I was relieved when the band finished around 10:30. The lead singer's screaming was driving me nuts!

Fifteen minutes to 11, there was a ripple in the atmosphere. A noticeable elevation in mood around the restaurant as a group of three guys came in the front door, rolling amps and guitar cases. Tables had been moved back in the large dining area to create a make shift stage.

Jordan hopped over the bar and went up to the three guys, giving them a fist bump, guy hug thing. These must be the other members of Generation Rejects. I watched Jordan interact his band mates and could see the easy camaraderie between them.

Jaz stopped and saw whom I was staring at. "The guy with the tattoo covering his head is Mitch. He moved to Bakersville a few years back. The guy with the longish blond hair and guitar case is Garrett, he's a townie. Then there's Cole. He's the lead singer, though Jordan sings sometimes too. Cole is a bit of jackass. He plays the whole lead singer thing up a bit. But they're all cool," Jaz told me.

The guys started hooking up their amps and began sound testing the equipment. There was a buzz of anticipation as people started crowding around the band. I handed my last two tables their checks. The kitchen closed at 11:00, so the crowd started clambering around the bar for drinks. Lyla was slammed, as she was the only one left with Jordan now out front. Jaz, Damien and I made our way to the bar to wait for the show.

Around 11:15, Jordan sat down at his drum kit and did a quick run. I couldn't help but be impressed by his obvious talent. Moore had come out from the back and grabbed himself a beer. Cole took the mic and turned it on, a squeal from the amp cutting through the noise of the restaurant. Everyone got quiet as the guys took their spots.

"Thanks to everyone who has come out to see us tonight. My name is Cole and we're Generation Rejects." And with that they launched into a metal version of the Rolling Stones' *Gimme Shelter*. I watched riveted as Jordan beat the hell out of his kit, sweat already dripping down his face. Cole's voice was almost a scream as he sang about girls in their summer clothes.

The crowd soaked it up. Girls had jumped up and started dancing to the music, yelling out the names of the guys playing for them. I had been to a fair number of live shows, but this was awesome. The vibe was intense and the band played like their lives depended on it.

And Jordan was...well, he was the sun in the middle of it all. It was impossible to ignore his presence behind the drums. Even though Cole was technically the lead singer, it was Jordan's voice that I focused on as it melded with the music. He was flipping fantastic.

They played three more covers, choosing obvious crowd-pleasers. Everyone ate it up. Jaz and Damien joined the dancing fans but I chose to stay in my seat, enjoying the view uninterrupted by swaying girls in halter-tops and too tight dresses.

After they finished a rowdy version of Bob Dylan's Rainy Day Women, the music came to a sudden halt. Cole held the mic between loose fingers and swayed his hips as he peered into the crowd. "I'd like to introduce you to the rest of my mates. On lead guitar, Mitch!" The crowd cheered. "And my man Garrett on bass!" The crowd continued to roar. "And on the skins, the fucking bandit, Jordan!"

The sound was deafening. I could hear "I love you's" and "Marry me's" interwoven together in the chaos.

"This next song is one of ours. Written by our own lyrical genius, The Piper, Jordan Levitt! I hope you like it," Cole yelled into the mic. The Piper? Then without any further preamble, Jordan began to pound out an intense beat. His body heaved with the wave of music that poured out of him. The guitar picked up and then the bass, mixing together in an intoxicating blend of sex and love and pain.

Then to my surprise, Jordan began a raspy hum that made my nipples harden. My panties had become instantly wet, I was so turned on. His voice was unbelievable. The noises he made were erotic. I watched his rippling forearm muscles as they beat against the skins in an almost violent passion. The sexy claustrophobic press of bodies and heat of the room caused sweat to drip between my breasts. The noises, the hot, suffocating pressure in the air aroused me in a way I didn't think was possible. And all I could imagine was Jordan making that same low rumble as he pounded into me.

My heartbeat hitched up a notch and my breathing became shallow. Was it possible to orgasm just from listening to someone sing? I was so lost in the spell he wove that it took me a moment to realize he was staring at me. He continued to beat his drums mercilessly but I knew he was watching me. And for a moment it felt like we were the only two people in the room. And I knew that the song was for me. Just for me.

And then he began to sing.

Desire drips off your tongue
Legs tangled and abused
Smoldering in the aftermath
Bodies tired and used
Your eyes hold a secret
that you will never tell
The fire inside consumes me
I will embrace your hell
Touch me,
Tease me,
Need me,
Hate me
In the silence of your arms
I almost feel like a man
You destroy my soul, you open me wide
You crumble me in your hand
Touch me
Tease me
Hold me
Want me
Gutless and hated
Ruined and sated
Lost and Jaded
Breath barely bated
My biggest regret is your face
The lie overcomes the truth
Shadowed and lonely I crawl
At the wasted feet of my youth
Touch Me
Tease Me
Need Me
Want Me
Hate Me
Love Me
Fuck Me!

Fuck Me!
Fuck Me!

My eyes widened in shock as Jordan screamed 'Fuck Me' into his mic. And not once did he take his eyes off of me. The song was dark and powerful and I absolutely loved it. I felt like I was witnessing a side of Jordan that I had no idea even existed. He was deep and mysterious and full of an intensity I couldn't even fathom. Everyone in the room responded to that song. The girls undulated their bodies and the guys pounded their fists in the air. Jordan held everyone in his sway and we were all powerless to stop it.

And just like that it was over and the band was taking a fifteen-minute break. I let out a breath that I had no idea I was even holding. My hands were clammy and I ran shaky fingers through my hair. I had a visceral response to Jordan's music and it had buried deep inside me in a way I didn't entirely understand. A way that I was almost fearful of.

Jaz came back to my side and sagged against the bar. "Aren't they amazing?" she sighed. I could only nod. Words weren't good enough to describe the way I was feeling. I loved music. I really did. But I had never felt so ready to submerge myself in it the way I had as they played. And I knew it was because of Mr. Jordan Levitt.

"Jordan!" Jaz squealed from beside me, pushing me out of the way as she launched herself at him. Jordan laughed and patted her back.

"I'm all sweaty," he apologized, catching my eye over Jaz's shoulder. I gave him a small smile. Jaz wriggled closer.

"I love your sweat," she purred and I rolled my eyes.

Jordan pulled away with an uncomfortable laugh. He looked at me again. "So, Maysie. What did you think?" he asked, grabbing the cold beer that Lyla handed him. I acted as though I were really thinking about his question.

"Not bad," I stated but I couldn't stop the grin that spread across my face. Jordan's answering grin lit up my insides.

"Not bad?" he clarified. I nodded and then I did something

that surprised me. I winked at him. And he loved it. I could see instantly the affect it had on him. Jordan swallowed and his eyes heated up. He opened his mouth to say something else when a guy came up behind him and put him in a headlock.

"Jordan, my man! You guys rock! When are you going to play at the house again?" I recognized the steroid looking jock as one of the brothers in Pi Sig.

Leaving Jordan to his conversation, I went back to my section and started cleaning my tables. The band came back from their break and played a few more covers and two more original songs. Jordan didn't sing again, much to my disappointment. But they were still great. They finally finished their set around 12:30. By that point, I had joined Jaz and Damien again down at the bar. I was on my third shot of tequila and Jaz was pounding beers like crazy. Damien was the only one still sober.

I watched the guys tear down their equipment and my stomach clenched as Jordan picked up the heavy drums of his kit. I could see his muscles rippling under his Barton's T-shirt. Damn, I had it bad. Girlfriend or not, all I could think about was having him down between my legs. I imagined clutching his hair as he did things with that mouth that should be illegal.

"You alright, Mays? You look a little flushed," Damien asked, shooting me a look. I cleared my throat and crossed my legs, trying to tamp down the throb that had started.

"Fine, just feeling my ass at the moment," I slurred. Crap, I was going to have to get a ride home. Riley would be pissed at me for leaving her car here. But there was no way I could drive.

Jordan had finished loading up the band's gear and came down to the bar. The kitchen crew had come out and joined us and now Jaz was in the middle of a serious game of Flip Cup with Pocco and Fed.

Jordan slung his arm around my shoulders and I struggled to ignore the instant physical response I had to his touch. "We're having an impromptu party back at my house. You guys wanna come?" he asked the group.

There was a collective "hell yeah" from everyone.

Jordan leaned in close to me and put his lips to my ear. "What about you, Maysie? Are you game?" His breath tickled my skin and I knew without a doubt that if I ended up at his house, my earlier resolve to stay away from him would be flushed down the toilet. Because I was way too attracted to him for my own good. And he was way too taken.

I pulled away from him and reached up to remove his arm from my shoulder. "I think I'll pass. I have to get up early in the morning. Second job," I explained, looking up at him. Jordan frowned.

"Come on, Maysie. Just come by for a little while. I'll make sure you're all tucked in tight early enough for you to go to work in the morning." His voice was like liquid caramel. And I knew that's exactly what I wanted to do with him. I wanted no holds barred, throw-me-against-a-wall-and-pound-me-within-an-inch -of-my-life-sex.

But that wasn't going to happen. So, despite the aching desire to give into those delicious base urges, I shook my head. "No can do. I really have to get home." I turned away from him before I could register the disappointment on his face. I tugged on Damien's sleeve. "Hey, can I get a ride? There's no way I'm driving." Damien grinned.

"Sure thing. Let me go get my stuff."

Jordan made a noise from behind me. I turned around to look at him and he was frowning.

"What?" I asked, confused.

"I could give you a ride home," he offered, looking insulted that I hadn't asked him first. He just didn't get the hint that I was trying to put serious distance between us.

"That's okay. You've got your party to get to," I said flippantly, getting to my feet. Jordan still looked bothered.

"Maysie. Don't be like this," he whispered so quietly that I wasn't sure I heard him correctly.

I was saved from having to respond by Damien's reappearance. "Ready?" he asked. I nodded and picked up my purse. I chanced one more look at Jordan as we headed toward the door but he had already turned away from me and I felt hollow as I left.

CHAPTER
6

The weeks started to fly by. I couldn't remember the last time I was so busy. Between Bibi's, Barton's and summer school I barely had time to breathe. But I was excited about how much money I had been able to save up. I had already sent $1,000 to my parents.

My mom had called when they had received the check in the mail. She made it clear that she and my father were still disappointed by my choices but she was glad I seemed to be on the right track. I hated talking to my parents. Nothing I did was ever good enough. Sometimes I really wondered why I bothered seeking their approval on anything.

Summer school finally finished up at the beginning of August. I was stoked when I received my grades and saw that I had gotten a solid 'B' in both classes. I had just finished a victory dance around my living room when the doorbell rang.

I skipped over to the door and swung it open. Eli stood on the other side, his guitar case in his hand. I hadn't really seen a lot of Eli over the last month. We texted back and forth some and there was the occasional late night visit but our relationship had seriously cooled down. So I was surprised to see him standing there.

"Eli!" I said; giving him a smile and holding the door open for him to come inside. Riley was at her lunch shift at Barton's and wouldn't be home for a few hours. Tonight was the first night in a while that I didn't have either homework or a shift at Barton's.

"Hey, babe. Haven't seen you in a while." Eli leaned in and gave me a kiss on the lips. I returned the kiss, feeling a little guilty that I wasn't more concerned than I should have been that it had been so long since Eli and I had spent time together.

And it wasn't because of Jordan, either. I was proud to say that I had held firm to my resolve to keep some distance between us. We continued to work together most nights, but his flirtation had died down. Probably because I didn't give him any sort of response when he tried. He seemed to have finally taken the hint that I wasn't going to go there with him. I could sense he still watched me while I waited tables, feeling the heat of his eyes, and there was still that undeniable attraction between us. But for the moment, we weren't doing anything about it.

I had overheard Jordan talking to Lyla about Olivia last week. He had been telling the other bartender that the president of Chi Delta was due home soon. When Jordan had realized I was standing there, waiting for a drink order, he had immediately stopped talking about it. He wouldn't meet my eyes and I couldn't help but feel the awkwardness between us.

Lyla had gotten my drinks as Jordan made an excuse to go the kitchen. I really wish we had been able to build a friendship as opposed to this weird discomfort we felt when we were around each other. But how do you move onto friendship when all you wanted to do was rip each other's clothes off? And his girlfriend would be back soon. So it was for the best we had minimal interaction.

Eli plopped down on my couch and pulled out his guitar. He tuned it and started to strum the opening chords to the Beatles' *Norwegian Wood*. I sat down beside him and listened for a bit. I couldn't' help but compare him to Jordan's musical talent and Eli was definitely lacking. Not that he sucked but his ability was a bit more forced and put on. It didn't flow naturally the way Jordan's did.

"So, what are you doing tonight?" Eli asked as he continued to pluck at the notes. I still held my grades in my hand. I held them up.

"I got B's in my summer school classes. So I'm thinking I need some serious celebration in my future." I grinned, unable to stop myself.

Eli nodded but didn't respond, which was so annoying. Why couldn't he just once act happy for me? Or seem remotely interested in something that was going on in my life?

"So you want to celebrate, huh?" Eli put his guitar back in his case and he scooted across the couch toward me. I tried not to roll my eyes. He really did have a one-track mind.

Eli's fingers slid up the front of my shirt and traced circles on the skin of my stomach and I couldn't stop laughing as he tickled me. Eli grinned down at me as he lowered his mouth to my shoulder and nipped me with his teeth. "Stop it, Eli! I can't breathe!" I shoved him in the chest and he leaned back.

"So, what did you have in mind? You wanna hang at Randall and Cicely's?" Eli asked; sitting back away from me, now that he could see fooling around wasn't on the agenda.

Go to his cousin's apartment? Uh, no thank you. I was sort of over hanging out while Eli got high and waiting until he was ready to make out in a darkened bedroom. It seemed like ages since that had seemed like a fun idea.

"No, I think I'd like to go out. I'll probably go meet Riley after her shift and hang at Barton's." Eli made a face.

"Seriously? You're not there enough?" he asked. I hated it when he seemed to be mocking me. I stiffened and I felt my face harden.

"Well, I really like the people down there. And I get a discount. So that's what I'm gonna do. You can join me if you want. If not, no biggie." I got to my feet and went into the kitchen to make some lunch.

My earlier good mood was effectively gone and I kind of just wanted Eli to leave. He was getting on my nerves. Eli followed me and leaned against the counter, watching me while I made a turkey sandwich. "You gonna make me something?" he asked. I grit my teeth but pulled out two more pieces of bread.

I grudgingly handed him his sandwich and started eating mine. "Well, if that's what you're going to do, I think I'll hang with Randall for a while. Maybe we'll meet you there later," Eli commented, talking with his mouth full, which totally grossed me out.

I hadn't expected him to offer to meet me and I was suddenly unsure if I liked that idea. I kept him completely separate from my college life. He was like my dirty little townie secret and I liked it that way. But he was offering to spend time together. And we hadn't seen much of each other lately. And I thought I still liked him.

So I found myself nodding. "Sounds good," I said, giving him what I hoped was a happy smile. Eli reached out and pulled me to his chest. He nuzzled my neck and I tried to relax into him. This would be good. Tonight would be fantastic. Even in my head, I sounded fake.

"*C*an't I go home and change first?" Riley whined as I ordered us two beers. It was 5:30 and Riley had just gotten off of work. I was already on my third drink and was feeling the warm fuzzies from the alcohol. I had to pace myself otherwise I'd be throwing up in the bathroom before 9:00.

"Fine! But hurry up! I'll get lonely if you take too long," I teased, swatting Riley's behind with my hand. She shot me a look and downed her beer.

"I'll be back in twenty," she assured me, heading toward the front door.

I was left sitting at the bar, shredding a napkin. "What did that napkin ever do to you?" a voice asked. I looked up to see Jordan leaning over the bar toward me. I gave him a saucy smile and threw the destroyed napkin at him. He laughed and tossed it in the trash.

Jordan must have just come on the clock. His hair was starting to grow out and was still wet from the shower he must have taken before he had come to work. He smelled amazing. Like musk and man. And I wanted to bury my nose into his chest and just breathe him in.

Jordan laughed again, interrupting my obvious ogling. "So, what brings you in here on your night off?" he asked me, wiping down the counter. I smiled, feeling myself relax around him for the first time in forever.

"I got my grades from summer school in the mail today. I did really well and felt like a little celebration was in order."

Jordan reached out and gave me a high five. "Nice, Mays!" He took my now empty beer mug and slid another one my way. It was a Sam Adams, my favorite. How did he know that? "This one's on me." He gave me a wink before going to tend to two guys who had just sat down.

I watched him while he poured their beers. And I watched him while he chatted up his customers, shooting them that sexy smile I had come to love so much. Hell, I couldn't keep my eyes off of him. And it wasn't just because of the alcohol.

I wanted him. The truth was I had never stopped wanting him. And I hated so much that he and I were not meant to be. Because I knew, deep down, that we could be beautiful together. And that just made me sad.

"Why do you look like someone just ran over your cat?" Riley asked, sliding into the bar stool beside me. I plastered a smile on my face and leaned over to give her a one armed hug. She patted my back soothingly.

"I'm fine! Just waiting for your sorry ass to get back," I teased. Jordan came back over then.

"Hey, Riley. What'll it be?" he asked her.

Riley shot me a look, as if to say she knew what caused my bleak expression. "Give me a G and T," she said. Jordan quirked his lips at her.

"Ah, living large tonight?" he asked. Riley just rolled her eyes at him, not bothering to respond. Chuckling, he went about making her drink.

"When will you stop being all depressed over him? I thought you were over that?" Riley whispered after Jordan had brought her gin and tonic. My eyes followed Jordan as he went into the kitchen to get someone's order.

"I'm not depressed. And I *am* over that. So just shut up about it," I snapped. Riley just raised her eyebrows and shook her head.

"Sure, you are," she said flatly. I was about to say something

67

else when I felt a pair of lips against the back of my neck.

I jumped and whipped around to see Eli standing there with Randall, Cicely and another one of their friends. Some guy they called K-dog. Though I wasn't sure why. "Hey! You made it!" I said overly brightly. I wrapped my arms around Eli's neck and gave him a hug.

Eli pulled up the stool on the other side of me and sat close. He laid his hand on the top of my thigh and kissed the corner of my mouth. "I told you I'd meet you here," Eli replied, snaking his arm around my waist.

It was then that I noticed Jordan was standing in front of us. He had a dark look on his face and I saw him dart his eyes from Eli to me and to Eli's arm encircling my middle. I sat up a little straighter and eye balled him. No way was he permitted to look like that when it was he who had the girlfriend.

"Get me a Budweiser," Eli told Jordan, not looking at him. Jordan's eyes met mine, his expression not happy.

"Yeah, sure." Jordan turned from me and took Randall and Cicely's orders. Riley cleared her throat.

"This should be interesting," she muttered, downing her drink.

"Whatever," I replied flippantly, not wanting to admit that my stomach had suddenly tangled in knots.

Jordan slammed Eli's beer glass down on the bar and quickly walked away. "What the fuck?" Eli snarled, mopping up beer that had sloshed out of the mug. I laughed uncomfortably and drank the rest of my own drink.

The next hour consisted of Eli and his friends getting lit and Eli spending the entirety of the time trying to get his hands up my shirt. On what planet had I thought meeting Eli here was a good idea? I glanced at Jordan periodically and he was looking more and more pissed off. I would catch him watching Eli as he tried to kiss me and then he would turn away, his shoulders tight.

I was about four drinks in when Eli put his lips to the side of my neck and flicked his tongue along my skin. "I think it's about time we get out of here," he growled in my ear, his hand heavy on my upper thigh. I laughed a little uncomfortably and removed his fingers from my leg.

"I don't think either of us is driving anywhere," I told him.

Eli's slobbery mouth moved to my chin and I tried not to cringe. He was a mess. "Well, I wanna go back to your place and fuck you senseless." He removed his mouth and grinned suggestively. The whole thing was comical considering Eli could barely sit up straight and was swaying in his seat. Dear lord. It was suddenly hard to remember when I had found his drunken idiocy remotely attractive.

"Um...I don't think so. Let's just hang out for a while longer." I did not want to go anywhere with him right now.

Eli tugged at the collar of my shirt, pulling it down so that the top of my bra showed. Crap, he was trying to give me a Janet Jackson moment! I shoved at his hands but he had already put his lips right above my barely covered breasts. This was deteriorating into bad amateur porn territory and fast.

My face flushed hot in embarrassment as I tried to shove him off. "Get off, Eli. This is where I work! Not cool!" My voice was hard and I was getting very, *very* angry.

Eli laughed it off and continued to assault me with his mouth; the other people around the bar were openly staring at us with barely veiled disgust. "Get off, Eli!!!" I shoved at him again. One minute he was there and the next he was on the floor. The stool he had been sitting on toppled over and his beer glass shattered on the bar.

"Get the fuck away from her!" I heard a voice say dangerously low. I blinked in surprise to see Jordan standing over Eli, the veins on his neck noticeable.

Eli sat up on his butt and sneered at Jordan. "And what the hell are you gonna do about it?" Bad move, Eli. Jordan reached down and hauled Eli up to his feet and held him by the front of his shirt.

"I will shove my fist so far down your fucking throat that you'll be shitting my fingernails for a week. I believe she told you to back off. Now back the fuck off or I will throw your ass out, after I use your face as my punching bag. And I will enjoy every second of it." Jordan gave Eli a little shake. Eli looked pale and was visibly retreating. Not that I blamed him, Jordan looked ready to kill.

Randall and Cicely were laughing their asses off and K-dog wasn't even paying attention. *Nice friends there*, I thought. Riley was looking conspicuously the other way. Eli's pride kicked in and he wrenched himself backwards out of Jordan's grip, stumbling a bit.

He sort of swayed on his feet, too drunk to stand still. "Don't tell me what I can do with *my* girl," he yelled.

His girl?

Since when?

This seemed to set Jordan off even more and he started for Eli again.

That was it, I'd had enough. I jumped down off of my stool and got between them. I turned to Jordan and held my hands up. "Stop it, Jordan! I don't need you assaulting Eli. Go back to work. I can handle myself." I was shaking from the adrenaline overload. I was pissed at Eli and I was pissed at Jordan. What the hell was with the He-Man show? I felt like a bone two dogs were fighting over. And it was seriously wrong. Jordan was still staring down Eli but then his eyes flickered to me. And I saw them soften marginally.

"Sorry, Mays," he said quietly. My shoulders dropped but I didn't relax my defensive stance. "Just go back to work," I told him tiredly. Jordan looked like he wanted to say something else but I turned away from him. I put my hand on Eli's arm.

"You okay?" I asked.

Eli pulled back from me. He was obviously still angry and probably pretty humiliated as well. And macho pride wasn't something you messed with. "I'm fine. But I need another beer." He sat back down at the bar and waved down Lyla, who brought him another Bud. She looked at me with her eyebrows raised.

"Interesting night, huh?" she said, looking back at Jordan who was slamming glasses down onto a tray. I didn't bother to answer her. What was the use? We had just become a three-ring circus. It was mortifying.

One thing definitely needed to happen; I had to get *extremely* drunk. So I slammed back two shots of tequila and ordered another beer. Jordan stayed away from me, so Lyla handled our drinks from there on out. I wouldn't look at him. I was too irritated by the earlier fight, and I didn't particularly want to talk to Eli either for causing the whole thing to begin with. With his groping hands and inability to take no for an answer. Luckily, his slobbery, amorous advances seemed to have cooled significantly and he spent most of his time with his back to me, talking to his friends.

A half an hour later, I realized I had to pee. I grabbed Riley's hand and dragged her to the bathroom with me. She had been suspiciously quiet after the Eli/Jordan smack down, which was highly unusual for her.

"Go ahead. Say it," I said after we stepped into the bathroom. Riley took down her ponytail and used her fingers to comb through her dark hair.

"What are you talking about?" she asked innocently, glancing at me in the mirror.

"I can't believe you don't have some sort of witty commentary on the bullshit macho spectacle earlier." I leaned back against the sink and crossed my arms over my chest. Riley laughed.

"Well, it was certainly something," she said dryly with a sardonic grin. "And that's it?" But the truth was I actually wanted her insight into what was going on with Jordan. What he had done, that unexpected possessive aggression freaked me out. And not because he almost beat Eli to a bloody pulp.

"What do you want me to tell you? That Jordan is insanely crazy about you? To the point that he'll take down a room full of guys if they look at you funny? I don't need to tell you that, because you already know it." I started to protest. But she gave me a look that shut me up.

"Stop playing stupid. He likes you. From the look on his face as he watched Eli maul you at the bar, I'd say he feels a lot more than *like* for you. I know you're hot for him. So I don't know what else to tell you. He has a girlfriend, Mays. Not just any girlfriend either. But one you know pretty darn well. I don't know what to tell you to do about that. I'm not even sure what *I* would do if I were in your shoes. But you definitely have yourself a situation here and you need to sort it out before you become collateral damage." Riley ran her hands under the tap and grabbed a paper towel.

I followed her to the door. "Well, that wasn't even remotely helpful," I joked. Riley laughed.

"Sorry chickadee. I'll work on my sage advice and figure on some sort of Dear Abby answer for you later," she said. I patted her back.

"That would be greatly appreciated." I chuckled as we left the bathroom, my mood already improving.

"Maysie, you got a minute?" I looked over to the door of the men's room and saw Jordan leaning against the wall. And my restored good mood evaporated just like that.

"I'll go keep the masses entertained," Riley said and left us. Jordan pushed off the wall and walked toward me.

"I don't have anything to say to you, Jordan." I felt wobbly on my feet and it had everything to do with the boy standing in front of me. But I tried really hard to keep my voice disinterested and my eyes cool. He scanned my face and I flushed an even brighter red.

"Well, I have stuff I need to say to you and you're going to listen," Jordan's voice had an edge to it and I bristled at his audacity.

"Screw you, Jordan. I don't need to stand here and listen to your bullshit after the crap you pulled out there." I jerked my head in the direction of the bar. I could see Eli talking to Randall. He apparently didn't realize I hadn't come back from the bathroom with Riley.

"Look, I'm sorry, Mays. I didn't mean to lose my cool like that. But he was touching you and I could tell you didn't want him to. And...well...fuck...he was touching you!" he said in an agonized tone. His obvious jealousy fueled my anger. I leaned into him and dropped my words to a whisper.

"And what's it to you?" Was that seductive voice mine? I licked my lips and saw Jordan's eyes drop to my mouth.

"Maysie." His voice was husky and he moved in closer to me. I should back up, move away. This was everything I didn't want but everything I craved.

"Why should it matter to you what he was doing? You and I have nothing, are nothing. More to the point, there is *no such thing as you and I!*" I hissed. Then my shoulders relaxed and my gaze dropped to the floor.

"You have a girlfriend, Jordan," I said softly, my fury fizzling out the longer we stood close together in the dark space. That pull I always felt around him was back in full force and I placed my palm on his chest and felt the hammering of his heart beneath my palm. It was dim in the tiny hallway and I had a momentary flash of concern that someone would see us like this. Because we didn't look very innocent, nearly pressed body to body as though we needed each other to breathe.

"It matters to me, Mays. It matters a lot. I don't like seeing some other guy touching you. Not when it should be me touching you." His hand slithered up my side, until he was cupping the back of my neck. I wanted to say something about Olivia. I wanted to yell at him for continuing to mess with my head like this. "I hated him calling you *his girl.* Because I want you all to myself," he dropped his voice into a seductive growl.

At that moment all I could think about was the fact that Jordan's lips were moving toward mine. "I want to kiss you. More than I've ever wanted anything," he murmured, stopping just shy of my mouth. I held my breath, waiting for him to make a move because I was too scared to do anything. I was terrified of this irresistible force that was building between us. And then I shocked us both.

"Then do it," I whispered, licking my bottom lip in anticipation. Something sparked in Jordan's eyes a split second before he slammed his mouth down on mine. He pushed me back into an alcove, pressing my back against the wall.

His traced his tongue along the seam of my lips and I opened them, allowing him access. Inviting him. Welcoming him. His tongue plunged inside and I made a noise deep in the back of my throat that sounded an awful lot like a whimper. Jordan's hands dropped down to cup my ass and haul me up against him. I could feel his erection against my leg as our mouths mated with one another.

My hands slid up under his shirt and my nails dug into his back. Jordan moaned into my mouth, his lips becoming more frenzied. His kiss more urgent. I wanted him to drag me to the floor and have his way with me. I wanted to feel him buried deep inside me and yelling my name.

What I wanted obviously didn't matter, because we were suddenly interrupted by a group coming to the bathrooms. The girls chuckled as they caught sight of us tangled up in each other. I pulled my mouth away from Jordan's and tried to push him back with trembling hands, only gaining a few inches of separation.

"We can't do this," I whispered unsteadily. Jordan's breathing was ragged and he rubbed his hand over his face. Then he stared at me and moved his hand so it ran down the length of my cheek.

"I've never felt this way about anyone. Ever," he told me. The heat in his eyes had simmered down and now all I saw was tenderness. And that scared me a hell of lot more than the passion from just moments before.

"Not even with Olivia?" I cringed internally, hating myself for bringing her name into this. But I needed to. It had to be dealt with. Jordan needed to be reminded that what we were doing was behind his girlfriend's back. He closed his eyes and leaned his forehead against mine. Our noses rubbed against each other and I didn't' have the strength to move away from him. He held me captive.

"Yes. Even with Olivia. Maysie, I have a girlfriend. A girlfriend I've been with for three goddamn years." I felt tears burn my eyes as the nasty reality of the situation I found myself in washed over me. Because hell if I wasn't falling for him. And falling hard.

Jordan opened his eyes and looked at me as he grabbed my face between his hands and held me perfectly still, not letting me move. "But tell me, Mays, why is it that all I can fucking think about is you? Why am I so eager to take another guy's head off for touching you? Why is it when I lay in bed at night I dream that it's you there beside me?" he demanded almost angrily, his words causing my heart to skip a beat. His fierce expression then relaxed into that beautiful tenderness again.

"Come home with me tonight. Please. Let's figure all this

out...together," Jordan pleaded, his hands sliding down my face until they rested on either side of my neck. They felt so warm, so natural there. Slowly, he leaned in to kiss me again.

God I wanted to go home with him. I wanted to forget that there even was an Olivia. But there *was* an Olivia. And she would be home in a week. And he would go back to her. And I would become a shameful, dirty secret to be forgotten. Jordan would most likely feel guilty and what if he told Olivia about me? Where would that leave me?

I would lose my sorority, my new friends, the life I had created for myself at Rinard. I was pretty damn sure that I was just a passing fling to Jordan Levitt. A flash in the pan. I was also pretty damn sure that he didn't feel the same depth of emotion for me that I was starting to feel for him. Sure he was attracted to me. We had this undeniable physical chemistry. Chemistry that was impossible to ignore. But that didn't equate to anything resembling love. And I think I wanted that. No, I knew I wanted that. And that frightened me. A lot.

I also knew, without a doubt, that he would crush my heart. Destroying my soul, my will, my entire being. And I couldn't let that happen.

So I finally forced myself to push him away. Jordan looked hurt as I shoved his chest with my hands. "No, Jordan. I won't go home with you. I won't go anywhere with you. This can never happen again," I told him firmly, feeling our separation like a physical ache. A new emptiness. A hollow sense of loss for what could never be.

The fire in Jordan's eyes dimmed until it was as though it had never existed at all. "But I thought..." Jordan started, trying to reach for me again. I held up my hand to stop him.

"I don't care what you thought. This thing going on between you and me ends here, tonight. You are not going to do this to Olivia. I know you love her." Swallowing hard as the words got stuck in my throat. I felt sick.

Jordan shook his head. "I don't know how I feel about Olivia anymore. But, Maysie. I *do know* that what I feel for you is real. And it's not something I can ignore," he implored, his eyes desperate. I felt myself weaken but then I stiffened my spine and went in for the kill.

"It'll pass. Now, I've got to get back to Eli. He's probably wondering where I am." Jordan's eyes went hard as he let me edge around passed him.

My lips were tender and swollen from kissing him and I hoped Eli wouldn't notice. I wanted Jordan to try and stop me from walking away, and I hated to admit that I was extremely disappointed when he didn't. So that just proved I had done the right thing even as I felt my heart breaking into tiny little pieces.

CHAPTER
7

I called in sick to Barton's the next afternoon. I knew I was avoiding Jordan. I just couldn't stomach seeing him after the turmoil he unleashed inside of me the night before. I also couldn't stop thinking about the way his lips felt on mine. It had been perfect for all of thirty seconds before reality had kicked in and had stomped on any chance there had been that something might have happened between us.

After my epic make out session outside the bathroom (how romantic), I had returned to the bar, feigning sickness. Eli, who was still unfairly miffed with me, said he wanted to stay. Asshole. So Riley drove me back to the apartment and, for once, didn't grill me about what had gone down between Jordan and me. I couldn't tell her. I wasn't ready to talk about it. I felt too emotionally raw.

So instead of going to work, I lay in my bed, watching re-runs of Beverly Hills 90210 and ate a gallon of mint chocolate chip ice cream. I went into Bibi's the following day, which was a welcome distraction. Layne had known something was off with me, though she didn't question too closely. I gave the excuse that I was just tired from working so much. She urged me to take it easy and ended up letting me go home early.

So what did I do? I crawled back into my bed and ate another gallon of ice creamy goodness and tried to forget the tattooed bartender who had bulldozed his way into my life. Stupid dick wad.

I hadn't heard from Eli, so I finally texted him saying I thought we needed to take a break. Yep, I broke up with him over a text. I was a serious jerk. But I stopped feeling bad when all I got in reply was a short message with *whatever*, fifteen minutes later. I may be a coward for ending things via text but Eli was a jackass so I was glad to be done with him. Sure, he had had moments where I thought there was more to him than the slacker stoner. That maybe he cared about me. But after his fantastic showing at Barton's last night, I forgot about that other stuff and I was pretty sure that I didn't want to see him for a good long time.

I had finally returned to Barton's a few nights later. I was both glad and disappointed that Jordan wasn't scheduled to work. At least I was off the hook with trying to act normal around him. I'd like to shelf that awkwardness for another time, thank you. To the rest of the world, I was Maysie happy-go-lucky, sweet-as-pie, Ardin. No sense in anyone getting wind of how close I had been to becoming Jordan's road kill.

Though, for all my bravado, I couldn't get the image of him out of my head. The way he had looked at me as he told me I was all he could think about. I couldn't stop the yearning to give into him and everything his eyes had promised.

But as the days passed and Olivia's arrival loomed large, I tried to put my desires out of my mind. Because when it came down to it, it didn't matter what I wanted in all of this. Jordan was with Olivia. Case closed.

It was a Thursday evening, almost a week since my kiss with Jordan and I was clocking in at Barton's. I hadn't realized I was just standing there, staring at the clock until I heard him come up behind me.

"You alright there, Mays?" Jordan asked. I peered at him over my shoulder and wanted to puke on his Adidas sneakers. He smiled at me and I couldn't summon the strength to smile back.

"I'm fine," I mumbled and made room for him to clock into the computer. He looked at me with an unreadable expression but didn't say anything else. It was obvious we were all done with talking.

I stood there another moment, waiting to see if he would say anything more. When he didn't, I suppressed a sigh and went into the dining area.

My shift passed quickly enough. Before I knew it, the clock read 6:30 and I already had $70 in my pocket. Cold, hard cash was a great way of forgetting about an aching heart.

I was hanging out at the hostess station during a lull in my tables. Normally I would have been by the bar with Jaz, who was continuing her endless flirtation with Jordan. But I couldn't face all of that. So instead I hid out with Laura, the sixteen-year-old hostess, as she folded up kids' menus.

"Maysie Ardin! I didn't know you worked here now!" I looked toward the door that had just opened and my stomach dropped to my feet. Olivia Peer walked in with Milla and Tabby, another sorority sister. Olivia gave me a quick hug and I felt worse than something you scrape off the bottom of your shoe.

Well, hello guilt. I had missed you.

"Yep, just started this summer," I told her. Olivia gave me a big smile and I hated myself even more for lusting after her boyfriend. Olivia glowed with a golden tan. Her long legs accentuated by her minuscule jean skirt. She was one of those girls blessed with a tiny waist and huge boobs, which were currently on display in a low cut tank top. Her long black hair hung perfectly brushed to the middle of her back and her big blue eyes sparkled as she scanned the restaurant until she found what she was looking for.

Or more specifically, *who* she was looking for. And the way her entire face lit up as she saw Jordan made me want to crawl into a hole and die. Olivia looked at me again, the happiness emanating from her made me want to gag.

"It was good to see you, Mays. Don't forget about the rush meeting tomorrow. Our first event is in three weeks so we need to start planning." She gave me another hug and then hurried to the bar. I watched, like the masochist that I am, as she squealed Jordan's name. I tried not to stare as he smiled at her; a little stiffly I thought (though that was probably wishful thinking) and came around the bar to see her.

I finally had to look away as Olivia leaned up on her tiptoes to kiss him. Ugh, I *did not* need to see that. I turned to give my other sisters a hug. Milla seemed to be looking at me a little oddly but I ignored it. Milla looked at *everyone* oddly.

"When did Olivia get back?" I asked in what I hoped was a light tone. Tabby flicked her hair off of her shoulder and shrugged.

"Only like an hour ago. But she had to get down here to see Jordan. They're so cute it's disgusting." Even I could hear the jealousy in Tabby's voice and I followed her eyes back to the reunited couple.

God I hated how great they looked together. Olivia was the perfect height for him. The top of her head fitting perfectly underneath his chin. You'd have to be an idiot to not see how much she loved him. I couldn't look at Jordan's face. Scared to see the same expression mirrored in his eyes as he looked at his girlfriend.

I hated her. In that moment I wished the worst possible plagues on her. I wanted her to wake up in the morning covered in zits. And for all of her perfect hair to have fallen out. And for her to have gained thirty pounds. I hated that I hated her. Because she was seriously one of the nicest girls I had ever met (though it was a fake sort of niceness, if you ask me). But right then, I didn't care if she was Mother-fucking Teresa, I just wanted her hands off of him!

"Mays! Are you listening?" Milla's voice cut through my Olivia induced misery. I tore my eyes from the happy couple to look at my sorority sister.

"Sorry, what?" I asked. Milla narrowed her eyes at me.

"I asked when you got off of work and whether you wanted to have a few drinks with us," she spoke slowly as though I were low functioning.

I wanted to smack her face but instead I put on my best saccharine sweet smile. "I'm done in an hour. If you guys are still here, I'll come over for a round," I said, hoping the urge to bitch slap her wasn't evident as I answered.

Tabby looked back over at Jordan and Olivia. "Oh we'll be here. I don't think we'll be able to tear her away. He's all she talked about the entire summer. It was ridiculous," Tabby remarked, rolling her eyes. Olivia had her arms wrapped around Jordan's waist and was resting her cheek against his chest. Jordan held her back lightly and said something that made her laugh.

Gah! Enough! "Alright ladies, I'll see you in a few." I marched back to my tables, which were thankfully empty and started straightening the salt and peppershakers.

By the time I was done, my five tables looked as if someone with OCD had laid them out. Jaz came up as I was wiping down their surfaces again, and sat down in a chair. "I really want to dislike that girl," she sighed, looking over her shoulder at Olivia.

She, Tabby and Milla sat talking at the bar while Jordan tended to other customers. It was crazy the way everyone around her seemed to dim in comparison. Olivia was way too pretty for comfort. And seeing her again reinforced why I never had a chance with Jordan to begin with. There was no way someone like me could hold his attention for long. Not when he had a girl like Olivia in his life.

I wasn't used to this level of negative self-talk. I had never felt so down on myself. And it disgusted me that it was all tied to a guy. Even if said guy had the face of a god and the lips made for sin. Shit! I was making myself nauseous. I mentally smacked myself in the face.

"Yeah, Olivia is *really* nice," I said to Jaz, noticing how even without trying, I sounded completely sarcastic. Jaz looked at me a little funny.

"Yeah. I mean, you want to hate any girl that is able to snag a guy like Jordan. But she's so sweet. Never has a hateful thing to say about anyone. Makes me feel like a conniving slut for wanting to get down on all fours in front of her boyfriend," Jaz giggled.

"Wow, I had no idea you were such a perv," I joked, tossing a sugar packet at my friend. Jaz caught it and opened it up, pouring the contents into her mouth.

"Yuck! You are disgusting!" I screeched, blanching.

Jaz laughed and got to her feet. "Yeah, well let's go talk to Moore. The place has really died down and I just saw Dina and Leo come in for their shift. No sense in us staying on the clock." I followed her into the back, where we found Moore on the phone.

"Moore. Our tables are empty and we haven't had any new

customers in ten minutes. Can we leave?" Jaz whispered loudly. Moore barely looked up, waving us on. Normally I would have been stoked to cut out early but today I'd actually rather be working. Because now I had to go out in the bar and have a drink with Olivia. I'd rather slide down on my back over razorblades into a giant vat of rubbing alcohol. Okay, I was a little morbid in my metaphors, but whatever.

After saying goodbye to Jaz I headed back out to the bar, and almost turned around and headed back the way that I had come. Olivia was leaning over the bar, her hand fisted in the front of Jordan's T-shirt, kissing him passionately while Milla and Tabby hooted at them.

Jordan broke away with a chuckle and Olivia sat back down, clearly a little breathless. She looked up and saw me. "Maysie! Come on chica! I've got a beer with your name on it." Olivia waved me over. Jordan looked up as I came over. Our eyes met and he looked a little sheepish. Embarrassed even. Which was stupid. I mean he was just kissing his girlfriend. Nothing wrong with that, right? Only it didn't feel alright. It felt horrible.

"Hey," I said quietly as I hopped up on the stool beside Olivia. Jordan looked as sick as I felt. His eyes darted between Olivia and me.

I picked up my beer and held it up in a mocking salute. "Cheers," I said coldly as I downed it in one go, never breaking eye contact with him.

He frowned but didn't say anything. "Hell yeah!" Olivia shouted, draping her arm around my shoulders in a show of affection. Olivia and I had never been close but she had always gone out of her way to be nice to the new pledges. She was a senior, as was Jordan, so we ran in different social circles. But we still got along. Which is what made this whole situation completely messed up.

"So, how's it working with our girl, Maysie?" Olivia asked Jordan. She was obviously a little buzzed. I saw Jordan swallow. His Adam's apple bobbing up and down.

"Uh, it's fine," he answered noncommittally. I wanted to smirk at him, treat him with a cold indifference. But I didn't think I could pull it off. So instead I simply looked away, feeling uncomfortable.

Olivia had already turned to say something to Tabby and Milla, leaving me all but forgotten. Jordan had picked up my empty glass and put it in the sink behind the bar. He met my eyes again and I saw *it*. The simmering heat that left me panting for more. It hadn't dimmed in the slightest. Not even with his girlfriend sitting two feet away.

I broke the eye contact and joined in the conversation between my sisters, making a point to ignore the bartender who had unbeknownst to him, had stolen my heart. "I think we need to have a final party before school starts back up. I mean we only have a week and a half before classes start. Let's plan something," Milla suggested. I nodded in agreement, not into the discussion at all but not wanting to be rude. Olivia squealed and clapped her hands.

"That's a wonderful idea! Jordan!" she called out.

Jordan looked up at her. "Yeah?" he asked from across the bar.

She crooked her finger at him. "Get your fine ass over here, baby. I want to ask you something." She waggled her eyebrows seductively, laughing huskily. And I wanted to crawl under my stool and lay there in a fetal position.

I didn't miss the exasperated sigh Jordan let out before making his way over. "What is it Olivia? Some of us have to work, you know," he stated a little shortly. I was surprised by his terseness but Olivia seemed oblivious to it.

"I want to have a party. So we're having it at your place. Tomorrow night. K?" She didn't ask, she told him. Was this how their relationship worked? She said it was so and he just agreed?

Jordan's mouth tightened and was clearly not pleased with her suggestion. "I have to work tomorrow night, Liv," he said, his words clipped. Olivia waved away his objection.

"So? I can take care of it. I know Fred and Gio would help me," she said, mentioning the Pi Sig brothers who shared the house with Jordan.

Jordan's shoulders stiffened. Olivia batted her eyelashes at him. "Please, Jordie. I promise to show my gratitude," she teased, running her finger up his arm.

Oh yuck. And what was up with calling him *Jordie*? It made him sound like he belonged on the Jersey Shore or something. I saw Jordan glance at me quickly. He needed to stop doing that. He was being way too obvious.

"Who would you invite?" he asked, looking back at Olivia.

She squealed again (how much could she do that in one night?). "Just my girls and the Pi Sigs of course. Only the best. Come on, it'll be fun." Tabby and Milla had started pleading with him as well and he finally gave in. Holding his hands up to stop them, he nodded.

"Fine, whatever. I don't get off until midnight. Just keep it cool, Liv. Nothing like last time, alright," he said, shooting her a pointed look.

She dismissed his words, focusing on his acquiescence. "Oh, thank you, baby. You're the best." She turned to Tabby and Milla, immediately starting to make plans. Jordan leaned on the bar and looked at me again.

"So, Mays. Are you gonna come to my raging party?" he asked sarcastically.

I shrugged. "Don't know. It all depends on what I have going on." Jordan tipped his head toward me and dropped his voice.

"Oh, come on. Don't leave me to deal with a house full of sloppy drunks by myself," he pleaded teasingly.

I couldn't help but laugh. "Please. You deal with sloppy drunks almost every day. By now you have to be a pro."

"That's why I shouldn't have to suffer it alone on my off time. Please come," he said softly. I looked over at Olivia and the girls but they were too wrapped up in their party planning to pay us any mind.

This felt sneaky and underhanded but oh so delicious. When Jordan looked at me like that, it was frighteningly easy to throw my morals and resolve straight out the window. I sighed heavily. "Fine. I'll come. But only for a little while," I conceded. Jordan's mouth stretched into a dazzling grin.

"Excellent. See, I knew you'd never let me down," he said, tapping the back of my hand with his finger, shooting electricity through my skin where he touched me.

"We'll see," I muttered, trying not to look as pleased as I felt by his words. Jordan smiled again and then had the audacity to wink at me. His flirting knew no bounds. But before I could say anything else, he moved away and went about his job.

I was only able to stomach another thirty minutes of watching Olivia and Jordan as they bantered back and forth. I couldn't deny the connection they shared. One that obviously came from a shared history. Sure, there were times Jordan seemed annoyed by his girlfriend but she also made him laugh and he interacted with her on a level that was impossible to ignore.

It sucked. I slammed back my beer and got to my feet. Olivia looked up in surprise. "You leaving, Mays?" she asked, giving me a smile that was so sweet it made my teeth ache. Jordan's eyes flicked over to me and I immediately looked away. Something stirred in my gut as I realized Milla was watching me.

"I've had a long day, I'm beat. I'll see you guys tomorrow. I'll be over to the house around lunch time, cool?" I said, grabbing my purse and digging for the keys.

"Sounds good. We'll see you then." Olivia got to her feet and gave me a hug. I patted her back awkwardly and threw out a final goodbye to Tabby and Milla before heading to the door.

"Maysie! Hang on a sec!" I froze as Jordan jogged to catch up with me. I painted a smile on my face and stood rigidly as I waited for him.

"Yeah?" I asked, almost scared of what he would say.

"You forgot your debit card," he said, handing out the thin piece of plastic between two fingers. I laughed nervously. God, I was such an idiot. What did I think he was going to do? Profess his undying love to me in front of his girlfriend and my sorority sisters? I needed to get a grip.

"Thanks. Guess I need that." I laughed shortly and reached out to take it from him. He put it in his palm and pressed it into mine. He held my hand almost intimately. The feel of his skin against mine was too much. We stood like that, our hands together, for longer than was appropriate. Realizing he had made no effort to move away, I snatched my hand back and gripped my card tightly in my fist.

"Thanks," I said, refusing to meet his eyes.

"Sure," he said quietly. I darted a quick glance back at my sisters. Olivia and Tabby were talking, oblivious to our little moment. But we did have a witness. Milla watched us closely and I tried not to shiver at the calculation I saw in her eyes. She met my gaze and lifted her drink toward me, arching her eyebrow.

Shit, I had to get out of there. "See ya," I told Jordan quickly, hurrying out the door.

"Don't stand me up tomorrow night! You promised!" he called after me as I crossed the parking lot. I couldn't help myself; I just had to look at him again. So I stopped and turned to face him. He stood in the open doorway, watching me.

"Sure, wouldn't miss it," I called back, feeling the beginning of rain pelt down around me. Jordan smiled. The most perfect, amazing smile ever. And this time I fled as fast as my legs could carry me.

CHAPTER
8

"*I think* we should do some sort of skit. You know for the rushees. Something that shows them how awesome Chi Delta is. We have to stand apart from the other sororities on campus," Vivian enthused, as I looked through albums of pictures from past rush events. We were brainstorming ideas for the upcoming rush week. So far all we had come up with was a beach party theme and a biker babes night. I thought both were a little lame, but Vivian was all about it. I had yet to learn the fine art of speaking my mind at sorority meetings. I was still trying to figure out my place in this group of girls and didn't want to rock the boat.

"Like what kind of skit?" I asked apprehensively, shuddering as I came across a series of pictures with past sisters dressed in zebra and leopard print outfits. A banner that read "Welcome to the Jungle" hung on the wall behind them. Dear lord.

"I don't know, maybe we could do something that's like Chi Delts through the ages. We could have sisters in different time periods. Like flapper girls, then hippies, disco. We could have killer music and everything," Vivian suggested. I actually thought the idea was pretty cool.

"Yeah, I like that one. Let's start drafting a skit," I said, standing up. I went over to the bookshelf and pulled a spiral notebook down. We were sitting in the common room at the Chi Delta House. It was a beautiful room. There were three huge picture windows that overlooked the quad. The colors were a combination of warm golds and soft greens. I was camped out on one of the three plush couches that sat in a semi-circle around a large oak coffee table. Two walls were covered with built in bookshelves and the other two walls were covered in pictures of the campus and Chi Delta members.

I had opted out of having a room at the house. Sometimes I worried that this made it even harder for me to bond with my new sisters, but I had made the commitment to live with Riley. I would never have gone back on that.

Vivian pulled out her own notebook and started writing down ideas for the skit. We were so into what we were doing that I jumped when the front door opened and a group of sisters came in. They had obviously been to the campus gym because they were all dressed identically in tiny work out shorts and barely there tank tops.

Olivia was with them. When she saw us, she broke away from the group and came over. She sat down on one of the couches. "How's it going girls? Any ideas for rush?" she asked, taking a drink from her sports bottle.

"Vivian came up with a great idea for a rush skit," I said, letting Vivian have the spotlight.

"Oh, yeah? Do tell," Olivia said, sitting up. Vivian launched into an overly detailed description of the skit. I sort of zoned out. I couldn't help but watch Olivia as she spoke with Vivian.

And I couldn't help but compare the two of us in my head. And so far I was coming up seriously short. How sad was it that I was creating a fictitious competition with this girl in my head? I needed to get over my ridiculous fixation with her boyfriend. The quicker I did that, the better off I'd be.

"Don't you think, Mays?" Vivian asked suddenly, pulling me out of my thoughts. I blinked in confusion.

"Huh?" I asked stupidly. Vivian rolled her eyes and Olivia chuckled. A low rich sound that probably made guys go instantly hard. Man, I hated her.

"I said, we should probably start thinking of a play list for the skit and then we can build the dialogue around it," Vivian said with irritation, clearly annoyed that I hadn't been paying attention.

I nodded. "Yeah, that sounds like a plan," I said as Olivia got to her feet.

"You girls should talk to Jordan. He has an insane amount of music. He probably has everything from the last fifty years. He'd be a great resource for you to use. And I have it on good authority that he'll help out. You know; if he wants to get any later." I tried not to gape at Olivia's sexual comment. Then I couldn't help but think of the two of them together. Naked. And I felt sick.

"Really? Can you call Jordan and ask when we can meet with him?" Vivian asked, a little too eagerly.

"Sure, I'll let you girls know," Olivia told her, walking out of the room.

"That'll be awesome! I'm sure Jordan will have a bunch of great ideas," Vivian gushed and I gave her a weak smile.

"Yeah, I'm sure," I replied, none too enthusiastically.

"Don't forget about the party at Jordan's tonight! Everyone is expected to be there!" Olivia said, peeking her head back around the door.

"Of course we'll be there!" Vivian chirped. I gave a thumbs up as Olivia disappeared.

"I've got to find something to wear for tonight!" Vivian squeaked, picking up her notebook and bag. For a girl who was about to enter her senior year, she came across as extremely juvenile sometimes.

"Viv, you've got like eight hours before the party. I'd say you have time," I said as she hurried to the stairs to go up to her room. She turned around and placed her hand on her hip.

"Girl, it'll take me that long to be perfect. There will be some fine Pi Sig ass there tonight and if I want to secure a date to our first mixer, I have to look drop dead gorgeous." She gave me a once over. "You might want to head home and start getting ready yourself. Maybe you'll find a guy you like tonight," she offered.

Oh there would be a guy I liked there alright. Just not one that I would ever have any claim to. "Eh, I've got time to wax and primp. No worries." I followed Vivian up the stairs and headed to Gracie's room.

"There's never enough time to make sure you look amaze!" I tried not to roll my eyes as she walked away.

I went into Gracie's room without knocking. I never knocked. Unless there was a scrunchy on the doorknob. Then I knew she was otherwise indisposed and to come back later. Gracie was ironing a shirt when I walked in. Her music was cranked up. She had on that horrible rap crap that she insisted was the only music worth listening to.

She looked up as I came in and grinned. "Hey girl!" she shouted over the stereo.

She thankfully turned the music down. "How did the meeting with Vivian go? She's not having everyone dress like biker sluts for the first party is she?" Gracie asked.

"Ah, so you've heard the fantastic biker babes concept already," I surmised, lying down on her bed. She moved a pile of clothes onto the floor so I could put my feet up.

"Yeah, we had to hear about it all last week. She seems to think it's the best idea EV-ER!" Gracie mimicked Vivian's high-pitched voice perfectly.

I laughed. "Yeah, well it looks like you're going to have to suffer through black leather and fishnets like the rest of us," I told her.

Gracie threw a shirt in my direction, which hit me in the face. "Why didn't you tell her that idea sucked? That's what you're supposed to do, Mays!" Gracie argued.

I shrugged. "I don't know, maybe it won't be so bad," I offered. Gracie looked at me pointedly.

"No, you just didn't want to speak up. Girl, you have to learn to say what's on your mind. We're your sisters. We're not going to feed you to the lions if you disagree with us. That's the whole point of sisterhood. We stick together." I sighed. I could tell she really believed what she was saying, but I wasn't so sure. I still felt a little out of place in Chi Delta at times. Some of the girls, like Gracie, had become real friends. The rest were still virtual strangers.

Looking at Gracie, she was the epitome of the sorority chick. Her long hair was straight and the color of wheat. Her eyes a pretty light green eyes and she sported a thin figure despite the fact that she ate more than most guys I knew. She was classically pretty, with a cute little nose and rose bud lips. If I looked up sorority girl in the dictionary, I was sure Gracie's picture would be there. And her effortless ability to fit into this life was something I envied.

"Yeah, well, next time," I said noncommittally. Gracie didn't say anything, just turned back to her ironing.

"So, do you have an outfit picked out for tonight?" she asked me, putting her shirt on a hanger and placing it in the closet. She shared her room with Milla and you could see the divide between their two personalities in that closet. Whereas Gracie dressed conservatively but cute, Milla's clothes were trampy and revealing.

"Not yet. What's the big deal? It's just a party," I said, not really getting the hype over it. Gracie turned around to face me.

"Just a party? Girl, this is a party at Jordan Levitt's house. His parties are epic. This is the first official social event of the year. It sets the precedent for the entire fall semester. You have to look perfect! And more importantly, you have to find your date for the Pi Sig mixer in three weeks! I mean, you can't go by yourself!" Gracie sounded appalled at the idea. I wondered when I had stepped into the 1950's. I couldn't believe that people still hinged their entire life on finding the perfect guy. And herein lies the biggest difference between these girls and me.

Because I'd much rather go to the mixer by myself. I didn't like the thought of scrounging for a date with some random guy and then having to suffer through an entire night of awkward conversation. But apparently that was a serious social faux pas.

"Okay, okay. I'll make sure to look Barbie doll perfect," I said sarcastically, though Gracie didn't pick up on it.

She breathed out a sigh of relief. "Good. If you need any help getting ready, I can come over and we can hit the party together," she suggested.

"That sounds good," I responded. It's not as if I needed help getting ready. I could put myself together pretty damn nicely. I had style and I always looked good, but Gracie had a need to put her touch to things. So I figured it was just easier to let her.

Gracie came and sat down beside me on the bed. She grabbed my ankle and gave it a little shake. "Have you finally ditched the townie? You ready to find yourself a decent guy?" Not her too! Gracie had met Eli a couple of times and had never seemed bothered by our relationship. Apparently she had disapproved as much as Riley had. She was just less vocal about it.

"Yeah, we're done. But I don't think I'm looking for anyone either. I might take a bit of a break from the whole dating scene for a while," I said, knowing that I couldn't even think of hooking up with anyone while Jordan was still front and center in my mind.

Gracie made a noise of disapproval. "No, no, no. You have to find someone to take you to the mixer! It's important, Mays!" she implored.

"Well, what about you? Do you have your sights set on anyone?" I asked, trying to move the topic away from me and my love life.

"I don't know, I have some potentials. I'm thinking of checking out Gio. I mean, he's cute, he lives with Jordan so you know he's really popular and he's a senior." She ticked off each characteristic as though she were buying a car. What a sterile way to go about deciding whether to go out with someone.

"Sure, Gio's nice," I replied, though truthfully I had always heard he was a bit of a dog. A love 'em' and leave 'em' sort of guy. Gracie was too nice to be another notch on anyone's bedpost. But I didn't say anything. Who was I to tell someone whom they could and couldn't like?

We hung out for a while longer before she finally kicked me out, saying I had to go home and start prepping for tonight. I had the obstinate desire to show up to the party in my rattiest pair of jeans and a damn T-shirt. But I knew my sisters wouldn't be happy with that. They wouldn't be able to see the funny of it.

But Jordan would get it...

Okay, I had to stop that. Every thought seemed to find its way back to him and I was driving myself crazy. I let myself into my apartment and found Riley watching television, still in her pajamas. She had come home late last night. I had heard her letting herself in around three in the morning. Looking at her now, I could tell she was feeling rough.

The blinds were still drawn across the windows and I felt like I was walking into a tomb. I sat down beside her on the couch. "How's it goin' Riley?" I asked too loudly. I couldn't stop grinning at her. Normally our roles were reversed and I was going to enjoy this.

Riley gripped her head. "Ugg! Volume, please!" she whispered hoarsely.

I slung my arm around her shoulders and squeezed. "Feeling a little crappy today?" I asked more softly this time, taking pity on her miserable state.

Riley groaned. "I am never drinking again!" she swore, turning the TV off and laying down.

"Have you eaten anything?" I asked her.

Riley shook her head. "The thought of food makes me want to puke." I got to my feet and headed into the kitchen.

"Well, you have to eat something, or you'll feel worse," I called out as I put two pieces of bread into the toaster and got the ibuprofen down from the cabinet.

I took the dry toast, a large glass of water and the bottle of pain meds into the living room. "Drink all of this and take three ibuprofen. Trust me, if there's anything I know how to deal with, it's a hangover." Riley gingerly took the capsules out of my hand and put them in her mouth. Then she drank the entire glass of water.

"Now eat. Dry toast is the best thing for an upset stomach." I shoved the plate into her hands and she took it, glaring at me.

"You're enjoying this way too much." She accused, nibbling on the bread. I smiled at her as I took a seat again.

"Well, considering it's usually me in a fetal position on the couch, I don't envy you. But I must say it's not like you to over indulge. I've never seen you like this. So what gives?" I ask her.

"Stupid boys," Riley muttered and my smile became even wider.

"Did you go out with a boy last night, Riley?" I goaded. She gave me the middle finger.

"Yeah, I hung out with Damien and a bunch of his friends after work. I got a little too drunk. Who knew a Green Eyed Monster was so vile coming back up." Her face had gone pale.

"Well, no wonder you feel like shit. Everclear is some hard shit if you're not used to drinking." I pointed out.

"Says the girl with the pickled liver," Riley snarked. I ignored her, knowing she was feeling touchy.

"So, you and Damien, huh?" I asked, watching her to make sure she finished the toast.

Riley shrugged. "We've hung out a few times," she said.

My eyes widened in surprise. "You have? What happened to not dating guys you work with?" I asked, giving her a smug smile.

Riley shrugged again. "Yeah, well my advice sucks. Forget about the shit I say. I know nothing," she said sarcastically. I snorted.

"Do you like him?" I asked her, trying really hard not to yell told you so in her face.

Riley smiled a little and I knew she did. "He's really cool. Did you know he started an eco-group back in his hometown? He recruited like fifty people and started an annual recycling campaign. He really gets things. And it's nice to talk to someone who's on the same wave length, you know?" She finished her toast and put the plate on the coffee table. I didn't want to tell her that he sounded boring as snot. So instead I grinned for her.

"Wow, Riley. I don't think I've ever heard you talk like this about a guy. I'm happy for you," I said sincerely. Riley looked at me shyly. A first for her.

"Yeah. I really like him. But who's to say he feels the same way. I mean we kissed last night, but..."

"You kissed?" I screeched, bouncing up and down on the couch.

Riley laughed and then groaned, pressing her hands to her stomach. "Please stop making the couch move or I'm going to barf in your lap." I stopped instantly. Upchuck and Maysie were not friends. Riley leaned back and pulled a fleece up over her. "Yeah, we kissed. Most of the night actually. But we were both pretty drunk. So who knows if he really wanted to or if it was the booze talking?"

I wasn't used to hearing such insecurity from my friend. She was one of the most self-possessed, totally sure girls I had ever met. It just goes to show how boys can bring you low without you realizing it. I laid my head on Riley's shoulder. "Of course he wanted to. What guy wouldn't want to kiss you? You're the most awesome person I know," I told her.

Riley sighed. "Thanks, Mays." We sat quietly for a moment and then Riley turned the conversation around to me. "So what's up with you and our resident rock god?"

I stiffened at the mention of Jordan. She noticed immediately and nudged my head with her shoulder. "You know Olivia's back in town, right?" I asked. Riley nodded. "Well, all of the Chi Delts have to go to a party tonight...at Jordan's," I said miserably.

"It's just a party, Mays. It's not like you're going to watch them star in an adult film together. It'll be alright," Riley assured me, being brutally honest as always. I couldn't help but laugh.

"Yeah, but the whole thing just sucks. I really like him, Riley. I mean, I thought I could make myself stop once I knew he had a girlfriend. But it's almost like my feelings are getting stronger. And all I want to do every time I see Olivia is pull every strand of hair out of her stupid, perfect head." I sat up and crossed my arms over my chest.

Riley snorted. "Well, if there's one thing I know about you, Maysie is that the more screwed up the situation, the harder it is for you to resist it. I mean, look at your little, whatever it was, with Eli over the summer. That guy was bad news. And an asshole. But you still went after him anyway. So now there's Jordan, and he's taken and that is completely irresistible to you." I bristled at her words.

"So you're saying that I don't really like Jordan? That it's more about the fact that he's unattainable?" I bit out, feeling a little insulted by her opinion of me.

Riley shook her head. "No, okay, that came out wrong. What I'm trying to say is the more hopeless the situation, the more you try to change it. And I know you feel something for Jordan, just like I know he has feelings for you. You'd have to be blind not to see it. But you say you're keeping your distance and pushing him away, but are you really? I mean, I see the looks you give each other. You practically orbit around each other. What you both are doing is engaging in nonphysical foreplay." I swallowed audibly.

Riley raised her eyebrows. "You know I'm right." Damn her, she probably was right. I hated how perceptive she could be at times.

"Yeah, well that doesn't mean I'm going to do anything about it. I have no desire to be the hussy home wrecker," I said sharply.

Riley patted my arm. "And that is what makes you better than your sorority sisters and most of the girls we know. Because they would jump at the chance to get with Jordan Levitt, girlfriend or not. But you're better than that. And that's why I love you." Her compliment took me aback. And it felt really good, if a little undeserved. Because I still thought about doing Jordan every which way to Sunday.

"Love you too, girlie," I said. We hugged each other for a moment. Which was unusual for us because Riley was not a touchy feely kind of gal. Maybe the whole Damien thing was breaking through her guard a bit. And I for one was happy to see it.

"Okay, you rest. I'm going to go take a shower and start the waxing process." Riley shuddered.

"How you can torture yourself like that is beyond me," she said. I ruffled her hair in a way that I knew annoyed the shit out of her.

"If you need anything, just holler," I told her before heading down the hall.

CHAPTER

9

*A*n hour later I came out of the bathroom, tweezed, shaved and waxed within an inch of my life. My legs were smooth, my skin had been buffed and I had even taken the time to wax down south, leaving only a thin strip of hair. I had conditioned my hair and plucked my eyebrows. Surely, this would pass Gracie's hawkish inspection.

"No wood picks underneath your fingernails?" Riley asked from the couch. She still hadn't moved from the spot where I had left her. She did not wear hangover well.

"Shut it. There's nothing wrong with wanting to look nice," I retorted, turning to head into my room, not waiting for my roomie's response.

It was only 4:00. I had four hours until the party. Gracie had sent me a text while I was in the shower saying she and Cira, another one our pledge sisters, would be over around 5:30. She said they'd bring their outfits with them so we could all get dressed together. If there was one thing I had come to learn since joining Chi Delta, was these girls took their parties seriously.

I spent the next hour and half watching TV with Riley, who was finally almost human again. She had stopped groaning and even allowed me to open the blinds. "You want to come to this party tonight?" I asked her.

Riley looked at me like I was crazy. "What part of me throwing up all night and feeling like my brains were being pulled out of my ears, makes you think I want to go anywhere near a party?" she asked.

I laughed. "Just thought I'd ask. Maybe we could have a few Green Eyed Monsters..." Riley jumped up and ran to the bathroom. Okay, maybe the hangover wasn't completely gone. I heard a knock at the door and jumped up to answer it.

Gracie and Cira came in with their arms full of bags. "What is all this stuff?" I asked, leading them back to my bedroom.

"The essentials of course," Gracie replied, dropping it all on my bed. Cira immediately went to my closet and started rooting through it.

"You have to wear this!" she said, pulling out my sexy short white denim skirt and dark green tight fitted tank with spaghetti straps.

"Yes! That's perfect!" Gracie enthused as she started sorting my shoes, finally holding up my black, strappy Stella McCartney sandals. "You will look so hot in these! I need to borrow them sometime." Gracie slipped off her shoe and tried them on.

"Okay, let's do your hair first," Cira said, pulling me by the shoulders until I was seated at my vanity table.

"I am capable of doing my own hair, you know," I joked as Cira started separating large sections of my dark hair.

"Just let Cira do it, the girl is a genius," Gracie said, pulling her own outfit out of one of the bags.

"Cute," I commented, looking at Gracie's yellow summer dress that would wrap around her chest. Cira plugged in the two-inch curling iron and I tried not to groan. I liked wearing my hair straight. I wasn't one to change up my style too much. I knew I looked good how I was.

But my friends were determined, so I gave in. "Now hold still, I don't want to burn you," Cira warned as she started winding chunks of my hair around the hot iron. The next twenty minutes were punctuated only with Cira's orders for me to move my head this way and that. After she finished with my hair, she started doing my make-up. And I had to admit, it was kind of fun to be pampered. Finally, she declared that she was finished.

I looked in the mirror and I gaped in surprise. I didn't even look like me. My long hair fell in a mass of waves around my shoulders and my makeup, while less subtle than I was used to, looked good. Cira had ringed my eyes in liner, giving them a smoky look that made them stand out. She had used more coats of mascara than I typically did, but she had made my normally short eyelashes look much longer.

My lips were red and full and kissable, if you asked me. Not that I planned on kissing anyone, but still. "Damn, lady. You clean up nice!" Gracie piped up from behind me. She had changed into her dress and she looked adorable. She was in the process of putting her hair in a complicated updo.

I got to my feet and gave Cira a hug. "Thanks," I said sincerely.

"No, prob. You look good enough to eat," she teased, pulling on the hem of my shirt so that my chest popped out even more than it already did.

My friends finished getting ready and when they were done, it was time to leave. Riley had returned to her spot on the couch and looked up when we came into the living room. "You guys look nice," she said, though I could hear the sarcasm.

Gracie grinned, obviously not picking up on Riley's lack of sincerity. "Thanks, Riley."

"Let's go. I'm ready to get my party on," Cira called out from the front door. Riley tossed me my keys from the coffee table. I had offered to be sober sister tonight. Since all of the girls would be at the party, I didn't have to sit at home waiting for them to call me.

It was hard not to get excited with Gracie and Cira blasting One Direction and singing as loud as they could. The girls had started pre-gaming in the apartment while we were getting ready and they were already good and lit.

We pulled into the driveway of the house Jordan shared with two of his Pi Sig brothers. It was a good-sized two-story home, three blocks from campus. There were people everywhere. "This is going to be awesome!" Gracie cheered, climbing out of my back seat.

We made our way up to the front door. Olivia swung it open and gave each of us a hug. "More of my sisters! Yeah!!!" She hung on my arm as though I could help her stay upright. Jeesh, I had never realized Olivia was such a sloppy drunk.

Looking around as we made our way inside, I felt bad for Jordan and his roommates having to clean this up in the morning. The place was already thrashed. There was a group of people around the pool table in the living room using it to play beer pong. Drinks were getting knocked over and the green felt was soaked.

There were Solo cups everywhere and puddles on the floor from people spilling their drinks. The couches had been tipped onto their backs and shoved to the wall to make room for dancing. Gracie pulled on my hand and led me into the kitchen.

A wave of smoke hit me as I walked in and I could see a couple of guys at a table smoking a joint. I waved my hand in front of my face and coughed. It smelled like a skunk. There were three kegs and a plastic kiddie pool filled with Jungle Juice in the corner.

I took a beer, just so I'd have something in my hands and waited while Gracie and Cira got their beverages. "Maysie Ardin, lookin' fine." I rolled my eyes as I looked over my shoulder at Gio Bovalina, one of Jordan's roommates and the guy Gracie had her eye on.

He was cute in a Guido kind of way with his black hair slicked back off of his forehead and his polo shirt with the popped up collar. Personally, I didn't see the attraction. I thought he was kind of a sleaze. He flirted with anything that moved.

And his eyes were currently trained on my chest. I pointed to my eyes. "I'm up here, Gio," I said dryly.

"Yes you are," he said in what I guess was meant to be a seductive voice. He moved in closer to me and I couldn't help but back up.

"Gio!" Gracie squealed, coming up beside him and looping her arm with his. She looked between us, still smiling; unaware that the guy she wanted to hook up with had been seconds from drooling all over my boobs.

"Let's go dance," she purred and Gio laughed in a self-satisfied way.

"What the lady wants, the lady gets," he put his arm around

her shoulders and looked at me again. "I'll make sure to save you a dance for later." He raised his eyebrows at me and licked his lips. Gross.

Gracie was frowning, clearly a little confused by Gio's blatant interest in me. "No thanks. I'll pass," I said, moving away from them. Gio's response was lost in the din of the crowd as I went into another room. Watching people I knew getting wasted while they desperately searched for someone to rub against was mildly nauseating. At what point did parties go from 'hey lets hang out' to 'I'm gonna drink shots from between your boobs?' Probably around the time that we all discovered the embarrassment inducing effects of alcohol and recreational drugs.

I was normally a partier by nature. I loved to go out and drink. It was one of my favorite pastimes and what had drawn me to the whole Greek system to begin with. I'm not going to be one of those assholes and pretend I did it for the philanthropic opportunities. People that actually spewed that crap were either complete losers or knee deep in serious denial. Because being Greek was all about the parties. And the keg stands. And the ice luges.

But tonight I stood in the middle of this crazy college level debauchery and I felt a little empty inside. My eyes followed Olivia as she danced on the coffee table, her skirt barely covering her ass as Pi Sigs leered up at her. Milla and Tabby were grinding against each other while guys urged them to make out.

Gracie was trying desperately to look sexy as she writhed against a disinterested Gio. And Jordan's house was getting trashed. These people really didn't give a shit about the destruction they were unleashing in someone else's home.

When had I grown a fucking conscience? It was sort of annoying and making enjoying the party next to impossible. I found myself a spot in the corner and sat down on one of the chairs that hadn't been upended. I sipped from my cup, grimacing at the taste of cheap beer.

A few of my sisters came up and chatted. I engaged in a rioting debate about the superiority of the thong as opposed to the less sexy boy shorts with several inebriated Pi Sigs. I even joined in one game of beer pong. But by midnight I was ready to call it quits and head home. But I couldn't. Because I had stupidly volunteered to be the goddamn sober sister.

I had already made four runs back to the Chi Delta house, threatening bodily harm on my sisters if they threw up in my car (which was finally fixed and road functioning). I had resumed my spot by the back door, still sipping that god-awful beer when my eyes zeroed in on the living room.

Jordan had walked in and stood there, looking around at the complete and utter chaos that had taken over his house. He looked tired. His hair that had started to grow out was sticking up on all sides of his head. Even from this distance I could see the dark circles under his eyes. As well as the bulging vein on the side of his neck. He was pissed.

Not knowing what possessed me, I got up and edged closer to him. Some sick part of me wanted to witness his detonation. "Olivia!" I heard him call out. I could barely hear him over the noise level. My eyes darted around the room, finally locating our illustrious president as she licked a line of salt from a random Pi Sig's neck and then proceed to take a shot of tequila.

Jordan stalked toward his girlfriend. I inched behind him, curious as to what was about to go down. Olivia was trying to balance a shot glass in her cleavage when Jordan grabbed her by the upper arm and swung her around. "Jordan!" she shrieked. In her drunken state it actually sounded more like "Jahhhdunnn."

Jordan reached down and pulled the shot glass out of her shirt and threw it on the floor. "Hey," she pouted but then tried to put her arms around his neck. Jordan reached up and untangled her hands and put them firmly by her side.

"I told you to keep it under control. You fucking promised me, Liv," he said tiredly. My heart wrenched for him.

Olivia rolled her eyes and pressed against him. "We're having fun. Don't be such a party pooper. Now come on and do some shots with me." I could see the tip of her tongue glide along his neck and I wanted to punch her in the face.

Jordan stepped away from her. I wondered if he would go off. He looked like he wanted to. But then he just shook his head.

"Enjoy the party," he told her. He grabbed a beer from the table and walked away, heading for the stairs. I watched him disappear around the corner. I turned back to see what Olivia would do, but she had already forgotten about him. I watched in disgust as she crawled around on the floor looking for her lost shot glass.

I had had enough. I put my cup down on the windowsill and found myself climbing the stairs to the second level. I didn't know what the hell I was thinking. I had been adamant in my resolve to stay away from Jordan. I didn't want to play this game with him while he was involved with someone else. But after witnessing the fucked up dynamic between he and Olivia, my heart hurt for him.

I didn't want to find him to hook up or anything. I kind of just wanted to hang out with him. For a little bit. As a friend. If that were possible.

There were four doors in the hallway and I had no idea which one was Jordan's. So I started opening them. The first was a bathroom where a girl was puking her guts out in the sink and a guy was passed out in the tub. I closed that door quickly.

The next was a bedroom and it was currently being used. I caught sight of two girls and a guy naked on the bed before I slammed the door shut. I might have to bleach my brain when I got home after the shit I had seen go down this evening.

I opened the third door and knew instantly I was in the right place. A drum kit sat in the corner and a guitar rack hung from the wall above a double bed. There were a few posters, each of a different band. I recognized one of my favorites, the Pixies.

A door to the right opened up and Jordan stepped out of an adjoining bathroom. He looked up and stopped short, seeming surprised. "Maysie. What are you doing up here?" he asked, turning off the bathroom light.

A heated look crossed his face as his swept over my body. "You look amazing," he murmured, his stare searing holes through my body. I coughed in nervousness and Jordan looked away. I watched him cross to the other side of the room. He picked up one of the guitars off the rack. He slipped the strap around his neck and sat on the bed as he started to tune it.

"Well, I promised you I'd come," I said, still looking around his room. I noticed several framed pictures on his dresser. Walking over, I picked up one of him and Olivia at some formal. They looked younger and were smiling at each other in a way that made it obvious they were in love. I quickly put it down.

"Yes you did. Glad to see some people keep their promises," he replied darkly, running his hand down the length of his shiny Ibanez guitar.

"A little crazy down there, huh?" I asked, watching him. He started twisting the tuning pegs, while plucking the strings. Jordan grunted something unintelligible but otherwise didn't comment.

"I didn't know you played the guitar," I said, tentatively pulling up his desk chair and having a seat. He looked up at me and gave me a halfhearted smile.

"Yeah, I don't play that well. The drums are definitely more my thing. But sometimes I just like to jam out for a bit. It's kind of a stress reliever." He looked back down at the guitar in his hands and started to move his fingers over the strings. I was tickled to realize he was playing the opening chords of *Tangerine*, one of my favorite Led Zeppelin songs.

"Don't play well my ass," I teased, mesmerized as I watched him pull notes from his guitar. Jordan looked at me and I couldn't help but smile at him. Gone was the flirty, intense Jordan Levitt. This Jordan was quiet and collected and perhaps even harder to resist. He suddenly got up and shut his bedroom door.

My face flushed and I felt like I might hyperventilate. Jordan must have recognized the look of panic on my face because he put his hand on my shoulder and squeezed lightly. "The noise out there is giving me a headache. Is this okay?" he asked and I appreciated him wanting my permission. It was sweet.

And right then, I forgot about everything but being here with him...right now. So I nodded. Jordan dropped his hand and sat back down on his bed.

"You ever thought about learning to play?" he asked me as he continued to strum a tune.

I put a hand to my chest in mock horror. "Dear God, no! I'm

musically challenged in the worst way. Tone deaf doesn't even start to cover how bad I am when it comes to anything instrument related," I explained adamantly.

Jordan waved his hand, gesturing for me to come over to him. When I didn't move he smirked. "I'm not going to bite," he taunted, though his words seemed to hold the hint of a promise. So against my better judgment, I stood up and sat down beside him on the bed.

Jordan lifted the guitar over his head and slid the strap around my neck and under my arm. "I know you're a righty, so hold it like this." How in the world did he know I was right handed?

Jordan couldn't miss the question in my silence. "When you write down orders, it's always with your right hand," he explained, looking a little shy by the admission.

I knew he watched me sometimes, but knowing he paid that close of attention was more than a little flattering. He leaned behind me and propped his chin on my shoulder. His arms came around me and he took my right hand and placed it over the strings. Then he wrapped his hand around my smaller left one as we gripped the fret board together.

"You have to loosen up. The first thing about music is you can't think too much about it. You kind of have to feel it. Does that make sense?" His breath tickled my ear as he spoke. I had to force my body not to shiver as I became entirely too focused on the feel of his chest pressed against my back. I could smell the grease from his shift at Barton's mixed with a scent that was undeniably Jordan.

I swallowed thickly and nodded my head. Jordan lifted my forefinger and held it down over one of the strings. Then he took my middle finger and placed it one string down. Followed by my ring finger that he positioned below that one. He pressed my hand lightly into the biting metal. He lifted my right hand in his and took my fingers, running them along the length of the guitar, top to bottom. The sound it emitted was pretty.

I turned my head a bit to look at him and grinned. "That was cool!" I enthused.

Jordan smiled back. "That was an A chord," he said, obviously enjoying my excitement. His smile slowly faded and I became very aware of how close our faces were. Our lips were almost touching and all I could do was stare into his beautiful blue eyes.

If I moved forward just a fraction of an inch I could kiss him. God I wanted to kiss him. No, I needed to kiss him. Needed it like I needed the air that I breathed. How had I never noticed how incredibly amazing Jordan's eyes were? They weren't just blue; they were this molted blend of light blue and darker cerulean. Someone could get lost looking in those eyes. And for a second I did.

Until I realized what was happening and I pulled myself away. I cleared my throat and looked down at his hands holding mine over the guitar. "Can you show me a different chord?" I asked, my voice trembling as I tried to steady myself.

Jordan took my cue and backed up a bit, putting some space between our bodies. But he didn't drop my hands as he held them tightly, moving my fingers into another chord position.

Fifteen minutes later and he had walked me through the opening chords of *Stairway to Heaven*. I had this incredible moment of accomplishment. I couldn't stop the goofy smile that made its way across my face. Jordan was smiling too and I felt like we just sort of clicked. We got each other on a level I had never experienced with another person other than Riley.

And then it all fell spectacularly apart. "Jordan!" I heard Olivia call from the hallway. Suddenly the door flew open, bouncing off the wall. I jumped up, the guitar swinging heavily off of my shoulder. Jordan got to his feet as well, running his hands through his hair.

"There's my baby cakes," Olivia slurred, falling into Jordan and wrapping her arms around his waist. I stood rooted to the spot. I was helplessly immobile as Olivia started slobbering all over Jordan's chin, trying to reach his lips.

Jordan seemed kind of disgusted by her and tried to gently move her away. "Baby, I need you. I want you to fuck me," she whispered loudly as she shoved her hand down Jordan's pants. He flushed a bright red, which would have been funny if my heart wasn't being shred to pieces.

He looked up at me in apology. I quickly pulled the guitar over my head and dropped it unceremoniously onto the bed. "I guess I should get going." I hated how shaky my words were in my own ears. Jordan pulled Olivia's hand out of his pants and tried to get around her.

"Jordan..." Olivia whined. Jordan made a grunt in frustration.

"Mays, wait," he started but I just shook my head.

"Thanks for the guitar lesson," I muttered, turning to leave.

"Jordan...I think I'm gonna be sick." Olivia ran into Jordan's bathroom and then all I could hear was the sound of her retching.

Jordan ran his hand over his face in agitation. "Maysie, I'm sorry..." he began.

I raised my hand to stop him. "You have nothing to be sorry about. Now, go take care of your girlfriend," I emphasized the word girlfriend and I couldn't stop the sound of my bitterness.

Jordan stared at me and looked as though he wanted to say something. But the moment was broken by Olivia's miserable moans from the bathroom. Jordan sighed and with a final look in my direction, followed her, closing the door. I stared into the space we had occupied only a few minutes before. How different things seemed now than before Olivia came bursting into the room.

Jordan had a girlfriend. And I was a fucking fool.

CHAPTER
10

I had about four stops to make before I had to head over to the Chi Delta house in an hour. This afternoon was our third party for rush week. The first two had gone off without a hitch and we had found some girls that would fit in with our group perfectly.

Today was the infamous skit. Vivian ended up writing most of it. I didn't feel comfortable going to Jordan's house to work on it after the party incident. Things had gotten pretty intense between us and I was back to trying to maintain distance. Which was easier now that school had started. I had to cut back my hours at both jobs, so right now I was only working at Barton's one shift a week. My schedule hadn't coincided with Jordan's in quite a while.

Though I wouldn't be able to avoid him forever because this weekend was the Pi Sig mixer. I still hadn't found a date, much to my sisters' horror. But I decided to screw it and go stag. The thought of scrounging up a date and forcing myself to interact all evening with someone I barely knew sounded exhausting. But I had gone out and bought myself an adorable little dress that was a deep red with an awesome skirt that flared out around my upper thighs.

I know, I know, I shouldn't be spending. But I figured with the way I had been busting my ass, I deserved it.

I was walking down the aisles at the Super Wal-Mart

downtown, trying to find tiny cocktail umbrellas and pink party napkins. The only thing I was finding so far was tacky and not at all with the pink and punk theme we had going on for today's rush event.

Feeling frustrated I decided to head over to the pharmacy section and pick up a few items I needed. I grabbed a box of tampons, some Midol and some super absorbency maxi pads. Because of course my period had to fall on the most important week of my fall semester. My uterus seemed to be plotting against me. Then on a whim, I grabbed a giant bag of Swedish Fish just because I loved them. And having your period called for copious amounts of sweets.

I was holding the items precariously balanced in my arms when I tripped over a cart that was conveniently left in the middle of the aisle. As if in slow motion, I fell face first to the floor and my feminine hygiene items sailed into the air, landing at the feet of none other than Jordan Levitt.

Of course! It just made sense that he would be the one to share my embarrassment. Because the universe wasn't kind enough to allow me be alone in the aisle when I face planted.

"Are you alright?" he asked, leaning down to take my hand. I wished I could tuck my head into my shirt like a damn turtle. Just so I wouldn't have to look at him standing there, holding my ginormous assortment of maxi pads with new super strength absorbent wings for your heavy flow.

Just kill me now.

"Here you go," Jordan said, dropping my humiliating grocery list into my basket. He didn't look embarrassed in the slightest. As though he were used to girls throwing their tampons at him.

"Thanks," I mumbled, feeling like the biggest tool on the planet.

I peeked up at him and saw him smile at me. I couldn't help but smile back, even as I tried to hide my basket behind my back. It had been two weeks since I had seen him and it might as well have been a year with the way my body responded to his presence.

"So, stranger, how've you been?" he asked, falling into step beside me as we headed toward the shampoo and conditioner.

I lifted my shoulders. "You know, busy and stuff. School is crazy right now. With classes and rush, I barely have time to sleep," I told him, picking out my brand of shampoo and tossing it into the basket.

I watched Jordan choose some deodorant and put in with my items. I felt all warm and fuzzy, like we were a married couple doing our shopping together. Married couple? Hell, we were barely friends. I needed a serious reality check.

"So, how's Olivia?" I asked, slamming both of us back into that reality. Jordan's shoulders tensed a bit but I may have imagined it because his voice was even and unaffected when he answered me.

"She's fine, I guess. But you probably see more of her than I do. She goes into sorority hibernation the week of rush. Nothing can deviate her focus from all things pink and frilly." I thought I heard a twinge of annoyance in his statement. But again, I was most likely searching for something that wasn't there.

"Yeah, the girls go a little nutso with all of it." I picked out a new toothbrush and put it in the basket while Jordan tossed in some mouthwash.

"And you don't?" he asked, looking down at me.

I shook my head. "No way. I mean, I love being in Chi Delta, but there's more to life than cupcakes and talking to random people about how much I love sparkles," I said sarcastically. Jordan laughed. He seemed to like my answer, which was odd considering he was as entrenched in the Greek system as his girlfriend.

"How's rush going for the Pi Sigs?" I asked as we made our way through the Wal-Mart.

"Same as every other rush, I suppose. I've been pretty busy so I've missed a bunch of the events actually."

I looked at him in surprise. "I thought you were the president. Aren't you kind of required to be there?" I asked as we got in line to check out.

"Well, funny you mention it; I stepped down from my position earlier this week." My eyes widened.

"You did? Can you do that?" I asked, taken aback.

Jordan shrugged. "Of course I can do that. I just have too much going on with this being my senior year. Plus the band is picking up more gigs and I didn't have the time for Pi Sig stuff. Plus, I'm sort of over the whole Greek thing. But don't say anything," he whispered conspiratorially.

Jordan Levitt was full of surprises. "I won't breathe a word. Cross my heart." I traced an 'x' over my chest and I saw Jordan follow the movement. I flushed as his eyes darted from my boobs back up to my face. "Will you be at the mixer on Saturday?" I asked, handing him his stuff from my basket.

He took the items and waited as I unloaded my crap. "Yeah, I'll be there. Wouldn't miss it," he said, grinning. I tried not to read too much into it, but it was hard when he was looking at me like that.

"Yeah, should be fun," I replied lamely.

I turned away from him and paid for my stuff. When I was finished, I grabbed my bags and started to leave. "Well, I'll see ya later," I called to him. Jordan handed the teller his debit card and then reached out to grab my hand.

"Wait for me. Why don't we go get a coffee or something?" he said. I was torn. I wasn't sure Jordan and I hanging out was a good idea. But what could it hurt? It was just coffee.

"Sure, that sounds good." I held my bags and waited for him to finish up. When he was done, he grabbed his items and then reached over and took mine as well. My heart swelled at the gesture. We walked out of the store and stood on the sidewalk.

"Where are you parked?" he asked me. I pointed to the aisle three rows over. "I'm right here. Why don't you meet me at the Cup and Crumb," he suggested.

I nodded and went to take my bags from him. He reached out at the same time and our hands brushed against each other. I tried not to sigh at the physical contact as I took my things. "Thanks for carrying them for me," I said quietly.

"Sure," he remarked nonchalantly. "See you in a few minutes," he called over his shoulder as he headed toward a Ducati motorcycle. Of course he had a motorcycle. Could he fit the bad boy image anymore if he tried? If he wasn't so delicious I would have laughed at how trite it was.

I hurried to my car, slinging my bags onto the back seat and threw the car into reverse. I realized once I pulled out onto the road that Jordan was behind me. It was hard to focus on the road when I really wanted to stare at him riding his bike in my rear view mirror. He looked dangerous and more than a little lethal, his face obscured by the dark helmet and his strong hands gripping the handlebars.

I was so screwed. Because I couldn't stay away from him, no matter how much I knew I should. And I was starting to not give a shit about the consequences. The fact that he was dating Olivia started not to mean so much. Because I wanted him to be mine. And that was clouding my better judgment.

I pulled into the Cup and Crumb, Jordan parking his bike beside me. I held my breath as I watched him take off his helmet and tuck it under his arm. I wiped my mouth, sure that drool had dribbled down my chin. He waited for me to get out of my car then followed me into the coffee shop.

The Cup and Crumb was a popular hangout for Rinard students and it was pretty busy. We approached the counter and I pulled out my wallet. Jordan put his hand on mine. "I've got this, Mays," he said and I slowly put my wallet back in my purse.

"Hey Jordan!" The girl behind the counter squeaked. Her nametag said Molly and she was batting her pretty little eyelashes at him as he looked at the day's specials.

"Hey, Molly. How's it going?" he asked her.

"I'm good." Molly puffed up at his attention before shooting a strange look my way. Everyone on campus probably knew who he was dating and she was wondering who the hell I was.

"What are you getting?" Jordan asked.

"Caramel latte with extra whipped cream, and two of the mini chocolate éclairs, please," I said, giving him my normal order.

"Sweet tooth, eh?" he teased. He ordered a black coffee and we stood to the side while we waited for our order.

"So will Generation Rejects be playing Barton's again anytime soon?" I asked him as we waited. Jordan cocked his eyebrow.

"Why, have you decided to become one of our groupies?" he asked jokingly.

I huffed. "No way. I don't do the groupie thing. I was just wondering because you guys are sort of entertaining," I told him coyly, shooting him a small grin.

"Sort of entertaining? You're breaking my heart, Maysie." He clutched his chest dramatically. I smacked his arm.

"Here you go, Jordan." Molly appeared suddenly, handing him our drinks while I took my plate of pastries. The girl shot me another look, this one not at all friendly, before turning to the next customer.

"I think she likes you," I said as we made our way to a booth near the back.

Jordan rolled his eyes. "Whatever. Molly is in my poly-sci class, she's just being nice." He dismissed my statement. I slid into the booth and sipped on my latte.

"Are you blind, Jordan, or just oblivious?" I asked, shaking my head.

"Uh, neither," he replied, looking at me over the lip of his mug.

I laughed but it came out as a snort. "Okay. You just choose not to acknowledge when girls practically fall all over you." My lips quirked in a smile.

"If that were true, I wouldn't feel as though I were chasing you all the time," he murmured, taking a sip of his coffee. I choked on the éclair I had just taken a bite of. Was he being serious? I had no idea how to respond.

The air was thick with the sexual tension between us. I tapped my fingers on the table. "So, tell me why are you so done with Pi Sig? I thought you were Mr. Fraternity," I asked, trying to refocus the conversation on something with less potential for an explosion.

Jordan cleared his throat. "I used to be. I mean, I like the guys alright. But I get sick of the backhanded bullshit that goes on. Do you know what I'm talking about? I mean, you've got to see it over there with the Chi Delts," he said.

I nodded, understanding him exactly. "Yeah, it's kind of like swimming with sharks at times. I worry they're going to take off my foot if I don't toe the line," I joked.

Jordan frowned at me. "Well, why do it then? You don't seem like you belong with Olivia's herd." I didn't know if I should be insulted or not.

What was he trying to say?

"Well, I wanted to make some new friends. So I figured why not. And I like the girls in Chi Delta. Most of them are really nice," I said defensively. The truth was, I got what he was saying and I wondered how I would survive in the dog eat dog environment the school's Greek system bred. You had to fit the mold or get out. Which was so against everything I had always stood for. But now, I was doing nothing but spending my energies on trying to fit in.

"Well, I guess that's what's important," Jordan mused, looking as if he didn't believe me. His attitude was making me a little angry. Nothing pissed me off more than when people questioned my choices. It made me feel inferior and insignificant. As though I were incapable of making a reasonable decision.

"What does Olivia have to say about you stepping down as president?" I asked sharply. Jordan's face darkened a bit.

"She doesn't know," he said, taking another drink of his coffee.

"She doesn't know? You didn't tell her you were going to do it?" I scoffed, not believing he could keep something like that from his girlfriend.

It was Jordan's turn to get defensive. "Yeah, well, Olivia has her own shit going on. I knew she'd freak out if I told her, so I just did it. I don't need to hear about how stupid I am for giving it up," he said bitterly.

I couldn't cover up my surprise. Jordan met my eyes. "I told you before that things have been strained with Olivia and me," he said quietly, reminding me of our disastrous conversation after he had asked me out and I had discovered he was taken.

This time, I didn't want to shut down the conversation because of my fears. I wanted to hear from him what was going on. "What do you mean?" I asked, moving my empty coffee mug to the edge of the table and taking another bite of an éclair. Jordan leaned back in the booth with a sigh.

"Have you ever been close to someone for a while and then realized that the two of you had absolutely nothing in common?" he asked me. I shook my head.

"No, not really. What are you getting at?" I asked him pointedly.

Jordan sat up and crossed his arms on the table. "I started dating Olivia when we were freshmen. We met the second week of school. She was a different person back then. Over the years I've realized we want different things. I mean, I care about her. But I just don't think we fit in each other's lives anymore." His words left me raw. Was he saying that he planned to break up with Olivia even before he asked me out?

So where did I fit into all this? I really wanted to know, but I was too much of a chicken to come out and ask that. "Does Olivia know you feel this way?" I asked, feeling a little sorry for my sorority sister. Because I knew she loved Jordan. You could tell that when she talked about him. But I had also seen the way she so easily disregarded his feelings. I understood what Jordan was saying about them being two different people. Because while they may look like they belonged together, personality wise they just didn't fit.

Jordan looked frustrated. "I don't know. I mean, it's not like we talk about anything that isn't Greek related." He shook his head slightly as if to clear his thoughts. "Enough about my Olivia drama. How are classes going?" I was thrown by the sudden change in topic, but I allowed it. I didn't want to focus on Olivia any more than he did.

We spent the next twenty minutes talking about school. Jordan revealed that he still had no idea what he wanted to do when he graduated. He was an Accounting major, mostly because his dad wanted him to become a CPA, like he was, and partner with him at his accounting firm. I could *not* see Jordan as an accountant. Didn't they wear glasses and buttoned collared shirts with Chinos? How could his dad even begin to think that would be a suitable career path for Jordan? I had known the guy for all of two minutes yet I knew unequivocally that he was meant to do a hell of a lot more with his life than crunching numbers.

Jordan explained that his mom owned her own chocolate shop and imported sweets from all over the world. He spoke warmly of his mom and I knew that even though his feelings for his father were strained, his mother was his rock.

He talked about staying in town after he graduated and playing with Generation Rejects. That seemed to be where his passion lay. His face lit up when he talked about playing shows and his dream of making music for a living.

"My dad would never go for it though. I've been told enough times, by a lot of people, that I need to concentrate on making a proper living and not put my energies into something that will never happen." He sounded sad and I couldn't help myself from reaching over and putting my hand on his. Jordan turned his hand so that he pressed his palm against mine and laced our fingers together. It felt right. As though our hands were meant to hold each other.

"Are you an only child? Or do you have any brothers or sisters?" I asked. Jordan shook his head.

"Nope, just me. So I am the lone recipient of my dad's disappointment." He let out a frustrated breath. I squeezed his hand before pulling away.

"The only child club kind of sucks sometimes, huh?" I asked lightly. Jordan cocked his head to the side.

"You too?" he asked. I took another bite of my éclair.

"Present and counted for. My parents were older when they had me. My mom was forty-two, my dad almost fifty. They didn't think they'd be able to have any kids. So when I happened, I became their sole focus. Their last ditch effort at realizing their dreams," I admitted harshly.

Jordan's eyes didn't hold an ounce of judgment and he looked at me as if he got what I was saying. "My dad is this uber successful guy, you know? He has this amazing career that he worked his whole life to have. He came from nothing and he thinks I'm throwing away all of the opportunities he never had. He calls me a fuck up because I'd rather play drums than stare at math problems all day," Jordan said, sounding unhappy. I understood exactly where he was coming from.

My whole life I had tried so hard to be something my parents could be proud of. I could never be enough or do enough to make them happy. My dad hated the fact that I was in a sorority and that's why he refused to help pay the dues. My mom, while she loved the thought of me finally being popular, sided with my dad in thinking it was a foolish waste of time. They never failed to let me know that they thought I should be 100 percent focused on school. My dad was a teacher and my mom was a nurse. They were totally dedicated to what they did. So having a daughter who sort of flew halfcocked through life wasn't their ideal.

"Disappointing your parents sucks," I said softly. Jordan's eyes sparkled at me and I felt we connected in that moment.

"It sure does," he agreed quietly, staring into my eyes intently before I finally had to look away.

I cleared my throat, trying to dispel whatever was building between us. I gripped my hands tightly together, staring down at the tabletop. "You know, I say do what you want. You have to do what makes *you* happy," I said.

Jordan smiled. "That's what I'm trying to do," he said quietly and I had a feeling he was talking about more than just his music.

My phone started vibrating in my pocket, the sound of Blue Oyster Cult's *Don't Fear the Reaper*, blaring.

"Love the ring tone," Jordan said smiling as I pulled out my phone. I looked down and saw that it was Gracie.

"Hello?" I had an overwhelming urge to throttle Gracie for interrupting such a great moment.

"Where the hell are you?" she yelled into the phone.

"Whoa, calm down. What's up?" I asked, shooting Jordan an apologetic smile.

"The rush event starts in two hours and Vivian is freaking out. Nothing is set up and the costumes are a mess. You've got to get to the house right now."

I sighed. "I'm on my way," I assured her and hung up.

I tucked my phone away and got up. "Sorority crisis?" Jordan asked.

"As always," I deadpanned, grabbing my purse. We left the coffee shop and headed to our respective vehicles.

"Thanks for the coffee. I enjoyed hanging out," I told him sincerely. Jordan leaned against his motorcycle, balancing the helmet against his thighs.

"Me too. It feels like it took too long to get here. I hate that things have been weird between us. I never wanted that," he said a little sadly.

"Me either," I admitted, feeling that magnetic pull between us intensify. My phone buzzed in my pocket again and I pulled it out. I didn't bother to read the text that Gracie had just sent. "I've gotta go. Duty calls. I guess I'll see you on Saturday?" I asked, before getting into my car.

"Yep. See ya Saturday," he called back, throwing his leg over the seat of his motorcycle and revving it up. He gave me a final wave before taking off down the street and I headed toward the Chi Delta house and two hours of drama.

CHAPTER
11

Rush week was a raging success. We had sent out eight bids and each girl had accepted. I finally, after months, felt like I belonged with my sisters. It felt good to help contribute to something that benefited the sisterhood. Most of the girls had made it a point to tell Vivian and me how great of a job we had done. The skit was fantastic and it had all fallen into place. Even with the massive amounts of anxiety and stressing. I had even received a call from my Big Sis in Chi Delta, Caryn, who had graduated last year and now lived in California. She wanted to congratulate me on completing my first rush week as co-chair. So all in all, I was feeling pretty damn proud of myself.

And seriously exhausted. By Saturday afternoon I was ready to drop. But my day was far from over. I had just gotten back to my apartment after being at the house all morning for Bid's Day activities. The new girls had been excited and their enthusiasm reminded me of why I had joined Chi Delta in the first place. I hated to admit that I had started doubting my reasons for signing on with a sorority. But today reaffirmed that these girls were my friends and I belonged.

"You look wrecked, my friend," Riley said from my doorway. She was dressed for her shift at Barton's. I hadn't seen much of her since school started. Partly because I was so consumed with all things rush and partly because Riley was spending every free minute with Damien.

"I wish I could just lie down and take a nap," I groaned, throwing my shoes out of my closet trying to find the pair I wanted to wear tonight.

"You're going to burn out if you don't take it easy once in a while," Riley warned, dropping to her knees beside me and pulling out the other wedged sandal I was looking for.

"Thanks," I told her, taking the shoe from her hand. Riley sat cross-legged on my floor as I got to my feet and started getting my outfit together.

"So what's on your epic social calendar for the evening?" Riley asked.

"It's the Pi Sig mixer. I have to be back at the house around 7 to pre-game," I muttered, focusing on my search for my silver hoop earrings. "Agg! I feel like I'm losing my mind! Where are my silver star earrings? I can't find anything!" I cried, throwing my hands into the air.

Riley got to her feet and gently pushed me out of the way as she started to root through my jewelry box. "Go sit down, you need a breather. I'll find them." I took her advice and lay down on my bed.

"Here they are loser." Riley tossed me the earrings and they landed on my chest.

"I'm a mess! What would I do without you?" I asked tiredly, my eyelids drooping heavily.

"Not be able to find your earrings?" Riley asked and we both laughed. I patted the bed beside me and Riley came and sat down.

"How are things with Damien?" I asked her, wiggling my eyebrows suggestively. Riley blushed. Dear God, she must have it bad if she was actually getting red at the sound of his name.

"Good. After work tonight, he's taking me to the midnight showing of that comic book movie I wanted to see that you refuse to go to." I pushed her arm.

"Sorry if I can't sit through two hours of guys in really tight spandex talking about their crystal of power or whatever." Riley widened her eyes.

"You just don't get its complexity," she intoned dramatically. I chuckled.

"Sure, that's it. So, Damien's taking you out on a date. Things seem to be moving along nicely," I said. Riley smiled softly.

"Yeah, he's pretty great. You know, he has a few cute friends if you want me to hook you up," Riley joked. She knew how I felt about blind dates.

I made a rude noise. "I'll try internet dating first, thanks. Besides, I'm not looking, remember," I reminded her. Riley looked at me knowingly.

"Well you're not looking if that guy isn't Jordan Levitt," she said. I smacked her with a pillow and she laughed. "You know, he talks about you a lot," she said suddenly.

I sat up on my bed. "Jordan talks about me?" I asked dumbly. Riley rolled her eyes.

"No, the Pope talks about you...yes Jordan!" My throat felt tight.

"What does he say?" I shouldn't want to know this. I knew better than to ask. But damned if I didn't want to hear every tiny detail.

"He makes every excuse to mention you in some way. 'Oh, Maysie must have rearranged the salt shakers.' 'I wonder if Maysie knows where the phone book is?' It's almost pathetic." I forced myself to laugh, though I really felt like throwing up. "Yesterday, he was telling me about how he taught you to play the guitar at his party. He said you're a natural."

It was my turn to roll my eyes. "He clearly has a different memory of that than I do. I sucked." Riley shrugged.

"Hell, you could probably sound like a dying cat and he'd think you were amazing," she teased. I shot her a look.

"What's that supposed to mean?" I asked. Riley picked up the pillow I had thrown at her and hit me in the face with it.

"Don't fish, Mays. It doesn't suit you." I stuck my tongue out at her. Riley flicked my nose. "You know exactly what I'm talking about. That boy has it bad. You can see it every time someone says your name."

"But Olivia..." I started and Riley cut me off.

"Fuck Olivia." I gaped in surprise at Riley's forcefulness.

"Wow, tell me how you really feel," I said dryly. Riley got up off of the bed and stood there for a minute.

"Seriously. Jordan has major feelings for you. And he's a good guy. I have never endorsed a guy you dated because so far they've been a bunch of dick weeds. And I know what I said about dating him before. But I was wrong because Jordan's different. And Olivia's a bitch." I automatically opened my mouth to defend my sorority sister.

"You know she is, Maysie. And Jordan sees that too. He wants you, my love. I say stop worrying about Olivia. She'll move onto the next sorry ass frat guy in no time. But you deserve to be with someone who looks at you the way Jordan does." I blinked, shocked by her statement.

"But, whatever. It's your life. Have fun at your 'mixer'." There she went using those stupid air quotes again. I didn't say anything as she left. I couldn't say anything. She had given me a hell of a lot to think about.

I proceeded to get ready in a bit of a daze. Riley had called out a goodbye before she left for work. I put on my cute little cocktail dress and opted to leave my hair straight. I applied very little makeup and deemed that I was presentable.

I arrived at the Chi Delta house a quarter after seven. I found a bunch of my sisters hanging out in the common room. They all called out a greeting as I came in. I couldn't help but feel warm at the recognition. It's not like the girls had ever been anything but nice to me. Otherwise I would never have pledged to begin with. But I had always felt a little outside of it all, despite my every effort to the contrary.

"Damn, Mays. You look hot!" Gracie called out, hopping up from the couch to give me a big hug. I did a little twirl and then a short little curtsy.

"You know it, babe," I replied, grinning. Cira came up and put a cup in my hand. I took a tentative sniff. "What is this?" I asked cringing. Cira giggled.

"I think it's every liquor we had in the cabinet and a little bit of 7-Up. Drink!" I took a sip and coughed.

"Are you trying to give me instant alcohol poisoning? I think I'll just have a beer." I handed the drink back to Cira who only laughed.

"Come on lets get you a beer then." Gracie tugged on my

hand and I followed her into the kitchen. We had about an hour before we were all heading over to the mixer. It was taking place at another off campus Pi Sig house. It was only a couple of blocks away, so we would be walking.

Olivia was in the kitchen embroiled in an intense looking conversation with Milla when we came in. "Hey Maysie," she said, throwing me a distracted smile as she turned back to her discussion. I lifted my hand in a quick wave before grabbing my beverage. Olivia looked stunning, as always. She wore a purple halter dress so tight it looked as though it had been painted on her body. The bodice apparently had a push up bra built in because her boobs looked like they were about to spill out from the top. Her legs looked ridiculously long in her black hooker shoes.

She was beautiful and I felt anything but standing near her. *Jordan's a lucky guy to have someone like her,* I told myself harshly. Gracie was talking to me about some guy she planned to hook up with tonight, even though she was the date of Eric Lewis, a Pi Sig sophomore. I tried to listen but I was completely distracted by the conversation going on behind me.

It seemed that Milla was giving Olivia a pep talk. Olivia's voice sounded strained and when I took a peek at her, she looked as though she had been crying. "I just wish I knew what he was thinking. He's just been so distant since I got back. I thought it was just me, that I was being paranoid. But it's not in my head. We haven't had sex since I got back." I heard Milla gasp in surprise, though looking at the other girl's expression; she seemed pleased with the news. Who was that bitch kidding? She *loved* that Jordan and Olivia weren't doing it. For her it was the probably the best news of the night.

Olivia sniffed and rubbed her nose with her hand. "Last night, I went over to his house after he got off of work. I was wearing his favorite lingerie. You know the red one with the nipple tassels?" Milla nodded.

Nipple tassels? Uh, gross.

"So, I'm all laid out on his bed when he gets out of the shower and he tells me to move over, that he needs to get some sleep. Can you believe that?" I felt bad for her as I could tell she had started to cry. Milla patted Olivia on the back.

125

"It's like he doesn't want me anymore. How could he not want me? He used to never be able to get enough! Don't you remember that time everyone walked in on us having sex on his pool table in the middle of the mixer?" Gag! I tried to control the upchuck reflex at her pornographic reminiscing.

"That's how it used to be all the time. Now I can barely get him to kiss me. Do you think he's seeing someone else?" Olivia sounded terrified at the possibility.

"No way, Liv! How could ever look at anyone else when he has you? Put that thought out of your head." Milla was saying exactly what a supportive friend *should* say. But I couldn't miss the fakeness of it. I knew with a certainty that had Milla been in my shoes with Jordan this summer, she would have been all over him like white on rice. Great friend there.

Gracie snapped her fingers in front of my face. "Earth to Maysie!" I blinked and stared back at her.

"What?" I asked, embarrassed at being caught snooping. Gracie sighed in exasperation.

"Never mind. Just drink up. You can't go to the mixer without a pre-buzz." She put my bottle to my mouth. "Now drink." Isn't this the very thing we were forced to watch videos about in high school? It had been the subject a myriad of after school specials. But how many college-aged student succumb to it each and every time? Gotta love peer pressure!

Olivia seemed to have gotten herself together and joined us in a round of Kings at the kitchen table. By the time we were ready to go, most of my sisters were well and truly lit. I hadn't ended up drinking that much, so I was still relatively sober. Gracie and Vivian held onto me as we made our way to the Pi Sig house off campus. They laughed a little too loudly and were told by some of our other sisters to shut up or we would all get busted for drinking.

"Shh," Gracie whispered dramatically, putting her finger to her lips. Vivian and I laughed, earning us another glare from our less than tolerant sisters. The guys were waiting for us when we arrived. Jordan was at the door when we arrived, holding it open for us. He looked ah-maz-ing. He wore a deep blue button down shirt with the sleeves rolled up to reveal his toned arms. He wore a pair of dark jeans and had changed the barbell in his eyebrow for the hoop again. His hair had been freshly buzzed and the whole affect was heart stopping.

I gripped Gracie's hand tightly. Even though I was the one who was sober, I was I afraid I'd fall over.

"Ouch, you're crushing my fingers, Mays," Gracie whined, pulling her hand away. Olivia led us up the stairs and stood on her tiptoes to give Jordan a kiss on the lips.

Jordan pulled away a short second later, his smile now tight. "Welcome ladies, come on inside."

The girls filed into the house. Music was blaring and my bones reverberated with the bass. I tried to slink passed Jordan without him seeing me but his voice stopped me.

"Good to see you, Mays." I looked up at him and gave him a weak smile. His eyes were sparkling as they took me in and I had to force myself to look away.

"Thanks," I mumbled before hurrying after Gracie and Vivian.

The Pi Sig guys converged on us as we entered the house. Soon, people began pairing off to dance. Gracie had gone off with Eric, her date, and Vivian had latched herself onto some guy I didn't know that well, leaving me the lonely wallflower. Just fantastic.

I felt a little out of place and I wished I had taken Gracie's advice and come with a date. Arriving solo to these events sucked giant monkey cock.

I found the keg on the screened in porch. I poured myself a cup and took a few sips. Ah, cheap beer. I'd rather drink cat piss.

"You gonna drink that or what?" someone asked. I turned around as Gio came in. He really was one of the smarmiest guys I had ever met. He just oozed cheese.

I tipped my cup in his direction. "Cheers," I said, emptying some of the crappy beer into my mouth. I tried not to grimace at the taste.

Gio took my cup and put it down. "Come dance." He pulled on my hand and I let him. I tripped over a piece of linoleum popping up from the floor in his haste to haul me out of the kitchen. I toppled forward but Gio caught me around the waist.

"Easy there, babe," he teased, leaning into me. Oh crap was he trying to make a move? The sound of giggling snapped Gio out of it. I used Gio's arms to right myself and looked over at the doorway. Olivia and Jordan had come in. Olivia was hanging off of Jordan's arm.

"Gio, your moves are worse than ever. Leave poor Maysie alone." She laughed and I gave her a smile.

"Oh, I can handle him. No worries." Oops, that came out all wrong.

Gio wound his arm around my waist. "Oh, you can handle me alright," he purred in my ear. Yuck! I tried to shove him back.

"I think she wants you to let her go, G," Jordan said tightly. Gio dropped his arm and I looked at Jordan. His face was dark and if looks could kill, Gio would ten feet under by now.

Gio laughed. "No harm, no foul. Can't blame a boy for tryin'." Gio put his hands up in mock surrender. "I still want that dance though. I promise to be good." Gio grinned at me and my eyes darted to Jordan again.

Our eyes connected and he looked pretty pissed. For a second I wavered, tempted to tell Gio to forget about it. But then I looked down at Olivia wrapped around his arm like a fucking octopus and felt my own anger flare up.

"Sounds good Gio. But only if you promise to be naughty." I dropped my voice into a seductive whisper, never taking my eyes from Jordan. Something sparked in his deep blue eyes and I swallowed hard.

"Hell yeah!" Gio hooted; pulling me out of the kitchen before Jordan could react. Was I imagining the hurt look he gave me as I was pulled out into the living room? What the hell did he have to be hurt about? Stupid boy with his stupid girlfriend.

Okay, leading Gio on to make Jordan jealous was definitely one of my more idiotic ideas. Because once encouraged, the boy just wouldn't give up. I danced with him for one song, but when I declined a second he wouldn't take no for an answer.

"Gio, give it up. I'm done dancing with you!" I told him harshly, shoving him in the chest as he tried to mash our bodies together. He was wearing way too much cologne and it made me dizzy.

"But you told me to be naughty, Mays. I ain't shown you nothin' yet." He licked his lips and I tried to back away again. Suddenly a hand came around and pulled Gio by the upper arm.

"I believe she said to back off, Gio. Now stop being a fucking rapist and get the hell out of here." Of course it was Jordan. Who the else would come riding to my rescue while his drop dead gorgeous girlfriend looked on with obvious confusion?

"Dude, what's with the cock block?" Gio asked, his face going red and I worried there was about to be a fight. Both guys were obviously inebriated. And if I knew anything, it was that alcohol and testosterone did not mix. I wedged my body between them, facing Gio.

"Cock block, really? I don't think your cock is getting anywhere near my block. So don't worry about it." I flicked my hands in a shooing gesture. Gio's eyes narrowed.

"Whatever, bitch," he said and he stormed off.

"I need to go teach that shit some manners," Jordan growled, ready to go after him. I grabbed a hold of Jordan's arm to stop him.

"Jordan. Chill out." He stilled and looked down at me. We stood there staring at each other for a minute and I realized I was still holding onto his arm. Feeling self-conscious, I dropped my hand and wiped my clammy palm on the skirt of my dress.

"Thanks," I said a little shyly. Jordan gave me cute half smile.

"Anything for you, Mays," he said quietly and I had to seriously suppress the urge to jump up and down. This boy was my complete undoing.

"Thanks for helping out our girl, Mays. But I think she could have handled herself," Olivia said a little coolly, appearing beside us. I took a quick step back, making sure there was an appropriate amount of space between Jordan and me.

Olivia, flanked by Milla, was looking at me in a way that made me anxious. I had to defuse this situation and fast.

"You're right. I could totally have taken him. But guys like Jordan have to step in and ruin our female empowerment, right?"

Okay, so my attempt at lightheartedness was going down like a lead balloon. Jordan gave me a funny look.

"Well, thanks again, Jordan," I said one last time and then got the hell away from all of them. I found Gracie in the back corner of the room, tangled around her date.

"Gracie, could you help me find the bathroom?" I asked her, looking away as I saw her tongue fly into the guy's mouth. I stood there awkwardly for a few minutes before calling her name again. She finally pried her lips from Eric's, a trail of saliva connecting them. That was just nasty.

"What?" she asked shortly.

"Can you help me find the bathroom please?" I asked nicely. I had to pee, but more than that I needed some girl talk. If I didn't unload some of this bullshit going on with Jordan I thought I might explode. And I trusted Gracie. I knew she'd listen and not gossip behind my back later.

But I had caught her at a very bad time. She gave me the look of death. "I think you can find it yourself. Later, Mays." She gave me a very pointed look before returning to the full examination she was giving Eric's tonsils. Sighing heavily, I made my way to the staircase. I figured going upstairs would be the best bet at getting some quiet.

I just needed a moment to get my whirling thoughts straight. Jordan was wreaking havoc on my head and my heart. One minute I was determined to do the right thing and stay away, the next he was making that very resolve next to impossible.

I hurried up the stairs and found the bathroom. I splashed some water on my face and took a dozen deep breaths. *I can do this! I am not a slutty backstabber!* I chanted to myself.

When I thought I had composed myself enough to return to the party, I opened the door. And ran smack into Jordan. My hands flew up in front of me and braced myself against his chest. His hands came up and gripped my upper arms, holding me in place.

In my wedged sandals, I was almost at eye height, and it was nice to look at him without getting a crick in my neck. I tried to move to the side to let him by.

"It's all yours," I said, motioning to the bathroom.

Jordan didn't let go of my arms. Instead he pushed me backwards so I had to stumble into the bathroom. He flicked the light on and closed the door behind us. I backed up into the wall and stared at him. I was acutely aware of the fact that we were in a tiny space. Alone. Together.

I knew Jordan was drunk but the intensity in his eyes made my stomach flip over. "What can I do for you, Jordan?" I asked lightly, trying to alleviate some of the crazy tension crackling in the air between us.

Jordan ran his hands over his head and clasped them together behind his neck. His eyes bored into mine. "I can't keep doing this, Maysie." I coughed to cover my discomfort.

"Can't keep doing what?" I nervously started twirling a strand of hair around my finger.

Jordan reached out to touch the hair that I was frantically wrapping around my finger. "*This*. I can't keep doing this. I can't keep pretending that I don't want you. That I can handle seeing other guys watch you and look at you. Jesus, Mays, I wanted to beat the shit out of Gio! And I would have! I see fucking red when another guy even breathes in your direction! I can't keep lying to myself that I don't care about you. Because I do. So damn much." Okay, I had officially stopped breathing.

"Jordan..." I started but he shook his head, stopping me.

"Just let me finish, alright." I shut my mouth. Jordan closed his eyes as though it hurt to look at me. "I know I'm with Olivia. I know that was a deal breaker for you. But goddamn it, I don't want to be with her. I only want you. It has only been you from the moment you walked into Barton's." He opened his eyes again and took a small step toward me.

I couldn't back away, I had nowhere to go. Though I had to admit that I didn't want to.

"What are you saying, Jordan?" I whispered, not trusting my voice.

"I'm saying that I want to do *this*." And just like that, Jordan's mouth was on mine. He made a primal noise deep in his throat and my panties went instantly wet.

131

His tongue darted passed my lips and I could feel the cool metal of his barbell slide against my teeth. I twined my arms around his neck and Jordan lifted me up and put me down on the sink. I wrapped my legs around his waist, my dress pulled up to my hips and I could feel his hard on though my soaking wet panties. He rubbed against me with small little thrusts and it was my turn to moan into his mouth.

"My God, Maysie. You're killing me," he rasped as he pushed his hands through my hair, pulling my head back so he could attack my neck. His tongue ran along my collarbone as he suckled and nibbled his way back up to my mouth. He held me tightly in his grasp, his fingers gripping my hair so that I couldn't move my head. I was at his mercy. He slanted his mouth over mine again and I moved my hands up to the buttons of his shirt.

Slowly and deliberately I unbuttoned the first one. Jordan pulled my mouth away from his and his eyes smoldered. He watched me in the mirror behind my back as I opened up his shirt, one button at a time. Finally, I discarded the piece of clothing and let it fall to the floor. Then I slowly lowered my mouth to his chest. Kissing softly and carefully until I touched his nipple. I was being swept away in a tidal wave of lust. Rational thought and good decision-making had gone right out the window.

"Fuck," he groaned as my tongue swirled around the tight bead.

Jordan gripped the back of my head again and roughly pulled me back. Jordan's hand shook as though his control was quickly slipping away. The affect I had on him was a serious turn on. He pushed my shoulders so that I rested my back against the mirror. My ass was precariously propped on the edge of the sink but at that moment I didn't care. Jordan spread my legs apart his rough hands moving up my inner thighs.

Jordan kept his eyes on mine as he flicked up the skirt of my dress and ran a finger along the length of my very wet panties. "You're soaked, baby," he whispered, rubbing me more forcefully. My head fell back and smacked into the mirror.

"Touch me, Jordan. Now!" I cried out desperately. Jordan's lips quirked up in a taunting smile.

"What; like this?" His forefinger slipped underneath the edge of my underwear and slowly rubbed my throbbing clit. "Do you like it when I touch you like this, baby?" he whispered, watching me as his finger slid into my warmth. He stared at me as I clutched his hand and guided his movements in and out of my slippery folds.

I met his eyes and whispered, "Yes, I love it."

Jordan groaned and thrust another finger inside me and I arched off of the sink. Jordan's other hand roughly pulled down the neck of my dress so that my breasts were on full display. In one movement, he tore my bra from my body and I couldn't even register the fact that I would have to be braless the rest of the night.

With my breasts heavy and aching from desire, he cupped first one, then the other as he started rubbing my nipples. His callused fingers pinched and teased as his other hand manipulated my saturated heat. He had lit a fire inside of me and I was ready to go down in the flames.

"Oh God, Jordan!" I gasped as his fingers increased their rhythm.

"Come for me, Maysie. Please." His voice was a strangled plea and I was helpless to resist him. It was the rawest and intimate experience I had ever had with a guy before. Jordan watched me as I started to clench around his fingers and he continued to thrust them inside me. He licked his lips as I lifted my hips and pressed into his hand. I cried out his name, feeling myself shatter into a million tiny pieces.

Then Jordan picked up every one of those pieces and put me back together again. He removed his fingers from my dripping center, putting my panties back in place, his hand lingering between my legs. Then he gripped my waist, pulling me toward him again. He rested his forehead against mine and looked at me with an expression that made my heart twist up.

"I can't turn my back on us now. Don't fucking ask me to!" he demanded, looking almost angry. I closed my eyes and felt the first tears prick behind my eyelids.

Jordan put his lips to mine again and this kiss was less hungry than before but no less intoxicating. His hands came up to cradle my face and we kept kissing. It was almost as though we couldn't bear to be separated.

"Oops. Am I interrupting?" Four words and my life just got ripped in half.

CHAPTER 12

I *tore* my mouth from Jordan's and looked over his shoulder in horror to see Milla leaning against the door jam, her arms crossed over her chest. I shoved Jordan backwards and got down from the sink, straightening my shirt.

"We were just..." I tried to think of something to say, but it was useless. She had seen us together, kissing. I knew my mouth was swollen and bruised. There was no way I could whitewash that. Jordan didn't seem as bothered by this latest development as I was. In fact he looked annoyingly relaxed.

Milla clicked her tongue. "What would our lovely president say if she could see the two of you like this?" Jordan opened his mouth to respond but I cut him off.

"It was nothing! I swear! We're both just drunk!" I cried out desperately, lying through my teeth, as Milla started back down the hallway. God, if only I could blame alcohol on my behavior. But I was stone cold sober and I knew that I had no one to blame but myself. I started to run after her but Jordan grabbed me from behind, holding me in place. I twisted in his grip, trying to get away.

"Let me fucking go, Jordan! She can't tell Olivia!" I was panicked but Jordan continued to hold me still.

"So what if she tells Olivia? I'll go scream from the rooftops that I want to be with you and only you! I don't care!" he said angrily.

I pushed at him as he tried to pull me closer. Tears started running down my face. I was an emotional wreck and I had just gotten caught messing around with my sorority sister's boyfriend behind her back. I felt like such a slut.

"You don't get it, Jordan! I *do* care!" I screamed at him. Jordan looked shocked by my words. He began to rub my arms slowly, as if he were trying to calm a skittish animal.

"Why does it matter what anyone else thinks? We want to be together and that's what's important," he said softly, tucking a strand of hair behind my ear.

I should have felt soothed by his words. Isn't this what I wanted? Right then all I could think about was how wrong this situation had become. I was freaking out. I couldn't listen to this right now. Not when I had to do damage control.

"Who says that's what I want, Jordan? I don't know that I'm ready to shit all over my friends for some guy! Now, just leave me the hell alone!" I yelled, wrenching myself free and stumbling down the hallway, leaving him standing alone.

I was scared to go downstairs. No, I take that back. I was freaking terrified. I knew Milla would waste no time in telling everyone about what she saw. What was I going to do? Dear flipping God!

WHAT WAS I GOING TO DO?

I headed down the stairs, peeking into the living room. The party was still going on in full force but then I saw it. Little groups of my sisters huddled together, talking animatedly. My eyes darted around, trying to find Milla. And there she was her arm around Olivia who had her face buried in her hands. A self-satisfied smirk danced across Milla's face. This was so much worse than I could ever have imagined.

I gnawed at my bottom lip. They still felt tender from kissing Jordan only minutes before. Had it only been minutes? It felt like a lifetime ago. I hit the bottom stair and it was like one of those movies when everything goes in slow motion. I saw a few of my sisters look up at my entrance into the room and everything just stopped.

And their faces were anything but welcoming. I had to find

Gracie. I needed to explain to someone who would listen to me. Then the whispering started. The buzz of hushed voices filled my ears and it was deafening.

I practically tip toed further into the room, feeling exposed and on display. Everyone was staring at me. Everyone knew! You didn't have to be the most observant person on the planet to see that. It was on every one of their faces. My supposed friends all looked the same. They looked disgusted. Outraged even. A few of them looked almost jealous.

And the guys leered at me as though I had come in with my clothes off. "Having a good time tonight, Maysie?" Gio sneered as I tentatively headed to the kitchen. I didn't even bother to respond. I needed to find Gracie. I needed to talk to Olivia. I needed to pick my dignity up off the floor.

My eyes flickered up and found Olivia watching me. Our normally happy, party loving president looked at me as though I had just killed her favorite pet. Anger and betrayal painted her face in an ugly mask. I couldn't deal with her right now.

I bolted toward the kitchen, hoping to find Gracie there. Cira and Vivian were at the keg, talking with their backs to the door. I took a deep breath. Here goes nothing.

"Hey girls. Have you seen Gracie?" I asked; tacking the fakest smile I could muster onto my face. The girls stopped talking, the responding silence louder than anything else. Cira looked over her shoulder at me, her eyes cold. She traded glances with Vivian who looked a little more sympathetic. But both of them ignored me, turning their backs again as they filled their Solo cups with beer.

I grit my teeth and tried again. "Look, I'm not sure what's going on. But have you seen Gracie? I need to talk to her." I figured feigned ignorance was the best course of action. Cira flicked her hair over her shoulder and turned to face me. Her look of disdain cut me to the quick and took the air from my lungs.

"You don't know what's going on? Really? Are you stupid as well as a slut?" she asked hatefully. I reared back as though she had slapped me. I felt my face go pale.

"What the hell?" I hissed, feeling my anger start to simmer.

Who were they to judge me? I chanced a look at Vivian and she looked less disgusted. In fact, she seemed almost sad. Cira took a step toward me and for a moment I wondered whether my "sister" would strike me.

"I think it's time you left," she said in a quiet voice.

I drew myself upright, finding it hard to say anything. I had made my bed, I supposed. It was time for me to lie in it. I had allowed things to get out of hand with Jordan and now I was paying the price. I knew I was playing with fire but for those few minutes upstairs I just hadn't cared. It had only been Jordan and me. And for a brief time, that was all that had mattered.

But now I had woken up in the middle of a very real social nightmare. I turned on my heel and started to leave the kitchen when I heard hurried footsteps behind me and a hand grab me by the elbow. I looked up in surprise to see Vivian. Her eyes flashed in sympathy as she dropped her hand.

"I think Gracie's out back. But you should probably get out of here. Otherwise I'm pretty sure it's going to get ugly." I gave her a weak smile.

"Thanks, Viv," I told her sincerely. She smiled in return but it was full of pity.

I had to go back out through the living room to get to the door that led to the backyard. Going through the crowd of Pi Sigs and Chi Deltas was like trying to navigate through a room full of vipers. I heard someone snickering from behind me and a coughed "skank" said a little too loudly.

My eyes started to sting and my cheeks burned. *I will not cry! I WILL NOT CRY!* I screamed at myself as I walked, with my head held as high as it would go. I didn't look anyone in the eye. I moved by them all as if I were the Queen of fucking Egypt. Bunch of hypocritical bastards. Like none of them had ever made a mistake in their lives. How easy it was to judge others when really they should be examining themselves.

I pushed through the screen door and looked around for Gracie. I found her talking to a few of our sisters at the patio table. I walked toward them. The girls looked up as I came closer and every last one got to their feet. Gracie looked startled and more than a little concerned.

"Later Gracie," Bella, Victoria and Taylor said as they pushed past me. At least they refrained from calling me any derogatory names as they left.

Gracie grabbed my arm and squeezed. I winced. "What the hell is going on, Maysie? It's not true is it?" she asked in hushed panic. I could see that she had sobered up but she looked at a complete loss. I sank into the chair beside her and put my face in my hands.

"Did you really hook up with Jordan Levitt in the bathroom?" Gracie asked, putting her hand on my shoulder. I couldn't say anything; my throat felt like it had closed up.

So, I simply nodded. "Well, shit," was all she said and then she put her arm around my shoulders. Her act of compassion was all it took to unleash my tears. I started to sob. Deep, ugly crying. And Gracie let me. She didn't say anything until I had finally calmed down.

I looked up at her, hiccupping. "What happened?" she asked me. I clutched at her kindness like a lifeline. In that moment I knew with absolute certainty that most of my so-called sisters weren't my friends. I paid all of that damn money to hang out with girls who would turn their backs so much as look at me. What a depressing realization.

"I don't know. It just sort of happened," I said lamely. Gracie shook her head.

"No. Jordan Levitt doesn't just sort of happen. Now spill." I took a shaky breath and sat back in my chair.

"I really don't know how to explain all of this. Jordan and I work together at Barton's. You know that." My explanation wasn't explaining anything at all.

"Yeah, well that doesn't tell me how your lips ended up on his. Not that I blame ya, girlfriend." She gave me a small smile and I couldn't help but chuckle. Man, I loved her. Our smiles disappeared as fast as they appeared, as we both grew serious again.

"Jordan asked me out while Olivia was away this summer. I didn't know who he was when I met him. I had no idea he had a girlfriend when he asked me out. You know me, Gracie! I wouldn't do that! Especially not to one of my sisters!" I said, my voice rising in desperation.

Gracie squeezed my shoulders. "I know that, Mays," she said quietly. I shook my head again.

"I found out that he was Olivia's boyfriend when you, Vivian and Milla came into the bar that first night. And I told him to back the hell off. That nothing was going to happen between us," I said. Gracie nodded.

"That sounds like you." I appreciated her believing me. I had a feeling that that was going to be in short supply over the next few days.

"I tried to keep my distance! I really did! But there's something between us. I can't explain it. It's like this crazy connection that is impossible to resist. It was harmless flirting for a while. But then tonight..." My words trailed off. No need to explain what had gone down this evening. She already knew.

"So you like him. I get that. But, Mays. He's Olivia's boyfriend. They've been together forever. The other girls aren't going to take this well. You could get blackballed for this," she told me matter-of-factly.

Blackballed? Christ! I hadn't even thought about that. I could get kicked out of Chi Delta. But after seeing the way the other girls were treating me already, I wasn't sure I even wanted to be a part of the sorority anymore.

"He said he wanted to break up with Olivia," I whispered. Gracie gasped.

"Are you serious?" she squeaked. I put my head in my hands.

"Jordan told me he wants us to be together. But I can't do that. Not now." It all seemed so hopeless. How had I made such a mess of things in such a short amount of time? Gracie tugged on a piece of my hair and I looked up at her.

"Maysie, I think you need to get out of here. They're probably lying in wait to attack in there. You need to give everyone time to cool off. And stay the hell away from Jordan. Don't even entertain the idea. No guy is worth losing your friends over," she said with such surety.

But at that moment, I wasn't so sure I would be losing anything.

But I agreed that I had to leave. I needed to get out of the fire. And I sure as hell needed to keep a healthy distance from Jordan fucking Levitt. He made everything way more complicated than I could handle. And I wasn't sure that was something I could deal with now or maybe ever.

I got to my feet and Gracie followed suit. We looked at each other for a minute before she pulled me into a hug. I tried to choke back the tears that threatened to resurface. Gracie rubbed my back comfortingly.

"It'll be okay. It will all blow over." She sounded as though she didn't believe her words any more than I did.

We pulled apart. "I can't go back in there," I whispered, strangling on the reality of the screwed up situation. I had to hide from my friends. I had to hide from everyone. Gracie pushed me toward the garden gate.

"Go through there. Do you have your cell phone? Can you call Riley to come and get you?" she asked me. I shook my head.

"I didn't bring my purse. But I'll just walk. It's only five blocks to the apartment." I just hoped I wouldn't get jumped on my way home.

Gracie gave me a little shove. "Well, get out of here. I'll try and do some damage control. I'll call you tomorrow," she assured me, though her smile was a little hollow. I reached out and squeezed her hand in silent thanks and then slunk through the gate like a goddamn criminal.

Who gives a damn about their reputation? Oh, that would be me. Especially since mine had gone straight to hell in the span of thirty minutes. I walked toward the sidewalk, shooting a panicked look back toward the house, hoping no one could see me.

"Maysie!" Someone screamed. It was official; I was having the worst night ever. I thought about not stopping. I should have just run for it. But my sense of guilt and even greater sense of pride brought me to a halt. Olivia came hurrying down the path from the front door of the Pi Sig house, Milla hot on her heels.

"You fucking bitch!" she shrieked. And then she slapped me. I mean, she put every ounce of strength behind that slap. My head swung to the side and I put my hand up to my burning cheek. My eyes watered and my teeth crunched together painfully. That would bruise. Just fabulous.

"How could you do this to me? We're sisters! Sisters don't screw each other's boyfriends behind their backs!" she yelled in my face. Screw their boyfriends? What the hell had Milla told her that she had seen? What Jordan and I had done was bad enough, but I sure as hell didn't sleep with him!

"Wait a second, Olivia. I didn't..." I didn't get a chance to finish because Olivia launched at me like a damn monkey. She jumped on me, taking us both to the ground. I tried to fend her off, but she grabbed a hunk of my hair and pulled as hard as she could.

"Stop it, Olivia!" I screamed as I felt my hair being yanked from head. My scalp was on fire. Her fingernails scratched down the side of my neck and she pushed her knee into my gut.

"You stupid, fucking WHORE!" she screeched into my ear. I rolled us both over until I was on top of her, holding her arms off to the side. My breath was coming in pants as Olivia thrashed beneath me, her heels digging into the back of my calves.

"Get off of me you skank!" Olivia moved her head to the side and bit into my arm.

"Ow!" I yelped, dropping her wrist. Olivia slithered out from underneath me and was on me again. I knew she wanted to do more than maim. She wanted to freaking kill me! I had never seen such hatred in someone's eyes before. It was chilling.

People came filing out of the house and formed a circle around us.

"Chick fight!" The guys yelled and started chanting as though we were in bikinis and wrestling in Jell-O. None of my sisters came to my aid. Instead, they stood silently and watched our president assault me.

"Olivia! Get off of her!" There was a murmur from around us and suddenly Jordan was pulling Olivia back by her shoulders. Gracie appeared beside me and put her arms around me, moving me off to the side. I felt battered and bruised and the tears started again. I couldn't stop them. And I hated these people for witnessing my weakness. I had never been brought so low before. And they all had a front row seat.

"What the hell are you doing?" Jordan yelled, holding Olivia firmly. She started smacking at his chest.

"You stupid asshole! How could you do this to me? You've humiliated me! And with *her?*" Jordan lifted his eyes to meet mine.

I looked away, not wanting to see him hold *her*. I sort of hated him right then. If I hadn't wanted him so badly, none of this would have happened. It was so much easier to place blame anywhere but on myself at the moment.

I heard Olivia start to sob. "Why?" she wailed. I couldn't help but look up and saw Olivia bury her face into Jordan's chest, her body shaking as she cried. "Why?" she screamed again into his shirt. Jordan looked at a loss. But I felt my heart being ripped out of my chest as I watched him put his arms around her and slowly lead her back to the house.

"This party is over," he called over his shoulder. Olivia wrapped her arms around his waist and Jordan supported her as they disappeared into the house without a backward glance. He hadn't looked at me again. And that was all I needed to see to know I had ruined everything for *absolutely nothing*. My shoulders sagged in defeat and I wanted to curl into a ball and die.

Most everyone gave me the evil eye as they started to disperse. "Bitch" and "slut" were on everyone's lips.

"Let's get you home, Gracie said, keeping her arm around me. Gracie and I walked the long five blocks back to my apartment and I think I cried the entire way.

By the time I let us inside, I was all cried out and just felt empty. I was glad Riley hadn't come home yet. I didn't think I could have dealt with her questions. Gracie turned the lights on and sat me down on the couch. She went into the kitchen, opening cabinets and making a lot of noise. She came back a few minutes later with a glass of water and three ibuprofen as well as some antiseptic and Band-Aids.

"Take these and let me put some stuff on those scratches on your neck. They look brutal." I took the ibuprofen and swallowed them, trying not to wince as she started dabbing my war wounds.

"Well, it doesn't look like you have a bald spot. With the amount of hair she pulled out of your head, I wasn't sure." Gracie tried to crack a smile but I just gazed at her numbly.

"Maysie, I'm so sorry," she said, putting her hand on top of mine. We sat like that for a few minutes but then I got achingly to my feet. There was no doubt I'd be feeling shitty in the morning. And not just from the bitch fight.

"I want to go to bed," I rasped, my voice sounding like I had been gargling with glass. Gracie got to her feet as well.

"Do you want me to stay? I mean, I could keep you company," Gracie offered, looking worried about leaving me by myself.

But I just wanted to be alone. I didn't want to talk. I didn't want the looks of sympathy and concern. I only wanted to sleep and pretend that this was all a bad dream. At least for a little while.

"No, that's okay. You head on home. Riley will be here in a bit I'm sure," I told her. Gracie gave me a quick hug.

"Olivia was wasted. I'm sure she'll feel like shit in the morning for attacking you," Gracie said. I shook my head.

"I hooked up with her boyfriend. I'm sure she'll just regret not doing a better job." I touched the scratches on my neck and grimaced.

Gracie sighed. "You'll ride this one out. Give it a few days and everyone will move onto another scandal. It's the nature of the college gossip chain. You'll see," Gracie promised. But I didn't believe her.

Though I tried to smile, for her sake. "Thanks, Gracie. You're a good friend." Gracie hugged me again.

"Okay, well then, I guess I'll talk to you tomorrow. If you need anything, call me, okay?" I nodded, following her to the front door. "You're one tough cookie. You'll come out of this swinging. I know it!" I wished I shared just a fraction of her positivity. But I was all tapped out.

"Sure thing," I replied, closing the door behind her. I went to my room, not bothering to turn on the light. I took off my dress and threw it on the floor. I lay down on my bed, too exhausted to turn back the covers. I stared at my ceiling, my mind going a thousand miles a minute. My life was over. I was sure of it.

My phone chirped from my bedside table. I wanted to ignore it, but instead I leaned over and grabbed it, turning the screen on. A text from Jordan waited for me.

Are you alright? Please let me know you got home safely! I'm so sorry about all of this. We need to talk.

I debated whether I should respond. But finally, I caved.

I'm fine. Talk soon.

Then I deleted his message and turned my phone off. Because right now, I was done with talking.

CHAPTER 13

It was day one of "Maysie goes into hiding." It felt like being in a leper colony. Or having some sort of serious social phobia. But I had to stay in my safe little bubble. Off the grid. Until everything blew over. Or the world ended in a fiery apocalypse. Whichever came first.

I woke up Sunday morning, my body aching and sore from my brief stint as a WWE wrestler. I debated whether I should turn on my phone. Then even more strongly debated whether I should just chuck it out the window. But I wanted to make sure I answered it if Gracie called. She was my lifeline to the outside world at the moment.

So I powered up my phone and chewed my thumbnail while I waited to see what would greet me. And I was both relieved and depressed to see that there were no missed texts. No new voice mails. Nothing. It *was* like I had fallen off the face of the Earth.

I had really thought that Jordan would try and contact me again. No, let me take that back. I had *wanted* Jordan to be blowing up my phone, desperate to get in touch. I had told him we'd talk but then I'd heard nothing. His disturbing silence was all the proof I needed that our brief saliva swapping was a complete mistake. One that would be much harder for me to come back from than him.

I was pretty sure Olivia had already forgiven Jordan of our little transgression. They were probably back to being the most perfect couple ever. And here I was, in my Scooby Doo pajamas looking like I had lost a round with Rocky Balboa. If that wasn't karma, I didn't know what was.

Tucking my phone into the pocket of my jammie bottoms, I went to the bathroom, refusing to look at my reflection. No need to depress myself. There would be enough time for self-recrimination later. Now, I just wanted a bowl of Cocoa Puffs and hours of Gossip Girl on the DVR.

I parked myself on the couch with a mixing bowl full of my favorite chocolate cereal and I loaded up the first eight episodes of my running guilty pleasure. And that's how Riley found me two hours later. Well, at that point I had curled into a fetal position on the couch. I was so miserable I was practically comatose. And all I could think about was that I had fucked up everything in my life for a guy who didn't bother to call me again.

Sure he had texted but if he really cared about me, wouldn't he have responded to my last message? No, he had only been doing the decent thing. I'm sure he and the tragically betrayed Olivia were all wrapped up in each other while he made up for allowing himself to be tempted by the evil skank in Chi Delta clothing.

I would not cry damn it! I was chanting this to myself over and over again to little avail when Riley breezed in, looking happy. I felt like the shittiest best friend on the planet because I couldn't think about what it was that put that huge smile on her face. My only thought was that I wanted her to comfort me.

Once she got a good look at my tear stained face and the fact that it was almost noon and I was still in my pajamas, her smile faded. "What the hell happened to you?" she asked in concern, coming over to the couch. I tucked my knees up to my chest and gave a shuddery little sob.

"Mays. What is it?" she asked, putting her hand on my leg. I pulled up into a sitting position and looked at her, feeling the tears slip down my cheeks.

"I fucked up, Riley. Fucked up big time." And then I unloaded everything. The whole horrible night.

When I was done she looked at me in shock. "Well, damn.

Maysie, that's some messed up shit," she said matter-of-factly. I couldn't help but laugh a little maniacally. Because she had hit the nail right on the head, as always.

"I can't believe I was so stupid! I had told myself time and time again to leave it alone. To stay the hell away from him! And what do I do? I jump in lips first!" I growled, throwing a pillow across the room in frustration.

"Now, now. No sense in destroying the decor. First things first, you need to get a shower because I am not going to sit here and smell you a moment longer. You reek of desperation and b.o." She tugged on my hand, pulling me to my feet.

I whined as she shoved me into the bathroom and turned the shower on. "Now strip and wash the guilt off. And then I can spend the rest of the day telling you how ridiculous you're being for allowing those ass hats to dictate your life like this." And with that she slammed the door.

I didn't want to get a shower. I wanted to marinate in my shame. But even I could smell myself and I figured I'd take pity on the person who had to share a personal space with me. While in the shower, Riley dropped a pile of clothes on the floor and scooped up my pajamas.

"Hey! I want to wear those!" I yelled, peeking my head around the shower curtain.

"No, these need to be disposed of as biological waste," she responded, closing the door again. After I got out, I put on the change of clothes Riley had provided and went out into the living room. She had made us cups of tea and sat at on the couch, deleting my Gossip Girl episodes from the DVR.

"What the hell, Riley? I was watching those!" I shrieked, diving for the remote. She held it away from me.

"If you don't want your brain to rot out of your ears, then you don't need to watch anymore of this cultural strain on society." She flipped the TV off and turned to face me. I crossed my arms over my chest and pouted. Real mature, I know. But at that point, I didn't care.

"So, tell me. How long do you plan to hole up in our apartment, channeling Morrissey? Because if you decide to morph into Goth girl, I'm looking for a new roommate," Riley warned, pointing her finger at me. I rolled my eyes.

"Dude, I'm allowed some time to hide out...Christ! My life just went up in flames. I have serious processing to do," I huffed. Riley snorted.

"Processing? No, what you need to do is get your ass out there and show those sheep that they cannot scare you off! You are way above this. I've always thought you were better than those stupid Chi Smelltas or whatever the fuck they're called."

"Chi Delta," I corrected automatically. It was Riley's turn to roll her eyes.

"Whoever the hell they are, they suck. And you suck for letting those girls, or Jordan for that matter, get to you. I know what happened was horrible. I know you feel like Elizabeth Taylor, but seriously, do you think for one flipping minute that Olivia is crystal clean? The lot of them have more dirty laundry than a damn laundry mat. Grow a spine, Maysie Ardin!"

Wow, she was ruthless. And right then, I appreciated her tough love approach. I needed to be reminded that I wasn't this horrible human being. Because right then I felt up there with Gadhafi or at least Paris Hilton.

But it wasn't just the fact that I had hurt Olivia. I mean, I hated that. I really did. I wasn't a complete jerk. But the truth was, my heart hurt. I couldn't help but let my mind wander back to last night and watching Jordan lead Olivia away as she clung to him. The fact was, seeing them together; I couldn't deny how they just *worked*. They looked like they belonged together and I had no place in that pretty little picture.

Riley smacked the back of my head. "And stop obsessing about Jordan Levitt. If he can chase after you like that and then drop you on your ass once the going gets rough, then seriously, you're better off." Damn her and her all-knowing ways. I picked up my mug of tea from the coffee table and took a drink.

"Why the hell did you make me tea? You know I'm a coffee drinker," I complained, grimacing at the taste.

"Because tea is soothing," Riley retorted primly. I could use some soothing, that's for sure. I put my cup back on the table.

"Okay, okay. I hear you and make note of your suggestions. But have you ever heard that it's easier said than done? Well, there you go. It's easier said than done," I spat out.

Riley's face softened. "I know, Mays. I don't expect it to be easy. You had your heart stomped on. You had your pride slapped in the face like a little bitch. You deserve to lick your wounds. Just don't let it become an indefinite sabbatical. I want you to come back swinging. Go Muhommad Ali on this shit!"

I laughed. I couldn't help it. Riley was good for that. Our moment of levity was interrupted by the sound of *Don't Fear the Reaper*. My phone vibrated around the coffee table and I grabbed it like a live grenade. It was Gracie.

"Hey," I said a little breathlessly after I answered it. Riley gave me a look and then got up to give me some privacy.

"Hey chica. How are you today?' she asked sympathetically.

"Well, I'm better than that time I had mono. So I guess that's something, right?" I said lightly. Gracie chuckled on the other end.

"That's the spirit," she said. Then we fell silent.

"Okay, Gracie. Just give it to me straight. How bad is it?" I asked in a rush, wanting to get to the point. Gracie sighed and I could practically hear her wheels turning as she questioned how much she wanted to tell me.

"Gracie. Seriously. I can't feel any worse. So just tell me the truth, please," I begged, knowing I was a complete liar. Because I *could* feel worse. A hell of a lot worse.

Gracie sighed again. "It's bad, Maysie. Most of the girls are pissed. Some of them are being extremely vocal about wanting you out." I closed my eyes. I suspected this could be a possibility but some part of me hung onto the hope that "sisterhood" would be stronger than my current drama. Guess not.

"Okay," I said softly.

"But, not everyone feels that way, Maysie. You still have your friends here and they are just as vocal that we should let you and Olivia sort this out between you, and that the rest of us need to back the hell off." I felt a glimmer of hope that not all was lost. And I was relieved that I did have friends at Chi Delta. Bonds that went a little deeper than coordinating our mixer outfits.

"Have you seen Olivia?" I asked, bracing myself. Gracie cleared her throat.

"Well, um. She didn't come back to the house last night. Apparently Milla spoke with her this morning and she stayed with Jordan." Well shit. I felt like I had been punched in the gut. Really, really hard. I felt sick and those stupid tears started welling up again.

"I see," I responded evenly. I was proud of how calm my voice sounded, even as I was screaming inside. That dumb, two timing ass munch! I should have known better! I HAD known better! And now I would be the one with the ruined reputation and nothing to show for it. I hated Jordan Levitt!

"Yeah. My Jordan worship is at an official end. Sad to know he's just like every other douche bag out there," Gracie said a little sadly and I had to smile.

"He gives douche bags a bad name, Grace," I muttered and Gracie laughed.

"We're going to have to come up with a new name for Jordan that truly reflects his level of douchedom...something like douche hole or fucktard. Give me a few hours and I'll think of something," Gracie assured me.

I was laughing so hard by then that for a second I had forgotten about how much I wanted to run away and join a nunnery. We calmed down and I gripped the phone in my hand as a new wave of pain swept through my body.

"But you need to talk to Liv, Maysie. You're sisters. This will rip the house apart. I don't want to lose you in the sisterhood. You deserve to be here as much as anyone else. What happened was NOT your fault. Jordan played you. And if Olivia can't see what a lying asshole her boyfriend is then let her have him."

My heart constricted at her words. My first instinct was to defend Jordan. That he wasn't an asshole. That he had wanted to be with me. Then I remembered my quiet phone and the fact that he was right now, with Olivia, instead of trying to talk to me. I *had* been played. Goddamn it!

Gracie was still speaking and I had to refocus on our

conversation. I zeroed in on her words "chapter meeting tonight."

"Wait, wait, wait. I can't come to the chapter meeting. That would be like walking into a lynching. You can't be serious?"

"Oh, I'm as serious as a heart attack, Mays. You *will* be at that chapter meeting tonight. Even if I have to drag you there by your hair. It is essential for you to come. You have to show the girls that you want to be in Chi Delta. That the sisterhood *does* matter to you. Consider this your first step in polishing your public image, girlfriend." I groaned my stomach already a twisted knot.

"Fine. I'll go. But if it's a bloodbath, it's all on you," I intoned miserably. Gracie clucked her tongue and I could hear her frustration.

"Stop being so dramatic. Vivian and I will come and get you and escort you there ourselves."

"Vivian?" I asked in surprise. But then I remember how nice she had been when I was trying to find Gracie last night. My heart warmed at knowing she was willing to put her neck out there for me like that. As surprised as I was, I wouldn't look a gift horse in the mouth.

"Yeah. She feels bad for you. Apparently, she knows how it is to be on the receiving end of Chi Delta bullshit. She wouldn't really go into it. I guess it was something that went down when she and Olivia were sophomores. But anyway, she's one more on team Maysie." I rolled my eyes, though I know she couldn't see me.

"Should you get T-shirts made?" I asked dryly.

"Not a bad idea. We could do cute little tanks and they could be pink and gold like our colors..."

"I was joking, Gracie," I cut her off.

"I know, Miss Serious. We'll be at your apartment at 6:30. Wear something cute. You are to go in there looking fantastic and untouchable, do you hear me? You cannot show any weakness. It will be fine! I promise."

"Sure. It will all be fine," I responded tiredly. We ended our conversation after that. Neither of us had much more to say. After getting off the phone I went into my closet and unearthed my best, no nonsense, black skirt and conservative green shirt. It was cute but appropriate. No high slits up my thigh or heaving cleavage. Nothing that made me look like the slut everyone thought I was.

I spent the rest of the day alternating between napping and gorging myself on Ben and Jerry's Phish Food that Riley had so considerately gone to the store to get for me. I didn't care about the fact that all of those calories would migrate down to my thighs. All I could focus on was the sweet, ooey gooey goodness that was a complete endorphin rush in every delicious spoon full.

Riley stayed with me, refusing to leave me alone. "I'm not on suicide watch, Riley. You don't have to hang around here all day. I'm sure you'd rather be with your hot new boy toy than playing babysitter for your judgmentally challenged bestie," I said blandly after finishing my second pint of ice cream.

Riley pried the empty cardboard container out of my hands. "Okay, enough. You're making me want to puke with the amount of junk you're eating." She made a gagging face and I threw my spoon at her retreating back as she went into the kitchen. "Don't you have to get ready for the super fantastic chapter meeting?" she called from the other room.

I stuck my tongue out at her even though she couldn't see it. It was already 5:30. I knew Gracie and Vivian would be there in about twenty minutes. I guess I should pull myself together. I got to my feet and shuffled off toward my bedroom.

"And get another shower, Mays!" Riley yelled down the hallway. I let out a deep groan and changed my course to the bathroom. Okay. Time to put my game face on. I could do this. I could go there tonight and take whatever they wanted to dish out. I mean, I wasn't alone in what went down. I can't take all the blame, right?

I went through the paces and got my shower; blow dried my hair and put it up in a sensible bun at the nape of my neck. Going into my room, I put on my skirt and blouse and opted for a very minimal amount of makeup. Looking in the mirror I couldn't help but grimace. I looked like I was heading to church with my parents. Yuck. This was so *not* me and I knew my sisters would see straight through my attempt at a good girl image.

I was tempted to change when my doorbell rang. I heard

Riley let Gracie and Vivian in. I waited for the two girls to come down the hall but they didn't. After five minutes, I went to find out what was keeping them. Not surprisingly, Riley and Gracie were in deep conversation. Three guesses as to whom they were talking about.

"So have the two of you figured out how to fix my shit hole of a life yet?" I called out. Vivian, Gracie and Riley looked up and I almost laughed at the near identical fake smiles they each wore. If I wasn't so damn depressed I'd find the fact that they were conspiring behind my back really amusing. Gracie and Riley didn't get along at the best of times. Riley found Gracie's pro Greek stance obnoxious and vapid. Gracie found Riley to be pretentious and snobby.

"There you are! You look great!" Gracie chirped, coming over and giving me a hug.

"Don't lie. I look like I'm going out to sell encyclopedias," I grumped. Vivian chuckled and I gave her a smile over Gracie's shoulder. "Hey Viv. Thanks for coming tonight," I said sincerely after pulling away from Gracie. Vivian nodded.

"You don't need to thank me. I've been there; done that, have the emotional scars. These girls are ruthless when they want to be. You'll need all the backup you can get."

Riley made a noise. "Now why isn't that on the school's Greek living brochure? I think that's a fantastic sound bite," she snarked. I thought my sisters would get pissed, but instead they laughed, shocking the hell out of me.

"Okay, let's do this," I said with more determination than I felt. Gracie pumped her fist into the air. I didn't miss the look she exchanged with Riley but I pretended not to notice.

"Good luck, Mays. If you need me to beat someone up for you, just let me know!" Riley called out as we left the apartment. I shook my head but couldn't help but feel a little warm and fuzzy at the support I was receiving from my friends. It made me feel like perhaps I could come out of all this with my skin intact.

CHAPTER
14

Our ride to the campus was quiet. We didn't talk at all. Which I was fine with; I didn't know what to say anyway. Vivian pulled into the parking lot outside of the Chi Delta house and for the first time since I had pledged, I didn't want to go inside. This place that had been source of happiness for me had now become something much more sinister.

"Come on, Maysie," Gracie said softly, getting out of the car. Not being able to put it off any longer, I got out and followed my friends up to the front door. We had five minutes until the meeting started so I hoped most of the girls would be in the chapter room.

Clearly luck was not on my side tonight. Big surprise. We walked in and it was like the sound evaporated from the room. At least twenty of our sisters were in the common room. Every single one of them stopped what they were doing and looked up as we entered. Not one of them said anything. They glared at me as though I had walked in with a scarlet 'A' branded on my forehead.

My palms began to sweat and my heart started to palpitate uncomfortably in my chest. Gracie reached down and took my hand in hers'. I looked at her gratefully as she pulled us down the hallway toward the meeting room. Milla stood in front of the door, not letting us enter.

"What the hell is she doing here?" she hissed, giving me a once over and sneered. I straightened my back and looked my "sister" straight in the eye.

"I'm here for the sisterhood meeting. Isn't that why you're here, Milla? For the sisterhood?" I goaded. We had a thirty second stare down before Milla looked away, her lip curling in disgust.

"Move, Milla," Vivian grit out, shouldering passed the other girl so we could make our way into the room. I wanted to train my eyes on the floor, not wanting to look at anyone. But I couldn't. That would be acknowledging my shame and I wouldn't do that. Not here.

My eyes fell on the head of the table, where Olivia held court. She looked stunning, as always. Nothing let on to the emotional turmoil of the last 24 hours. Her black hair was shiny and perfect. Her skin fresh, her eyes free of the black circles that ringed mine. She looked...happy?

Olivia raised her chin as I made my way to my normal seat, flanked by Vivian and Gracie. Our eyes met and I could see the anger there. Her lips quirked in revulsion before she looked away. I swallowed thickly and sat down. This was going to be a long evening.

Ten minutes later, the rest of the sisters had filed in and we were ready to start the meeting. All eyes rested on Olivia Peer and waited for her to begin the meeting. Slowly, she got to her feet and slammed the gavel in her hand down onto the table. "I call this meeting of the Beta Pi chapter of Chi Delta to order," she said with authority.

The first part of the meeting ran like any other. Details of upcoming mixers. Discussions about the Fall Ball. Ideas for increasing our philanthropy efforts. The president of our new pledge class gave a rundown of their meeting minutes. Maybe this wouldn't be as bad as I had feared.

"Now, I think we need to talk about rush week and what we can do to improve things next for spring," Olivia announced. I blinked in surprise, sharing a shocked look with Vivian. What we needed to change? Rush had been a roaring success. No one could deny that. We were able to recruit every girl we had wanted.

"We've had some complaints that our themes were trite and clichéd. That leadership was somewhat lacking. I think we need to take a look at the way things went and whether this was how we want Chi Delts to be perceived by potential pledges." Olivia didn't look my way, but her words were meant for me alone.

So this was her plan. To make me look even more like an idiot in front of our sisters. I had already been branded the slut, why not the moron who couldn't chair a rush event as well? She wanted to tear me down so far that there was no way I could ever climb up again.

Looking around the room, most of the girls were nodding, refusing to look at me. I noticed there were a few that looked unhappy with our president's announcement. "This is bullshit," Vivian growled under her breath. Because of course this wouldn't just affect me; this would impact Vivian as well.

"Well, I really wonder if maybe we need some new blood handling rush for the spring. Come up with some new ideas," Milla suggested sweetly, not shying away from looking at me. She was enjoying this. Stupid bitch. Vivian gripped the arms of her chair and sat forward.

"We had the highest turn out for the fall than any other year. Every single girl we offered bids to accepted. Our skit kicked ass. I don't see what the problem is," she said sharply, staring down Olivia and Milla.

I hated that there was a division happening there. These girls had pledged Chi Delta together. Vivian, Olivia and Milla were always together. And now they were split apart. Because of me.

Olivia flicked her hair back and waved her hand in dismissal. "Don't get so defensive, Vivvie. It was just a suggestion. I know a bunch of us had concerns over doing the same things again. Thought we'd shake it up a bit. It's nothing personal," she said innocently, smiling our way. I ground my teeth together.

"Not personal my ass! You know exactly what this is about. If you want to address your beef with Maysie, then do it on your own time. Do NOT bring the rest of us into it. And don't you dare sit there on your throne and think you can tear me, Maysie or any of us down!" Vivian had gotten to her feet and looked prepared to do battle. I was shocked to see perky Vivian seething with anger.

I had a feeling that these thoughts spewing from Vivian's

mouth like vomit had been festering for a while. I should say something. I couldn't let Vivian fight my battles for me like this. But right then I just wanted to disappear.

Olivia narrowed her eyes at Vivian then turned her steely gaze on me. Her face relaxed and she started laughing. Milla joined in, followed by most of the sisterhood. Vivian's face was a scary shade of red. "Oh, Vivian. Chill out already. I think you're reading too much into things. But since you brought it up, I think we should address the huge elephant in the room." Olivia stopped laughing and turned to look at me.

I withered a bit under her stare. "Everyone knows what happened last night. Everyone on campus knows what happened last night. But none of that matters." Olivia's words were clipped. "Maysie, what you did was wrong. More than wrong. It was a complete violation of everything our sisterhood stands for," she admonished me harshly and I felt like a little child. How could this girl make me feel so horrible? Oh, wait...because I was so horrible.

"I know, Olivia. And I'm so, so sorry," I told her, hoping to make this right in some small way.

Olivia's eyes held mine and I saw no warmth there. No understanding, no compassion. I only saw the same anger and betrayal that I had witnessed last night. "I'm not sure what to do about all of this. But Jordan and I talked a lot last night. We hashed out a lot of our problems. And I think we're in a really good place now. So in a way, I should thank you, Maysie. You helped Jordan realize how much he wanted me. Wanted *us*. And now we're stronger than ever." Her eyes glittered coldly and I felt like I might pass out.

Olivia finally looked away from me and turned her attention to the rest of the sisterhood. "So, you see...the best woman won. And we can put all of this behind us." What a backhanded way of putting me down. Everyone looked at me and I knew there would be no putting this in the past. Hell no. If anything, Olivia's words only fanned the flames.

Just fucking fabulous. The rest of the meeting passed in a blur. I didn't hear anything else, Olivia's words ringing in my ears.

I should thank you, Maysie. You helped Jordan realize how much he wanted me. I felt like such an idiot.

I practically ran from the chapter room at the end of the meeting. I needed to get out there. I wanted to go back to my apartment and work on that whole hibernation thing again.

"Maysie, wait up!" Gracie and Vivian ran to catch up with me.

"Sorry, I just needed...ah, never mind." I pulled my hair down from the tight bun and rubbed at my scalp.

Gracie put her hand on my shoulder. "That could have been... worse," she offered half-heartedly. I gave her a sideways smile.

"Sure, if I was on trial for murder," I muttered. I turned to Vivian and hugged her. "Thank you so much for sticking up for me like that. I'm sorry if this makes things harder for you. And just so you know, I won't hold it against you if you need to keep your distance from me. Both of you. Don't let being my friend ruin things for you with the sisterhood." I rubbed my eyes tiredly, just wishing I could rewind time and undo the last three months.

Because I sure as hell would undo Jordan Levitt. I would erase his sorry ass from my life.

Vivian and Gracie looked at me like I was crazy. "We're sisters. Friends. We're not going anywhere," Gracie said firmly and I could do little more than nod, all out of words.

"Do you mind if I just head home? I'm tired and I have an early class tomorrow," I asked, already heading toward Gracie's car. The girls followed me.

After I got home, I ignored the pile of homework I had yet to do. I feigned a headache so I didn't have to go back through my night with Riley. I went into my room, took off my clothes and fell on my bed. I wanted a do over.

The next two weeks of my life fell into a sad little routine. I went to class, came home. I went to work, came home. I did the one thing I swore I would never do, no matter what happened. I quit my job at Barton's. I just couldn't be around Jordan after everything. I knew I was being a coward but I just didn't have it in me to see him. Because he hadn't tried to contact me since the night of the mixer.

Not once. No texts, no phone calls. Nothing. Talk about making a gal feel special.

My life had become an endless source of misery. I knew people were talking about me behind my back. I could see the stares I got when I walked into the commons to eat lunch. The whispers that would suddenly go quiet when I would enter a room.

Jordan's fraternity brothers were the worst. They leered at me as though they were picturing me naked. And they didn't stop there. One of the guys, a new pledge, came up to me while I was reading my Shakespeare homework on the quad before class.

I had looked up in surprise as he dropped down beside me on the bench. I didn't even know the guy's name. He smiled at me and I smiled back, unsure what was going on. "You're Maysie Ardin, right?" he had asked, his smile wide. I had frowned, not sure where he was going with this.

He had put his hand down on my upper thigh, his fingers brushing the edge of my shorts. I moved backwards in shock. "Get your hands off of me," I had told him angrily, swatting his hand away. The guy had only laughed and pressed toward me again, his hand snaking around my waist and pulling me toward him.

I pushed on his chest. "Who the hell do you think you are? Get the fuck away from me right now!" I said as calmly as I was able. I had started to tremble, my anxiety peaking precariously.

I darted a look around, there were people everywhere. If I screamed, a hundred people would be there to help. The guy leaned toward me and stopped just short of my lips. I clenched my mouth shut, prepared to bite him if he tried to kiss me.

He pressed something into my hand and then put his lips by my ear. "I'd like to use this sometime. My name is Derek. I'm over at Olin Hall. Room 312. I want to see what those lips could do for me."

Then he had pulled away, got to his feet and walked toward a group of Pi Sigs who were howling with laughter. A few of the guys clapped him on the shoulder. The guy had puffed up his chest and threw a look my way as if to say, *you know you want this.*

I had looked down at what he put in my hand and I blanched.

It was a condom. A fucking, foil wrapped, ribbed for her pleasure, condom. The Pi Sigs were heading across the quad. I wasn't sure what had possessed me but I had run after them.

"Hey!" I called out. The douchy pledge had turned around, a look of pure arrogance on his face. As though I were going to blow him right there on the quad. I flicked the condom at him and it hit his chin before falling to the ground. "I'd rather staple it shut than let your tiny penis anywhere near me," I yelled.

"Denied by the skank!" one of the guys, who I recognized as Greg, a Pi Sig senior, taunted the pledge. I shrank at the word he used to describe me. Skank. They thought I was a skank. But then I got mad.

"Skank? Says the guy who pays for fucks." Greg turned red and he clenched his fists. I laughed harshly. "Yeah, everyone knows about that," I mocked. The rest of the Pi Sigs were in fits of riotous laughter.

I turned to the pledge again. "So take your condom and use it to go fuck yourself," I spat out. Wow, where had that come from? I had been kind of proud of myself. The pledge leaned down to pick the condom up off of the ground.

Tucking it into his pocket he sneered at me. "As if I'd let my dick anywhere near that. I have standards." And without another look in my direction, the guys turned and walked away. Leaving me standing in the middle of the quad pissed but completely humiliated.

I had turned around and ran across the grass. I blew off the rest of my classes that day and gone back to my apartment. I wouldn't leave for another two days. My show of bravado faded as quickly as it had come and I was done with it all.

I was depressed. Hurting. I stayed away from the Chi Delta house. I stayed away from people in general. I ate my meals at home, avoiding the commons. I didn't hang around after classes like I typically did. I had become a damn pariah. Nobody spoke to me. It was like I had a contagious disease. And as much as I wanted to scream and yell at each and every one of them, I kept my mouth resolutely shut. I convinced myself that doing that would only make things worse. No matter how good it may have made me feel.

Rinard was a small campus. Only 700 students. It was that reason that I had chosen the college in the first place. I wanted the intimate class sizes and more hands on learning. I wanted to feel that sense of community. Now, I wished nothing more than to be lost in the crowd. Instead of being stuck in a place where everyone knew my business and judged me for it.

"You need to leave this apartment!" Riley declared one evening. I was on the couch, my normal place of occupancy over the last few days. I scowled at my roommate.

"I'm perfectly happy right here, thank you very much," I mumbled, turning my eyes back to the television.

Riley grunted in disapproval and turned off the TV. "Enough! Go get dressed! Gracie and I are taking you out. She's going to be here in ten minutes, so go get dolled up." She pulled on my arm, yanking me to my feet. I gave her my best evil glare.

"Since when do you and Gracie talk? And when do you ever go out together socially?" I asked, annoyed that my evening of sedate nothingness was being foiled.

Riley pushed me toward my bedroom. "Since we are both sick and tired of your depressed moping. Now, do I need to dress you myself? Because, so help me God, if I have to, I will put you in my black cargo pants and combat boots," she threatened.

I shuddered. Those cargo pants should have been burned a long time ago. But I knew Riley meant business. So I put my hands up in defeat. "I'm going, I'm going. Back off killer." I went into my room and halfheartedly unearthed something semi-decent. I emerged from my room five minutes later, wearing a pair of skinny jeans and a short sleeved dark green knit top.

"Do something with that mop on top of your head. Have you even brushed your hair today?" Riley asked.

"Ugh! Alright, already!" I complained, going into the bathroom. Three critiques later, and I was deemed ready to mingle with society.

Gracie showed up a short time later, looking cute and perky as always. With Gracie on one side and Riley on the other, they shepherded me out to Gracie's Jeep. We made a motley crew. Gracie in her conservative prettiness, Riley looking like a Goth diva in her short black skirt, black top and knee high laced black boots. Then there was me. Well, the less said about that, the better.

"Where are we going?" I asked as Gracie pulled out of the apartment car lot.

"We're heading downtown. You need to do some dancing. And some drinking. Time to get your happy on, my friend," Gracie chirped. I crossed my arms over my chest. I did not feel like dancing. And don't even get me started about putting my *happy* on (were we in the fourth grade here?). And drinking would just make me more depressed and miserable. I didn't like this plan at all.

But I didn't say anything. I knew it would be pointless. My two friends were determined and they were a wall of solidarity against me. Bitches.

We pulled into a downtown dance club called The Boogie Lounge (lame name, I know). It was pretty crowded for a Thursday night.

"Wow, what's with all the people?" I asked, getting out of the car. Riley shrugged. Her face lit up suddenly and she started waving frantically. Looking over my shoulder I saw Damien and a few of his friends in line to get in the club. I tried to suppress my groan. But I wasn't very successful. Riley gave me a dark look.

"Just suck it up and have fun, Mays. It won't kill you," she told me firmly.

I gave her a sardonic salute. "Aye, aye, Captain," I bit out sarcastically. Gracie looped her arm through mine and pulled me toward the entrance of the club. We paid our cover and went inside. The place was teaming with people. We had to do some serious shoving to get to the bar.

"Go find a table if you can. I'll get the drinks." Riley whipped out a fake ID and flashed us a smile.

"Awesome! Get me a cranberry and vodka," Gracie yelled to her. Riley knew my usual, so she headed off to the bar. Gracie and I were able to find a small table toward the back. Gracie found a napkin and wiped spilled beer off the surface before sitting down. The stage was set up, so that must be the reason for the crowd.

"I wonder who's playing?" I mused, watching the people start to push toward the front of the room. Riley had just gotten to our table with our drinks when a familiar voice cut through the noise.

"Thanks for coming out to see us tonight! We're Generation Rejects!"

NO, NO, NO! I could not be here!

I gripped Gracie's hand tightly. "We have to leave, NOW!" I said desperately. Gracie winced and then pried her hand away from my tight grasp.

"Now, you can't avoid him forever. We'll just stay here in the back. Jordan will never know we're here," Gracie reasoned.

I whipped my head around to look at Riley suspiciously. "Did you know Jordan would be playing here tonight?" Riley looked at me with irritation.

"Would I do something like that, Mays. Get real." She sounded miffed that I had even suggested it. I started to say something else when the music began. And just like the first time I saw them play, I couldn't help but watch. They were intense and raw. And Jordan was a demon on the drums.

I hadn't seen him in weeks and my eyes thirsted for the sight of him. Even after everything, I couldn't stop the crazy pitter-patter of my heart as I watched him. His forehead was furrowed as he beat the skins frantically. The tight material of his T-shirt strained over the muscles of his arms and I couldn't help but remember the way they had felt holding me.

I had tried so hard *not* to remember any of that night. Particularly the part he played in what went down. The hurt, anger and embarrassment washed over me again and all I wanted to do was leave. But the place was packed and getting out the door would be difficult. Plus Gracie and Riley were boxing me into the corner.

So I sat there and tried to control the physical response I had to the music reverberating around me. I tried not to look at Jordan and how insanely sexy he was up there. But I loved the music and I loved the sensual beat he added to the mix. He was an amazing musician. Despite everything, I could still admit that.

They played almost the exact same set as they had that night at Barton's. I braced myself for Jordan's solo. When the song began

I looked anywhere but at the stage. If I wouldn't have looked like an immature idiot, I would have put my fingers in my ears to stop the sound of his gravelly voice.

So, instead I watched the crowd undulate to the band's music. They ate up whatever the band threw at them. It was like watching a religious experience. And on some small level, I gave into it. And it was liberating. To be able to let go of all the negative shit I was feeling and for a moment, just enjoy myself.

When they were done, I was left feeling bereft. Because then I had to return to feeling like crap again. "Wow, they *really are* good," Gracie said, looking a little in awe. I could only nod.

"Can we go now?" I asked, wanting to get out of there and go back home.

"Come on; just hang out for a little while longer. I know you want to dance, Maysie," Riley teased, motioning for Gracie and I to follow her onto the dance floor.

The techno music had started up now that the band's set was finished and I had to admit, I wanted to get my groove on. So the three of us went and got lost in the throng of moving bodies. I danced until sweat poured down my face and my shirt clung to my skin. Gracie and Riley could dance, but they had nothing on me.

I rolled my hips to the beat, moving my hands up my sides, scaling my body until they reached above me. I tossed my head back and forth, my hair flying in my face. I was lost in my own little world. Dancing did that for me. I forgot about everyone and everything else.

After a few songs, I was parched. "I need a drink," I rasped, tugging on Gracie's hand. Riley and Damien had found each other and were currently clutched together, rocking slowly to the upbeat tempo. There was no interrupting that. Gracie and I, holding each other's hand so we wouldn't get separated, made our way to the bar.

"Hang back over here, I'll get our drinks," she told me. I went to the end of the bar and waited, my eyes darting around the room. Yes, I was looking for Jordan. But I guess the band had left right after their set.

Or maybe not.

"Hey, Mays." I didn't need to turn around to know who spoke. My entire body lit up and every nerve and synapse responded to those two words.

"Hey," I said casually, not looking at him. Jordan was suddenly in front of me and my mouth went even drier. He had no right to look that hot. It pissed me off.

"You looked good out there," he said, looking at me with the thousand things unsaid between us.

"Thanks," I replied, glancing over his shoulder, as though I'd rather be anywhere but standing there with him. I was very good at lying apparently. Because in truth, there was nowhere I'd rather be.

"How've you been?" he asked, pulling my attention back to him. Okay, his question made me mad. *How had I been?* Really? I felt the chill spread outward from my heart at his callous question.

"Oh, just fucking peachy," I snarled, throwing every ounce of hurt and anger at him.

Jordan frowned. "What the hell, Maysie? It was just a damn question," he bit back sharply. That was it. I was going to explode. And it wouldn't be pretty. I was saved from committing malicious wounding by Gracie handing me my soda.

She looked back and forth between Jordan and me, a concerned look on her face. "Um, hey Jordan," she said; clearly not sure what to make of the dark expressions we both wore.

"Hey, Gracie," he said shortly, and then continued to look at me. Our eyes never left each other. I was so upset and enraged that I could feel my hands shaking as I clutched my drink. Jordan looked frustrated and confused.

Finally, he dropped his eyes and shoved his hands in his pockets. "I've got to get back to the guys. See you later," Jordan said, his voice sounding strangely thick. He looked at me one more time but I purposefully glanced away.

"Woah. What was all that?" she asked, sipping her water. I rolled my eyes.

"He was asking me how I was," I answered, slamming my full glass down on the bar, not bothering to finish it.

"Okay. Well. That was...nice?" Her statement came out more as a question. I started to stalk away.

"Nice? No, it wasn't fucking nice! He has no right to even ask me that, when my life is in shambles because of him. So screw him and his stupid kissable lips and the fact that he couldn't be bothered to try and talk to me at all. No, he had to go jump back in with Olivia and forget all about me. Just like I knew he would." I stopped when we got back to our table. I threw myself down in the chair and glowered.

"But I thought you didn't want to talk to him." Gracie sounded confused. Not that I blamed her.

"No, I didn't want to talk to him. I just don't know what I wanted him to do!" I felt those damnable tears again. I had to get home. I was a mess.

My eyes flitted around the room and found Jordan, again by the bar with a throng of girls around him. His band mates were living it up. Jordan looked less than happy, but that didn't stop a chick with seriously huge tits slide up beside him and curve into his side. He looked down at her as she spoke to him, her fingers trailing up his arm. And he let her touch him. Yep, time to get the fuck out of there before I flew into a demon rage and ran across the room to claw that bitch's eyes out.

"I need to get out of here. Please, Gracie." She didn't try to convince me otherwise. She must have seen how close I was to losing it. We went to find Riley who was wrapped around Damien as though they were one freaking person. She started to insist on coming with us but I had simply held up my hand to stop her. I told Damien to make sure she was taken care of and then with a hug to my best friend, Gracie and I left.

When we got back to the apartment I insisted on Gracie heading on home. It was after midnight and I didn't feel like being around people anymore. "Okay, well as long as you're okay." Gracie looked at me skeptically.

"I'll be fine. I'm just going to go inside and put my facemask on and go to bed. I'm exhausted." I faked a yawn. In truth, I was the farthest thing from tired. I was so keyed up I thought I would blow a gasket. But the last thing I wanted was small talk or my friend's efforts to make me less miserable. As well intentioned as they were.

Gracie nodded. "Alright, girlie. I'll call you tomorrow and we can get lunch or something." I gave her a small smile.

"Sounds great." I got out and slammed the car door. I waited until she had driven off before making my way into the apartment. Where I was left alone with my bitterness.

CHAPTER
15

I changed into my tiny little pj shorts and a tank top. Pulling my hair into a high ponytail on top of my head, I grabbed my basket of nail polish and accessories and headed back out to the couch. I started to give myself a late night pedicure, choosing a garish red. Might as well look the part of the harlot if I was going to be labeled one.

I had finished the final coat on my nails when there was a loud knock on my door, startling me. I peered up at the clock on the wall. It was almost 1:30 in the morning. Who the hell could be beating my door down at this time of night?

Whoever it was wasn't very patient as I heard another pound on the door. "Alright!" I called out, getting up off the couch. I sort of waddled to the door, careful to keep my newly painted toenails up off of the floor.

I unlocked the door and pulled it open. And almost dropped dead right there. "What the hell are you doing here?" I asked in shock, coming face to face with a very pissed off Jordan. His jaw was tense and he was clicking his tongue ring back and forth over his teeth in agitation.

"Can I come in?" he asked, his calm voice at odds with the tension radiating from his body. I blocked the doorway, not sure what to do.

"Don't you have some groupies to keep company?" I asked and hated how jealous I sounded. Jordan shook his head.

"Don't start this immature shit, please. If I gave a damn about any of those girls would I be here right now?" he asked, clearly frustrated. Hmm. Do I get annoyed that he called me immature? Or giggle like a schoolgirl because he admitted to wanting to see me? Ack! I needed to get it together!

So I tamped down both reactions and concentrated on the matter at hand. "How did you find out where I live?" I asked, suddenly very aware of my barely there shorts and shirt and the fact that I wasn't wearing a bra. I tried to discretely cross my arms over my chest.

"Does it matter?" he asked tersely. I frowned at his attitude.

"Well, actually it sort of does." Jordan ran his hands over his buzzed head and I could see the fine tremors in his arms. He was very worked up. He braced himself on the door jam, leaning into me. I backed up a fraction, uncomfortable with our close proximity.

"You think I'd let you hide from me forever?" he asked softly, his eyes sparking with an intensity that took my breath away.

I swallowed and moved aside, letting him come in. There was no point in having this conversation in the hallway. And I had the feeling he wouldn't leave, even if I slammed the door in his face. He had a look of pure determination.

"I was getting ready to go to bed," I replied, trying to put a serious time limit to this little discussion he seemed insistent that we have.

Jordan stood in the middle of my living room, his back to me. I couldn't help but check out the strong muscles of his shoulders and upper back. I had never found the back of someone's neck to be sexy before. But damn if Jordan Levitt didn't have a sexy neck. I wanted to put my lips right below the hairline.

I shook my head, trying to clear my thoughts. "So, um, can we make this quick? Because I'm super tired." And suddenly super horny, but he didn't need to know that. Jordan turned around to look at me. He clasped his hands on the top of his head, and stared at me for a moment as though he were trying to work something out.

"What did I do?" he asked, taking me by surprise.

I blinked. Once, twice, three times.

"Huh?" I asked, dumbfounded. Jordan sighed and started clicking his tongue ring again.

"I asked what the hell did I do? I thought...I don't know...that we had something." He sounded so vulnerable and more than a little hurt. I know my mouth gaped open. Was he for real? After blatantly blowing me off and jumping cock first back into things with Olivia, he had the audacity to come to my damn apartment in the middle of the night to ask *what he did?*

My face started to flush and I felt my temper rise. Jordan clearly didn't realize the dangerous waters he was swimming in. He took a step toward me, dropping his arms to his sides, hooking his fingers into his belt loops as he regarded me with an aching tenderness that would have made my toes curl had I not wanted to bash his freaking head in.

"Please, Mays. I'm miserable here. Tell me what I can do!" he pleaded with me and I finally lost it. I shoved him in the middle of his chest. He stumbled back and looked at me in shock.

"What the hell, Maysie?" he demanded, furrowing his brow.

"You fucking bastard!" I yelled, letting loose all of my anger, my humiliation, my gut wrenching sadness at being shoved aside for Olivia Peer. I let it all out in those three words.

I shoved him again, feeling the urge to hurt him. "How can you stand there and ask me something like that after EVERYTHING?" I was being loud. I knew my neighbors were probably getting an ear full through our paper-thin walls. But at that moment, I didn't care.

Jordan held his hands up, trying to stop me. "Why are you so mad at me? I'm in the dark here." He sounded genuinely perplexed, but I was passed hearing any of it. I took a threatening step toward him and got right into his face.

"Why am I mad? Are you stupid? Or just blind? Maybe it's the fact that I've been branded the college whore after hooking up with you? Or maybe it's the fact that you went right back to Olivia after telling me..." I drew in a shaky breath; my anger starting to fizzle out and being replaced with the overwhelming need to cry.

I bit my lip to stop the tears and squeezed my eyes shut. "You text me telling me that you want to talk. I text back. And then I hear nothing. And then the whole time I'm dealing with the fact that most of my sisters now hate my guts and everyone is talking about what a skank I am. *You've* been miserable? Give me a damn break." I couldn't stop the traitorous tears that escaped behind my closed eyelids.

I furiously wiped them away, hating the show of weakness in front of Jordan. I bowed my head refusing to look at him. There was absolute silence between us. I was acutely aware of Jordan's breathing and my heart pounded in my chest so hard that I was surprised it didn't come flying out and smack him in the face.

Then I felt his hands on my upper arms. His thumbs caressed my bare skin and I loathed how much I loved it. He tilted my chin so that I was looking at him. His eyes were sad as he stared down at me. "Maysie, I had no idea..." I barked out a laugh.

"Have you been living under a rock?" Jordan frowned.

"No, Garrett's house, actually. I haven't been back to my place but to get some clothes and books for class. I've been purposefully staying away from the house."

"But, what about Olivia then?" I couldn't help the bitterness that was obvious in my question. Jordan cupped my cheek and stared me straight in the eye.

"I broke up with Olivia the night we were together," he told me quietly.

My heart stopped. That couldn't be true!

"But she told me you were together. And she stayed with you that night..." my voice trailed off. I was completely confused.

Jordan wrapped his hand around the back of my neck and tugged me closer. Our chests pressed against each other and our faces were less than an inch apart. I looked up at him, not knowing exactly what was happening. "She was lying, Mays. I haven't talked to Olivia in over two weeks. And I don't know where she stayed that night, but it sure as hell wasn't with me. After I texted you, I headed to Garrett's house. That's where I've been staying ever since. So I had no idea all of this was going on. I have barely talked to any of my brothers, so I didn't know shit was being said about you. But I swear to God, that crap ends now!" His face turned red and his nostrils flared. I knew he meant it.

He took a few deep breaths in an effort to calm himself down. "Why didn't you call me and tell me this was going on? Didn't you think I'd want to know?" he asked after a few minutes. I dropped my eyes, not wanting to look at him.

"Because it was my problem. And I thought you and Olivia... well you walked off with her. And then she said..." I couldn't finish. I didn't know what else to say. Jordan let out a deep breath and it fanned across my face, smelling like beer and peppermint.

"You thought I had chosen her." His hand, still clutching around the back of my neck, tightened. "I'm such a fucking asshole," he growled. I couldn't help but smile.

"Yeah, you kind of are," I agreed. Jordan tapped his forehead against mine.

"Watch it," he warned, his eyes sparkling.

I sobered then and pulled away, forcing him to drop his hands. "Then why haven't I heard from you, Jordan?" I asked him with all the hurt I had felt the last few weeks. This time, Jordan didn't tentatively reach for me. He grabbed my arms and pulled me tightly against him. He held my face roughly between his hands and forced me to look at him. His cheeks were splotched red and his eyes snapped with a fire that threatened to engulf me.

"What are you talking about? After you sent me that text I thought I'd give you the night to deal with stuff. But I drove my ass over here first thing the next morning. But no one was here. So I waited until I had to leave for class myself. Then I came back. And came back. I've been by here at least three times a week since I last saw you! Every time, you either weren't here or Riley has empathically told me that you did *not* want to see me. I begged her to let me talk to you but she was pretty insistent that I needed to leave you the hell alone. And what I had to say to you couldn't be said over the phone." I closed my eyes. Damn my well-intentioned but seriously misguided best friend.

"And what did you need to tell me that couldn't be said over the phone?" I asked my voice weak. Jordan took a deep breath, his eyes never leaving mine.

"I wanted to tell you that I couldn't stop thinking about your face. That you had burrowed your way so deep into my veins that I would fucking bleed *you*. That if I died tomorrow, I could go a happy man for having felt your lips on my skin."

Shit. Well, what was there to say to that? The man was a poet. It was no wonder girls practically dropped their panties in his presence.

"Just so you know, I had no idea you had been coming by," I told him, putting my hands up to cover his as they held my face. Something instantly changed in Jordan's expression. No longer did he look fierce and angry. Now he looked relieved and almost happy.

"You didn't?" he clarified. I shook my head.

"Nope. Had no clue," I responded, smiling a bit.

"And would you have seen me?" he whispered, inching his mouth towards mine until we were breathing each other's air. I looked into his eyes. This was the moment. The one where everything would change in an instant. How I handled the next thirty seconds was crucial. Did I back away and force myself to deny what had always been there between us? Or did I finally allow myself to accept it...and him?

So, I put my lips to his and whispered back, "Yes." Jordan gripped my face as our lips crushed against one another. His tongue begged entrance into my mouth and I happily complied. The moment our tongues collided, Jordan groaned heavily in the back of his throat. His hands cupped my ass and lifted me up so that I could wrap my legs around his waist. He started walking me down the hallway.

"Which one is yours?" he asked against my mouth. I pointed to the door on the left. Jordan kicked open the door and carried me into the darkened room. He laid me down on the bed and his mouth moved to my neck, suckling my skin and tracing his tongue along my collarbone. My hands ran up his back as I pushed his shirt up. My legs remained wrapped around him and I rubbed myself against the obvious erection he had underneath his jeans.

"I have wanted you from the minute I saw you," Jordan

murmured into my mouth as his hands started to slide up my tank top. I arched off the bed as his hands cupped my breasts, his thumbs rubbing circles over my hardened nipples. "I have *only* wanted you since June 18th at 3:45 p.m.," he said huskily as he continued to palm my aching breasts.

Even as turned on as I was, I couldn't help but laugh at what he said. "Wow, you remember the exact hour we met?" I asked, gasping as he lowered his mouth to my breasts, his tongue gliding between them before pulling a nipple into his mouth. He bit down lightly, causing me to moan.

"I remember every moment with you, Maysie. Every single time I touched you. Every time I heard you laugh. The way you taste in my mouth." He kissed my breasts reverently. "From the second I saw you, it has *only* been you. Even when I tried to force myself to forget you. I couldn't." He breathed as he kissed a line down my body, his tongue blazing a hot trail along my skin.

I could barely focus on what he was saying to me, I was too fixated on the fact that he was ever so slowly, pulling my shorts and underwear down over my hips. He continued to kiss and lick every inch of my skin from my belly to my hips.

He pulled my bottoms off and tossed them on the floor with an enthusiasm that totally aroused me. He returned his attentions back to my body as he started to kiss my inner thighs, his fingers digging into my hips as he worked his way north.

"Ahh. Jordan," I hissed as he blew across my wet center. Slowly, his tongue darted out and flicked against my clit. I bucked like crazy, already feeling the stirrings of my orgasm. "I have wanted to taste you so badly." His tongue came out of his mouth again and he circled my throbbing clit. I could feel the metal of his tongue ring as he licked me. Fuck, that was incredible.

"Mmm. Just as sweet as I imagined," he groaned, his tongue piercing me with abandon.

He spread my legs wider and his fingers suddenly replaced his tongue as he rubbed my sensitive flesh. Then slowly and with careful precision, he pushed his finger inside me and began to suck on my clit as he penetrated me. I had never experienced anything like this before. Jordan was merciless in giving me pleasure. My hands gripped his head as he alternated between his tongue and his fingers fucking me. The feel of the barbell in his mouth was incredible. People weren't lying when they said it made things much more intense. That damn barbell hit just the right spot for me to go completely, stark raving wild.

The orgasm came on like a volcanic explosion and I felt myself shudder and release. And Jordan continued to lap at me with his tongue as I came; taking everything I had to give him. My legs felt like jelly. I think I literally started twitching. Jordan kissed me once more between my legs before moving back up my body.

I realized he was still dressed and my tank top was still on. Dear lord, I *was* a hussy! Jordan kissed my lips softly and I could taste myself. It was strange, but not unpleasant. We lay there together, Jordan wrapped around me as I tried to get my breathing under control. He brushed the hair back from my forehead and nuzzled my ear. I was very aware of his hard on pressed against my hip. I felt a tiny bit bad that he hadn't gotten off. But only a little, because that was freaking amazing!

Jordan kissed my temple, his nose buried into my hair. I felt sort of awkward. Sure, that had been the most mind-blowing oral sex I had ever received, but what did it all mean? Jordan had said he had broken up with Olivia...but was I to assume that we were together now?

Jordan must have sensed my tension because he pulled back and looked down at me. The street lamp outside lit my room in a hazy sort of light, making it hard for me to see Jordan's face. He caressed my jaw line with the tips of his fingers. "What's wrong?" he whispered, rubbing his hand down the side of my neck.

I shivered involuntarily at his touch. I closed my eyes so I could steel my courage to speak my mind. "This was great..." I began. Jordan chuckled. I opened my eyes to see his amused expression.

"Well, that's good," he replied, nipping my bottom lip with his teeth and giving a playful growl. I laughed and pushed at his shoulders.

"But what does this all mean, Jordan? Don't think I'm not appreciative of your superior oral techniques. I'm just not sure where we go from here." Christ, I sounded like one of those pathetic girls who read too much into a one-night stand. Oh god, what if he was one night standing me?

Jordan tugged on a strand of my hair, breaking me out of my panic induced thoughts. "This means that you're my girl," he said seriously, pulling me as close to him as possible. I couldn't help but smile.

His girl.

I liked the sound of that.

But what about Olivia? And my sisters? And his brothers? And everyone else who had so quickly labeled me the campus home wrecker? I'd be playing the part perfectly, wouldn't I? I wasn't so sure I could deal with all that.

Jordan kissed me, slowly at first and then his tongue mated with mine. He held me perfectly still as his mouth ravaged mine desperately. He broke away suddenly, leaving me panting. "Stop over thinking it, Mays. Don't think about Olivia, or your sisters, or anybody else. I want you to *only* think about me. And us. And what my fingers are doing right now. The rest we can figure out later...together," he said huskily as his hand moved between my legs again.

I sighed, my head falling back as his mouth found my skin. Screw everything else, this was all I needed.

CHAPTER 16

I woke up the next morning with a big smile on my face. I'm sure the fact that Jordan's arm was wrapped around my waist and his face pressed against the back of my neck had a lot to do with it. Also the three orgasms he had given me the night before weren't bad either. I didn't want to move. Not wanting to destroy this perfect moment where everything in my life finally made sense.

Wow. I let a guy sleep in my bed. And I liked it. No, I *loved* it. I didn't care that he was all up in my personal space. In fact, it made me feel warm and secure and safe. I knew that even in my sleep I couldn't be away from him.

My mind replayed last night and I could hardly believe any of it. Jordan showing up at the apartment. Telling me he had broken up with Olivia. That he had been trying to see me for three fucking weeks! And then his mouth and his hands and oh, god, his tongue. We hadn't had sex, but dear god everything else had been the closest thing to heaven I could imagine.

Then he had told me I was his girl.

I was Jordan Levitt's girl!

I clamped down on my lips so I wouldn't squeal like a pre-pubescent girl at a boy band concert. I squeezed my eyes shut and prayed this wasn't a dream. Slowly I opened my eyes again. Yep, Jordan was still there. I could feel his even breath against my skin.

But after a few minutes I had to move. My left arm was going numb from lying on it. I slowly wiggled out from underneath Jordan's arm. "Oh no you don't," he murmured, squeezing me tightly and hefting me up against his side again. I squealed as he pushed my hair to the side and started kissing the side of my neck.

"Stop it. I really have to go to the bathroom." I pushed against his arm but he only laughed.

"Then I guess it would be really mean to do this." He started tickling me and I swear I was seconds away from losing all dignity and wetting myself.

"Seriously. Stop!" I screeched. Jordan was laughing hard by this point, but finally released me. I smacked his chest. "You are a malicious jerk!" I said not unkindly. Jordan continued to laugh as I scrambled out of the bed and practically flew to the bathroom.

While I was in there, I quickly brushed my teeth and pulled my hair into a ponytail before heading back to my room. Riley's door was still closed, so I wasn't sure she had come home last night. Jordan was sitting up in my bed checking his phone when I came back in. He looked downright edible first thing in the morning. Girls had to worry about crazy bedhead and raccoon eyes if we forgot to wash off all of our makeup the night before. Guys could just wake up and look ready to go. It wasn't fair.

I stood awkwardly just inside the door. I know he had said I was his girl and all, but I was still unsure as to what to do with that. Do I crawl back into bed with him? Do I just go ahead and get dressed? Do I offer to make him breakfast? Oh god, I hope he doesn't want breakfast...I had the amazing ability to burn even water.

Jordan was frowning at something on his phone. That wasn't a good look. I edged around my dresser and finally sat down on the bed, folding my legs beneath me. He looked up as the mattress sank underneath my weight. "Hey," he said softly with an adorable smile.

"Hey," I said back. He put his phone on the bedside table and reached out to grab me by the wrist.

Jordan pulled me and I found myself sprawled across his

chest. He wrapped his arms around my back, my front pressed against him. He placed a kiss on the top of my head. "Everything okay?" I asked, kissing the bare skin of his chest.

"Yeah. Just a text from one of my brothers. Nothing important," he replied. I didn't really believe him but decided not to push it. Jordan squeezed me tight. "I could get used to this," he whispered as I buried into his side.

"Oh yeah?" I asked, tilting my head back so I could look at him. He clicked his tongue ring along his teeth and grinned down at me.

"I love the feel of your tight little ass against my cock first thing in the morning. Makes me think of spreading those gorgeous legs of yours and..." I smacked his arm, cutting him off as I flushed a bright red.

Jordan chuckled and nudged my chin up with fingers. He kissed me slow and deep. "What time is your first class?" he asked me when we finally came up for air. I looked at the clock on my dresser.

"I have World Religions in an hour and a half. What about you?" I asked.

"I have Business Finance at the same time. Do you want to get dressed and head over to campus? Maybe get some breakfast?" His lips went to my ear and he sucked the lobe into his mouth, making me moan. Then I realized what he was saying. He wanted to go into public. Together.

I pulled away from him. "Um. I'm not sure..." I began. Jordan pulled my face back around so I would look at him.

"Maysie. If we're going to be together, that means we have to be seen together. Who cares what anyone thinks," he said with such assuredness that it was hard to deny him anything.

"Okay. Yeah. Let's go get something to eat." I said, trying to put some enthusiasm into my words, even though I really felt like jumping out the window and making a run for it. I got out of bed and went to my dresser, pulling out a pair of jean shorts and a t-shirt.

I could feel Jordan's eyes watching me as I got dressed. It was such an intimate feeling, having him in my space like that. But I had to admit, I liked it. A lot. Jordan got up and put his clothes on and I had a difficult time keeping my eyes off of that magnificent body. He really was beautiful. Cut and toned in all the right places without being overly muscular. I hated super muscly guys...but Jordan was downright perfect.

I was putting a pair of hooped earrings on when I felt Jordan's hand on my lower back. I watched him in the mirror as he dipped his head and placed a soft kiss to where my shoulder joined with my neck. I tried not to shiver, but I failed miserably. He grinned at my reflection. "Ready, baby?" I nodded, my voice having left me.

I grabbed my book bag and purse and followed him out of the apartment. "Do you mind if we swing by my house so I can change my clothes? I've run out of clean stuff at Garrett's and really need to pick up a few things," he said, leading me to his truck.

"Why aren't you staying at your house?" I asked.

Jordan's lips thinned. "Just needed some space," he answered. I guess I could understand that.

"That's fine, we can swing by," I told him, though it was anything but *fine*. I didn't particularly want to head to the house he shared with his Pi Sig brothers. But I had agreed to give this thing with him a shot. So I suppose I had to face everyone at some point.

I had just hoped it wouldn't be so soon.

I got into the passenger side of Jordan's truck as he slid into the driver's seat. "Not ridin' the hog?" I asked. I loved his motorcycle and had many a fantasy of being wrapped around him on the back of his bike.

Jordan chuckled. "Not today. But you can be my biker babe whenever you want. I'd like to see you in some sexy black leather," he said, cupping the side of my neck, his fingers squeezing lightly. I couldn't stop my grin. When he turned on the truck, the radio blasted Motorhead. That will wake you up in the morning.

"This music will melt your brain!" I yelled over Lenny's screaming vocals.

Jordan held his hand around his ear. "Huh, can't hear you, brain melting here." I chuckled as I watched Jordan sing Ace of

Spades along with the music. He had a really nice voice. Rich and smoky. It made me think of sex and his fingers and the way his eyes looked right before he put his mouth between my legs. Oh crap, I was going to have an orgasm just listening to him sing.

The volume of the music left little room for conversation on the way to Jordan's house. Which was fine with me, because I was trying to calm down my raging hormones. And stop the very real freak out about going into Pi Sig territory as his girlfriend for the first time. Jordan reached over and squeezed my upper thigh, his fingers pressing into my skin. He didn't move his hand; instead he kept it there for the entire ride.

Pulling up to his house, I wondered if I could get away with just staying in the truck. "You coming?" Jordan asked, getting out of the vehicle. I sighed and climbed out. He took my hand as we entered the front door. Several of his brothers were in the living room and every single one of them looked up as we came in. The looks they gave us ranged from surprise, confusion, to outright leering.

"Hey, man. Where've you been hiding?" One of the guys asked as we headed toward the stairs. Jordan slung his arm around my shoulders.

"Ah, you know. Here and there," he answered vaguely. The guy, I think his name was Derek, looked between Jordan and me. His lip curled a bit when he took in the possessive way Jordan held me. I tensed and tried to move away, but I was held firm.

"You know Maysie Ardin, right?" Jordan asked, a little confrontationally. Derek's eyes flicked to me but then looked away.

"Yeah, sure. Maysie," he said. But I could hear the chill in his voice. It made me feel like absolute shit. Jordan didn't miss the way his "brother" greeted me. His jaw hardened and he pushed passed the other guy and led us to the stairs.

"Asshole," Jordan muttered under his breath as he dropped his arm from around my shoulder and took a hold of my hand. I squeezed his fingers but didn't respond. What could I say? This was not a good beginning to our first venture into public as a couple. I had a feeling this was going to be a long day.

Jordan and I went into his room and I sat down on the bed while he found some clothes to change into. "Like what you see?" he asked huskily as he took off his shirt, catching the way my eyes clung to his every movement. He was so damn mouthwatering, and hell if he didn't know it. For the first time I was able to see the tattoo on his back that spread up toward his neck. It was a black Celtic sun in the middle of his shoulder blades. The flames leaping up to wrap around his neck and arms. It was amazing. And hot. And I wanted to trace it with my tongue.

"Not bad," I said noncommittally, though I had to swallow around the lump that had formed in my throat just by looking at his naked torso. Jordan arched his eyebrow at me, not fooled in the slightest. Then with careful slowness, he pulled on a gray Generation Rejects t-shirt. I felt like I was watching a strip show in reverse. He was so freaking sexy, even when putting his clothes *on*. I was debating whether we should just skip our classes and spend the rest of the day in bed, getting better acquainted when the door burst open.

"Jordan! Where the hell have you been, man?" Gio came into the room and punched Jordan good-naturedly on the shoulder.

"I've been at Garrett's. We've been putting in a lot of practice time so I needed to be over there." Jordan answered dismissively. I watched the two of them and I realized Jordan didn't like Gio *at all*. Not that I blamed him. Gio was a jerk. And he just earned the title all over again when he realized I was sitting on Jordan's bed.

"Well, that's not Olivia," he said with a sneer. Jordan's shoulder's tightened.

"Shut up, Gio. That shit's uncalled for," Jordan said in a dangerously soft voice. Gio put his hands up in mock surrender.

"I was just making an observation, man. Just a little surprised to see the swap in bed partners. After all, it was Olivia's fine ass up in here just a few weeks ago. Though pussy's pussy, right?" Gio grinned nastily in my direction. The acid bubbled in my stomach though I was proud of the hateful glare I threw in his direction. Gio purposefully licked his lips, his eyes raking over my body as though he saw straight through my clothing. This guy had date rapist written all over him. What a creep.

Jordan got in the other guy's face. "That's enough. Get out the fuck out," Jordan growled, his face a scary shade of red. Gio looked at Jordan with a twinge of disgust.

"Whatever. It's your dick. You can dip it wherever you want. Though I'd be sure to wrap it with that one." I barely had time to register the insult before Jordan's arm reared back and swung around to connect with Gio's jaw.

Gio went to the floor. He held his hand up over his face. "What the fuck man?" he screamed, trying to get to his feet. Jordan hauled him up and threw him out into the hallway. He stood over Gio, his hands clenched by his side, ready to do more damage if necessary.

"Don't you *ever* fucking talk to my girl like that again! DO YOU HEAR ME?" Jordan roared.

A few of their brothers had appeared. One was trying to pull Jordan back while two others got Gio to his feet. Gio's jaw had blossomed in to a bright red and I knew he'd have a serious bruise in a few hours. Gio spat at Jordan's feet.

"Bros before hoes man. Or have you forgotten? No chick is worth it," he yelled, throwing me a look that made me want to crawl into a hole and hide.

Jordan tried to lunge for him again, but their other roommate, Fred, pulled him back into his bedroom. Fred slammed the door and shoved Jordan back. "Don't bring your shit into this house, Jordan! I don't know what is up between you and Gio, but it ends now!" Fred was a big guy and manhandled Jordan with ease. I knew Fred played on the school's lacrosse team. He had always seemed like a sweet person but now he just looked pissed.

Jordan turned and slammed his fist into the wall, plaster falling in big chunks to the floor. The whole time, I sat there on his bed, too freaked out to move or make a sound. It was like Jordan had forgotten I was there. Fred looked in my direction and gave me a tiny smile. "Sorry about that, Maysie. You okay?" he asked. I was shocked by the concern in his voice. I nodded.

"Yeah," I was able to squeak out.

Fred turned back to Jordan. "Calm down. I'll talk to Gio. But this shit cannot happen again. We have to all live together. I think we need to have a house meeting tonight," he said. Jordan didn't say anything and Fred didn't wait for a reply. He left the room after giving me another comforting smile. Once Fred had left the room, Jordan seemed to try and get himself under control. I didn't know what to say, but I got to my feet and tentatively walked toward him.

I put my hand on his arm. "It's okay," I said softly. Jordan grabbed my hand and pulled me to him in a tight hold.

"No, Maysie. It is NOT okay! Is this the shit you've been dealing with?" he asked in a pained voice. I didn't say anything. I didn't want him to get even more fired up than he already was. Jordan must have taken my silence for acquiescence because he tightened his hold on me. "I'll fucking kill them all! They cannot talk about you like that!" he said angrily.

I pulled away from him. "Stop it, Jordan. I don't need you to fight my battles for me," I assured him. Jordan shook his head and looked so upset that it wrenched at my heart.

"This is my fault! I created this stupid mess. If I had just broken up with Olivia in the first place..." I put my fingers over his mouth to quiet him. His eyes held mine and I hated to see him like this.

"Yeah, the situation sucks. I won't lie and say it doesn't. But I'm a big girl and I made the choices that I did knowing the consequences. It is not entirely your fault. It takes two to tango, Jordan. We got into this together and we'll handle it together. Right?" I asked. Jordan nodded; kissing the fingers that still covered his lips.

"Then, we'll be alright," I said confidently. Jordan pulled my hand from his mouth and roughly kissed my lips. His hands came up to tangle in my hair as he ravaged my mouth. He always kissed this way. Like he was trying to eat me alive. Pulling away, he dropped his forehead to rest against mine.

"I mean it when I say I won't tolerate the kind of bullshit people are saying about you!" he said emphatically. I held his face with my hands, touched that he wanted to defend me like that. But also feeling sad that he had to in the first place.

I placed my lips to his and he softened immediately. His arms came up to hold me and we stood like that for a while, not saying anything else. I looked up at the clock on his wall.

"Well, I'd say breakfast is out of the question," I said, indicating the time. We had thirty minutes before our classes started. Jordan grabbed his messenger bag and slung it over his shoulder and then he took my hand in his.

"I can't have my girl going to class hungry. Let's at least stop and get a bagel." His earlier anger had dissipated and he smiled down at me in a tender way so at odds with his bad boy appearance. With his facial piercings, buzzed head and tattoos he looked like the quintessential bad ass. But I was beginning to see the soft heart underneath it all. And it was safe to say I had already fallen more than a bit in love with him.

A few of the guys said goodbye as we left but Jordan ignored them. After we got back into his truck, I felt the need to address the icy vibe between him and his fraternity brothers. "I hate to see you so mad your friends," I said, watching him as he concentrated on the road. He glanced at me and frowned.

"If they were my friends, they wouldn't look at you the way they just did. So fuck 'em." He said it with a conviction that I wished I felt.

But I didn't want to be the reason there was a rift between him and his Pi Sig brothers. "I'm sure it's just weird seeing you with someone who isn't Olivia." I had to force her name out of my mouth. I hated bringing her up at all. Jordan snorted.

"It's not like any of them were particularly fond of Liv, sweetheart." I blinked in surprise. Hmm, I had always thought Olivia got along well with the Pi Sig guys. Maybe not.

"No, they're just being a bunch of bitches. And I don't have time in my life for bitches," he said shortly, making it clear he was done with that particular subject. We stopped and got bagels from The Cup and Crumb before making our way to campus. The ugliness from the morning, while not entirely forgotten, was at least pushed to the side. And I was able to see what a relationship with Jordan would be like.

We got along so well, it was a little scary. Despite the amazing sexual chemistry, I found we actually had a lot to talk about.

Jordan was smart and funny and damn near irresistible. "We have a gig coming up this weekend at Dave's Tavern. I'd love for you to come and see us play." Jordan commented, pulling into the parking lot in front of the freshman dorms.

I picked up my stuff from the floor of his truck. "Yeah, I think that can be arranged," I responded coyly as Jordan reached over to curl his hand around the back of my neck, pulling me toward him.

"Yes, please pencil me into your busy schedule," he said with a grin before kissing me soundly. I wanted to melt into a puddle on his leather seats. This boy could kiss. And kiss well.

"Now come on, can't have us late for class," Jordan said, running his thumb along the curve of my bottom lip as I tried to get my bearings.

"Um, yeah. Class," I mumbled as he chuckled, opening his door. I followed him up the path that led to Randolph Hall, where my class was held. Jordan made a point to hold me close, rubbing his hand up and down my arm. I couldn't ignore the looks we got as we made our way along campus. I hated this feeling of being on show. That everyone was a little too focused on the two of us together.

If it bothered Jordan, he didn't let on. We stopped in front of Randolph Hall, toe to toe, holding each other's hands and grinning like the crazy fools we were. "I'd like to take you out to dinner tonight. What do you say?" he asked, swinging my hands back and forth. I laughed, enjoying the lightness that unfurled in my chest. Jordan lifted our joined hands and laced his fingers with mine. Slowly and deliberately, he brought my knuckles to his lips, kissing them softly.

"It's a date," I replied softly, watching him as he held my hand against his mouth. I felt his smile as much as I saw it. His face lit up and he reluctantly released me to head toward his own class.

"That's right babe. It's a date. And tonight, you're all mine." He promised with a devilish twinkle in his eye. I giggled as I turned and walked inside. I was on cloud 9. Well, until I saw three of my sorority sisters giving me the evil eye.

"Hey, Maysie," Milla said snidely, giving me a hateful smile. I nodded in her direction but didn't say anything, moving passed her. Milla fell into step behind me and I suppressed a groan. "Saw you with Jordan. So are you two...together?" she asked as though it were something lewd. I turned and faced her.

"What do you want Milla? If you want to say something, just say it." I knew I was setting myself up for it, but at that point, I just didn't care.

Milla moved in closer. She was quite a bit taller than me and I hated how I had to look up at her. "I've never liked you, Maysie. If it were up to me, you'd be kicked out of Chi Delta so fast your head would spin. But that's not how we do things. Some of us are classier than that." I snorted.

"Classy? You?" I scoffed, giving her short skirt and revealing shirt a critical once over. Milla's face darkened.

"Well, I wasn't the one fucking Olivia's boyfriend behind her back, was I?" I opened my mouth to give a snappy comeback but stopped myself. What was the point? I wasn't in the mood for a round of verbal jousting.

"I think you have some nerve prancing all over campus with him like that. Olivia has been nothing but nice to you. And this is how you repay her? By jumping in for her sloppy seconds?" Milla pushed passed me then stopped and looked back. "But I guess it's easy to land a guy when you're so willing to lay on your back for him. You are nothing but a whore and the whole campus knows it. So enjoy Jordan while you have him. Because I can guarantee it won't be for long." She flipped her hair behind her shoulder and walked off, our two sisters following behind her not bothering to acknowledge me.

I stood there, dumbstruck. Was that bitch for real? It didn't take a scientist to see that jealousy motivated everything with Milla. She reeked of it. I didn't want to listen to any of the bullshit that came out of her mouth. I wanted to dismiss her outright. But the sucky thing was that she was right. It was crappy to walk around with Jordan, blissful in the newness of our relationship while Olivia nursed her wounds over their recent break-up. It was kind of heartless and more than a little selfish. And I didn't want to be that girl. But maybe I had unwittingly already become her.

CHAPTER
17

The rest of the week went by in agonizing slowness. Every day I had to walk onto campus knowing I was the talk of the town. I suppose I could have been flattered that people were so interested in my life. It would have been great to look at the catastrophic mess in something semi-positive. But the truth was that the rumors, the whispers, the hateful looks, were like a knife to my gut. I had gone from being a happy, popular sorority girl, to public enemy #1. I had known Olivia was well liked but I had a feeling that my descent into villainy had more to do with the public's need for a juicy scandal. The parts had been given out and I was cast as the conniving slut.

I sat in my classes, trying to pay attention to my professors' lectures but I all I could hear were the hushed voices swirling around me. I overheard a couple of girls talking about how I had purposefully gone after Jordan while Olivia was away for the summer. The words "slut" and "disgusting skank" had been thrown in for good measure and I had immediately stopped listening.

Jordan wasn't immune to it either. He had shown up at my apartment for our date looking majorly pissed off. I had asked him what was wrong but he had only shaken his head, saying it didn't matter. After some more prodding, I had gotten out of him that there was a "house meeting" with his roommates. It had gotten ugly. Nasty things were said (though he wouldn't elaborate what they were) and he had left before anything had been resolved.

I felt horrible. I hated that I was the source of such dissension in his life. Jordan wouldn't let me apologize, emphatically telling me I had nothing to be sorry for. But I *was* sorry. So, horribly, terribly sorry.

How could we have any sort of meaningful relationship when it was founded on so much drama? I had asked if we could rain check on going out to dinner and instead suggested ordering in. Jordan had argued that he wanted to take me out. That we had nothing to be ashamed of. I didn't agree. Now more than ever, I wanted to hide away from it all.

Jordan had eventually caved and we ended up ordering Chinese and watching a movie. I tried to forget about everything outside of he and I and this great thing we had going on. I had also come to find that while we were alone, forgetting was surprisingly easy.

Because we had fun together. More than that...we just sort of *fit*. And that made me think that it was definitely worth the heartache.

So, while we ate our cheap Chinese food, Jordan had tried to get me to eat some his spicy pork. I refused, resulting in Jordan shoving a piece into my mouth while he pinned me to the couch. Soon a food fight had ensued and by the time we called cease-fire, the living room walls were painted with sweet and sour sauce and bits of chicken hung from my hair. Jordan was trying to lick the remnants of our dinner off of my neck when Riley had walked in with Damien.

They took one look at Jordan kneeling over top of me on the couch with his mouth sucking on my chin and had turned around and walked right back out. Jordan and I had started laughing until he pressed his mouth to mine and then there wasn't any more laughing. Or talking. Only kissing. And a lot of touching.

The insatiable physical attraction only grew stronger the more time we spent together. And it was this need to be with him in every way possible that made our situation all the harder to handle. Because I wanted to yell from the rooftops that Jordan

Levitt was my boyfriend. I wanted to go out on dates and walk across campus together. I wanted to take him to mixers and announce to the world that he was mine.

But it still felt like we were each other's dirty little secret. Because Jordan didn't offer for me to come hang out at the Pi Sig house. We avoided places where there was a chance of running into Olivia and my Chi Delta sisters (which was pretty much everywhere). Instead, he came to my apartment in the evening. We fooled around and he usually fell asleep wrapped around me. And that was nice. Just not what I had dreamed it would be like.

Because Olivia was still a major problem. She wasn't going away quietly. And hell if she wasn't bent on making my life miserable. She was calling Jordan...constantly. His phone would often beep several times a night. He was always honest in saying that it was her and never made any effort to respond. He usually deleted the texts without reading them. I was dying to see what she had written and I considered snooping. But we were really working on building trust between us, especially given our shaky start. And reading his text messages behind his back wouldn't help with the whole honesty thing.

So, Jordan would eventually turn off his phone, then assure me that it didn't matter. But it *did* matter. Because I was insanely jealous. And worried. Worried that he'd wake up one morning and tell me that being with me was a big mistake.

My insecurities were driving me crazy and Olivia did everything she could to dig my doubts in a little deeper. She was sneaky; none of her attacks against me were overt. I had avoided the Chi Delta house for the few days after the chapter meeting. But Gracie had insisted I come and hang out Wednesday after my last class. I had put up a bit of a fight but she reasoned that I was still a sister and had every right to be there.

I finally agreed, not wanting to argue about it anymore. I had gone over to the house and at first it wasn't too bad. A few of the other girls came and hung out with Gracie and I while we watched re-runs of America's Next Top Model in the common room. We had laughed together and made cutting commentary as we watched the show.

Then Olivia had shown up and with one look at the girls, everyone got up and made excuses to leave. I had no power against Olivia's popularity. She controlled the house with an iron fist and I had been firmly allocated outsider status.

I seriously questioned why I was still apart of Chi Delta when it was so obvious I wasn't wanted there. When I brought this up to Gracie and Vivian, they both staunchly refused to hear what I was saying. "You are a Chi Delt! Don't you dare let them make you feel any different! Olivia is out of here after this year and next year will be all about us!" Gracie argued. Vivian had nodded adamantly.

"This will blow over. I promise you," Vivian assured me.

That's what they *always* said. And so far, that day when it would all be behind me, had yet to come. Though, I never called them on their well-intentioned bullshit. Because, I didn't think Olivia would just *get over* what had happened. She and Jordan had been together for three years and I understood her feelings of hurt and betrayal. And I knew without a doubt that she loved Jordan. I just wish I could stop feeling like Kelly Taylor splitting up Dylan and Brenda. Oh crap, I was totally Kelly! I hated Kelly!

My own feelings of shame and guilt were burning a hole through my heart. I was ready to pull my hair out by Saturday night. I had promised Jordan I'd come to the Generation Rejects gig at Dave's Tavern but I was so anxious I felt like I would come out of my skin. Riley had agreed to come along so I wouldn't have to go by myself. Gracie and Vivian were busy doing sisterhood stuff. Sisterhood stuff that I hadn't been privy to. Gracie had assured me that it was just planning for the upcoming Ball Blast; the semi-formal Chi Delta hosted every November. Whatever, I knew I was left out on purpose.

So I found myself in my room, twenty minutes before we had to leave, trying to decide on what to wear. I was dangerously close to calling Jordan and plead some sort of illness that required me to spend the evening in bed, when Riley knocked on my door. "Come in," I called out, throwing a pair of black heels across the room.

"Woah, Babe Ruth, watch it!" She dodged another pair of

shoes that I hurled as she walked in. I sighed in frustration and sat down on the floor, pulling my knees up to my chest. "Is that what you're wearing?" Riley asked, indicating my sweat pants and torn t-shirt. I couldn't help but laugh.

"Why, you don't think I look hot in this? I thought I'd try and bring sleep deprived college student back as a legitimate style. What do ya think?"

Riley pulled on my ponytail. "Well, I guess the coffee stains and torn elastic could be considered trashy chic." We laughed together.

"I can't find anything to wear, Riley. I mean what do you wear to a biker bar?" Dave's was a pretty rough place to go. I had heard of numerous stabbings there over the years. I had never dared to venture to Dave's myself, but I had been told it was pretty hard-core.

"Come on, you've got to have some black leather in there somewhere." Riley peered into my closet.

"Actually..." I got to my feet and dug around in the pile of clothes on the floor and pulled out a short red leather mini skirt that I had gotten for the Chi Delta "Biker Babes Bash" last spring. Riley gave me a thumbs up.

"That's more like it!" She enthused. I found a black halter-top with a collar and open sleeves and then pulled out my black ankle boots to finish the ensemble. Okay, I felt better. Nothing like a killer outfit to pull me out of my doldrums.

"Now get dressed, the band goes on in thirty minutes. There isn't enough time for your marathon primping. Just hurry up," Riley told me blandly. I waved her out of my room and went about making myself look bikerlicious. When I was done (in record time, I might add), I took in my reflection and had to admit that I looked damn hot. Hell, *I'd* do me if I could.

I had put my hair up in a teased ponytail on the top of my head and left some chunky strands around my face. I did my makeup a little heavier than normal, rimming my eyes in dark liner. My lips were a deep, but I thought kissable, red. The tight mini skirt and even tighter top made my body look awesome. The whole process of getting ready to go out had done wonders for my spirit. I found I was looking forward to my evening. Ready to go see my man's band and enjoy hanging out with people who weren't there to judge or look down on me for my choices.

Tonight was supposed to be my first time hanging with Jordan's band mates. Garrett was having a party at his house after their gig. Jordan warned that they usually got a little wild. I hadn't really met the band yet, but Jordan had assured me that they were nothing like his brothers in Pi Sig. These were a bunch of guys who didn't do the whole college scene. It was a little weird how Jordan had these two totally different lives. On one end you have Jordan #1. Mr. Pi Sig, the most popular guy at Rinard College. On the other, there was Jordan #2. The hardcore rocker who played music and went crazy with a bunch of townies. I wasn't sure what to expect with Jordan #2. But I was excited to find out.

Riley had promised she'd come too. That made me feel better. She and Damien had been attached at the hip lately and I was with Jordan constantly. Our friendship had its ebbs and flows, but we had never gone this long without spending time together. I missed her.

We got to Dave's with only ten minutes to spare. The place was packed. I had gotten my obligatory underage stamp on my hand. I intended to wipe it off using the small container of salt I had brought in my bag for such an occasion. This crowd was quite different than the ones I was used to. I didn't make it a habit of hanging out in biker bars and as I took in the scary looking dudes and even scarier looking women, I knew why.

Riley pushed her way through the crowd to a table near the back. Damien had saved us a spot and we sat down, taking it all in. "Hey ladies. Lookin' fine as always," Damien yelled over the noise. Damien was cute in a math geek with an edge sort of way. He wore black-framed glasses and had messy brown hair that fell nicely over his forehead. What was most important was the way he looked at my best friend. I knew love when I saw it and that was what was painted all over both of their faces. It warmed my heart.

Damien had brought his friend, Adam. Adam nodded in

greeting, but was more interested in nursing his rum and coke than having a conversation, so we left him to it. "Hey, I'm going to head to the bathroom and try to get this off." I held up my hand, indicating the huge green 'x' that let everyone and their brother know I was underage.

"You want me to come with?" Riley asked from her perch on Damien's lap.

"No, I'm cool. I'll be right back." I made my way, very slowly, through the heaving crowd. I was knocked sideways a few times and almost lost my footing. I was finally able to push my way into the bathroom. I pulled out the tiny bottle of iodized salt and poured it on the back of my hand. Then I turned on the water and started scrubbing. These underage stamps used serious ink and this was a little party trick I had learned very early on in my college years.

I stood there at the sink, rubbing my skin raw in an attempt to get rid of the annoying x when I heard a very familiar voice. "I think this is the bathroom." Olivia's voice filtered in through the door and I hurriedly turned off the tap and bee lined to one of the stalls. Yuck. The stall was foul and I had to hold my nose so I wouldn't breathe in the stench.

I heard the bathroom door open, the commotion of the bar wafting in. The stalls on either side of me opened and shut and I waited. What the hell was *she* doing here? I heard Olivia and at least two other girls leave the stalls and turn on the faucets. "Are you going to go back and see him before the show?" I recognized Milla's voice. Great. The bitches were all here.

Then I realized what Milla had asked. There was no question as to whom she was referring to. "No, I'll see him afterwards at Garrett's party. He said he'd be there." I know I made a noise and I clamped down on my lips to stop myself. Oh god, Jordan had invited Olivia to Garrett's party? What the hell was going on?

The girls got quiet and then the water turned off. "Do you think they'll play your song tonight?" I recognized the voice as Talia's, one of the new pledges.

"Which one?" Olivia giggled. I thought I would gag.

"You know, *the song*. The one Jordan wrote after you guys...

you know..." Milla said suggestively. I could feel the acid in the back of my throat and I really thought I would lose my dinner. I could just picture Olivia's dainty little blush at Milla's comment.

"They always play that song, Milla. It's Jordan's favorite." Olivia's voice became husky, as though she were turned on or something. What fucking song were they talking about? Now I had to know, even though I knew when I heard it, I would wish I hadn't.

My reaction was ridiculous, because I knew Olivia and Jordan's history was as deep as it was long. But the thought of him writing songs about her was too much for my delicate self-esteem. Without a thought to the massive amount of germs living on the toilet seat, I sat down heavily and waited for them to leave.

They spent a few more minutes talking about how Jordan apparently wanted to meet up with Olivia at Garrett's party. Milla was certain he had finally come to his senses and would be throwing that skank (aka, me) to the curb where I belonged. Olivia gave a non-committal response to that but even I could hear the undisguised hope in her voice. They spent a few more minutes talking smack about me. Everything from the clothes I wore to the way I styled my hair. Apparently I had nothing going for me and the fact that Jordan looked at me at all was a testament to his temporary insanity. As I sat on that disgusting toilet, I became more and more enraged. I was sick and tired of being their target. My blood began to boil and my fists started to clench in my lap.

But it was when they were devising a plan of attack on how to get Olivia and Jordan alone together that I officially had enough. I sucked in my anger and blanked my face into a picture of calm collection. Then I left the safe confines of the hepatitis-infested stall and walked brazenly to the sink. The looks passed between Milla and Olivia made it clear that they had been very aware of my presence the whole time. So I was positive that their conversation had been for my benefit alone.

"Howdy, girls," I said flippantly, scrubbing at the back of my hand again. Milla made a noise of revulsion and Olivia looked away. Talia was the only one who wanted to play the two faced game. She gave me a smile and I struggled with the urge to smack her. Particularly after what I had just heard the three of them say.

"Hey, Maysie! I didn't know you'd be here tonight." I pulled my lip-gloss from my purse and started to reapply, making eye contact with Olivia in the mirror.

"Yeah, I'm dating one of the guys in the band." I said pointedly. Okay, maybe I was being an insensitive bitch, but their cattiness had finally opened the gate to my inner Rocky. No way was I backing down without a fight. Talia cocked an eyebrow.

"You are?" she turned to Olivia. "Didn't you date the drummer?" she asked our president, who looked like she had swallowed a lemon.

Olivia and I were locked in a deadly stare down, neither one of us looking away. I tuned out Talia's passive aggressive nastiness. Milla was being suspiciously quiet but I ignored her as well. I was too focused on the battle of wills being waged in the bathroom mirror. Olivia purposefully pulled the scooped neck of her dress down to reveal even more cleavage. She fluffed her hair and rubbed excess lipstick from around her lips. "If you think you can hang onto a guy like Jordan Levitt, you're more delusional than I thought." She turned to face me head on and I stood up as straight as I could. No way would I back down.

"Oh really? Then maybe you could explain why I've been the one in his arms each and every night." Olivia's eyes narrowed and I could practically see the steam coming from her ears. She inched forward and I worried for a second that she'd hit me.

"You are nothing but a man-stealing bitch. I can't believe we didn't see it when we gave you our bid." I couldn't help but flinch. I hated that anyone saw me that way. There was that huge part of me that wanted to be liked, no matter what. Scratch below the surface and I was just a girl who cared what people thought of her. I liked being popular. I liked being in a sorority full of ready-made friends. I didn't like knowing that the image I was so proud of had become completely tarnished.

And the whole thing was more than a little unfair, if you ask me. Because the way these girls looked at it, I had maliciously and with calculation gone after a sister's boyfriend behind her back. If Olivia only knew how horrible and guilt ridden I had felt and how much I had resisted. But there was no point in trying to explain it. It didn't matter. She would never believe me. It was like every Jerry Springer episode I had ever seen. The "other woman" was always the one at fault.

I blinked, taken aback by the blatant loathing on Olivia's face. I didn't want this to hurt so much. But damned if it didn't. Olivia put her hand on her hip and leaned into me. Her lips peeled back from her teeth in a hateful grin. "But like it or not, Maysie, Jordan and I have a bond you can never get rid of. We have a past. A history. We have loved each other faithfully for three years. Sure he's into you now...but where do you think he'll end up when he's grown tired of the Maysie Ardin tramp show?" She smoothed her hair down, affecting disinterest. She seemed so calm and collected and I knew she truly believed her words. She had no doubt that she and Jordan would end up together. And her conviction started to sway even me.

She flicked her blue eyes back at me before turning to leave the bathroom. "He'll always come back to me. Because that's where he belongs." Then without another word, she slung her purse over her shoulder and left the bathroom. Milla curled her lip in disgust and followed her. Talia flicked her hair back and gave me a fake smile before leaving. And I was left standing there, feeling like a complete idiot.

I was mortified that I had sunk to that level. I had just become "that girl." The nasty, tear another chick's hair out, you-were-looking-at-my-man, kind of girl. I *hated* those girls but damned if I hadn't morphed into one. Just call up and get me a seat on Maury. Because that's where I was headed. So not only had I gone all territorial over a flipping guy, but I had also just rubbed my "sister's" face in the fact that I was currently dating said guy, her very recent ex-boyfriend. It was like tap dancing on someone's grave. It wasn't right. What happened to chicks before dicks? Oh that's right, Jordan Levitt happened. Jordan and his beautiful face and his stupid hot tattoo and piercings. I grumbled at my foolishness. Then I just became depressed.

I forgot about scrubbing the rest of the stamp off of my hand

and headed back to Riley and Damien. "What took you so long? I thought one of the bikers had eaten you," Riley quipped as I sat back down. I gave her a wan smile and she frowned at me.

"What's wrong?" she asked, cutting straight to the point.

I opened my mouth to answer her when the lights dimmed and a guy announced Generation Rejects. The spot lights shown on the stage and Cole grabbed the mic, growling low. The crowd pushed its way to the front and I could see Milla, Talia and Olivia at the foot of the stage. I had to admit, Olivia looked hot in her tiny black dress, her hair falling perfectly down her back. I hadn't really taken stock of her get up while we were shooting eyeball daggers at each other in the bathroom. But now, looking at her with her perfect little body and effortless beauty, I felt kind of slutty in my outfit.

The band launched into one of their many covers and the place went wild. I tore my eyes from my sorority sisters at the front of the pack and tried to focus on the four guys on stage. Because they were good. Damn good and I couldn't deny the raw magnetism they exuded. Cole was a looker alright and he played front man with aplomb. His dark, shaggy hair and five o'clock shadow were sexy as hell. Mitch and Garrett weren't hard to look at either. Mitch had the whole dark and mysterious thing going on while Garrett was the wild man of the group, bouncing to the music and wagging his tongue suggestively at the girls in the crowd. But it was the drummer who maintained the heartbeat of the music. It was impossible to look anywhere but at him.

Jordan wore a collared button down white shirt with the sleeves ripped off. Very Patrick Dempsey in *Can't Buy Me Love*. Retro and hot. His face glistened with sweat as he beat the hell out of his drums. His transformation into rock god was fascinating. It was so complete and total that it was hard to imagine him as anything else. It was like he lived and breathed the music he played.

I allowed myself to get lost in their performance. I loved seeing Jordan like this. His passion was evident, even from this distance. I wanted to push myself forward and dance with the rest of the people here. But I didn't want to deal with Miss Too Tight Dress and her cronies, so I stayed where I was. I couldn't stop myself from watching *her* watch *him*. She obviously knew the set well, singing along to most of the songs. She looked the part of the rock star's girlfriend, whereas I looked like a child playing dress up in my stupid leather skirt and trying too hard boots.

About thirty minutes into their set, Cole addressed the crowd. "Now we'd like to take it down a notch. This next song was written by the resident sex god himself, Jordan Levitt!" The crowd roared and my stomach clenched tightly. I had almost allowed myself to forget the bits of the conversation I had overheard in the bathroom. The part about the song. The one Jordan had written for Olivia. Fuck.

Milla and Olivia were going crazy, dancing their asses off as Jordan started to beat out a sensual rhythm. The muscles in his forearms stood out as he smashed his drumsticks down onto the kit. The song started slowly, like the slide of a lover's hand down your body. It was tantalizing and seductive. Music meant to turn you on and get you wet. And Jordan had written it for Olivia. This *would not* make me feel the warm fuzzies. Of that I was sure.

Riley and Damien had gotten to their feet, their arms curled around each other as they swayed together. Couples were pairing off, touching and grinding. Everyone responded to the primal beat Jordan laid out. If just the music made me feel like this, I knew the lyrics would destroy me. Maybe I was being overly sensitive but something instinctual took over when I realized Jordan had written a song for Olivia. Even though it happened way before I came into the picture. I felt an irrational sense of betrayal. And if I took the time to examine it closely I would realize it was because I loved him, sort of desperately, and I wanted all of his songs to be about me. And only me.

I was nuts. That's all there was to it. I had to get my head together or I would lose my shit right there.

I watched in transfixed horror as Cole wrapped his hand around the mic and bent it low, looking into the crowd as he began to sing.

You lie your head on my arm
your heart in my hand.

Lost in your eyes,
I have become a man.
Your body sings a song
Only I can hear,
Etched in the dark of my soul
Losing you is what I fear.
I've searched so long
for the promise of you.
Enthralled by your silence
I've got everything to lose.
Lost in your eyes
I have become a man.
Lost in you.
Lost in you.
Lost in you.
You moan my name
I play your game
I struggle to breathe
You're all that I need
You've become my forever
All I know is you
Enthralled by your silence
I've got everything to lose.
Forget the past
Hold on to me now
All we need is this
All we need...
Don't ask me to leave
I don't know that I can.
Lost in your eyes,
I've become a man.
Lost in you.
Lost in you.
Lost in you.

Cole's voice trailed off into a whisper as he sang intimately to the frantic crowd below him. The song was beautiful. No, beautiful didn't even begin to describe it. The love that had gone into writing those lyrics made me feel raw and vulnerable. Because it came back to the fact that Jordan had written them about someone else. Someone who had shared his life for three fucking years. How the hell could I ever compete with that sort of devotion?

I watched Olivia sway to the music as though it were calling to her personally. I could see that she was singing along with Cole and I felt tears sting my eyes. I knew she watched Jordan as he played his drums. Playing the song he had written just for her.

Oh god. I was done. So 100% done! I was a freaking idiot! What Jordan and I had was nothing compared to that. The fight I had felt earlier when confronting Olivia fizzled out in a sad sort of whimper. Did we really have anything worth fighting for? Listening to that damn song, doubt spread like a cancer through my mind. So what was I going to do? Run and hide. Because that's what I did best, and when you were good at something, why change it?

I got to my feet. "I'm going home," I announced as the band began to play a rowdy version of the Beatles' *I Wanna Hold Your Hand*. Riley looked at me in surprise.

"What? But they're only half way through the set. What about Garrett's party?" I looked up at the stage. At Jordan who was completely immersed in his music. Nope. I couldn't do this. I didn't belong here. I didn't belong with him. Who was I kidding?

"I just want to go," I said shortly. I was angry and hurt. However nonsensical my feelings were, they had a death grip on my heart and wouldn't let go. This whole thing with Jordan had been a big heap of angst from the very beginning and right then I was so over it all. Damien looked from Riley to me in confusion.

"Is everything alright?" he asked with concern. I gave him, what I hoped was a convincing smile.

"Yep, everything is just peachy. But I'm heading out. You guys can go to Garrett's without me, it'll be cool." Riley got to her feet.

"What about Jordan? What do I tell him?"

My eyes trailed over to Olivia who was thoroughly enjoying herself. Riley followed my gaze and a knowing look crossed her face.

"Mays..." she started but I held my hand up to stop her.

"I think he'll be busy. So, don't bother to say anything. Later." And with that, I turned on my heel and left the bar. Outside, I pulled out my phone and called a cab. I was a big, fat wimp. I knew that. But I didn't care. Because my new boyfriend had just played a song he wrote for his ex-girlfriend and I felt like total crap. I knew I was probably being very immature about the whole thing. But again, I didn't fucking care.

So I went home, put on my comfiest pjs and went to bed. I put my phone on my dresser. You know, just in case Riley needed something. Oh, who was I kidding? I wanted to see if Jordan would call. I was beyond ridiculous.

My phone stayed conspicuously silent.

CHAPTER
18

I *woke* up the next morning entirely too early for a Sunday, feeling very unrested. I had tossed and turned most of the night, my ears pricking up at the slightest sound. I couldn't help but obsessively wonder whether Jordan would call or come by. He had to recognize my very purposeful burn by not waiting for him after the show for what it was.

But, I didn't hear from him. Finally, after checking my phone for the thousandth time, I turned it off around five in the morning. I was driving myself certifiably crazy. So at an ungodly 9:00, I got out of bed and what was the first thing I did? I grabbed my phone off the bedside table and turned it on, only to find that there were no texts. No missed calls. Zilch. Nothing. Nada.

I angrily pulled my robe of the hook on the back of the door and shoved my arms through the sleeves. I didn't know what to do with this desolate feeling inside. But one thing was for sure, I was sick of moping over some stupid guy. The whole thing irritated me to no end. I was sick of guys and the way girls forgot all sense when they were in the picture. It was beyond annoying and completely degrading.

I opened my bedroom door and saw Riley coming down the hallway. "Just getting home?" I asked, smiling at her. At least one of us got lucky last night. Riley shrugged and looked like she was about to drop.

"Long night. I need sleep," she mumbled, heading into her room.

"Hmm, now what could have kept you up all night?" I teased. Riley rolled her eyes.

"Save your sexual innuendos for when I can respond with my normal sarcasm." She opened her door and started go into her room when I reached out to grab her arm.

I needed to know if she had talked to Jordan. I was downright desperate to find out his reaction to seeing I had left. Had he gone to the party with Olivia? Ugh! Should I just have Riley pass him a note in study hall asking him to check a box if he liked me?

So instead I played it safe. "How was the rest of the show?" I asked as casually as I was able. Riley gave me a smirk and then snorted out a laugh. What was so funny?

"Why don't you go ask Jordan," she said shaking her head as though she were talking to a very small child. What was with the condescending bullshit first thing in the morning?

"Huh?" I asked in confusion. Riley shook her head again and went into her room, closing the door behind her. Okay, enough with the cryptic messages. It was way too early and I was entirely too sleep deprived. I went to the bathroom and brushed my teeth. I looked exhausted, dark circles ringing my eyes. I needed coffee, stat.

I trudged out to the living room and froze. Jordan was sitting on the couch, his arms hanging limply between his knees, a hard look on his face. I took a deep breath. "Uh, what are you doing here?" I asked, though I couldn't help but feel the first twinges of hope mixing with the anxiety and anger in my belly. Jordan looked at me, an unreadable expression on his face. He didn't get to his feet; he stayed seated, tension radiating from him.

"Chasing after you...again," he replied coldly. Oh, whatever. He could chase himself right out the door. I didn't need this. I blew out a breath and waited for more of an explanation. Hell if I would ask him for one.

Jordan grunted in exasperation. "Riley let me in when she got home a few minutes ago. I've been waiting outside since about four this morning." What? That was the most moronic thing I had ever heard.

"Why didn't you just knock on the door like any sane person would do?" I asked him sharply.

"Because I had to make sure I didn't come in here and scream my fucking head off, alright!" he raised his voice and then struggled to get himself under control. Oh shit, he was pissed. But that just made me even more irritated. I shoved my hands into the pockets of my robe and leveled my own frosty glare in his direction.

"Well, no one asked you to come here," I pointed out. Jordan rubbed his buzzed head in frustration.

"What the fuck, Mays? Is this how it's going to be every time you get a tiny bit mad? You're going to run and hide like a twelve year old and wait for me to come and plead forgiveness for some crime that you've invented in that messed up head of yours?" He bit out.

What the hell? There was no need for any of that. "Fuck you, Jordan! If you're just going to come into my home and lob insults at me, you can turn around and leave." I felt my face heat up and my blood pressure rise. The skin tightened around his eyes and he took a deep breath.

"Okay, I admit, that was uncalled for. But can we talk about this like rational adults, please?"

"Talk about what?" I asked snottily, refusing to back down an inch. Jordan's eyes snapped to mine as the veins on his neck bulged. He got to his feet and stalked toward me. I backed up until I was up against the wall. He put his hands on either side of my head and leaned in close, our faces mere inches apart. I felt dizzy at his proximity. And I wanted to kiss him.

"Can you stop with the shitty attitude for two seconds? Or do I need to hogtie you to the bed to get you to listen to me?" he whispered, leaning in dangerously closer. My heart began to race and I felt my traitorous body begin to respond to him, just like it always did. He was even more gorgeous when he was angry. He oozed alpha male and it made me want to tangle myself around him like an octopus and never let go.

"Why should I listen to anything you have to say? I wasn't the one that invited my ex to a show where my current girlfriend was also in attendance. And I wasn't the one who played a love song in front of a room full of people that I had written for said ex-girlfriend." I hated how jealous I sounded. But I couldn't stop the words pouring out in one long stream.

Jordan's brow knit together. "So that's it? You're just going to make your ridiculous assumptions without even talking to me first?" he asked, his eyes boring into mine. I held perfectly still.

"Can you deny any of it?" I asked, my eyes going steely. Jordan let out a deep sigh and backed away, leaving the space he inhabited cold and bereft.

"Maysie, I can't do this if you're going to let everyone and everything dictate what happens between us. Relationships are built on trust and communication. If something upsets you, you have to tell me about it then we work it out together. But this running away and hiding crap has to stop. We're not in high school anymore. When will you understand that I can't control what people say and do? I wish I could. What we have going on isn't going to be easy. It will be downright hard. But I believe it's worth it. That *you* are worth it. But if you're going to throw a temper tantrum every time you feel threatened we might as well call it quits right now."

I tried to think of some smart-ass thing to say. I wanted to shove his self-righteous BS down his throat. As if I was the only one that had messed up here. Sure I had acted a little childishly. I wasn't denying that. But that didn't change the fact that Jordan had invited his bitch ass ex to his concert and didn't tell me. Oh then there was that damn song...okay I was starting to seethe again.

Jordan's jaw set and I knew he could see how pissed I was. "Liv called me yesterday afternoon. She was kind of a mess. She was begging to talk to me. Jesus, Mays, I was with her for a long time. Even if we're not together anymore, that doesn't mean I don't care if she's hurting. I'm not that kind of guy. She asked if it was alright if she came to see us play. I said sure because I didn't think it was that big of a deal. I was going home with *you*. *That's* what was important." His face was drawn and I could see how tired he was. It was obvious he hadn't gotten any sleep last night. Probably because he had been camped outside my apartment for most of it.

"But you told her to meet you at Garrett's," I said, feeling the hurt all over again. Jordan scrubbed his hands over his face in agitation.

"Christ. I never told her to meet me anywhere! It's not like Garret's parties are a secret. Half the fucking county knows about them. And yeah, I knew she had some things to say to me. And why wouldn't I let her? I haven't given her much of a chance to say her piece since we broke up. To be honest, I've been a bit of a dick to her about all of it because my entire focus has been on being with you, Mays." Okay, way to make me feel guilty.

Jordan rubbed the skin between his eyebrows as though he were getting a headache. "So maybe I should have taken the time to think about how you would feel when I said she could come to the show. But I wasn't really thinking about Olivia. All I could think about was you and knowing that in a few short hours I would get to see you again. What Olivia had to say was of little importance to me. Yeah, I feel like shit that she's hurting. I wish I had handled things differently. But that doesn't change the fact that I was spending my night with *you* and only *you*. And I can't feel bad about wanting this the way I do. So, why can't that be enough?" he asked angrily.

Was he that stupid that he didn't see that Olivia wasn't ready to let him go? That there was no way in hell she would just sit back and let us have our happily ever after? Sure, he was being a nice guy but it didn't change the fact that he hadn't had the decency to let me know his ex would be at his show. That was not cool.

"You should have told me she was coming. I was a little blindsided." I said, looking away from him. Jordan was quiet for a moment and then his fingers were on my chin, pulling my face back around to look at him.

"You're right, Mays. I should have told you. That was supremely uncool. But like I said, I wasn't thinking about Olivia at all last evening. I was only thinking about showing everyone my girl and how freaking good that felt. How good I was going to make you feel."

I gulped, feeling the heat rise in my face. His words had come out like a seductive growl. Yeah, that's all I had been thinking about too...until I heard that stupid fucking song. "What about that song? The one you wrote for Olivia?" Who was this whiny chick with my voice? It couldn't be Maysie Ardin asking such a silly question in the most pathetic way possible. Why did I have let that song bother me? It shouldn't bother me. It had been written before Jordan and I even knew each other. But it made me feel incredibly small.

Jordan rubbed his forehead again. "What song, Mays?"

"You know what I'm talking about! That damn *Lost in You* song! I know you wrote it for her. She was bragging about it in the bathroom." Jordan barked out a humorless laugh.

"I wrote that song almost three years ago. And yes, it was about Olivia. At one time. But now, it's just another fucking song. It doesn't mean anything." If only that were true. I moved away from the wall and went into the kitchen to make myself coffee. I needed caffeine fortification immediately.

I knew Jordan followed me because I could feel the heat of his body as he crowded into my personal space. "Maysie. Seriously, you can't get pissed off about a song I wrote years before I knew you. It's a fan favorite, so we play it at our shows. I really don't get what the big deal is." He sounded lost and that just irritated me more.

I dumped coffee grounds into the machine and turned it on. I braced my hands on the counter, not turning to face him as I unloaded my juvenile insecurities. But I needed to say the words or I would choke on them.

"That song, Jordan, was beautiful. Those words, I could see how in love you were with her when you wrote them. It just made me feel like there was no way I could ever compete with those feelings. I mean, what chance do you and I have when you had that with *her?*" Jordan gripped my shoulders and turned me to face him. His face had relaxed and his eyes had gone tender. He reached out and ran his fingers down my cheek.

"Baby, I'm sorry you feel that way, but you are so freaking deluded." I started to get angry again when he gripped the back of my neck and tugged me forward. His eyes were intense as he stared down at me. "Yes, I loved Olivia. Yes, I meant those words when I wrote them. But I was nineteen years old. She was my first serious girlfriend. I was an immature college freshman getting my first regular piece of ass so I thought she was *it.*" My throat seized.

Jordan kissed my nose softly. "But that was a lifetime ago. And I've grown up a lot since then. I'm not saying that I didn't feel strongly for Liv, but stuff has seriously changed since then. And I've learned that the love I thought I felt was more of an infatuation with the *idea* of her. I told you before that things had been messed up between us for a while. I wasn't just talking out of my ass. It's the truth. She and I were not a functional couple. She is selfish and self-involved. If something didn't relate to her Chi Delta world, she didn't care about it. You know last night was the first time she had been to one of my shows in over a year? She couldn't give a shit about my music. It was more of an inconvenience for her and she was constantly trying to get me to leave the band. Now does that sound like a healthy relationship to you?" Wow, even I knew that music was an integral part of who Jordan was. I couldn't imagine him not playing. It was like telling someone to stop breathing.

Jordan kissed the corner of my mouth. "But you get it. In the four months I've known you; you see more of me than she ever did. For the first time I feel like I can be myself and let loose with someone. We connect on a level Olivia and I never did." He placed his lips on mine in a gentle kiss that made my toes curl. "I feel like you were made just for me, Maysie Ardin. Everything about you makes me want you more. Even your jealous little snits have me wanting to haul you over my shoulder and take you back to your bedroom just to show you how much you mean to me." Well crap.

"That's just lust. I mean yeah, we have a serious physical attraction, but..." Jordan's mouth cut me off and I forgot what I was saying. He kissed me roughly, just the way I liked it. After a few seconds he ripped his mouth from mine and he breathed heavily as he gripped the sides of my face with his hands.

"This is more than just physical attraction and you know it.

I have NEVER wanted someone the way I want you. This thing I feel for you isn't rational. It doesn't really make sense, but it's there. And I'll be damned if I let you run away from it just because you feel insecure. Because there is no other girl for me, Mays. You are *it*." Wow. Um, just wow. I had no words.

My coffee was forgotten as I wrapped my arms around his neck. "No more running," he murmured as his mouth met mine again. He ran his hands down my back and I shivered.

"No more running," I agreed, letting him pick me up so I could wrap my legs around his waist. He carried me down the hallway and into my bedroom. He didn't kiss me again until he laid me down on the bed. He ran his hand down the length of my body as he lowered his lips to kiss the side of my neck.

"I'm sorry I was such an idiot," I whispered as his tongue slid upward to my ear. I gasped as he sucked my lobe into his mouth, sending an electric jolt straight to my vagina.

"I'll forgive you, this once," he rasped in my ear as his hand started to slide up the side of my shorts. "Kiss me, Maysie." Jordan demanded as his fingers pushed aside my underwear and started to tease the outer edges of my throbbing center.

"Yes, sir," I got out as his finger slid inside me. I attacked his mouth with my tongue and teeth. I bit down on his lower lip and he moaned deep in the back of his throat. He slipped a second finger inside me, pushing them knuckle deep into my core.

My tongue swept into his mouth and I spent a good deal of time exploring the barbell hidden there. God I loved his tongue ring. He withdrew his fingers to the tips and then pushed them back in with a force that made me arch my back. His thumb started circling my clit and I felt the slow burn start to smolder. He found a perfect rhythm and I became undone at the expert curve of his fingers. Our mouths were frenzied against each other. My orgasm came with an earth-shattering explosion. I was left panting and dear god, I wanted more.

Jordan withdrew his fingers and I watched in fascination as he put them in his mouth and sucked on them. He closed his eyes and moaned. "God, I wish I could keep your taste in my mouth all day long." He opened his eyes and grinned at me, making me blush. No one had ever talked to me the way he did. It was arousing and more than a little naughty.

Jordan leaned down and kissed the underside of my chin. "I'm nowhere near done with you," he promised as he took a hold of the hem of my shirt and pulled it over my head. I clumsily undid the buttons of his shirt and peeled it off of him. I traced the curves of his tattoo on the side of his neck. Yeah, it was time to taste that skin of his.

While Jordan slid my panties and shorts off, I put my mouth to his neck and lightly ran my tongue along the lines of his ink. I felt him shudder as he wrenched the clothing off my body. His hands ran along my stomach and upwards to my breasts. He cupped them in his hands and ran his thumbs along my hard nipples. I continued my torturous exploration of his skin, gliding my mouth along his shoulders and down into the hollow of his throat. He tasted salty and absolutely, 100 percent delicious.

I realized I was completely naked. Jordan had never seen me without my clothes in the light of day before. I felt a little shy all of the sudden; even with the crazy things we were doing to each other's bodies. Jordan lowered his mouth to my nipple, pulling it into his mouth and sucked the sensitive bud until I was gasping for breath. His one hand came up to the other breast and rubbed and teased, while his other hand went back between my legs to run along the wet slit. Crap, this boy was a multitasker. I was impressed.

His teeth nibbled at my nipple and damned if I didn't feel a second orgasm rolling through my body. He didn't put his fingers inside me; instead he rubbed my clit in slow, lazy circles and then moved downward to tease my wet opening without actually entering. It was maddening and so hot I thought I would die. And just like that, orgasm number two hit with a thunderous force that I think my heart stopped for a moment. Fuck, he was good.

I lay flat on my back, flushed and panting and Jordan still had his jeans on. There was something seriously wrong with that. Pulling together what little strength I had left, I sat up and reached for the button of his jeans. Jordan watched my hands as they unzipped him and pushed his pants down passed his hips, taking his boxers with it.

My vagina literally pulsed, as I took in the sight of him, hard and erect and ready for some attention. Using my feet, I pushed his pants all the way off and we were finally naked together. Jordan pressed his skin against mine and I let out a sigh at the beautiful intimacy of it. Touching Jordan was unlike anything I had ever experienced. We fit together in all the right places, like our bodies were made for each other.

He grabbed my face between his hands and kissed me slowly and softly. It was almost too soft after the intense sensations I had just experienced. I could feel his hardness pressed between my legs, just waiting for me to let him in. He rocked his hips a bit so that he rubbed against me and I spread my thighs, letting him rest between them.

Jordan propped up on his elbows and looked down at me. I touched his eyebrow ring with my finger, something I had wanted to do for a while now. "What is it?" I asked, when he continued to stare at me. He gave me the loveliest smile and my heart picked up a few extra notches.

"You are the most gorgeous woman I have ever seen. God, I could spend the rest of my life just looking at you," he said quietly, cupping the side of my face.

Jordan Levitt was the most romantic guy I had ever known. He knew just what to say to turn me into a pile of mush. "You aren't too bad yourself," I teased, wiggling my hips so that we pressed together without penetration. Jordan closed his eyes and held himself still.

"Are you sure you want to do this? Because if you keep doing that thing with your hips, Mays, there won't be any going back."

I leaned up and kissed the side of his neck. "You're naked. I'm naked. I think I've made myself perfectly clear that I *want* this to happen," I assured him, wrapping my legs tight around his waist and pulling him closer to where I needed him to be. Jordan took a shaky breath.

"Hang on a sec." He reached over the side of his bed and pulled his wallet out of his jeans pocket. He started rooting around. I knew what he was looking for.

I put my hand over his. "I'm on the pill, Jordan. And I've never had sex without protection before. So I know I'm clean," I told him. Jordan stopped and looked up at me in surprise. Now I felt embarrassed so I started to backpedal.

"I mean, it's fine, we can use a condom. I just wanted you to know that there wasn't an issue with me getting pregnant or me giving you the clap or something." Oh shit, I was digging a huge hole for myself. I had to stop...NOW!

Jordan dropped his wallet back on the floor and leaned over me again. "I'm clean too. So if you're sure..." he trailed off. I nodded enthusiastically, grinning up at him.

"Oh, I'm sure," I purred, my entire body quivered in anticipation. Jordan grabbed my hips and lifted my lower back off of the bed. He positioned himself and slowly sank into me. OH. MY. GOD! He was achingly slow as he allowed my body to adjust to his size. Because the man was large. Inch by excruciating inch he slid into my warm depth, his fingers digging into the flesh of my thighs.

I arched my back off the bed as he sank all the way in and started to move his way back out. He was going to kill me if he continued to go this teasingly slow.

I dug my heels into his backside, pushing him back into me. "Faster," I breathed, looking him straight in the eye. Jordan chuckled.

"I've never gone raw before, baby. I'm afraid it'll be over before we even start if I go much quicker." He slid half way in and then pulled out to the tip again. I was a quivering mess. "This feels fucking amazing. You're ruining me for life," Jordan choked out, his breath hitching as he held himself ready. Yep, I was going to die like this.

I pulled up onto my elbows and tossed my head back. "Fuck me, Jordan...NOW!" I demanded, pushing my breasts into the air. I heard Jordan make a strangled noise, his hand sliding down the middle of my breasts until it came to clutch my hip again. And he then did exactly what I wanted him to do. He slammed into me, the headboard of my bed hitting the wall with enough force that it knocked a picture onto the floor.

I didn't care. All I cared about was Jordan ramming into me over and over again, making the sexiest noises in the back of his throat that I had ever heard. His fingers started to rub my clit as he thrust into my body with complete abandon. Suddenly he pulled me up so that I was straddling him, his cock still buried deep inside me. His mouth came down hard on mine and he started moving me up and down his shaft. He penetrated me deeply and my orgasm came quickly as I shuttered around him.

Jordan pulled me roughly down on top of him and I felt his release inside me, his entire body trembling as he came with an intensity that set me on fire all over again. I laid my cheek against his shoulder and he wrapped his arms tightly around me. He didn't pull out; we stayed connected like that for a while as we tried to get our breathing back under control.

He pulled my head back and held my face as he kissed me gently. "God, that was fucking fantastic," he said, out of breath. It was my turn to grin, feeling incredibly proud of myself.

"Wanna do it again?" I waggled my eyebrows at him. He laughed and I felt him twinge inside me.

He kissed me and gave me a sexy smile. "I think that can be arranged."

CHAPTER
19

"**We're** having that date. Tonight. You can't argue your way out of it," Jordan warned as he pulled my feet off of his lap and sat up on the couch. I groaned good-naturedly but I was pleased at his suggestion. It had been three blissful days since the show at Dave's. Three days of all Jordan, all the time. He had spent the rest of Sunday at my apartment. And yeah, clothing was not required.

Riley had banged on my bedroom door around six in the evening wanting to know if we wanted to order dinner. Because surely we had worked up an appetitive by then. I had wanted to die of utter embarrassment, but Jordan had taken it all in stride. He had simply put on his clothes and gone out to the living room to look through the collection of menus Riley and I kept on hand.

I had blown off the weekly Chi Delta chapter meeting, sending Gracie a text using the age-old headache as an excuse. She texted me back with *Who are you kidding? :-)* Yeah, who was I kidding indeed? After a dinner of pizza and beer, Jordan and I had crawled back into my bed and worked on letting each other know just how much we enjoyed being together.

He was flipping amazing. And I was in so deep that I wasn't sure I could swim to the surface. Jordan walked me to class but I couldn't completely ignore the looks and whispers we received. Jordan seemed unfazed by it all and I tried really hard to follow his example.

I had caught a glimpse of Olivia watching us while we had lunch together in the commons. Our eyes met briefly and the hate in her gaze had me wanting to look away, but I didn't. Instead I met her stare head on until it was she that finally looked away. I had a momentary sense of triumph before I felt bad for feeling that way.

So, here we were, Wednesday afternoon. I had just gotten back from two painful hours of my English symposium class. I had decided on being an English major, thinking, hey I love to read, why not? What I hadn't counted on was having to read so much. A book a day was starting to kill me. I had curled up on the couch; reading about Milkman's crazy mother in Tony Morrison's Song of Solomon and Jordan had shown up with my favorite mini éclairs from Cup and Crumb.

He brought me chocolate. The man was a god. Then he had sat down beside me on the couch and pulled my feet into his lap and started rubbing the arches with the balls of his thumbs and I knew his deity status was firmly set in stone.

I was in the full-on throes of massage heaven when he announced his plans to take me out. I was still a little iffy about being too public with our relationship. Just because Olivia was a raging bitch, didn't mean that I liked the thought of flaunting our relationship all over the place. But I had to seriously stop worrying so much about what everyone else thought. But it was a weakness of mine. This incessant need to be liked. Though I tried to squelch it for Jordan's sake.

"So where are you going to take me?" I asked, tucking my feet underneath me and leaning into Jordan. He put his arm around my shoulders and pulled me tight against his side. He kissed my temple and I loved that we could be both wildly passionate and achingly tender. This was the best of both worlds, right here.

I put Tony Morrison down on the coffee table and let Jordan hold me close to his chest. "You'll see," he said mysteriously. I looked up at him and raised an eyebrow.

"I'll see? No hints then?" He kissed my mouth softly.

"Not a one." He let me go and laced up his Adidas before getting to his feet.

"Well, how should I dress?" I asked, following him to the door. Jordan pushed my hair back away from my face and cupped the side of my neck, his fingers pressed into my skin.

"Doesn't matter, because you always look beautiful," he commented, pulling me in for one last kiss.

"That doesn't help you know," I mumbled against his lips. Jordan chuckled and then our mouths fused together. It seemed like every time we tasted each other it took an act of god to pull us apart. This time it was Riley, throwing open the door and stomping inside.

"You have a bedroom, you know!" she called out, going into the kitchen.

Jordan groaned and dropped his hands from my face. I closed my eyes in annoyance but smiled anyway. "I'll pick you up at 7:00," he said, walking out the front door.

"7:00 it is." I replied, grinning as he walked backwards down the hall, his eyes still on me.

Closing the door after Jordan, I let out a contented sigh. "So things are good in fairytale land I see?" Riley asked, plopping down on the couch and turning on Myth Busters, her favorite show. I sat down beside her and laid my head back.

"Yeah, things are pretty great," I admitted, rolling my head to the side so I could give her a big smile.

She smiled back. "Good, it's nice to see you happy and not moping around here like some sort of Cure reject." I rolled my eyes.

"How's Damien?" I asked. I didn't see much of the two of them. Riley usually went to his house by campus. I secretly thought Damien was weirded out by all the girl stuff in our apartment. The last time he had come over he about had a coronary when I accidentally left a box of tampons on the kitchen island. He was so awkwardly cute that you wanted to pinch him.

"Eh, things are fine," she said a little moodily. I recognized that tone. She wasn't happy. I sat up and turned to face her.

"What happened, Riley? Spill," I urged. Riley sighed and flicked off the TV.

"It's nothing. I'm probably being stupid." She tried to wave it away but I wouldn't let her.

"If you're upset, it's not *nothing*. So what's up?" Riley let out an exasperated huff.

"Okay, so there's this awesome film festival down town this weekend. And I got us tickets because I thought it would be a pretty cool surprise. I mean, Damien is a freaking art major."

I nodded. "Sounds cool to me," I said supportively. Riley nodded her own head.

"Yeah, right? Well, I gave them to him last night after we were done with our shift at Barton's and he told me he couldn't go. That he promised his roommate they'd go to the driving range. Can you believe that? He's ditching me and a film festival for *golf*?" Her voice rose in pitch and I knew she was more hurt than angry.

I wanted to laugh. What I wouldn't give for simple disagreements like that. But it seemed when Jordan and I fought it was due to jealousy and insecurity. Maybe one day we could fight about him playing golf when I wanted to go shopping. It just seemed so nice and normal. But Riley was worked up and laughing would only earn me a seriously pissed off roommate.

So instead I patted her hand. "Well, he made a promise to his roommate, Riley. You wouldn't have any respect for someone who blew off their prior commitments. Because if he could do that to his friend, why wouldn't he do that to you? I think he's being kind of cool, actually. You know he'd probably rather go with you," I reasoned. Riley rolled her eyes.

"Yeah, yeah. I know. I'm being stupid." I squeezed her hand.

"Not stupid, you're being normal. What girl wants to be sidelined for sports? But at least he made his plans *before* you got the tickets. Otherwise, I'd tell you to kick his ass." We laughed together and I could tell Riley was over her irritation.

"So, what do you have planned this weekend? Wanna go to a film festival?" she asked, pulling the tickets out of her pocket.

"Sure, why not. Could be cool," I agreed and Riley smiled. "See, now we get a girl's day out of it! Score for both of us!" I enthused. Riley threw a pillow at me.

"As long as you don't try to give me a makeover, we're good." I pretended to pout but I knew any efforts to dress my best friend would be deftly evaded. The girl beat to her own drum, that's for sure.

"Jordan's taking me out on a date tonight," I said, after Riley had turned the television back on.

"Oh, yeah." she said nonchalantly. Okay, she sounded too blasé. Which could only mean...

"You know what he's planning, don't you?" I asked, grabbing the remote out of her hand and muting the television.

"Hey, I was watching that!" she complained but she couldn't contain her smile.

"What is it? Where's he taking me?" I jumped up and down on the couch, holding onto her hand. Riley laughed and shoved me away from her.

"Calm down or you'll have an aneurysm. Let's just say, the boy has romance in his soul." Now I was intrigued. And really, really excited.

Riley chuckled and rolled her eyes. "Just shut up and let me mong out please. Some of us have to work this evening." I snorted but slid down into the couch and propped my feet up on the coffee table. I watched three episodes of the most obnoxious program ever made. The dude with the beret had an obnoxious, nasally voice and made the most obvious and at times asinine observations. But Riley loved it, and swore the beret dude was one of the sexiest guys on TV. If Damien wasn't such a cutie, I would seriously question my best friend's taste in guys.

I pried myself off the couch around 6:00 and went and got a shower. Then I stood in front of my closet, trying to decide what to wear on my mystery date. I finally decided on a cute sleeveless maxi dress in off white with a brown belt around the waist. I had gotten the dress for a steal from Victoria's Secret and was looking for an excuse to wear it. Since we were experiencing a seriously hot Indian summer, I thought it would be perfect. I dug out some adorable brown-wedged sandals and completed the outfit with a chunky silver bracelet and some thin, dangly earrings with stars on the bottom. I left my hair down, spritzing it with some salt spray and running my fingers through it to help bring out my natural wave.

I opted out of a lot of makeup and just coated my lips with a pale lip-gloss. *Not bad*, I thought looking at myself in the mirror. I noticed the irises I kept in a vase on my dresser were officially dead. I scooped them out the glass and tossed them in the trash. I would have to remember to get some more. I was a sucker for fresh flowers, irises being my favorites. So, I tried to keep them in my room most of the time. At least until they died and I got around to getting some more.

I looked at the clock and shocked myself by seeing I still had fifteen minutes until Jordan was due to pick me up. I sat back down on the couch, smoothing my dress underneath me. Riley had left for her shift at Barton's thirty minutes ago, so the apartment was silent. I didn't feel like watching TV, I was too antsy. I grabbed my pack of cigarettes and went out onto the balcony. I was making a conscientious effort to minimize my smoking. But there were days when it proved difficult. I pulled a cigarette out of the pack and lit it up, staring out into the courtyard just behind our building.

I heard the sound of guitar music wafting up from below. I leaned over the railing, my hair dangling around me and saw Eli plucking at his strings just beneath my balcony. Well, crap. I hadn't seen Eli since I had text dumped him. Which was surprising, considering how much time he spent at his cousin's apartment just down the hall.

As if sensing my presence, Eli stopped playing and looked up. His face went perfectly blank and he lifted a hand in a halfhearted wave. "Hey," he called up. I gave a short wave back.

"Hey." We didn't say anything and I realized I looked like an idiot dangling over my railing. So I pulled myself up right and sat down in the white deck chair to finish my smoke.

"Maysie!" I heard Eli call out. I tried not to groan. But I didn't want to ignore him, so I got back to my feet. Eli had moved so that he stood out in front of my balcony. The guitar hung around his shoulders and I noticed off handily that he had let his hair grow out and that it was naturally curly. Interesting.

"What's up, Eli?" I asked, trying not to sound completely bitchy. But this was awkward. Eli reached up and scratched the back of his neck. He seemed nervous. Which was weird because I don't think I had ever seen Eli anything but high and laid back. Well except the night he and Jordan had gotten into it. But I didn't want to think about that.

"How've you been?" he asked, dropping his hand to rest on the front of his guitar. I took a last drag of my cigarette and knelt down to stub it out in the flowerpot I kept for my butts.

"Um, fine," I answered, standing back up and leaning my hands on the iron railing.

"Good. That's really...uh, good," Eli said. He was being strange. Maybe he was on something.

"So have you taken up serenading in your free time?" I joked, trying to alleviate some of the uncomfortable tension. Eli chuckled and tapped a quick beat on the hollow wood of his acoustic.

"Why not, the ladies love it. You always did." He glanced back up at me and I recognized that look. It was the one he always gave me before pulling me into a bedroom at his cousin's place.

I cleared my throat. "Well, I'd better get going." I jerked my thumb in the direction of the sliding glass door to make my point. I turned around to head back inside.

"So why haven't I heard from you? In my world, wanting space doesn't mean you pretend the other person doesn't exist," Eli called out just as I was about to open the door. I closed my eyes and leaned my forehead on the glass.

I turned around and went back to look down at Eli in the courtyard. "Can we not do this now? I mean, this isn't the best place to have this conversation," I said shortly, kind of annoyed he was putting our personal stuff on display for the neighbors. Looking over I could see old Mrs. Graves sitting on her balcony, pretending to read the newspaper. But I knew that nosy lady was listening to everything we were saying.

"Well, let me come up so we can talk," he insisted. Where was this coming from? I seriously thought he would be done with me by now. Hell, I strongly suspected he was hooking up with other girls the whole time we were "dating." So why the sudden need to hash shit out with me?

"Now's not a good time, Eli. I'm getting ready to go out,"

I said, trying to end the conversation quickly. I figured Jordan would be here any minute.

Eli ran his hands through his hair. "I know you're with that other guy. The dude from the bar. I've seen him coming out of your place. Is that why you needed *space*?" Eli asked sarcastically. Okay, enough was enough.

"No you self-involved prick. I needed space away from your sorry ass. Got a little sick of the drunken booty calls and then not hearing from you for days. And let's not forget your attempts to take my clothes off in my place of employment. Oh and how about going off to parties with girls practically shoving their tongues down your throat? Is that enough of a reason?" I bit off angrily.

Eli at least had the decency to look ashamed. "I guess I deserved that," he grimaced. I barked out a laugh.

"You think?" I scoffed. Eli ran his fingers along the strings of his guitar making them tinkle prettily.

"I'd really like to talk to you though. I mean, if that's cool with you." Before I could respond, someone else answered for me.

"No, she won't be talking to you, slick. Because she's gonna be with her boyfriend."

I whirled around and saw Jordan standing in the open doorway looking pissed. Well, he was hot too. He had dressed in a worn pair of jeans that hung perfectly on his hips and a fitted gray t-shirt that made his body look downright edible. But yeah, he was pissed. I saw him click his tongue ring along his teeth and he came up beside me and gripped the railing so tightly his knuckles turned white. He stared down at Eli, looking very intimidating.

Eli stiffened. "Man, I wasn't talking to you. So just back off," Eli warned. I saw Jordan's jaw clench.

"And *I'm* telling *you* that you're not gonna talk to Maysie. You got something to say, you say it in front of me, we straight?" I swallowed thickly. Damn, who knew Jordan was so freaking territorial. I glanced over at Mrs. Graves, who had stopped all pretenses of reading the paper and was watching the drama unfold with avid interest.

"This is not the place to be doing this. Jordan, go inside, I'll be there in a minute," I told him. Jordan's eyes flashed to mine and his jaw ticked.

"I am not leaving you out here to talk to that piece of shit. I'm staying." He crossed his arms over his chest and leaned on the railing. I sighed. I did not want to start our date like this so I didn't push him.

I turned to Eli. "I don't think we have anything more to say to each other, Eli. So I'll see ya around." Eli's head dropped and I almost felt bad for him. He looked back up and his eyes zeroed in on Jordan and they turned to ice.

"Well, when you don't have this jack ass speaking for you, maybe we could have that talk. It would be nice to hang out with you again. But until then, I guess I won't bother. Later, Mays." He swung his guitar around so that it rested on his back and stalked off.

I turned on Jordan, who was still standing there like a damn bodyguard with his arms folded over his chest. His muscles flexed in a way that made me want to touch them with my mouth. But that would have to be tabled for later because right now I was really mad. "He's gone. Happy?" I asked sharply, going into the apartment.

Jordan followed me and shut the sliding glass door. "Babe," he said and reached out to put his hand on my arm. I tensed under his touch.

"What was with the alpha posturing back there? Don't you think you went a little overboard?" I asked, refusing to look at him. Jordan let out a frustrated breath.

"Just like you went overboard when you stormed out of my show last weekend?" he reminded me. Damn him. He was right.

I looked over my shoulder and he wore an infuriating grin. "This isn't funny." I frowned and tried to hold onto my anger. Jordan shook his head and pulled me into his arms.

"I'm sorry if I pissed you off. I'm sorry if I acted like a fucker. But I'm not sorry for chasing off that pansy ass that used to have what's mine. Because you're my girl now and I won't have that asshole sniffing around where he doesn't belong." I didn't know if I should be thrilled or totally insulted by what he just said.

"Are you serious?" I asked with what I was sure was a stupefied look on my face.

Jordan sighed and held me tighter. "You and me, Mays, we're a fucking mess." He buried his face in my hair and I finally wrapped my arms around his back.

"I'm not sure that's a good thing, Jordan," I said, not being able to stop myself from pressing my nose into the front of his shirt. I loved his perfect guy smell.

Jordan pulled back, reaching up to run his fingers through my hair. "No, it's a fucking *great* thing! But, we've just got to learn to trust each other. And to remember that when it comes to you and me, nothing else, and definitely *no one* else matters." I couldn't stop the smile spreading across my face. I smacked him in the chest.

"It is impossible to stay mad at you!" I huffed out.

Jordan grinned again. "That's part of my charm, sweetheart." He pulled me forward and kissed my mouth hard. I nibbled at his bottom lip and he moaned. "No, you can't start that. I have plans for you," he said as I tried to rub myself up against him.

"Screw the plans. Right now, I just want to screw you," I said crudely. Jordan laughed in surprise.

"Damn. My Maysie has developed a dirty, dirty mouth," he said, his voice getting husky as he kissed me again.

It was my turn to moan as his tongue teased mine. Then he tore away and set me away from him. "We are leaving right now. There will be time later for, how did you put it? Oh, yeah. Screwing." I flushed red, totally embarrassed by the tart that showed her naughty head moments earlier. Jordan wrapped his arm around my middle and pulled me toward the door. He kissed the side of my neck as I locked up after us.

"There will be lots and lots of screwing. I promise you that," he whispered into my ear as I tucked my keys into my purse. I shivered as I felt his lips touch my skin again. I loved when he talked like that. It was like an on switch to my groin.

Jordan took my hand in his and walked me out to his car. We stopped when we got to his truck and he held me out at arm's length. "You look absolutely gorgeous, baby. I'm sorry I didn't say it sooner," he apologized, his eyes raking over my body. I couldn't stop the self-satisfied smile that lit up my face. He had a way of making me feel like the most beautiful girl in the world.

"Thanks. You clean up pretty nicely yourself," I said coyly, smiling at him as he opened my door for me so I could get into the vehicle.

"Only for you, Mays," he said. And I definitely liked the sound of that.

CHAPTER
20

Jordan didn't drop my hand as he maneuvered the truck out onto the road. "So, where are we going?" I asked, arching my eyebrow at him. He looked over at me.

"You'll see in about five minutes," he promised. Five minutes? Where in the world was he taking me that was only five minutes away? I was totally stumped.

And more than a little baffled when Jordan pulled into the parking lot at Barton's. He stopped the truck and unbuckled his seat belt. I hadn't moved, looking up at the sign in front of me. He unbuckled me and then smirked. "Well, aren't you gonna get out?" he asked. I peered out of the windshield.

"You're taking me to Barton's?" I asked, needing clarification.

Jordan opened his door and got out. "Yep," he replied, coming around to open my door for me. I was trying not to be disappointed.

"This is just so you can get your employee discount isn't it?" I joked as Jordan wrapped his hand around mine. Jordan snorted.

"Wow, you think a lot of me huh?" he teased, squeezing my hand.

He held open the door to the restaurant and let me go in first. I hadn't been there since I had quit. I still felt bad about leaving so abruptly. Because I had really liked working there. But with all the Jordan drama that had gone down, I had chickened out and shirked on my responsibility. Even now that Jordan and I were a couple, I knew working together wouldn't be very good for either of us.

"Maysie!" I heard a screech as we went inside. The place was packed, not surprising. Though it was just Wednesday. I watched Jaz come hurrying toward me. She launched at me and gave me a hug.

"Girl, where have you been? I feel like it's been years since I've seen you!" she said, giving me a full-lipped pout. I laughed.

"It's only been a few weeks, Jaz. I see you've survived though." She looked kick ass gorgeous as always.

She looked over at Jordan and gave him a flirty smile. "Lookin' good hot stuff." And she left it at that. Which shocked the hell out of me, considering she typically took every opportunity to plaster herself all over him. I must have been looking at her funny because she nudged me with her shoulder. "Honey, he's with you now, I'll back off." She winked, tossing her hair. And with a waggling of fingers in our direction, she went back to work.

Jordan leaned down close to my ear. "Huh, if I had known being with you would keep her at bay, I would have hounded your ass a lot sooner." I elbowed him playfully in the stomach.

"You know you love the adoration of your gazillion female fans," I replied dryly. Jordan kissed just below my ear and squeezed my waist with his hand.

"I only care about the adoration of one particular female," he murmured. Gah! He was almost too much sometimes.

Riley picked that particular moment to show up at the hostess station. "Hey guys! Jordan, the section is all yours." She motioned for us to follow her and I looked questioningly at Jordan. He shrugged and gave me a toothy grin, putting his hand at the small of my back as we made our way toward the back of the restaurant.

Riley stopped at a booth. "Here ya go, I'll be back in a few with your drinks." I looked around and saw that Riley's entire section was empty but for us. We were in the very back of the restaurant so despite the crowd, it was actually pretty intimate. Then I realized where she had led us. I looked up at Jordan and felt my stomach go all gooey. His eyes were soft as he watched me work it out.

"Have a seat, baby," he said softly, waiting for me to slide into the booth. This was the booth where Riley and I had sat during our very first shift at Barton's. The first day I met Jordan. The first time I realized how crazy I was about him.

I looked over and saw a large vase of irises sitting on the table. I reached out to finger the petals. "These are my favorites," I said, my heart close to bursting. Jordan smiled.

"I know. You always have some in a vase in your room." I met his eyes and his literally sparkled back at me. Did this guy miss anything?

"Wow, you pay a lot of attention to the little stuff, huh?" I was sort of in shock. Jordan grabbed my hand across the table and laced our fingers together.

"I pay attention to absolutely everything about you, Mays." I felt all tingly. This was turning into the best first date ever.

Riley came back a few minutes later with our drinks, even though I hadn't ordered anything. She put a Sam Adams in front of me and a Sierra Nevada IPA in front of Jordan. "Damn, I love this beer." I said, immediately taking a long drink.

"I know," was all Jordan said. Of course he did. Nothing got passed him.

I took another drink and looked over at Riley who was arranging salt and peppershakers on her empty tables. "You must be taking a hit on tips in order to give us our own section," I commented. Riley's eyes flicked over to Jordan and she gave a small smile.

"Eh, it's been taken care of." I looked at Jordan and my eyes widened. He looked pleased with himself.

"I wanted my girl to have a special night. And I wanted you all to myself. So I took care of Riley in order to get that for you." He said it like it was nothing. But I knew Riley could easily pull down $100 in tips during a busy dinner rush. I was sure Jordan made sure she was compensated for holding her other tables open. I didn't know what to say.

"Wow, who knew Jordan Levitt was such a romantic?" I teased, my hands a little shaky as I picked up my beer again.

Riley shot me a look that said "I-told-you-so," she wiped

her tables down and then turned to us. "I'll be back with your appetizers."

Jordan and I drank our beers in silence for a few minutes. "Thanks, Jordan. I wasn't sure what to expect when you pulled up at Barton's. But this is seriously cool," I admitted. Jordan shrugged.

"I wanted tonight to be special. And when I was racking my brain trying to think of somewhere to take you, I kept coming back to here. Because this is where it started for us. I couldn't think of a better place to take you. Back to where it all began."

"Jeez, Jordan. You're killing me here," I groaned, finishing my beer.

"You ain't seen nothin' yet, babe." He smirked. God, was that Stairway to Heaven playing over the sound system? I sat remembering when he tried to teach me to play it. Shit, it totally was. Then Riley brought out the appetizers, which consisted of Barton's bread sticks and chicken wings. Both were my staples when I worked there. I had them almost every night after a shift, Jordan often joining me. He had seriously thought of everything.

I picked up a bread stick and bit off a portion. "Maybe the bread sticks weren't such a good idea." Jordan's voice dropped low and his eyes were focused on my mouth as I put the bread stick in my mouth. He was practically smoldering so I made a show of sliding the long piece of bread between my lips. Who knew eating could be so dirty?

Jordan growled in the back of his throat. "Keep that up and we won't be having dinner. We'll skip straight to dessert." I laughed as I chewed. Moving onto safer topics, I asked him about Generation Rejects' next gig. "We're taking a few weeks off so I can focus on my mid-terms. And then Mitch lined us some gigs up until the holidays. I've got to do some thinking. You know about after graduation," he said, looking a little uncomfortable.

"What do you mean? Come on, tell me," I urged. Jordan rubbed his chin and looked heavy in thought. I hadn't really thought about what would happen after Jordan graduated in the spring. He had seemed so unsure every time it was mentioned that I hadn't bothered him much about it.

Jordan picked up a chicken wing and held it between his fingers. He stared at the tabletop. "Well, the guys really want me to stick around after May. They want to try and take the band on tour for the summer. Mitch has a cousin who's a club promoter in Washington D.C and thinks he can get us some gigs up north," he told me hesitantly.

Wow. That sounded amazing. "Jordan, that's great! You should do it!" I encouraged. Jordan smiled then, looking a little relieved.

"Yeah? That would mean I'd be gone a lot," he hedged and my stomach dropped a bit. I hadn't thought about that. Jordan on the road. Playing music. With girls throwing themselves at him. Ugh! I would not think about that!

"Don't worry about me. This is your dream. You've got to do it for *you*," I insisted, even if I didn't feel entirely sure. Jordan picked up my hand and kissed the soft skin on the underside of my wrist. Butterflies instantly fluttered their wings in my stomach.

"If only my parents could be as cool about it as you are," he said, his face darkening.

I squeezed his fingers. "They'll come around. Or they won't. But, Jordan, you can't live your life worrying about what they think," I said. Huh, if only I could take my own advice. It was so easy to say when it wasn't directed at me.

"Here you go guys." Riley appeared at our side and dropped two plates on the table. A bacon cheeseburger, fully loaded in front of Jordan and Tequila chicken in front of me.

"How the hell did you know that I love tequila chicken?" I asked, more than a little in awe of how thorough he had been this evening. Jordan's lips curled up in an easy smile.

"I have my sources," he teased. Riley coughed.

"He means me," she interjected dryly.

Jordan frowned at my best friend. "Way to ruin the mystique, Riley," he muttered. I chuckled and started eating my dinner. Riley rolled her eyes (her favorite expression) and left us alone. Before Jordan picked up his burger he looked at me intensely. I held a forkful of pasta poised at my mouth.

"What?" I asked. Jordan stood up and leaned over the table, cupping my face in his hands.

"Thank you for taking a chance on me," he whispered, dropping a kiss to my forehead.

Well, damn. My fork clattered to my plate and I covered his hands with mine and tilted my head back, capturing his mouth. We broke a part a minute later, each of us a little breathless. "What choice did I have?" I whispered back with a smile.

Jordan grabbed my chin between his fingers and pulled me forward so that our noses brushed against each other. "You've got that right, Mays." He grinned before sitting back down. We ate our dinner. We talked. We laughed. And we cemented why our relationship was worth the shit that came down like a firestorm around it.

I loved this man sitting in front of me. I loved him with every beat of my heart. Even though we had only been technically together for two weeks and known each other for less than half a year, there was no doubting what I felt. It was as clear as day.

It was hard to imagine what my life was like before he came into it. And I didn't want to even begin to contemplate an existence where he wasn't a part of it. It scared me with how entrenched he had become in my life. There was no ripping him out. Not now.

"Maysie Ardin! Please tell me you're here to take your old job back," Moore called out, coming out of the back.

I lifted my hand in a wave. "Maybe in the summer if you'll have me back," I replied. Moore walked over to the railing separating our booth from the bar area.

"I'm holding you to that, sweetheart." He looked at Jordan. "Any way I can talk you into playing a short set next Saturday?"

Jordan made a grimace. "I don't think so, man. We're on a bit of a hiatus. But I'll let you know when we start booking shows for the New Year."

Moore grumped but accepted his answer. "Fine, fine. But I best be first on your list," he warned, then reached over and gave Jordan an awkward fist bump. Moore looked as though he had never given anyone a fist bump in his life.

"That guy is relentless," Jordan said; taking a bite of his burger after Moore had left.

"You're telling me. I can't wait until you play here again, though," I remarked. Jordan raised his eyebrows.

"Will you actually stay for the whole show next time?" he teased. I kicked him lightly under the table.

"Low blow, Jordan Levitt. Low blow," I threw back at him. Jordan laughed.

"I know, I know. But I'm holding you to that. Next time your ass is in the front row. If I have to tie you to a chair, I will. I wanna see your sexy face when I'm up there. Knowing I'm the one that gets to see you naked will make it all that much better," he said softly, his eyes holding mine.

I didn't have anything to say. He had this crazy ability to make me lose all thought process. "Um, okay..." Then I shut up, any response quickly forgotten. Jordan laughed even louder, enjoying the fact that I was visibly squirming in my seat.

Riley took our empty plates. I had eaten everything and felt ready to burst. I leaned back in the booth and groaned. "I'm stuffed," I said, rubbing my stomach.

"You better have room for dessert," Jordan warned seductively.

"Oh, yeah?" I asked coyly, widening my eyes. Jordan smirked and the heat in his eyes made my body tingle.

Riley and Jaz came to the table, each carrying a tray. They started laying plates and bowls on the table. "What is all of this?" I asked, not believing my eyes. There was a plate of my favorite mini chocolate éclairs from Cup and Crumb. In a bowl was another of my weaknesses, Swedish Fish. Then there was a plate of chocolate croissants, something I kept in the apartment for breakfast at all times. Then lastly, there was a huge slab of Barton's six layer chocolate cake, my favorite on the menu.

"Oh my god, Jordan!" I couldn't believe how incredibly thoughtful he was. Jordan's watched me warmly as I picked up a green Swedish Fish and popped it in my mouth.

"I've never seen someone get as happy as you do when there's junk food to eat," he teased, grabbing one of the éclairs.

My stomach felt all mushy. This guy was too much. How did I ever get lucky enough to be with him? And the way he watched me, I knew he was feeling the same about me. And I hoped like hell I would be able to keep him.

Jordan dropped his napkin on the table after we had polished through most of the food. He picked up the boxes with my left over dessert and pulled me to my feet. "Let's get out of here. I have something sweeter to give you," he said, dropping his voice low and brushing his nose along the side of my neck. I turned to look at him as a gripped his hand with mine.

"Lead the way," I whispered, knowing I'd follow him anywhere.

CHAPTER
21

*T*oday was the day. The beginning of the dreaded Parents' Weekend. The two days that invited misery and discomfort to every college student in existence. Well, for those that wanted to hide their slacker debauchery from the rose colored glasses of their mom and dad.

My parents were driving up from South Carolina that morning. They never missed an opportunity to come up to campus, do the dinky tour and remind me of how important it is to make good decisions. They were probably about three hours into their five-hour drive. Giving me exactly two hours to clean through the apartment like a mad woman and prep myself for Dad's infamous interrogation.

"Woah, I've never seen this place so clean!" Riley gave a low whistle as she surveyed the spotless living room. I had gone all out, even going so far as to Windex the sliding glass doors. I had hidden my ashtray under an overturned flowerpot. My parents didn't know I smoked and I'd like to keep it that way.

"So I'm guessing your parents will be here soon." Riley surmised, watching me fluff couch cushions for the millionth time.

"That would be an affirmative," I mumbled, straightening the coffee table.

"Okay, Mays. You're channeling some serious OCD. It's okay. Your parents aren't near as hard core as you make them out to be." Riley loved my parents. Probably because they loved her. Her no nonsense, focused academic outlook as well as her stellar show of responsibility, had them eating out of her black nail polished hand.

"Of course you'd say that, Riley. I think they wish we had somehow been switched at birth," I said, wiping the coffee table with a dust rag.

Riley snickered. "I seriously doubt that. You need to stop taking things so seriously," she suggested. Easy for her to say. She didn't have to live under the umbrella of parental disappointment on a daily basis. Her parents doted on her.

"So, what do you have planned for the parentals?" she asked, flopping down on the couch. I made a noise as she messed up the immaculately positioned pillows I had just straightened. I sighed but chose not to say anything.

"Well, we're scheduled for the campus tour at 11:00. Then I'm taking them out to lunch. Figured we'd go to the Bakertown Deli. Jordan is supposed to meet us there," I added. Riley's eyebrows rose so high they disappeared under her bangs.

"Dang, meeting the parents. That's serious, Mays," she said. My gut twisted at the mention of it. When I had brought up the fact that my parents would be coming up for the weekend, Jordan had immediately suggested that he join us for lunch. I tried not to sound as freaked by the whole thing as I actually was.

Jordan and I hadn't been dating that long and I felt it was a little soon to do the whole introduce the boyfriend to your folks thing. Plus I was dreading the reaction my conservative parents would have to my guy with his facial piercings and visible tattoo. But I didn't want to hurt Jordan's feelings, so I had reluctantly agreed.

Jordan seemed strangely excited about it. He had called late last night after his shift at Barton's to confirm the plans. I wanted to tell him to forget about it, but it was obviously important to him.

"I guess," I hedged. The truth was it gave me a bit of whiplash at how serious Jordan and I were. We went from zero to joined at the hip in no time. I loved being with him. I loved how we could spend time together and it was so comfortable, as though we had always been together.

But...

"Stop stressing. Your parents will like him. You need to stop building things up unnecessarily in your head. You'll end up in the loony bin at this rate," Riley told me, giving me a sharp look. Introducing Riley Walker, my good sense.

"You're right. Turning off my overactive mind now." I tapped my head and gave her a smile. Riley snorted. She watched me continue my one-woman whirling dervish as I flitted around the apartment, making it as clean as humanly possible.

Finally it was time for me to get showered and dressed. I chose a simple, knee length flowered skirt with a short-sleeved pink shirt. Virginia was enjoying unseasonably warm weather; fall hadn't begun to move in. I loved it. I hated when I had to start cramming my feet into closed toed shoes and cover my legs with pants and leggings. I was a summer gal and I would live it up while I could.

I had just finished putting my hair back in a braid when the doorbell rang. Riley answered it before I could and I listened to my mom and dad's voices drift back from the living room. Riley must have said something amusing because I could hear my dad's rich laugh.

I walked down the hallway and saw my roommate and parents talking animatedly. My parents may be older but they still looked great. I got my long, dark hair from my mom. She wore hers down and it curled around her shoulders. Her face was only just starting to show signs of wrinkles, primarily around her eyes and her mouth.

My dad was a big dude. He towered over my mom's 5 foot 3 frame. He was clean-shaven with a strong jaw and dark brown eyes. His thick, black hair was peppered with white and his mouth was smiling. I wasn't used to my dad looking happy. He was serious guy. Being a high school English teacher, his thought process often went right over my head. He had always had high expectations for me and I knew I often fell short of them.

"Hi Mom. Dad," I said, joining the trio in the living room. My mom's face lit up when she saw me and immediately enveloped me in a warm, rose-scented hug. My dad gave me a small smile, nothing like the one he had been wearing seconds earlier. My mom pulled back and patted my cheek before my dad leaned in to pat my back.

No hug. Just a freaking pat on the back. What was I a dog?

My mom looked around the apartment. "It looks so clean in here. I'm glad to see you guys aren't like other college students living in squalor," she stated. I shared a look with Riley. If she only knew that on a normal day, our coffee table was covered in used glassware and empty pizza boxes. And our kitchen would have dirty dishes piled in the sink. We weren't complete slobs, just lazy about housekeeping.

"Thanks," I said. My dad was looking around, and I knew he was trying to find something to criticize. I hated how inadequate that man made me feel.

"So what exactly did you spend all of your money on? Because I'm not seeing anything here that cost more than fifty bucks at a garage sale," my dad asked coldly.

I tensed and my mom hissed out, "Dan!" Two minutes in and I was ready to cry. This was going to be a long day.

"Well, you know our Mays. Giving to the homeless and feeding stray animals." Riley jumped in. "So, Mr. Ardin, how are those Gamecocks doing this year?" she asked, steering the conversation away from my spending habits to the football team at my dad's alma mater, the University of South Carolina. Another reason for my dad's chronic disappointment where I was concerned. He wanted me to go to USC; I wanted to come to Rinard with their awesome English Program. That hadn't gone over well.

I gave Riley a look of intense gratitude as my dad launched into a detailed stats rundown of his favorite college football team. "Do you want anything to drink, Mom?" I asked, heading into the kitchen. My mother followed me.

"I'd love some iced tea if you have it." Of course I had iced tea. I'd stocked up because my mother drank it by the gallon.

I got a flowered glass down from the cabinet and poured her

some tea. "I love these glasses, Maysie. They're adorable," my mother said a little too enthusiastically. I knew she was trying to make up for my dad's nastiness. That was the way of our family. I was the royal screw up, my dad got pissed and my mom worked her ass off to smooth it over, even as she drilled in her own guilt trip.

"They're Riley's actually," I said a little shortly. We fell into a kind of awkward silence. My mom finished her iced tea and put the empty glass in the sink.

"Maysie." She began, facing me. My shoulders sagged in preparation of whatever she was about to say. She must have recognized me bracing myself because she took a hold of my hand. "I know your father can come across a little gruff." I wanted to roll my eyes at *that* understatement. "But he loves you. Very much. And he just wants what's best for you." I nodded, not trusting myself to say anything positive.

My mom leaned in and dropped her voice to a near whisper. "We've been getting your checks, sweetheart. And even though we were disappointed with your irresponsibility with the credit card, I think it's wonderful that you're taking care of that." Backhanded compliment number one. Check.

I gave my mom a fake smile. "Just doing what I should do. I'm sorry I messed up," I admitted honestly.

My mom squeezed my hand. "I know you are, honey." She reached out and brushed my bangs back from my face. "I wish you'd let your bangs grow out. They cover up your beautiful face." Back handed compliment number two. Check, check.

Riley and my dad coming into the kitchen saved me from getting defensive. I got my dad a glass of iced tea and I spent the next fifteen minutes trying to withstand the cutting commentary on my college life. Riley, bless her, tried to intervene where she could. But there was only so much she was able to accomplish when faced with the full force of my father's attack.

"Wow, look at the time. Don't you have to get over to campus for your tour?" Riley interjected during one of the many awkward silences that filled the kitchen.

"Oh, wonderful! I do so love the campus tours. So fascinating!"

My mom enthused, grabbing her purse off the counter and following my dad out the door.

I turned to Riley before leaving. "Thanks for the help in there," I whispered, so my parents wouldn't hear me.

Riley's eyes widened a bit. "I don't remember your dad being so...um..."

"Dickish?" I added before Riley could finish.

Riley choked on a laugh. "Well, I was going to say intense. But sure, whatever works." I grabbed my purse and slung it over my shoulder. "Good luck at lunch," Riley said quietly and I had to suppress a groan. Lunch. I had almost forgotten. Given the mood my dad was in, that was going to be a damn blood bath.

I followed my parents out to their car, a brand new Jeep Cherokee. "Nice car, Dad," I commented, hopping in the back. My dad adjusted his mirrors and turned the air conditioner on.

"Yes, maybe you'll be able to afford something like this someday. That is if you can get through college without some sort of catastrophe." Ouch. That hurt.

I bit on my bottom lip to stop myself from yelling at him. Was it any wonder my self-esteem sucked? I had been dealing with this sort of shit my entire life. And my mom just sat there, smiling like he had just commented on the fucking weather.

After the dreaded lunch, I was expected to bring my parents around to the Chi Delta house. Not that I wanted to do that...*at all*. Not only because things were so tense with the other sisters. But because my parents made no effort to hide how much they despised the whole concept of Greek life.

"Um, Mom, Dad. There's this cook out thing this evening for parents and I thought we could go," I ventured vaguely.

My mom perked up. "Oh, that sounds lovely. Where is it?" I took a deep breath. Here we go.

"It's at the Chi Delta house," I let out in a rush. I could see my dad frowning in the review mirror and my mom's mouth formed a little 'o' as she took in what I had just said.

"Well, that sounds...nice," my mom said hesitantly, looking at my father's reaction.

"A bunch of the sisters will be grilling out. You know

hamburgers and hot dogs. That sort of thing. And there will be music. And it's just a way for the parents to see the house and to meet some of the girls," I hurried on.

My father cleared his throat. "I think we should go," he said finally.

My mom looked over at him in surprise. I had to say, I was completely shocked as well. "You do?" I asked in a small voice.

My dad nodded his head as we pulled into one of the parking lots on campus. "Yes, I'd like to see what my daughter wastes her money on every month. Should be an eye opening experience," he bit out dryly.

Okay. I was done with this already. "Dad. Please just go in there with an open mind. I like being a sister. It's important to me. So just don't ruin this for me." I begged. My voice had gotten high and I hated how much I sounded like a little girl.

But I was relieved to see a momentary softening in my dad's features. He let out a deep breath and met my eyes in the rear view mirror. "Fine, Maysie. I'll have an open mind." He conceded and my heart did a little tap dance. That was the closest to compromise I had experienced from my father in a long ass time.

And then I remembered I had yet to broach the topic of Jordan with either of them. They had no idea who he was and that he'd be joining us for lunch. Maybe while my dad was being semi agreeable, I should let them know I had a) a boyfriend and b) he was crashing our lunch date.

"So, guys. I wanted to let you know that we would be having company for lunch," I said lightly as we started heading toward the Administrative building to meet our tour group.

"Oh, is Riley joining us? I really like that girl. Good head on her shoulders," my dad said gruffly.

I looked at my mom, hoping to get some help from that corner. "Well, no. Riley's meeting up with her mom and dad downtown. Actually, a friend of mine, Jordan Levitt, is coming with us," I said, then watched my mom and dad process that tidbit of information.

"Jordan Levitt? I've never heard you mention him." My mom remarked. Well, no duh. I didn't need my relationship picked over the way they picked over everything. Pardon me for wanting to keep something of mine out of their controlling grasp.

"Yeah. We worked together this summer, at Barton's." I started but my dad interrupted.

"That bar?" he asked sharply. Oh crap. I forgot the bullshit I went through when they found out I was waitressing at a bar. My dad had given me so much grief about that. It didn't matter that I was trying to do the responsible thing. Nope. All my dad had heard was that I working at a bar. And of course, that had just been another example of how I was screwing up my life.

"Uh, yeah. But anyway. He's a senior and we've been seeing each other for a little while." My dad's jaw tightened. My mom's eyes got wide again. She did that a lot.

"Is he your boyfriend, Maysie?" she asked. I coughed and nodded.

"Oh," my mom said quietly. I peeked up at my dad. His shoulders were tense but he wasn't yelling at me. So that was a good sign.

"Is that okay? He's really nice and really wants to meet you." I said quickly. My mom nodded. My dad didn't say anything for a moment and when he decided to speak it was less than heartwarming.

"It would have been nice to have a little warning that we were going to be meeting the young man you're dating," my dad said coldly.

"I'm sorry, Dad," was all I could say. My dad gave a curt nod and nothing more was said about the matter. We joined our group and headed out for the tour. The same tour I took as a prospective student. The same tour I took my first week as a freshman. The same damn tour I took every flipping year with my parents. It's not like the campus had changed that much.

I was suddenly very resentful of having to suffer through the mind numbing boredom of that goddamn college tour. I'm sure it had everything to do with my mixed up feelings about the two people walking in front of me.

Why couldn't I ever be enough? Do enough? Growing up, my dad never seemed particularly interested in me. You'd think as a teacher, he'd understand how important parental involvement was. But he just never seemed to take the time to get to know me.

One of my earliest memories was at the age of five, asking my father to play a game of Candy Land. Do you know what he did? He told me he was disappointed that I wasn't playing with the chess set he had gotten me for my birthday. Who gives their five-year-old daughter chess for their freaking birthday? I wanted pink, sparkly unicorns and Barbie dolls. Not Chess! But that's the sort of thing I came to expect from my dad. He never got me something because *I* liked it. It had to be educational and meant to make me a smarter, better and an all-around perfect person. Too bad his money was spent in vain.

Because as I got older it became pretty damn clear that the daughter he wanted just wasn't me. I tried so hard in school to get good grades and participate in the activities he wanted me too. I suffered through four excruciating years on the debate team in high school, all because my dad had been the state debate champion when he was a teenager.

I had hated it. Every single, obnoxious moment of it. I twisted myself inside out trying to please that man and it was never, *ever* enough. What really hurt was when I had gotten to high school and realized that the relationship I longed for with my father, he was having with every single one of his students.

He was the most popular teacher at the high school. Everyone wanted to have Mr. Ardin for Honors English Lit. The kids loved him. He was funny, encouraging, motivating. Just not with me. His child.

I remember going to my dad's classroom one day at lunchtime. I had stopped just before going inside. I heard him talking to Sarah Keller, a girl in my grade. She was on the debate team with me and my biggest competition for becoming Valedictorian. She and my dad were talking about colleges that she had applied to and she mentioned USC, my dad's alma mater.

I had watched while my dad clapped his hand on her shoulder and gave her a supportive smile. Then he had told her how proud he was of her and how he knew she'd succeed. That crushed me. My heart literally fell to pieces right then and there. This girl was experiencing my dad's pride, something I had never had. He looked at her with all the warmth he never once showed me. And part of me died that day.

I wanted to give up on my need for my dad's approval. But it was so deeply ingrained that I couldn't shake it. And my mom, well, she did very little to curb my dad's militant need for perfectionism. She had her own critiques where I was concerned. Where my dad was obsessed with my academics, my mom was fixated on my popularity.

You would think, given that they were older when they had me, they wouldn't be as focused on that stuff. They should have just been thankful for the miracle that was me, considering they never thought they'd be able to have kids. But that wasn't my lot in life. Instead, I was born to parents who wished and hoped I'd be someone else. Anyone, but who I was.

Instead of going all rebel and becoming a crack-addicted prostitute, I became the hyper vigilant, overachiever. So when I came to Rinard College, the ties that had bound me so tightly had loosened their grip and I had finally been able to breathe.

For the first time in my life I could become somebody *I* could be proud of. So I joined a sorority and now I was dating a badass drummer with an eyebrow and tongue ring and a sexy as hell tattoo covering most of his back. My parents were going to hate him. And that juvenile part of me that so desperately wanted her parent's pride and approval, cringed at the thought. Then the other more rebellious side of that same girl, looked forward to watching their faces when they saw Jordan for the first time.

And as predicted my mom's mouth fell open and my dad's eyes narrowed. We were sat in a booth at Bakersville Deli, having just ordered our drinks when I saw Jordan pull up on his Ducati. Oh shit, he'd ridden his bike. My dad watched out the window as Jordan dismounted and took his helmet off. My father's lip curled in disgust. "How can anyone willingly ride around on those death traps?" he asked in disgust.

I, on the other hand had to discreetly wipe the drool that started to collect at the corner of my mouth. Jordan was gorgeous. And he was mine. And I didn't give a fig what my dad had to say about that. I followed him with my eyes as he tucked his helmet under his arm and raised a hand to rub it across his dark, buzzed head. He did this when he was nervous or anxious and I found the gesture endearing.

He had dressed in a dark pair of jeans that hung deliciously on his narrow hips. I could see a button down shirt peeking out from underneath his leather jacket. He came into the deli, looked around and when he saw us, walked over.

My parents looked horrified when he stopped at our table. I glanced from my parents to Jordan. He gave them a dazzling smile and held out his hand to my father. "Hello, Mr. Ardin. I'm Jordan Levitt, Maysie's boyfriend." Maysie's boyfriend. We had never exactly established what we were. I mean, I knew we were dating, but I had never dared ask him outright if we were a *couple* couple. Hearing him say he was my boyfriend caused my lips to stretch into the biggest grin I could muster.

My dad looked at Jordan's hand, outstretched in front of him. Then he looked up at my boyfriend. I saw my father taking in the eyebrow ring and the buzzed head. The leather jacket and motorcycle helmet and realizing his daughter was dating every single thing he hated.

But manners won out and my father shook Jordan's hand. Jordan turned his attention to my mother, who was still reeling from the shock that *this* was her Maysie's boyfriend. Jordan gave me a troubled look before sliding into the booth beside me.

He rested his hand on my thigh and gave me a comforting squeeze. It was all going to be okay. Jordan was here.

Things were awkward. We put in our orders with the waitress and got our drinks. I waited on pins and needles, wondering when my dad would start grilling Jordan. I could tell Jordan was uncomfortable but he was trying really hard to carry a conversation with my parents. And I loved him for his efforts.

"So, Jordan. What are you studying in school?" my dad asked, taking a long drink of his water while watching him over the rim of his glass. The rest of us were just starting to dig into the food that had just arrived. I was poised to take a bite of my chicken Caesar salad, but immediately lost my appetite when I realized the interrogation had commenced.

Jordan took a bite of his burger and wiped his mouth. "Accounting, sir," he replied. His answer seemed to shock the hell out of my dad. His eyes widened marginally.

"Accounting. Really? That's a respectable career path," my father acknowledged grudgingly.

Ha, take that Dad! I wanted to shout. *That's what you get for making your hateful assumptions.* I tried not to smirk. "Yeah, my dad has his own accounting firm up near the city and he'd really like me to come on as a partner after I graduate." My dad was even more impressed by this. But I could hear the mostly concealed wistfulness in Jordan's voice.

"That sounds wonderful, doesn't it Dan? It's nice to see Maysie spending time with someone who has such wonderful life goals," my mother piped in, seeming relieved that this tatted up bad boy was actually a worthwhile human being. As though becoming an accountant made you a productive member of society or something.

I started to relax, thinking this wouldn't be so bad when Jordan spoke again. "But what I'd really like to do is play music," he said. My dad, who was actually looking...not happy, but something less than brutally disappointed, frowned.

"Play music? Whatever for?" he scoffed as though that were the most ridiculous notion he had ever heard. My mom gave a nervous giggle. Jordan stiffened a bit and I gripped his hand under the table, trying to tell him through my fingers to give it up. This wasn't a conversation he wanted to have with my dad. Not when things were actually going kind of well.

"I play drums in a band and I love it. I think it would be fantastic to do that for a living. To devote my time to something I'm passionate about, not just crunching numbers to help rich people get richer," Jordan said.

And there it was again. My dad's disapproval. Oh how I missed you.

"Well, the likelihood of making any sort of living as a musician is highly unlikely. And what kind of life does that build for you and your future family? What kind of person willingly brings their children into contact with drugs and sex?" my father spat out. God, he sounded like an idiot. An ignorant idiot at that.

Jordan started dragging his tongue ring across his bottom teeth. He was pissed but trying really hard to rein it in. I closed my eyes, wishing I was somewhere else. "You know, Jordan's mom runs her own chocolate shop. Mom, you love chocolate. Isn't that cool?" I broke in desperately. My dad and Jordan were engaged in some weird macho stare off and I had to stop this before it got really bad.

My mom was equally as nervous so she made a show of being impressed with Mrs. Levitt's shop. She asked Jordan a million questions about the types of chocolates his mother imported. Jordan answered every question patiently and respectfully.

"What time do we have to be at that sorority of yours?" my father asked, dabbing his mouth with a napkin. God, would he ever stop?

"Uh, 6:00, I think," I told him. My father clicked his tongue.

"I'm not sure why you bother with all of that sorority nonsense. The Greek system is a ridiculous waste of time, wouldn't you agree, Jordan?" My father directed his question at my silent boyfriend. This was a test. And from his set jaw, I knew Jordan was about to fail miserably.

Jordan took a drink of his soda and looked my dad in the eye. "Actually, sir. I'm in a fraternity myself. And while I think a lot of the Greek system can be a bit over the top, you can't deny the sense of community that comes with being in a sorority or fraternity," he said evenly. Okay, I knew that was just to goad my dad, because Jordan had told me on more than one occasion that he had come to detest the Greek system.

"You're in a fraternity? Oh, well that's interesting," my mother offered. I thought my dad would keep up about the whole sorority thing, but thankfully, he let it rest. But that didn't mean he was finished with me.

Our dessert had just been served when my dad went in for the kill. "We got your last check in the mail a few days ago. I'm not sure how you think you're going to pay off that credit card bill with the paltry amounts you're sending us. I can tell you one thing, young lady; we will not be bailing you out of this mess.

We've bailed you out of enough in your life, and we refuse to do it anymore," he said curtly. Bailed me out of what? I had always been a model kid. Hell, I wasn't given a choice. My father was seriously deluded.

My face flamed red. I was embarrassed that Jordan had to witness this abject humiliation. I hung my head as though I were five years old again. I hated that I wasn't able to stand up for myself with him. But it was like he zapped any spine I had right out of me.

Jordan lifted our interlaced hands to his mouth and kissed the back of my knuckles. I blinked in shock at his overt display of affection in front of my parents. He put my hand back in my lap and crumbled up his napkin and put it on the table.

"Mr. Ardin, sir, I think you're being entirely unfair. Maysie works her ass off; at the same time she's in a sorority and has a full workload. She does ten times more than most college students. I think you need to recognize what she *has* done instead of telling her what she hasn't," Jordan's voice was clipped and angry.

My mouth fell open. So did my mom's. But my dad clenched his teeth and straightened his shoulders. "Excuse me, young man. But who are you to tell me what I can say to my own daughter? And how dare you talk to me with so little respect!" my father hissed out.

Jordan looked down at me and his eyes softened. "You want to know who I am? I'm the guy who's crazy about your daughter. And when you can talk to Maysie with respect, then maybe you'll earn mine." He leaned over and kissed me gently on the mouth. "I'm sorry, baby," he whispered before getting to his feet.

"Mr. Ardin, I apologize that this didn't go as well as it could have. But I hope next time I see you, we can spend the time talking about how amazing your daughter is rather than tearing her down." His eyes bore into my father's and not once did he back down. Damn, I loved him. He turned to my mother. "Mrs. Ardin, it was a pleasure." Looking at me again, he smiled. "I'll call you later," he said quietly. Then he picked up his helmet from under the table and left.

When Jordan was gone, my father sputtered and fumed. He

went on and on about how disrespectful Jordan had been. My father didn't want me to have anything to do with him. That if that was the sort of person I chose to spend my time with, then I couldn't be trusted to make reasonable decisions and maybe college wasn't the place for me.

My mom had finally come to my defense and told my father to settle down. I was more than a little surprised by that. But I knew for all of his shocking exterior, Jordan had charmed my mother.

After lunch, I took my parents down town and they spent the afternoon going into the different shops. By the time we had to head over to the Chi Delta house, my father had simmered down and was his normal, unpleasant self.

My dad had hated every minute of being at the sorority, but had dialed down his outright distaste. I had dreaded going there. But all of the sisters were on their best behavior. Not one nasty look was lobbed my way and several of them made a point to speak to my parents. Gracie was her perky, wonderful self and my dad actually liked her. By the time we left, my father had three glasses of wine and a belly full of pulled pork and potato salad. So he was feeling less combative. When they dropped me off back at my apartment, we agreed to meet in the morning for breakfast. My dad patted my back and told me goodnight. Nothing more, nothing less. Though I was just thankful he hadn't used the opportunity to make any last personal digs.

My mom gave me a hug. "I like Jordan. I think you did well, Maysie," she whispered quietly before pulling away. I couldn't help but grin.

"Thanks, Mom," I whispered back. She kissed my cheek as I pulled back from her open window. I waved as they drove off. And despite the awfulness of the day I felt warm at the memory of Jordan telling my dad he was crazy about me. Yeah, I was one lucky gal.

CHAPTER
22

Several weeks had passed since Parents' Weekend. Jordan had apologized profusely for being disrespectful to my father. But before I could let him say any more about it, I had kissed him soundly, letting him know that I had appreciated the disrespect he had dished out.

No one had ever stuck up for me like that with my parents. And I realized, without a doubt, that I was with the most amazing guy ever. Because he was all about me. And I was all about him. And damned if weren't going to make this thing between us work.

Now it was another Saturday night and I was finally making it to one of Garrett's infamous parties. I was a little nervous. Garrett was definitely the wild one of the group and Jordan had regaled me of his after show exploits. He was probably the least good looking out of the four guys. Yet he apparently got more girls than any of them. I guess he had something going for him.

I hadn't been able to make Generation Rejects' show that evening because Layne had needed me to come in late to help unload some inventory. I had cut back on my hours considerably since school started, finding myself unable to juggle work and school very effectively. So any extra cash was a plus.

We had finished up around midnight and I had driven to the address Jordan had texted to me earlier. I found myself on the outskirts of Bakersville in a rundown area I wasn't familiar with.

I finally found the house at the end of a long gravel driveway. It was a non-descript two-story home that still had the 1960's German siding that was full of asbestos. Jordan had told me that Garrett's parents had been killed in a car crash when he was still in high school and had left him the house. Apparently, he had been in it ever since.

The place was heaving. Cars were along the driveway all the way down to the street. Other cars had driven right up onto the lawn. I could see a huge bonfire blazing in the back yard and people were hanging out on the porch.

Jordan wasn't kidding when he said these parties were nuts. As I approached the house, I saw a woman who had to be in her thirties, leaning over the railing, puking her guts out. The vomit splashed on the ground below and I had to scramble passed before it sprayed me. Gross.

The front door was wide open and I went inside. Looking around, this was clearly not my scene. This was a much rougher crowd than I was used to. I noticed some people I recognized from Rinard, but the rest were strangers. Some looked almost my parents' age. Others could still be in high school. And every single one of them seemed to be wasted off their asses.

I realized I probably stuck out like a sore thumb with my dark skinny jeans, off the shoulder midnight blue top, and knee high black leather boots with a three-inch stiletto heel. Especially when the dress code seemed to include clothing that would have been cool a couple of decades ago. I had felt really good when I had gotten dressed for my evening but now I wished I had gone for something a bit more low key.

I didn't see Jordan anywhere. In fact I didn't see any of the guys from the band. Though to be fair it was hard to see anything in this crowd. I was standing there like an idiot when a huge guy lumbered toward me. When I say huge, I mean *huge*. He was easily over 6 foot and he had the shoulders of a linebacker. His dirty blond hair came down the back of his head in a greasy mullet and his face was obscured by a Grizzly Adam's beard. He was fucking scary!

And he was bearing down on me. Shit! Do I run? And then he

stopped in front of me, grinned and shoved a red solo cup in my hand. "Here, sweetheart. You looked like you needed a drink." I blinked, having been rendered mute by this odd exchange.

"Uh. Thanks," I mumbled, holding the drink in my hand. I wasn't going to drink it. I had seen all the roofie videos in health class. I'm no dummy. But I didn't want to seem rude, so put the cup to my lips and pretended to take a sip.

The guy just stood there, smiling at me like I was something peculiar. I cleared my throat. "Uh, have you seen the band around?" I asked, feeling really dumb. I wished I had made Riley or Gracie come with me. Or maybe Vivian, she would have loved this.

Grizzly nodded and jerked his thumb behind him but didn't say anything. Okay. I guess that meant they were in the room down the hall. I tilted the cup in his direction in acknowledgment and followed his less than specific directions.

I came into a large rec room, complete with a pool table and Foosball. There was a bar to the right that had been built out of the wall. The room was packed. Scoping the place out, I finally saw Cole and Mitch. Cole was manning the bar and was slinging drinks to a large crowd.

Mitch was playing pool with two girls hanging off of his arm. Not wanting to interrupt that, I opted to approach Cole to find out where Jordan was. I had to push my way through the group circling the bar to reach one of the stools. Hopping up, I tucked my feet under the chair.

Cole was talking to a guy with dreads that had a joint tucked behind his ear. I waited for a lull in their conversation before I jumped in. "Excuse me," I called out.

Cole looked down at me and his mouth spread into a grin. "Hey there, pretty lady. What can I do for you?" He leaned over the bar, his dark hair flopping in his eyes. His smile was flirty as his eyes took me in.

I gave him a sassy smile back. "Well, you can tell me where Jordan is?" I asked. Recognition dawned on his face and Cole leaned back from the bar.

"Ahh. You must be the famous Maysie Ardin," he said, his grin getting wider. I laughed.

"Famous, huh?" I asked, wondering what exactly he had heard about me. It was sad to think that it could be any number of things. Not just the fact that I was his band mate's girlfriend.

Cole reached under the bar and grabbed himself a beer, he inclined his head my way in a question and I nodded. He popped the top off of second beer and slid it toward me. "Oh, luv, we've heard nothing but Maysie, Maysie, Maysie since this summer. Whatever you've done to our boy Piper, you've done it good." He chuckled, taking a swig of his beverage.

I swallowed a mouth full of my own drink. "Piper?" I asked, wondering where the hell that particular nickname came from. I had heard Cole use it during their performances but had never gotten around to asking Jordan about it. Cole laughed and the dreaded guy beside me guffawed. Clearly this was a private joke.

I arched my eyebrow. Cole shook his head. "Nathan, why don't you share that little golden nugget of info. That way when Piper gets pissed, he'll bash your face in and not mine. I'm a hell of a lot prettier than you," Cole said, rubbing his hand on his cheek.

The guy with the dreadlocks, Nathan, shrugged. "Whatever, it wouldn't be the first time he broke my nose," he said lightly and my eyes widened. What? Cole saw my face and patted my hand.

"Babe, don't worry, Nathan deserved what Jordan gave him." Both Cole and Nathan laughed as though the fact that the dude had his nose broken by my boyfriend was a huge freaking joke. These guys were mental.

Nathan pulled the joint out from behind his ear and lit it up. He passed it to Cole who took a drag. Cole then handed it in my direction but I waved my hand, refusing it. Drugs weren't my thing. Alcohol, yes. Other stuff, not so much. "Okay, so spill about the nickname. You've piqued my interest," I queried, drinking more of my beer.

Nathan toked on the joint a few more times before he responded. "Well, you know the story about the Pied Piper of Hamlin right? I mean, you're a college chick, you know all that history stuff," Nathan commented, his voice tight from holding in the smoke.

"Yeah, I know the story. The guy was hired to get rid of the rats and then took off with the village's children who followed him while he played the pipe. What does that have to do with Jordan?" I was a little shocked that these townie guys were able to place a nickname on someone that didn't have to do with a sport or a body part. And then I felt crappy for judging them like that. *What a snobby thing to think!* I chastised myself.

Nathan blew out a lungful of smoke. "Yeah, well Jordan is the pied piper of pussy." My eyes popped out of my head and I knew my mouth gaped open.

"What? Did I hear that correctly?" I sputtered. Cole was cracking up at my response. Nathan smiled in a stony kind of way.

Cole slammed his hand down on the bar top in his fit of laughter. "You should see your expression Maysie!" he said, snorting. My eyes narrowed. Nathan put his joint out and dropped the roach in his beer bottle.

"He plays and the pussy comes. These three sad sacks have gotten laid more since Levitt joined the band than they ever did before. The chicks love him. They would follow him off of damn cliff. So that's how he got the name Piper," Nathan finished, moving away from the bar. Clearly his storytelling was at an end.

"Wow. I'm not even sure what to say to that," I responded honestly. I didn't want to come across like a jealous shrew after just meeting Jordan's band mates. But there's something wholly unsettling about learning your boyfriend has been labeled some sort of pussy magnet.

I handed Cole my empty bottle and he threw it in the garbage can with a loud clang. "Shit, girl. He's never acted on it. The whole time he was with that other girl, Olivia, he never hooked up with anyone. And now he's with you. But the girls love that shit. Eat it up like it's a goddamn bowl of fucking ice cream. Think that maybe they're the one to get him to stray. It's like a fucking aphrodisiac. He gets more pussy flashed his way than a goddamn gynecologist and he doesn't do a thing about it. Has the will power of a saint if you ask me." Cole was a dog. There was no doubt about it. And I really didn't want to hear any more about girls throwing their girlie bits at my man.

I felt my hands curve into claws in my lap. Cole laughed again. "Girl, you need to settle. Jordan is as clean as they come. Sure he looks like a straight up badass motherfucker but he's way too soft for all that shit. Anyway...you've got him whipped, so I wouldn't stress about it."

I forced my hands to unclench and I gave Cole a smile. "Sorry. I won't go psycho girlfriend. I promise," I laughed, calming down. Cole smirked.

"Well, that's a nice change," he commented and I lifted an eyebrow.

"Oh really?" I asked; mining for the information Cole obviously had. Cole grinned, seeing straight through my dig for gossip.

He leaned in toward me again and dipped his voice down low. "Oh yeah. That last piece of work he was with was a straight up cunt. And I don't use the c word, well, ever. But that girl was all cunt. She hardly ever came out to our gigs. But when she did, she usually caused such a fucking scene; we'd have to ask her to leave. She was a jealous bitch, screaming and yelling if chicks even looked at Piper. He's in a fucking band! Then Jordan would get pissed and then there would be fucking drama. And sista, we *do not* do drama. And then there was that friend she would bring along with her. Now she was sort of fun. If you could get around the fact that while you fucked her she would scream out Levitt's name. That'll deflate your hard on in no time."

What the hell was this guy saying? I was totally and completely confused. "Wait...what friend?" I asked. Cole put his hand through his hair and seemed to be trying to remember something. "Fuck if I can remember her name. All I remember are her naked tits that she would shove in my face. They were nice. Real nice." Cole licked his lips lasciviously.

I groaned and rolled my eyes. Cole chuckled. "Wait. Her name started with an M, I think. She had dark hair and was like amazon tall." Milla. My eyes got wide. Milla had screwed Cole? And she had screamed out Jordan's name while she did it? This shit was messed up!

And Cole wasn't done with that particular story. He seemed

to be in some serious reminiscing. "Yeah. She loved giving it out. She wasn't picky about who she fucked. One night it would be me. One night Garrett. You get the picture. I guess sticking it where my boys have stuck it should have turned me off. But she was hot." OH. MY. GOD! Milla had not only slept with Cole, but Garrett and Mitch and probably half the county as well. I wanted as much information about this as possible.

"So, this 'M' chick. Did she come around just with Olivia?" I asked, trying to be nonchalant. Cole started picking up empty bottles from around the bar.

"Hell no! She was out here every time we had a party. Olivia never came. I always got the impression she thought she was too good for us. But whatever, we didn't want that bitch around anyway. She always killed Piper's buzz, so it was better when she wasn't here. But yeah, her friend showed up a lot. Usually looking for Levitt. We weren't stupid; we knew we weren't that bitch's first choice. She made no bones about letting everyone know it was Jordan she wanted. But he has never given her the time of day. And we didn't care, because bitch was nothing but kink." Okay I didn't want him to continue. I had heard enough. And if he wasn't talking about two girls I absolutely detested, I would be extremely insulted by his continuous use of terms like 'bitch' and 'cunt.' Cole had no couth.

But one thing was obvious; Milla had been trying to get with Jordan for a while now. Behind Olivia's back. And she had the nerve to start shit with me! It dawned on me clear as day that her pure motivation was jealousy. First of Olivia and now of me. Each of us had what she wanted desperately. Jordan Levitt.

Cole was still talking and I wanted to tune him out but he was being very animated. "She was all about doing it in public places. One time I fucked her on that stool you're sitting on with a room full of people watching us. It was hot!" I jumped up off the stool. Eww!

"And I didn't care if she called me Jordan. Hell, she could call me the fucking president. She was that good." Cole seemed a little wistful. Guys were disgusting. Yuck.

I smoothed my hair behind my ears. "So, when was the last

time you saw Mi...I mean, Olivia's friend?" I asked, trying not to sound too eager.

Cole frowned. "I guess it's been a few weeks." Hmm, interesting. Man, I would love to tell Olivia about her bestest buddy, Milla, who for years had been trying to screw Jordan behind her back. Then maybe I wouldn't be the bad guy.

But then I realized Olivia would never believe me over her friend. I mean, why would she? In the game of she said/she said I would definitely lose. But I tucked the information away, hoping I'd have an opportunity to pull out the big guns at some point.

Cole was sort of grossing me out by this point as he continued to try and tell me about girls he slept with and the crazy places he'd had sex. Like I cared about any of that. So finally I cut him off. "Cole, do you know where Jordan is? I should let him know I'm here."

Cole looked over at Mitch, who had given up playing pool and was watching the two girls he was with make out. "Mitchie! Do you know where Piper is?" Cole called out. One of the girls broke away from her lip lock and whipped her mouth.

"He was out by the bonfire when we left him," she smirked. I clenched my fists, not liking how she said that at all. Cole laughed beside me. This guy laughed...a lot.

"Don't mind Brooke. She's just some of the pussy the piper attracts. Obviously she didn't get anywhere or her tongue wouldn't be down Dalia's throat over there. But, Maysie, you've can't let that shit bother you. If I didn't love the guy so much I'd punch him in the face. He's that obnoxious about you."

Cole may be a bit of a douche, but I could see the nice guy underneath. I gave Cole a small smile. "Thanks. I'm off to find him.' Cole slung his arm around my shoulder before I could walk off.

"And just so you know, if you ever get sick of Piper, there's the really hot singer you could get to know. Just sayin'," Cole teased. I rolled my eyes and didn't bother to respond.

I made my way out to the bonfire and found my boyfriend sitting in a lawn chair, laughing with a group of people who seemed to be hanging on his every word. I took advantage of this opportunity to watch him. He was so charismatic and he seemed to suck people into his orbit without him even realizing it.

Girls and guys alike listened with rapt attention to whatever he was saying. He was talking very animatedly and I could tell he was drunk. I had never been around Jordan when he was overly inebriated, so I was a little nervous about that. Not that I was worried, just not sure what to expect.

There were three girls sitting at his feet. One of them had her hand curled around his ankle like a damn dog waiting to be petted. I was going to rip every one of those fingers off of him. White-hot jealousy flashed through me and I took a step forward. The other two seemed to be vying for the closest spot. I watched as they slowly edged closer to Jordan until they were practically on top of him. And my man was completely oblivious to the affect he had.

Though I didn't care about that, because aware or not, these girls needed to back the fuck off.

I walked up behind Jordan. He was saying something and moving his hands while he talked. I could see that his face was flushed. He was so sexy and damn cute too, with his excitable energy. The three girls at his feet looked up at me as I approached. Jeesh, it looked like he had a harem. Each of the girls wore way too much make up and way too little clothes. And then I didn't feel so much as jealous as kind of embarrassed for them.

All three glared at me and gave me the girl stare. You know the one where they give you to once over and calculate all of your flaws in point two seconds. They clearly felt threatened because they pushed closer to him.

Jordan was still talking, so I leaned down, ignoring the bimbette triplets and put my lips to his ear. "Hey, baby," I whispered. Jordan immediately stopped talking and whipped his head around. The grin that split his lips was breathtaking. Wow. He was beautiful.

He jumped to his feet, practically knocking over the girl on the ground beside his chair. She glared at me again and I smirked. "Mays! You're fucking here!" he said, picking me up and crushing me to his chest. He smelled of wood smoke and musky guy sweat and I loved it. "You took too damn long!" he told me before he pressed his lips to mine hungrily. Immediately his tongue swept into my mouth and his hands cupped my ass, hauling me up against him.

I almost forgot where we were until I heard a number of catcalls. I tore my mouth away, completely out of breath. My heart was hammering in my chest. Jordan's fingers dug into the flesh under my butt cheeks as he nibbled my neck.

"You look fucking amazing. I want to tear your clothes off and put my dick inside you right now," he said, his voice husky with desire. My panties went instantly wet and I couldn't help but press my hips against his.

"I don't think you want the entire party to see what goods your girlfriend is sporting under these clothes," I teased, pulling him by the hair so that he would look at me.

The skin around Jordan's eyes tightened. "Fuck no I don't. All of this is mine. And only mine. No one else sees it. Ever!" He tightened his grip on my body possessively and let out a low growl. Crap, he had gone all territorial. And it was hot!

"That's right, baby. Only for you," I murmured as he leaned in to kiss me again.

"Piper! Is this your lady? Let me have a look!" I heard someone say. Jordan rolled his eyes but moved his hands from my ass to my hips. I looked up at him and tilted my head.

"I've heard all about why they call you Piper. Really cute name," I taunted.

Jordan groaned. "Fuck, babe. It's a stupid nickname. I've tried to get them to stop calling me that..." he started to explain but I held my hand up, stopping him.

"Jordan, it's okay. You may be called the pied piper of pussy. But the only pussy you'll be touching is mine." It was my turn to go territorial and by the look on Jordan's face he really liked it. A lot.

"Damn, baby." He let out in a breath. I laughed. A wiry guy who I recognized as Garrett suddenly joined us. He was bouncing on his feet and his longish blond hair was in stringy disarray around his head.

Looking at him, I couldn't decide if I thought he was cute or not. But he was appealing with his deep, dark eyes and thick, almost girlish lashes. And when he smiled, it lit up his face. Yep, I could see why the girls liked him.

"Hey Piper, introduce us! I've been dying to meet the chick who has made you tolerable again." Garrett said, giving me a 100-watt smile. Wow, okay, he was sort of dazzling. And his personality was infectious. He was a live wire, that's for sure.

Jordan turned to me and gave the introductions. "Garrett, this is my girlfriend, Maysie Ardin. Maysie, this Garrett Bellows, lead guitarist and sometimes roommate." Garrett reached out and yanked me from Jordan's grip and then swallowed me in a huge hug.

I was a little taken aback by the overt show of affection from someone I had just met. Looking over Garrett's shoulder at Jordan, he just shook his head and mouthed, "Go with it." So I put my hands up and awkwardly patted Garrett on the back.

Garrett pulled back and held me by my upper arms. "You are fucking gorgeous, Maysie." My face flushed. I was flattered by his open appreciation. Then he turned to Jordan. "And I can tell she's a hell of a lot cooler than that bitch you used to date." Jordan just laughed and I didn't know what to say to that.

Olivia was obviously known as the "bitch" by Jordan's band mates and I loved how that proved that she was not a perfect fit in his life. And maybe that also proved that I was.

Garrett tugged on a strand of my hair in a familiar gesture, as though we were long lost friends rather than two people who had met literally thirty seconds ago. "Enjoy the party, Maysie. Anyone than can make that fucker start writing music again, is cool with me." He gave me a loud, sloppy kiss on the cheek and then left as fast as he had come.

Jordan swooped in and pulled me back into his arms. "Sorry about that. I should have warned you that Garrett is very...uh... hands on," he explained. I wrapped my arms around his middle.

I waved it off. "He's nice," I said honestly. Jordan kissed my neck and then was distracted by two guys who were calling his name. They held up a beer bong and were gesturing for Jordan to come over and try it out. He tugged on our joined hands. I pulled away and gave him a grin.

"Go ahead, I'll wait here." Jordan kissed me again.

"Just give me a sec. I'll be right back and we can get out of here." He flashed me a gorgeous smile before going to suck beer out of a funnel. I stood on the edge of the bonfire; hands shoved in my jean pockets.

"What's a girl like you doing at a party like this?" a voice asked over my shoulder. I looked behind me and saw a guy standing there. He was tall and skinny. Not bad looking, in a heroin chic kind of way. He had dark hair and dark eyes. And he was looking at me as if I were on the menu he planned to order from.

"Just waiting for my boyfriend." I replied, indicating Jordan, who was flat on his back with a length of plastic piping in his mouth. I could see beer rushing through it. Girls circled him, clapping as though they were watching an Olympic sport.

The guy didn't drop his smile. And for some reason he didn't take the hint about the boyfriend and instead took it as an invitation. Was he low functioning or something? "Well, let me keep you company then." He stepped in closer and swept his hand up my back, starting with my ass. What? Was this guy for real?

I moved away. "I'm fine, thanks. And I really think you should keep your hands to yourself." This dude was making me seriously uncomfortable. The guy closed the space between us again, his hand resting firmly on my left buttock and giving it a squeeze. I swung around and smacked his hand away. "I said, I'm fine. Now back the fuck off," I told him through gritted teeth.

This guy was either crazy or stupid. Because he just grinned at me again and reached out to touch me.

"I'm gonna cut those fingers off if you don't keep them to yourself, Amos," Jordan growled from behind me. My boyfriend stepped in front of me and grabbed a hold of the front of Amos's shirt and gave him a hard shove.

The guy went down like a ton of bricks, sprawling out in the grass. "Hey man, I didn't know she was yours. Sorry!" Amos held his hands up in surrender. Jordan took a threatening step toward him and I grabbed his arm.

"Enough Jordan!" I said sharply. Jordan was barely able to stand up right. I could see that the beer bong was taking affect.

Amos got to his feet and scurried away. Jordan then spun around to me, his eyes flashing.

"Did he touch you?" he snarled and I blinked in confusion.

"What?" I asked lamely. Was he mad at me because some loser tried to cop a feel? Jordan cupped the back of my neck and jerked me forward, his mouth so close to mine I could smell the beer on his breath.

"Did that asshole touch you?" he growled, his face dark.

I swallowed thickly. "Um, he tried..." I started but didn't finish because Jordan hefted me up, his hands cupping my ass and I had to wrap my legs around his waist so I wouldn't fall. He stalked off through the yard with me hanging off of him like a damn monkey.

"Where are we going?" I asked, not sure what was going on. Jordan seemed pissed. His vibe was fierce and intimidating. He didn't answer me, heading toward a huge out building at the back of the property.

"Answer me!" I demanded, smacking his shoulder, but his fingers only dug into my ass and he bit down on my shoulder hard enough to make me yelp. When he got around to the back of the building, he dropped me to my feet and then grabbed a hold of my hips roughly. He walked me backwards until my back was pressed against the wall of the shed.

He bent his head and captured my mouth with his, biting at my lips aggressively. My insides went instantly molten. His hand slid up my body to cup my breast through my shirt, his fingers rubbing into my fabric covered flesh.

I pulled back slightly, my lips feeling tender from his mouth. "What is this for?" Jordan's eyes glinted in the moonlight, an almost feral look on his face.

"No one touches you but me," he said in a low voice, the words tinged in a growl. I couldn't help but laugh.

"Baby, you think I wanted that asshole to touch me? Please, give me some credit," I scoffed. Jordan's hips pushed into mine again and his hand deftly popped the button of my jeans. Then he unzipped them and folded the waist down. My breath hitched as his hand slid down the front, caressing the soft silk of my panties.

His fingers found my wet center. I was soaked. His possessiveness was a serious turn on.

He slipped his finger under the edge of my panties and plunged inside me. I gasped and my hips arched to meet his hand. He bent his head and started sucking and nibbling at the skin of my shoulder. "I know you didn't want him to, babe. That's not the point. This is mine." Okay, so obviously he was feeling some sort of caveman need to mark me.

He thrust a second finger inside me and I groaned, my head falling back as he attacked my throat with his mouth. My body started to clench around his fingers and I felt my orgasm shudder through me. I cried out as Jordan continued to pump his fingers in a merciless rhythm.

"That's it baby, come for me," he whispered as the orgasm kept going and going. Fuck! I just kept coming. It was insane! When I was finally finished and my legs couldn't hold me anymore, Jordan withdrew his fingers and then suddenly my pants and underwear were pushed down to my ankles and I lifted my feet so he could get them off with his foot.

Jordan swiftly discarded his own pants and then I was up against the wall again, my legs wrapped around his middle as he shoved inside me. "Ahh!" I screamed as he thrust as deep as he could go into my hot core. My vagina pulsed around him as he pulled out and pushed back in, slamming my back into the wall.

"Fucking hell, Mays!" Jordan groaned as his hips moved frantically with mine, his knees bent so he could find the perfect angle to push into my body. The night air was punctuated with the slapping of flesh and our guttural cries as we both neared our shattering point.

My legs were trembling and I was finding it hard to hold on. Jordan hefted me up and pulled me down roughly onto his cock and I cried out. His fingers dug into my hips as he rocked into me over and over again. Finally, he slammed me into the wall of the building, burying himself to the hilt. I felt him release inside me as he yelled at the top of his lungs. I quivered and exploded with him in unison.

Jordan slowly let me down onto my feet as he withdrew from my body and my knees buckled. Jordan held me against him so I wouldn't fall on my ass. We were both out of breath and I couldn't even speak. I rested my head against his chest as I waited for my heart to slow down. Jordan rubbed a hand up and down my back.

"Wow. Not sure why you needed to do that right now, but thank you," I said, grinning, when I found my voice again. Jordan reached down and picked up my jeans and underwear. Holding my panties out for me I stepped into them and he pulled them tenderly up my body. Then he did the same with my jeans. He even zipped and buttoned them for me.

"Is it a crime to want to fuck my girlfriend within an inch of her life?" he asked as he pulled his boxers and pants back up around his hips. I pushed my hair back off of my face and pressed my cold hands against my flushed cheeks.

"Not at all, it was just sort of sudden," I replied as the sex euphoria started to fade. Damn, had he seriously just screwed my brains out behind a dilapidated old shed in the middle of a party? Yes. Yes he had.

Jordan kissed my mouth. "You're so fucking hot, Mays. When another guy comes on to you, it drives me crazy. You're *my* girl." I grinned. Who knew that Jordan Levitt was as insecure as I was? It was oddly reassuring.

He clasped my hand and we headed back to the party. Luckily no one seemed to notice we were missing.

Jordan led me into the house, where the party was getting a little out of control. Someone had punched a hole in the dry wall and a huge chunk lay smashed on the floor. Beer and booze were all over the place and the air reeked of pot smoke. I felt bad for Garrett having to clean the place up in the morning.

Jordan kept walking, waving at Mitch and then Cole (who winked at me as we passed making me wonder if I had SEX written on my forehead or something), until we were out on the front porch. Our bout of crazy sex seemed to have sobered Jordan up and he was at least able to walk in a straight line again.

He sat down on the porch swing and pulled me down on his lap, pressing his lips onto my collarbone as I fell into him. He kicked out his legs and the swing started moving back and forth. We weren't alone outside. There were people milling around the front yard but for the moment it felt like we were the only two people in the world.

"Garrett said you were writing music again. Why did you stop writing music?" I asked him, remembering my earlier conversation with the lead guitarist. Jordan dropped a kiss on the skin of my chest and turned his head to the side, laying his cheek over my heart.

He was quiet for a long time, as though he were listening to the heavy beating. His arms held me tightly and I began to wonder if he had fallen asleep or something. But finally he answered me.

"I finally have a reason to write music again. I've been inspired," he said quietly. I ran my hands over his head, the short hairs tickling my palm. My fingers came down and I rubbed the skin on the back of his neck. He moaned as my hands worked their magic.

"And what has inspired you, Jordan?" I asked, totally fishing. Jordan rubbed his nose into the hollow of my throat, his forehead butting my chin.

"As if you need to ask. Every song I write now is because of you. Every song I will ever write for the rest of my life will be because of you," he whispered, his eyes held an emotion that made my throat close up.

I shuddered. His words had hit me straight in the heart. I needed to get this man home and show him how much I loved him. I tilted his chin up so that he was looking at me. His eyes were a little bleary, but otherwise he was in full faculties. "You're coming home with me, right now. I think it's time for a repeat performance," I demanded, placing a kiss on him mouth.

He grinned under my lips. "I love it when you get bossy." He grinned as I pulled him toward my car.

CHAPTER
23

I'm not sure what woke me up. The room was pitch black so it was either really, really late. Or really, really early. Jordan's arm was around my waist, holding me tightly against his chest. I was sweaty from being pressed against him, our naked skin sticking together.

Jordan was making these adorable little noises while he slept and I couldn't stop myself from staring at him while he dreamed. Looking at him like this, vulnerable and relaxed, made my heart flutter painfully.

We had officially been together for over a month now. Our road had been decidedly smooth. Though I couldn't help but wait for the other shoe to drop. But also trying to *not* wait for the other shoe to drop. But all in all, I was happy.

We were riding the blissful waves of the honeymoon period. And things were close to perfect. As long as we stayed far away from anything and everything Chi Delta and Pi Sig.

It was sad how segregated our lives had become. I continued to attend to my mandatory responsibilities within the sisterhood but that was it. My life, that had six months ago, revolved around my sorority, was now tied up in this man lying beside me.

Jordan's ties outside of our relationship were a bit more consuming. He had bartending and his band aside from his responsibilities with his fraternity. We were both busy, but no matter how insane our days were, Jordan slept in my bed every single night.

I knew I loved him. I wanted to tell him. But I held back. I don't know why. Maybe I was being ridiculous and wanted to hear him say it first. Or maybe I was scared that if I let it out there, it would change things completely. That maybe he wasn't ready for that level of commitment.

Sure, he was the sweetest guy I'd ever met. He said and did things that made my inner pinky girlishness tingle. I knew he cared about me. But I couldn't stop myself from doubting that he could ever come to feel for me the way he had felt for Olivia. That girl he wrote that amazing song for.

Yes, I was still fixated on that stupid song. I don't know what was wrong with me and why I couldn't get over it. Maybe it was because I was still forced to see his beautiful ex-girlfriend several times a week. And seeing her flawless perfectness made it damn near impossible to stop myself from calculating comparisons. Plus, she was dead set on feeding my insecurities like a wild fire out of control.

It was in the way she casually mentioned something pertaining to Jordan, or their three-year history when she knew I was in earshot. Or it could have been the way his Pi Sig brothers acted as though she were the goddamn prodigal son whenever they saw her, showing how perfectly she fit into that area of his life. It didn't help that pictures of her and Jordan graced the Chi Delta walls. Collages of the girls during past formals and mixers. Jordan and Olivia, the most beautiful couple on the planet front and center in all of them.

Most of the girls continued their Maysie Ardin freeze out. I wasn't exactly persona non grata, but I was pretty darn close. I wasn't included in random drink nights during the week. I wasn't sent the sorority wide texts to coordinate outfits for mixers. I barely got a hello when I walked in the house on the few occasions I had dared to show up.

Gracie and Vivian tried their hardest to make it easier for me. And God love them for it. But I could see playing for team Maysie was weighing on them as well. Because of their association with me, our sisters were less friendly to them. At least when I was around. I suspected things were fine once I had left and the girls could pretend I didn't exist.

So herein lays the crux of the problem. Why didn't I just withdrawal? Why did I continue to subject myself to such pettiness? It seemed like a form of torture. And there were many days that I wondered this myself. At night when I'd lie in bed, with Jordan's warm body pressed against me, I'd think up the grand speeches I would give, announcing my formal withdraw from Chi Delta.

I had it all planned out in my head. I'd tell Olivia and Milla exactly where they could stuff their snotty little noses. I would look at the rest of them and call them a bunch of bitchy hypocrites. But then I'd wake up in the morning and swear to myself that I'd give it just one more day. One more day to see if things would be better. One more day to make things right again.

But as long as Jordan and I were together, that wouldn't happen. And I was torn between this fantastic new love I had found and my longing to return to the fold. The need to belong was strong in me and hard to quash. I knew in my psychobabble way, that this was firmly rooted in me wanting my parent's approval. It had simply morphed into all areas of my life. The constant worry about what other people thought was exhausting and I wished like hell I could just let it go. Riley thought I was an idiot and wasted no time in telling me that on a daily basis. And I understood why she thought that. Hell, most days, I thought that. But I had pride and it burned pretty damn bright.

So I stuck it out. Even as my life seemed to get uglier. Because the rumors were getting crazy. Last week, in my Shakespeare and Chaucer class, we were assigned groups to work on a comparative project between Canterbury Tales and Shakespeare's story telling in his tragedies. I was grouped with two girls, Cyndy and Aimee, who had lived on my floor freshman year and a guy named Charlie, who was a year below us. I knew their names, but knew nothing else about them. They weren't people I saw out and about in my normal, everyday routine.

But they knew me. Or knew *of* me. I saw it instantly when I pulled my desk closer to theirs to begin our work. It was in the curl of Aimee's upper lip when I sat down. It was in the look of barely concealed disdain in Cyndy's eyes before she flicked them back to her book. And fuck if it wasn't there in the openly lascivious look Charlie tossed casually my way.

"Hey, Maysie," Aimee had said. And the way she said my name made me feel like I had some sort of disease. She and Cyndy had shared a look and Cyndy covered her mouth to hide a mocking grin.

I had gotten pissed. I was sick to death of this shit. So I had slammed my book shut and looked at each of my group members. "Is there a problem?" I had asked. Charlie had looked startled and gave a mumbled, "no" before looking away. Cyndy and Aimee weren't as embarrassed by their behavior. Both were decent looking girls, but in a bookish kind of way. Definitely not sorority material. No, they were the girls, with their above average IQs, who looked down their noses and acted like anyone in the Greek system were barely functioning morons.

"Yeah, I guess there is a problem," Cyndy began and I gave her my best bitchy look of indifference.

"Oh, yeah?" I asked, trying really hard to act like I didn't give a crap about their opinions when deep down I was dying. Aimee snickered.

"I mean, can you be counted on to pull your weight or will it be interfering with your *extracurricular* activities?" The bitch had the nerve to use fucking air quotes.

"I'm sure I can fit you into my busy sorority schedule if that's what you're asking," I answered snidely. Cyndy's eyes had gone wide in feigned surprise.

"Oh no, that's not what we were referring to." Huh? The two girls looked at each other again.

"What?" I snapped, losing all patience with this entire conversation.

"We mean your *other* activities. You know. Your *fraternity* responsibilities," Aimee said and snickered outright. I looked at Charlie who had his mouth hanging open and was staring at me. What the hell?

Charlie sat up straighter. "I'm pledging Kappa Tau. Just so you know." It seemed really important for him to tell me this. What was going on here? Aimee leaned forward and dropped her voice into a whisper.

"We've heard you're part of the fraternity initiations. I've heard it's called, *pass the slut*. The guys say you're the best there is." Her lip curled again and she sniffed as though she smelled something foul.

I felt sick. My hands went clammy and I know my face had gone pale. "What?" I whispered, my voice gone. Charlie was practically fidgeting in his seat.

"We all know about *you*, Maysie. I hope I get to see you around the house soon. You know we're having a party this weekend. Maybe you could come," Charlie said eagerly. I looked from Cyndy and Aimee's disgusted expressions to Charlie's hopeful lustful one and I couldn't take it anymore. My snappy comebacks and snarky attitude were all dried up. I had nothing to say in the face of that. The fact that these three people, who I didn't know, had heard these horrible things about me, made me want to head straight for Timbuktu, or somewhere equally cut off from all civilization.

So, I had grabbed my books and my bag and got up. I fled the classroom. Yep, I ran. Like I said before, it's what I do best. The whole thing shook me. I knew people were talking about me. That I was the one labeled the whore because of what went down with Jordan. What I hadn't realized was the way it had grown into something else. Now, not only was I home wrecking bitch, but I was practically a prostitute being passed around by every fraternity on campus.

Where had the story come from? Even as I had thought it, I knew. Milla and Olivia. Where else? But I didn't have proof so there was no sense in confronting them. So I had gone home, waited for Riley and cried on her shoulder. The poor girl's clothes had been drenched in my tears on more than one occasion recently.

And I didn't tell Jordan. I didn't want him to go off on some one-manned vendetta to eradicate all the rumors going around about me. He didn't need the drama. Plus I was embarrassed that people were saying that about me. What if hearing it enough made Jordan think about me differently? Then I felt guilty for even contemplating that.

I wasn't entirely sure if Jordan had heard the rumors. If he had, he never mentioned them.

My mind was strangely full for having woken out of a dead sleep. So I slowly peeled myself away from Jordan, careful not to wake him up and tip toed out of the room. I grabbed my pack of cigarettes and headed out onto the balcony.

The air was cool and I wished I had thought to grab a sweater. Propping my feet on the railing, I lit my cigarette and took a deep drag. Everything was silent and I enjoyed the peace. I stared into the trees behind the apartment building. In some ways my life was everything I wanted it to be. I had friends who had my back no matter what. I had a great job. I was doing well in school. And I had a guy who I loved so much it was hard to breathe.

But then there was the flip side to the coin. The nasty ugliness of my reality that made the good stuff hard to remember. Deep down I worried that all of the shit, the horrible rumors, the despicable things people were saying behind my back, and hatefully to my face, would taint what Jordan and I had. What was that saying about if you hear it enough times; you start to believe it as the truth?

It sucked; this insecurity of mine. I had never really suffered from low self-esteem before. I didn't fixate on my flaws, real or imagined. But this whole thing with Olivia and Jordan and been a hard blow. I hated that I had become one of those girls who second-guessed herself all the time.

Because no matter how secure I felt in my relationship with Jordan, there was a black stain that threatened to spread over the whole damn thing.

"Hey, what are you doing out here?" I looked up, startled, to see Jordan leaning against the open door. He had thrown on a pair of basketball shorts and a gray t-shirt. He was warm and sleepy and smiling at me.

I lifted my cigarette. "Woke up, couldn't go back to sleep. Go on back to bed, baby. I'll be there in a few." I thought he'd go back to bed, but instead, he came out and closed the sliding door behind him. He sat down in the other chair and watched me as I finished my smoke.

"That shit'll kill you," he said good- naturedly, playing the reformed non-smoker. He had quit at the end of the summer and was very proud of himself.

"So will listening to you bitch about it," I volleyed back.

Jordan smirked and crossed his arms over his chest. "It's cold out here, Mays."

"Wimp," I teased, tossing my butt into the ashtray. I didn't move to stand up, enjoying the quiet of the night and the comfort of Jordan's presence. He looked back over at me and I could hear him clicking his tongue ring over his teeth.

"You looked pretty deep in thought out here," he observed. I shrugged, tucking my feet underneath me.

"Yeah. I guess I have a lot on my mind," I replied. I could feel my sleepiness kicking in again. Jordan scooted his chair closer to mine and rubbed his pinky along my arm, causing goose bumps to break out over skin.

"Wanna share?" he asked softly. I tilted my head in his direction.

"I don't know. It's a little early in the day to be delving into my crazy head," I joked, running my fingers along the side of his face. He captured my hand and brought it to his mouth, kissing it gently. He was quiet, not pushing. He was kind of great like that.

"Have you heard the shit people are saying about me, Jordan?" I asked in a hushed whisper. We hadn't really talked about any of this. It was like we tried to keep all of it outside the compact little world we'd created around us. I noticed Jordan tense and it confirmed my earlier suspicions that he was very aware. Aware of all of it.

"Babe, you can't listen to that shit. It'll eat you alive," he reasoned, gripping my hand tightly in his.

"Easy for you to say, you're not the one they're calling a whore," I said lightly, trying not to sound as pissed about that as I really was. It was unfair the way I got all of the blame. How easy it was to judge the girl and forget that the guy in the scenario was even involved. Not that I'd ever want people to say about Jordan the malicious crap circulating about me. But still.

Jordan gripped my chin and turned me to face him. "None

of this is your fault. If anyone should be called a fucking whore, it should be me. I chased you, pursued you, when I was with someone else. It pisses me off the way people can fucking judge you when they know nothing about what really happened." His eyes flashed with his anger.

I leaned in and kissed his mouth, loving the way his lips fit perfectly against mine. "Stop it, Jordan. I'm glad you chased me. I've never been so glad to be caught in my entire life," I murmured as his hands came up to tangle in my hair.

"I hate seeing you upset, Maysie. It guts me. If I thought it would help, I'd beat the shit out of every single one of those assholes," he told me, his eyes closed as he rested his forehead against mine.

"Do you ever worry that all of that stuff, that the ugliness will make what we have ugly too?" I asked quietly. I hated to ask it but it's what had been bothering me. It was so easy to say that none of it mattered, that it was him and me against the world. But the truth was those outside things could mess with the precarious happiness we had built together.

Jordan's hand gripped the back of my neck and he pulled me in close, his lips coming down hard against mine. I gasped at his forcefulness at the same time my body began to react to his passionate assault. He broke away from the intensity of his kiss and his eyes burned into mine. "Don't *ever* say that, Mays! What we have is too important to be ruined by petty bullshit. So take that crap out of your head right now!" he growled, pulling me into his lap so that I was straddling him. His arms came around me and held me tight against his chest.

He kissed the bottom of my chin and then put his lips to the hollow of my throat. His mouth stayed there, feeling the heart beat through my skin. "I wish I didn't care. That I could just let it slide off my back. But, Jordan. It bothers me...a lot. And I don't know what to do with that," I admitted. Jordan's hands began to gently rub my back.

"Does it change how you feel about me?" he asked me softly. I looked down at him and his eyes gazed back at me. I could see that the thought worried him. He was genuinely scared that I was having second thoughts about us.

I cupped his face in my hands and pulled him close so that our lips brushed against each other. "Never." I whispered. Jordan closed his eyes and let out a small sigh of relief.

"Then try to forget the rest. We have each other and, baby, and that's everything." He kissed me again and I felt myself melt into him. He was right. What we had *was* everything.

"Let's go back to bed, I'm freaking freezing," Jordan said, pressing his cold nose to the side of my neck. I squealed and tried to pull away. Instead of letting me go, Jordan lifted both of us up, carrying me inside. He walked us back to my bedroom, kissing me the entire time. And then he made me forget everything. My worries. My fears. My insecurities. They all disappeared as he showed me how much I mattered.

"*D*o you mind if we swing by my house? I left my biology book there." Jordan asked as we were leaving my apartment the next morning. We had made a point to spend a minimal amount of time at the house he shared with his Pi Sig brothers. After the crap with Gio a few weeks ago, it seemed like the smart thing to do. But I felt bad that Jordan was avoiding his friends because of me. So I sucked up my discomfort and nodded.

"Sure," I said as he took my hand in his.

"It'll be quick. I promise," he assured as we got into his truck.

"It's cool. We can't avoid people forever, Jordan," I told him, turning down the stereo as ACDC screamed through the speakers.

"Why not? Everyone else sucks," he joked. I rolled my eyes but grinned.

"That's right. There's only you and me, babe," I replied, blowing him a kiss.

His eyes stared at me warmly. "That's right. You and me." The way he said it made my insides all gooey. A few minutes later we were pulling into the driveway at his house. He held my hand as we went through the door. A few of the guys were in the living room and called out their greetings. They didn't stare at me the way they had that first time I had come there with Jordan, but they were still anything but welcoming.

We went up the stairs and started down the hallway toward Jordan's bedroom. Suddenly a door to the left opened up and a barely clothed Olivia came out. Her hair was rumpled like she had just woken up and her lips were red and swollen as though she had just been thoroughly kissed. She wore a guy's button up shirt and it fell to the tops of her thighs.

She stopped short when she saw us. Then her mouth lifted in a mean smirk. "Hey *guys,*" she said with a bitter edge to her voice.

I felt Jordan tense beside me. "Hey Liv," he responded and I just nodded. Then Gio came up behind her, slithering an arm around her waist and kissing the side of her neck.

Gio was only wearing a pair of shorts, his chest bare. His hair was rumpled and it was very obvious what they had done the night before. And probably that morning. I looked up at Jordan and he was watching them, his jaw hard. My insides froze a bit at his expression. Obviously this bothered him.

Gio looked up from slobbering all over Olivia's neck and grinned. "Hi Jordan," he said. He didn't acknowledge me, which was just fine. The smile on his face was brittle and challenging. I knew he loved the fact that Jordan was seeing the two of them together. My eyes flicked to Olivia and I could see she loved it too. What a sad pair.

"Didn't expect to see you." Olivia giggled; rubbing against Gio whose hands had started to slide up her front. I averted my eyes. This was becoming downright pornographic. Jordan pulled on my hand.

"Well, don't let us interrupt. See you later," Jordan said shortly. I followed my boyfriend down the hallway, with the sound of his ex-girlfriend's laughter floating behind us.

"Yeah, see ya later!" she called after us and then I heard Gio's door slam shut.

Jordan went into his room and he started rooting through his stuff, trying to find his book. I stood by the door and watched him. He seemed agitated. Clearly the run in in the hallway had gotten to him. And damn it that pissed me off!

"Where the hell is my book?" he grumbled, moving piles of

clothes to his bed as he searched. I walked over to him, grabbed the stuff he was holding and threw it on the floor. Jordan looked at me in surprise.

"What was that for, Mays?" he asked bewildered.

I pointed out into the hallway. "That upset you, didn't it?" I demanded. Jordan sighed and ran his hands over his face.

"Maysie. It's not what you think," he said, sounding annoyed. I went over and closed his door, then turned around to face him.

"Are you jealous that Olivia slept with Gio? Is that what your attitude is about?" I asked, unable to disguise the hurt in my voice. I knew rationally that of course he'd be weird about it. Even if he no longer loved her, he had to still care about her on some level. Yeah, rationalizations had no room in my brain at that particular moment. I felt tears prick my eyes and I tried to calm myself down.

I could feel my body start to tremble and I hated how upset I was over something so ridiculous. Jordan let out a frustrated sigh and turned his back to me. "This is stupid, Mays," he muttered, bending down to dig his biology book out from under his bed.

His flippant disregard for my feelings stung. I felt like a child being dismissed during a temper tantrum. I didn't think I was being entirely unreasonable. But Jordan had effectively shut me down. I stood there, watching him shove his book into his bag as he walked passed me and out into the hallway. I was left to follow him, feeling like an idiot.

We got back into his truck and Jordan didn't say anything. The air between us was decidedly cool and I didn't know how to thaw it. When he pulled into the parking lot at the school, we still hadn't said a word to each other. He threw the vehicle into park and grabbed his bag.

"Jordan, wait," I said before he could get out of the car. Jordan hesitated but didn't look at me. "I'm sorry, alright. I was being jealous. It's just really hard for me. You and Olivia have this history and we're so new. I just get intimidated by it," I admitted quietly.

Jordan's shoulders dropped a bit. "Maysie, I can't lie to you. Seeing Olivia with Gio bothered me." I sucked in a breath, his words like a knife to my heart. Jordan's jaw clenched.

"But not for the reasons you think. Gio is an ass. He uses girls and throws them away. I care about Liv. I always will. You don't share a huge portion of your life with someone and then discard them like it's nothing. I did wrong by her, Mays. What I did was fucked up. And I feel incredibly guilty. And that's what I felt when I saw the two of them together. Guilt."

He twisted in his seat so that he was facing me. His eyes were bright as they bore into mine. "I don't love her. Not anymore. I haven't loved her for a long time. But I feel bad. I feel like a total dick for being *that* guy. I cheated on her. It's hard for me to reconcile myself to that."

I swallowed. The shame of what we had done washing over me anew. I had no idea Jordan struggled as much as I did. He seemed so sure of us. Maybe he was starting to question whether he had made the right decision.

"I'm so sorry..." I started and Jordan cut me off, reaching out and pulling me toward him.

"No, Maysie. No! I don't want you to think for one second that I regret you. Regret us. I wouldn't undo anything that brought you into my life. I just hate that Olivia is reaping the aftermath of my decision not to be upfront with her. And now she's hooking up with douche bags like Gio Bovalina. It's just kind of hard not to feel like the biggest asshole on the planet," he said sadly.

I felt a little better, but I didn't like him beating himself up like that. I bumped my nose with his. "Olivia Peer is a big girl, Jordan. She makes her own decisions. Don't think for one second that you are in any way to blame for that. Guilt will suck you dry. I should know." Jordan rubbed his nose along my cheek, his breath sweet against my skin.

"Whatever I did in my last life to deserve you, I'm extremely grateful," he whispered, his lips tracing my ear. "I hope I always deserve you," he murmured before placing a soft kiss at the corner of my mouth.

"And I get what you're feeling. I really do. How many times have I threatened to put my fist down that jackass's throat that you used to date? We really need to learn to trust each other. We really, really do. Because you have become the most important thing in my life," he said, his voice husky with emotion.

I had no words. He had this crazy power to render me speechless. "Let's get you to class, baby," he said, pulling away and reaching for his bag again. I nodded, my tongue too heavy in my mouth as I tried to get my hammering heart under control.

We walked across campus, his arm slung around my shoulders and I knew that whatever else may be thrown our way, this is where I belonged. Right here, right now. For always.

CHAPTER
24

"*I need* to head over to the mail room. I haven't checked my box in forever." Riley commented, picking up her tray and going to drop it off. I followed her. We had met up for lunch in the canteen. We both had class in forty-five minutes so we were killing time until then. Jordan was in classes up until five, so I wouldn't see him until after his shift at Barton's that night.

I was still sort of reeling from our conversation earlier. It had the ring of things left unresolved. Yes, I knew he had made it clear I was what he wanted. But I couldn't forget the look on his face after seeing Olivia and Gio together. Why couldn't I get over my insecurities? Oh, that's right. Because I was a neurotic, self-sabotager extraordinaire. Hell, if ruining something great were an Olympic sport, I would have the gold medal.

Riley and I made our way across campus. The stares and whispering had died down some. Maybe everyone had moved on to some other tasty bit of gossip. I was less self-conscious about being in public. I had stopped looking over my shoulder for attacking groups of villagers with pitchforks. I took that as a positive step forward.

We went up the stairs to the mailroom. "Maysie! Riley! Hold up!" I looked over my shoulder and saw Gracie running after us. She was her typical cute self in a pink V-necked sweater, knee length jean skirt, polka dot leggings and brown Uggs. I wanted to put her on my key chain; she was so over the top adorable.

"Chicas! How've you been?" she asked breathlessly once she had caught up with us. Riley smiled at her and I noticed that their relationship had evolved from barely concealed loathing to polite civility. It was damn near heartwarming.

"Good. Same thing, different day," Riley quipped, pushing through the glass door. I held the door as Gracie followed close behind me.

"I hear ya. Maysie, you need to come to the house this evening. Olivia's called a last minute meeting. Not sure what it's about, but I'm guessing it has to do with the Ball Blast in a few weeks," she said, pulling off her puffy pink gloves.

"Great. I'll be there with bells on," I replied dryly. Gracie squeezed my arm.

"Girl, you've got to let it go. I haven't heard a negative thing about you in a while. I think everyone is moving on. So I think you need to as well. They're your sisters. That matters, you know," Gracie said convincingly.

Riley snorted, but otherwise kept her comments to herself. "Yeah, maybe you're right," I replied. And maybe she really was. Who knows? Perhaps I could survive this whole mess with my hide intact.

We each went to our mailboxes. I hadn't checked mine in at least a month and it was crammed full of junk mail and flyers. I tossed most of it into the trash. I was looking through a Sorority Life magazine when I noticed a commotion in the corner by the community message board.

Gracie came up beside me, thumbing through her mail and looked up at me. "What?" she asked when she noticed my attention was focused elsewhere.

"What's going on over there?" I asked, nodding my head in the direction of the crowd. There was laughing and whispering. Riley joined us. "I want to see what has everyone so interested," I said, moving toward the crowd.

Gracie and Riley followed me and we elbowed through the group. I should have known something was up when everyone parted for me. It was like one of those bad teenage dramas where people stop what they're doing just to look at you. That should have been my clue. The whispers were deafening, the laughter cruel.

But I didn't register it as directed at me until I got up to the big bulletin board covering the wall. Normally it held flyers for campus wide activities, help wanted ads, notices of people looking for roommates. Not today.

Today there was an eleven by fourteen picture that I recognized with mortified clarity. "Oh, shit," Gracie gasped as she took in the photograph.

"What the fuck is that?" Riley asked in horrified outrage. *That* was the sight of my reputation, my popularity, my self-esteem going down the fucking toilet.

The picture was one I hadn't known existed. But I would have recognized it anywhere. It was from my pledging days at Chi Delta. We had been made to dress in our bathing suits and go from fraternity house to fraternity house where we were "rated" by the brothers. It was a horribly demeaning form of hazing. I had hated every minute of it and that was the one time during my pledging experience when I really contemplated dropping out.

The other girls had been just as miserable as I had been. Gracie had broken down in tears. The sisters had taken us out and gotten us plastered afterward and the whole thing had been laughed off. But it hadn't been funny. And now, here was the painful reminder. You could see how unhappy I was in the picture.

But the worst part was the black rings drawn on the photo over my body. Circles around my thighs, my stomach, my upper arms. Beside them were numbers. They were the rankings I had been given that night by the fraternities. Four on my thighs. Three on my stomach, which had always had a little more flab than I was comfortable with. Five on my arms. My boobs had a big two written across them.

Someone had scrawled in big, black letters underneath it; *her face and body might suck, but we hear from the guys she's a solid ten in the sack. Give her a call and take her for a spin. Everyone else has.*

Then my cell phone number was written boldly at the

bottom. I choked on the tears in the back of my throat. I shoved forward, making my way through the other students standing there, laughing at that horrible picture. Laughing at my utter humiliation.

I ripped the picture down and tore it in half. One of the girls who were standing close by sneered at me. "Doesn't matter, I've seen at least six other posters around campus." She laughed before taking off with her friends, looking at me and whispering.

"Oh my God!" I cried, running out of the mailroom. "Maysie! Stop!" Gracie yelled from behind me but I kept running. I didn't stop until I got to the quad. Then I sank down to the ground and I couldn't stop the tears rolling down my face.

Riley and Gracie finally caught up with me and they went down to the ground beside me. "Maysie. That was awful!" Gracie said in a horrified voice. I couldn't look at her. I was so ashamed and embarrassed. Riley snapped in front of my face.

"Damn it, Mays. Don't you dare curl up into a ball and take this! Screw those jerks! Who cares what they think? I say we go find the rest of those posters and then track down whoever did this and rip them a new asshole," Riley growled.

Gracie made a noise of discomfort. "I'm not sure about the asshole ripping thing, but I definitely think we should find the rest of those posters," she agreed. She shared a look with Riley who was in full on militant mode.

"Come on, Maysie!" Riley said, getting to her feet and pulling on my hand.

I yanked my hand away. "Just stop it!" I yelled. Riley and Gracie stared at me and I could tell Riley wanted to shake me. I held up my hand. "I appreciate it, I really do. But we tear the posters down and then what?" I looked at Gracie. "We know exactly who is responsible for this." Gracie's fisted her hands at her side.

"Those bitches," she breathed out.

I shook my head. "So yeah, let's go tear them down and they'll just find some other way to humiliate me. Gracie, I really think I need to withdraw from Chi Delta," I said firmly. Riley was nodding as Gracie was shaking her head emphatically.

"This is freaking ridiculous! You need to confront them! They can't black ball you like this! I think you should file a complaint with the Panhellenic Council. They can't get away with this!" Gracie fumed. I felt the small flare of my self-righteous rage starting to simmer in my belly. Gracie was right. Fuck this shit. I couldn't sit here crying in the grass while Olivia and Milla systematically ruined my life. Enough was enough.

I got to my feet. "Let's go find the rest of those posters." I said with an edge to my voice that surprised even me. Gracie pumped her fist into the air while Riley gave out a loud whoop.

"Let's go!" Riley called out, dashing across the quad. And I raced off behind her, determined to take my life in my own hands.

CHAPTER 25

*M*y newfound sense of empowerment lasted a whole thirty minutes. We were only able to find three other posters. They had been strategically placed in areas that got the highest amount of traffic. It made me want to punch something every time we found one. People were milling about, laughing at that stupid picture and then their laughter would become louder and more pointed when I quickly tore the poster down.

It was draining, having a target on your back. It was hard to keep your chin up when you had so many people tearing you down. Riley, Gracie and I gave up trying to find the other posters after an hour of searching. Riley wanted to keep going but I protested. What was the point anyway? My anger had gone from a simmer to a full-blown forest fire level blaze.

And that's how I found myself storming my way toward the Greek quad. One of the posters crunched up in my hand and I'm sure steam was coming from my ears. Gracie trailed after me, practically running so she could keep up. Riley had continued the search after I declared I needed to settle things immediately.

"As much fun as seeing Olivia and Milla get their asses handed to them, I made a vow to never step foot into a Greek house. And even potential blood shed won't make me. So call me when you're done." Riley had said simply before heading off to scour the rest of campus.

I threw open the door to the Chi Delta house and the sisters looked up at me in surprise. "Where are Milla and Olivia?" I asked in lieu of a greeting. Vivian was in the kitchen and came out to find me, red faced and breathing heavily. She looked from me to Gracie, who looked a mixture of pissed and worried.

"What's going on?" Vivian asked. Not meeting her eyes, I held the poster out for her to take. I was still looking around the downstairs. "Crap," Vivian whispered, folding the picture back up. I started for the stairs.

Vivian caught my arm. "Girl, you need to settle for a moment." I glared at her and she lifted her hand from my sleeve in a placating gesture.

"I'm all for you giving the bitch sisters a piece of your mind. But you need to do it when you're calm and rational. Not when you're ready to take their heads off. They're more likely to trip you up. Don't give them a reason to throw you out of here. Come on," Vivian reasoned. But I didn't care anymore. I was sick of playing victim to their cruel games. I was confronting this now, before I lost my nerve.

So, I ignored Vivian and marched up the steps. Olivia's room was the largest in the house and situated at the end of the hallway. The door was open and I could see her, Milla, and two other senior sisters, Jadyn and Cici, inside.

Olivia looked up when I flew through her door. She seemed shocked at first but then her face smoothed out to a smirk. She looked gorgeous as always. Her long black hair was pulled back in a ponytail and she wore a pair of skinny jeans that fit her like a damn glove. A tight green sweater accentuated her too- perky- to- be- real chest.

I hated how pretty she was. I hated that she was popular and self- assured. I hated the crazy long history she had with the love of my life. And I hated that she had a song written for her. A beautiful song.

I don't know what came over me, but I lunged for her. Next thing I knew I had a fist full of her luscious, dark hair and I was pulling with all of my might. I hooked my leg behind her ankles and swept her down to the floor. I was on top of her, ripping at her hair and clawing at her face. "Get the fuck off of me, psycho!" she shrieked, pushing at me and flailing about.

But my anger must have given me super powers because I held on, taking out chunks of her hair as I pulled. "You are a NASTY, CRUEL, HATEFUL BITCH!" I screamed in her face.

Suddenly I was being pulled off of Olivia. I kicked out and tried to hit at her again. Vivian had me around the waist and was dragging me into the hallway. Milla had a hold of Olivia who started to run after me. "I'm gonna kick your ass, you man stealing whore!" she yelled. Milla and Cici held her by her arms, while Vivian and Gracie held me.

"I can't steal what doesn't want to stay, *Olivia!*" I yelled back, smirking at her. Olivia growled and wrenched out of Milla and Cici's grip. She came at me, her fingers swiping close to my face. I kicked up and my feet landed firmly in her chest, sending her sprawling to the floor.

I heard Jadyn and Cici scream and reach for our president, who was having a hard time getting to her feet. "How dare you come into the house, into *my* room and attack me! You are through!" Olivia threatened, breathing heavily.

I pulled the poster out of my back pocket and held it up in front of her face. "Well, I could report you to the Panhellenic Council for harassment! Then we'll see who's through." Even through my anger I saw Olivia's confusion as she looked at the mortifying picture. She looked as though she had never seen it before. Then my anger faltered. If she didn't do it, who did?

But that moment quickly vanished as Olivia laughed at the picture. "My God! You're pissed because someone put pictures of your skanky ass all over campus? Are you surprised people see you this way? After what happened with Jordan?" She looked at me in disgust. I blinked, feeling like an immature fool.

"Maysie, I've had it with your drama and all of the bullshit that goes with you. We're having a special meeting tonight. This has to be dealt with immediately," Olivia's words rang out with authority. And I felt as though I were being summoned to the principal's office. I felt Gracie grip my arm beside me and I really appreciated her presence at that moment.

"7:30, Maysie," Olivia said shortly, still trying to get her breath. Milla openly laughed at me, enjoying this way too much. Olivia and the other girls shoved passed me and went downstairs. I was shaking; the adrenaline in my system was going crazy.

"I can't believe I just did that," I said in a hushed whisper. Vivian and Gracie were quiet.

"I'm going to get kicked out. I physically assaulted the freaking president!" My voice hitched as I realized the huge hole I had just dug for myself. Vivian put a comforting hand on my shoulder.

"That was pretty righteous, Mays," she said with a chuckle. I looked at her in disbelief. I couldn't believe how tickled she seemed by the whole thing.

"Glad you think this is funny," I bit out.

Vivian covered her grinning mouth with a hand. "I'm sorry, Maysie. But if you knew how many times I fantasized about doing that." Her laughter broke through and I could only gape at her in shock as my life swirled down the toilet. Gracie shot her a look and then grabbed my hand.

"Let's get you home, Mays." She took me out the back door of the house. Vivian followed us as Gracie led me to her car.

"What happens now?" I asked, my voice deadened by the free fall I found myself in.

"Well, most likely you'll have mediation with Olivia and then the sisterhood has to vote whether to suspend you." Well, that's what I had expected. Even though I no longer felt Chi Delta was where I needed to be, I didn't like the decision being made for me. Call it stupid pride or whatever, but I didn't take a loss of control lightly.

"That's just freaking dandy," I muttered, propping my feet up on Gracie's dashboard and resting my forehead on my knees.

"We'll have your back, sweetie. I promise," Gracie told me, turning out onto the main road by the campus. My phone buzzed in my bag and I reached down to find it.

Pulling it out I saw I had two missed texts. The first one was from twenty minutes ago.

I'm heading into work. Leave the door unlocked for me tonight, because I'm comin' for you.

My stomach clenched up painfully after reading Jordan's text. I couldn't even smile at his message. I felt like my life had hit fast forward in the last half an hour. The girl who would have giggled at Jordan Levitt thinking about her was on vacation.

I deleted the first text and ran my finger over the second one. *Where are you? I tried calling.*

I turned off my phone. I should call him, but I couldn't deal with him. With *us*. Our relationship had been built on dishonesty and secrets. Right now, with my recent rumble with Olivia fresh in my mind, I didn't think that was particularly a good thing.

Gracie and Vivian got me home, deposited me on the couch with a bag of chocolate chip cookies and the TiVo remote before leaving. They promised they'd be back at 7:00 to take me to the house. They would have stayed but they each had an early evening class. Riley was still on campus and would be there for a while longer. So I was alone.

Alone with my less than pleasant thoughts and even worse feelings. My phone rang beside me. It was Motorhead's Ace of Spades, Jordan's ring tone. I had laughed at the inside joke when he programmed it a few weeks ago, remembering how he liked to make my eardrums bleed with that particular song. Now I just wanted it to stop. I hit ignore and focused on the television. The noise didn't penetrate and all I could do was obsess over tonight's meeting.

Riley came home a couple of hours later. She tried to talk to me but I wasn't much up for conversation. She quickly discovered I wasn't going to answer beyond monosyllabic responses. I got ready for the meeting with the grimness of someone going into battle. Ace of Spades rang out a few more times. But I continued to ignore it. I would have to talk to Jordan eventually. But right then I wasn't sure what I exactly wanted to say.

Part of me wanted to unload everything. I knew he'd listen. He'd hear me out without trying to give me ridiculous advice. He'd be everything I needed him to be. But I didn't really know what I actually needed him to be.

I didn't know anything.

Gracie and Vivian came and got me, just as they said they

would. Riley said something supportive but I didn't really hear her. We drove to the meeting in silence. Walking into the Chi Delta house was almost like the first time I went inside. The nerves, the clammy hands, the apprehension. But this time there wasn't the excited anxiousness and instead I just felt sick.

Gracie held my hand as we walked down the hallway and entered the chapter room. It was already full of our sisters. Everyone looked up when I came in. The quiet murmur of voices quieted instantly and silence descended like a blanket.

Gracie and Vivian pulled me toward three seats at the end of the long table that took up most of the room. At 7:32, Olivia hit the gavel and brought the meeting to order. I watched her, refusing to look away. No weakness. I wouldn't show an inch.

"I originally called this meeting to talk about some issues around the fall Ball Blast. But I think we need to table that discussion for another night. Instead, we, as a sisterhood need to address some serious issues that have recently arisen." Olivia said tightly as her eyes met mine. I tried not to flinch at the outright hatred I saw there.

Olivia coughed and clasped her hands together in front of her on the table. "Everyone is very aware of the...problems... that have come up between Maysie and myself. I know this is creating a very decisive division between us. This has gone on long enough. A decision needs to be made in how we can handle this and move forward." My jaw clenched and I hated that our lives were playing out in front of everyone like this. But like Olivia said, it was affecting everyone in this room. So they had a say in how it went down. As much as I hated that.

Gracie hadn't dropped her hand from mine and I felt her fingers tighten around mine. Olivia took a deep breath and continued. "I had hoped Maysie and I could resolve our differences. That things could be handled with maturity and respect." I wanted to laugh. Was she serious? But I could see how this would play out. My role as villain was firmly planted in these girls' heads and that wouldn't change. But damned if I would go down without a fight.

"This is sort of ugliness is unprecedented within the house. I wasn't entirely sure how this should be dealt with, so I made a call to the national headquarters this afternoon and they advised that we needed to have this meeting and that everyone had a right to voice their concerns and grievances. We need to deal with this like sisters." Olivia's malicious stare drilled through me and it took everything I had not to cower under it.

Milla stood up. "As the vice-president, I'd like to start by saying I'm appalled at how everything has happened. Sisterhood is supposed to matter to us. I'm greatly troubled by the way certain individuals were so willing to disregard everything we stand for. Trust has been broken. And just like in any relationship, once that is destroyed it's hard to come back from that." I clenched my teeth. Milla was playing her part well. Even if I could practically smell her hypocrisy. Olivia nodded in agreement and I heard the other girls give their acquiescence.

Milla took a breath and looked at me. Her face was somber but I could see the triumphant glee in her eyes. This is what she wanted. She was handing me my walking papers and she couldn't be happier to be doing it. "I feel that the source of this division, Maysie Ardin, needs to have her sisterhood stripped. The bonds have been broken. We cannot continue in this way anymore. Maysie has turned her back on her sisters and Chi Delta. There is no choice here," she said with conviction.

I heard Vivian mumble under her breath something that sounded like "fucking bitch." I didn't dare look at her. My eyes were focused on my persecutors. The witch-hunt was reaching its culmination, might as well see it through.

Milla sat down and crossed her legs, reaching over to squeeze Olivia's shoulder in a show of support. What a joke. Gracie suddenly got to her feet. "Look, I know what Maysie did wasn't cool," she began and I cringed. Where was she going with this?

"But Maysie has been a loyal sister and friend since pledging with Chi Delta. She is the one person in the sisterhood I always know I can count on. What happened with Jordan sucked." She leveled her steely gaze at Olivia who looked blandly back. "I know you're hurt Olivia. Maysie feels horrible about that. She always has. But what went down is between you and her and no one else. I just don't understand how this has become a 'Chi

Delta' issue," she stated, using her fingers as quotes to drive her point home.

I looked around at the group of my sisters. I noticed that the new pledges seemed uncomfortable by all of this and I felt a fresh wave of guilt. They were new to this, trying to establish their own friendships and loyalties within the sisterhood. And they now had a front row seat at how much of a farce it all was. Sisterhood didn't mean shit.

Maryanne, a junior, got to her feet then. I didn't know Maryanne that well and I knew instantly by the look on her face that she wasn't going to speak in my favor. I always got the impression that she was a giant butt kisser and the way she looked at Olivia with sympathy sealed that. "But this *has* become a Chi Delta issue. Everyone is upset. Everyone is on edge. Our relations with Pi Sig have been jeopardized and they are the best fraternity on campus," she protested. There was a universal agreement at her statement.

Great. Glad to know their priorities were in order.

Maryanne cast a quick glance at me before looking away. "I think Maysie is the problem here and I agree with suspending her," she sat down and several of the girls around her patted her on the back. I pulled my hand from Gracie's and gripped them tightly in my lap. I needed to; otherwise I'd start swinging. And that wouldn't help prove my case at all.

The next twenty minutes passed with each of the sisters getting to their feet and giving their opinions on my betrayal. Most were advocating for my removal. I was however, pleasantly surprised that a few actually stood up for me. I had thought that my only two supporters were on either side of me.

Then it was Vivian's turn. Vivian got to her feet and I couldn't help but watch her in a bit of awe. It was crazy to think that just a few weeks ago she had been annoying the crap out of me with her high maintenance, stressed out bullshit over rush. I had never been close with her before this. She was always firmly entrenched in Olivia's circle. I knew they had been tight. I still didn't understand what had possessed her to forsake that relationship in favor of championing me.

Well, I was about to find out.

Vivian leaned on the table, her dark red hair falling around her shoulders. She looked fiery and determined. "This is bullshit, Liv and you know it." Milla got to her feet.

"Don't start with your crap, Viv. This is not the time or place," she threatened and the two girls stared each other down. Vivian pulled back her lips in a snarl.

"Oh, I think this is the time and place. You are sitting there on your fucking high horse, painting Maysie like the worst kind of person. When you and I know that she hasn't done anything that the two of you haven't done," she hissed.

The room became eerily quiet. I looked over at Gracie who lifted her shoulders and widened her eyes. Olivia tensed and I could feel the ice wafting off of her. "Don't you dare," she said quietly, her meaning very clear. Vivian had better shut up or else.

Unfortunately for Olivia, Vivian wasn't done. "Oh, I shouldn't dare tell our beloved sisterhood how their perfect president slept with my boyfriend our sophomore year. While she was dating Jordan," Vivian spat out.

"Shut up, Vivian! You don't know what the hell you're talking about!" Milla yelled, pointing at her. Vivian laughed.

"Oh, I don't? So it wasn't you who slept with this same ex-boyfriend of mine two days after Liv?" Eww!

I knew my mouth was hanging open in shock. The room burst out in an angry buzz. "Did you know anything about that?" I whispered to Gracie.

"Uh, no," she whispered back. These girls were seriously twisted.

Olivia hit her gavel on the table and everyone stopped talking. "Vivian. We've talked about this a million times. Nothing happened with Ryan and me. You are completely delusional," she said flippantly. But I could see the quiet panic in her eyes. She was lying. She had totally slept with Vivian's boyfriend.

Vivian banged her hands down on the table. "You liar! I saw you together! I walked in and saw you fucking my boyfriend!" she screamed. I saw Olivia swallow and her mouth pinch.

"You were drunk, Vivie. And that was years ago. Your memory

is a little skewed," she said in a placating tone. Vivian crossed her arms over her chest.

"Not too drunk to know two people screwing like rabbits in my boyfriend's bed," she bit out angrily.

"This is playing out like a bad episode of the Young and the Restless!" Gracie said quietly.

"Or Jerry Springer," I added. Olivia stood up then.

"Enough Vivian. I'm not talking about something that you think happened two years ago. We are here to discuss the rift happening right now." Olivia effectively shut Vivian down. I could almost be impressed with her ability to make Vivian's claims seem irrelevant and immaterial.

Vivian looked like she was about to blow her top. "But that has everything..." she started.

"Enough!" Olivia yelled, her eyes flashing at her former friend. "You are not remembering things the way they are. But you and I can address that at another time," she said quietly. Vivian pushed back from her chair, sending it toppling to the floor.

"Screw this, I'm out of here," she fumed. She looked down at me and her face softened. "Sorry, Mays. But you'll get nowhere with this lot. They're a bunch of assholes." And with that, she stormed out of the chapter room, leaving everyone staring after her with their mouths open.

Eyes swung back to Olivia who had turned an interesting shade of purple. Milla looked livid as well and the two girls glanced at each other, a silent message being passed between them. I knew then that Vivian would be next. Once they had dealt with me, they'd be going full barrel after Vivian. What nasty, hateful people.

"Girls," Olivia said to the noisy room. Everyone quieted. "Don't let Vivian's bitterness taint your feelings. She clearly has unresolved issues she needs to address. Issues that have nothing to do with me, I assure you. But let's get back to the matter at hand." And like that, Vivian's claims had been dismissed.

Olivia put a hand to her chest and closed her eyes. When she opened them again, tears dripped down her cheeks. Crap, she was good. "Maysie. You've broken my heart. You've broken our friendship. And today you attacked me, physically, within the walls of this house. That can't be allowed or tolerated. I'm sorry if I've done something to make you turn on me this way. I have only ever wanted you to feel welcome and included in Chi Delta. I thought you were a perfect addition to our sisterhood. It pains me at how wrong I was." Her voice broke and Milla handed her a tissue. She dabbed her eyes. I bit my tongue to stop myself from calling her out.

"I love Jordan. He was everything to me. We had a future. And that's been taken away. Aside from losing the love of my life. I've lost a sister. And that is ten times more painful," she breathed out, her voice barely above a whisper. Damn, she was good.

Then the looks started again. Forty-five sets of eyes turned to me with disgust and betrayal. Okay, I couldn't keep silent anymore. I got to my feet and looked right at Olivia. "I'm sorry, Olivia," I began. I choked on my words and struggled to continue. But the truth was I *was* sorry. I hated hurting anyone. Even the biggest lying bitch on the planet.

"I never meant to hurt you. What happened with Jordan and me was in no way planned. We both tried to ignore it. Once I found out you were his girlfriend, I did everything to avoid him." I told her truthfully.

"But that didn't stop you from shoving your tongue down his throat behind her back," Milla called out with a sneer. I turned my eyes to look at her. This girl who had come to hate me with a passion that I didn't entirely understand.

"Yes, we hooked up. I don't know why I did that. All I can say is I love him too. This isn't some random fling." Olivia's eyes flared and I could see the hurt there.

"I'm sorry for that. We didn't mean for it to go down the way it did. I would take it back in an instant if I could. But what you've been doing is way worse." Olivia frowned.

"What are you talking about?" she asked. I glanced at Gracie who gave me an encouraging nod.

I took a deep breath and continued. "The rumors, the posters calling me a slut. All of it. I understand you're hurting, but that's no reason to rake my name through the dirt like that. I wanted to handle this privately. Between you and me. But you've made that impossible." Olivia opened her mouth, frowning.

Milla jumped in. "Don't blame Olivia for the fact that everyone on campus knows you're a whore. That's all on you, babe."

"Shut up, Milla!" Gracie yelled, jumping up beside me. The noise level in the room became deafening. And I couldn't help but notice Olivia sitting there quietly, her face a mix of emotions I didn't understand.

Olivia banged the gavel again. "It's time for us to vote. Tania is passing out slips of paper. As a group we have to decide whether Maysie will leave the sisterhood. You are voted coming in, and you are voted going out," Olivia said with an absolution that her face didn't mirror. She looked bothered. By what, I had no idea.

Ten minutes later, Randa, the treasurer, was adding up the votes. She got to her feet. "Thirty-five have voted for Maysie's suspension. Majority rules." Randa didn't meet my eyes. And like that, my days as a Chi Delta sister were at an end.

"Thank you, Randa." Olivia looked at me then and I saw something that looked like regret flash across her face, which confused me. "Maysie. The sisterhood has spoken." I nodded and got to my feet. I felt like I had faced a damn firing squad. I was ready to get out of there. Gracie was crying and I squeezed her hand.

"It's okay, hun," I assured her. Though I felt anything *but* okay.

I held my head high and walked out of the room. Gracie ran after me. "No, Maysie! This isn't right! You need to appeal this to the head council! You need to do something!" she implored as I opened the front door. I shook my head, too tired to hold it up.

"I'm not going to fight this. Those girls don't want me. I'm done. I'm out," I said. Gracie grabbed me in a hug.

"This doesn't change our friendship, Mays," she said emphatically. I didn't respond. I had nothing to say. "Let me grab my keys, I'll drive you home," Gracie said, turning around. I reached out to stop her.

"No, I'll walk. It's not far. And I need to clear my head." I told her. Gracie looked prepared to argue. "But it's dark," she reasoned.

"I'll be fine. You go do what you have to do. I'll talk to you later." I just needed to get out of there. The vibe of that place was killing me.

"Okay. Be safe, Mays. I'll call you," she promised, her eyes still wet with tears. God, this was depressing.

"Later," I called over my shoulder, letting myself out. Closing the door behind me, I sagged in defeat. I felt battered and bruised. I wish I felt relief or something other than the aching grief at how that just went down. Girls were brutal.

CHAPTER 26

*W*alking the six blocks home did little to clear my jumbled head. I opened the door with a slam kicking off my shoes. Riley came into the living room from the kitchen. She took one look at my face and came to grab my arm. "You look like shit," she told me matter-of-factly.

"Yeah, well I feel like shit, Riley," I said blandly.

"What happened?" she asked as I sat down heavily on the couch. I laid my head back against the cushions.

"Well, I've been officially suspended from Chi Delta. Sorority Maysie has died a tragic death," I muttered.

"What a bunch of ass hats!" Riley yelled. I wanted to laugh. Ass hats. What a great name for them. But I couldn't make my lips move.

Then just like that I was crying. "I feel like such an idiot," I wailed, covering my face with my hands, hiccupping as I tried to calm myself down. Riley put her arm around my shoulders.

"Why in the world would you feel like an idiot?" she asked softly. I dropped my hands into my lap and leaned my head on her shoulder.

"Because I actually thought those girls were my friends. And because I can't entirely blame them for what they did either," I admitted darkly.

Riley pinched my arm. "The hell you can't blame them!" she said, her anger obvious. I shook my head.

"No, Riley. I get it. What Jordan and I did was wrong. And because I couldn't keep my damn lips to myself, my life is in ruins. Everyone hates me," I moaned. Riley grunted.

"Not everyone hates you, Mays. Stop being so dramatic," she said harshly.

She got up and went into the kitchen. She came back with a glass of orange juice. I downed it in two gigantic gulps. "I just wanted to be part of something, you know? I really wanted those girls to like me," I said quietly, feeling the tears prick behind my eyes again.

Riley rubbed my back. "Babe, if they're so quick to turn their backs on you, then they aren't the kind of friends you want or need. Why are you letting it eat at you like this? Be relieved it's over and you can put it behind you," she reasoned.

"I don't know that I *can* put it behind me," I murmured, running my tongue along my lips. My phone beeped in my pocket. Pulling it out I saw it was another text from Jordan. I deleted it without looking at it.

"Jordan?" Riley asked and I nodded. She frowned. "Why didn't you text him back?" she asked suspiciously.

I didn't say anything, tossing my phone on the coffee table. Riley reached over and smacked my hand. "Hey!" I yelled. Riley glowered at me.

"I know what you're doing, Maysie Ardin, and you need to snap the fuck out of it!" she said, her voice hard. My eyes slid away from her.

"I don't know what you're talking about," I denied.

"The hell you don't! Don't you dare sabotage a relationship with a great guy because you feel guilty. You can't live your life worrying about what everyone thinks, Maysie. Otherwise you'll be miserable," she told me sagely. I smirked.

"Easy for you to say. You're not the one being bullied every time you step foot on campus," I said.

Riley sighed. "I know you don't want to hear this. But damn it, this once don't close those ears of yours and listen. Jordan Levitt is bat shit crazy in love with you," I snorted. Love? I wasn't so sure about that. Lust, yeah. That I could see. But why in the world would he love me?

"Maysie! Why are you so down on yourself? I had no idea all of this had eaten away at you like it has. Please don't self- destruct. Don't push him away. He is not your dad! He isn't going to turn his back on you the second you do something he doesn't like. If you screw this up, you'll regret it," she predicted. She had called me out pretty succinctly. She was right of course. I was trying to lump Jordan in with my parents. Expecting him to turn his back when I invariably disappointed him. I knew that wasn't fair. But my reaction was ingrained and hard to stop.

I was so mixed up. I had just had the day from hell. And some silly part of my kind of blamed Jordan for the mess I found myself in. I was so mad at him for pursuing me even though he had a girlfriend. I was mad at him for not breaking up with Olivia sooner. I was also mad at allowing myself to be led around by my hormones.

Riley sighed again, this time deeper and with obvious frustration. "Just don't do anything stupid while you're all emotional," she said, jabbing her finger into my chest. I swatted her hand away.

My body and head felt heavy. I was so freaking tired. "Whatever." I muttered, feeling an exhaustion that was bone deep. I lay down on the couch, bringing my knees up to my chest.

I felt Riley put a blanket over me and then I was asleep.

I wasn't sure how long I had been out. The next thing I knew I felt lips on my neck and warm fingers sliding up my shirt to tease my breast. I rolled onto my back and let out a moan. The lips came down on mine and I felt a tongue press into my mouth. My eyes opened in a slit and I saw Jordan leaning over me.

I closed my eyes again as he started rub my nipples, rolling them between his thumb and finger. "Sorry I woke you," he whispered, kissing the skin below my ear.

"Mmm," was all I could get out as his hand dropped to my pants as he pulled the zipper down. His hand slipped inside and he teased the edge of my panties as his mouth slanted over mine again. He nibbled at my bottom lip, his tongue thrusting inside my mouth. I tangled my tongue with his and shivered at the cool feel of his barbell.

His fingers moved my panties aside and he dipped inside my wet warmth. "Ahh, God!" I groaned into his mouth as he pushed inside my body while his thumb rubbed against my throbbing clit.

"Maysie," he rasped as his hand started to thrust in and out of my body. I arched against his palm and brought my hand down to shove him deeper inside me.

"You're always so wet for me, baby," he whispered as his fingers picked up the pace. My body started to tremble and I knew I was close. Jordan curved his fingers, finding the spot that would shatter me.

"Jordan!" I called out as I came all over his hand. Jordan moaned into my mouth, still rubbing my clit with excruciating slowness.

He pulled his fingers out of me and shed my pants and underwear. I lifted my arms as he took off my shirt. I was clumsy as I fumbled with the button of his jeans. Laughing, he finally took over and stood up, dropping his clothing to the floor. He lay back down on top of me; his naked flesh pressed tantalizing against mine.

I wrapped my legs around his waist as he trailed kisses along my collarbone. I could feel his hard erection pressed at my opening as he started to slide along my wetness. I thrust my hips up to meet his but he wouldn't penetrate. Instead he continued to tease me by taking his cock in his hand and rubbing it along my throbbing slit. He would push the head in and then pull out, sliding it along my drenched folds. "You're killing me," I groaned as he pushed part way in and pulled out again.

Jordan chuckled and brought his mouth down to my nipple. He sucked it into his mouth, his tongue lapping roughly. I moaned loudly and caught myself. Shit, Riley could come out here at any time! I tried to pull myself out from underneath but Jordan held me in place. "You're not going anywhere," he said softly, pushing his tip inside me and holding himself poised to thrust.

My breath was coming in ragged pants. "But Riley..." I was able to get out.

"She was leaving when I got here," he said, his tongue leaving a wet trail up between my breasts until he reached my mouth again.

"Ohh," was all I said as I arched again. Jordan pulled his cock out and I grabbed his ass in my hands. "God damn it, Jordan! Fuck me already!" I demanded.

Jordan threw his head back and laughed. I harrumphed at his amusement. "So demanding. Can't I have a little fun first?" he teased, his fingers replacing his cock between my legs. My thighs trembled as another orgasm started to brew in my belly.

"Please, Jordan," I begged, not caring how breathless and desperate I sounded.

Jordan lifted my leg and put it over his shoulder, his hand kneading my breast, his fingers still fucking me as he gazed down. "You are so damn beautiful," he whispered. Then he withdrew his fingers and suddenly his hard length was plunging deep inside my body. I groaned as he lifted my lower body off the couch so he could angle me just right. With one leg draped across his shoulder and the other wrapped around his middle he slammed roughly into me, over and over again. I gripped his arms, my head thrown back as the waves of my orgasm rippled through me.

Jordan shifted my hips slightly so that he could hit the sensitive spot inside me and I tightened around him just as I exploded. "Maysie!" he yelled as I came. His thrusts became wild as he pumped into me. I could barely hold on and we called out each other's names. His fingers dug into my hips and I briefly wondered if he had bruised me. I felt him grow thicker inside me and then just as another orgasm cascaded through my body, Jordan tensed and released himself.

I felt his body shudder and his chest was covered in a fine sheen of sweat. The room was dark but I could see the satisfied smile on his face. Fuck, he was fantastic. He leaned down and kissed my mouth tenderly before pulling out. I lay there, unable to move as he got up to go to the bathroom. He came back with a wet cloth and tenderly wiped between my legs, cleaning me with a gentleness that made my heart ache.

"What a way to wake up," I said smiling, my chest still rising and falling rapidly. Jordan dropped the cloth on the table and climbed over top of me, settling against my back. He placed a kiss on my naked shoulder and then pulled a blanket over both of us as he snuggled into me.

"Why didn't you answer my calls and texts?" he asked after a few minutes. I tensed beside him. The euphoria of really awesome sex was starting to subside and the evening's events started crashing back into me. And with it came my anger.

I couldn't help it, I pulled away from him. Jordan realized what I was doing and wrapped his arm around my middle, holding me still. "What is it?" he asked, his voice low. I tried to move against his iron grip. His arm tightened and I started to get pissed off.

"Let me go, Jordan," I said, pushing at his arm.

Jordan yanked me back and pushed me down onto the couch. He came up over me and looked down into my face, his eyes boring intensely into mine. "What the hell is going on, Maysie? I had my dick inside you ten minutes ago and now you're acting like you want me to get the fuck out!" he growled, leaning into me.

I wiggled underneath him. "Just move, okay. You're crowding me," I pleaded, not liking the way this was going. My mind was still muddled from the sex and the crazy emotions I had been feeling all evening. And being with Jordan made it impossible to think straight.

I remembered what Riley said about not pushing him away but right then, I needed space. Jordan sat up and lifted his hands. I slid out from underneath him and grabbed my clothes, quickly yanking them on. I pushed my hair off of my face with shaky hands.

Jordan grabbed my hand. "Maysie, please. Tell me what's wrong. I can't help you if you won't tell me," he said softly, his earlier irritation gone. Now he just looked confused and really worried. I let out a deep sigh.

"You can't help me, Jordan. It has gone way passed that," I said cryptically. Jordan frowned.

"What happened?" he asked me again.

"I've had a shitty day. There was some stuff that happened earlier, some posters that someone had put up about me..." I started but Jordan cut me off.

"Posters? What kind of posters?" he asked in a dangerously quiet voice. I looked at him and saw that his jaw had tensed. He looked scary and sexy and damned if I didn't want to jump his bones again.

"Posters of me during pledge week in a bikini. And there were these ratings for different parts of my body. And then it had my number at the bottom for guys to call if they...you know..." I couldn't even finish. I was too embarrassed. Jordan's fist slammed into the coffee table making me jump.

"WHAT THE FUCK?" he roared and I flinched at his anger.

"Do you know who did this?" he demanded. I took a tiny step backwards. His vibe was seriously angry and more than a little scary. I swallowed thickly and felt myself wobbling.

"Doesn't matter," I mumbled. Jordan got to his feet. He was still naked but his muscles were taught as though he were ready to do battle.

"The hell it doesn't matter! Who did this?" he demanded again. His anger made me angry and I glared at him.

"IT DOESN'T MATTER!" I screamed and Jordan went silent. But I went on. "Because then tonight I was voted out of Chi Delta. They kicked me out!" Jordan's rage melted away and he reached for me.

"Mays, I'm so sorry," he said, trying to grab a hold of me. I evaded his grasp.

"Yeah, well that came after I almost beat the shit out of your ex-girlfriend," I said darkly. Jordan's eyes widened in shock.

"You almost beat the shit out of Liv?" he asked, as though he hadn't heard me correctly. I smiled without humor.

"Yeah, she's sporting a wicked bald spot, I'm sure," I said a little too gleefully.

Jordan frowned again. "Mays, what the hell? Why would you do something like that?" he asked as though speaking to a child. Then I snapped. All of my anger, hurt, betrayal. Every horrible feeling I had had in the last few weeks came bubbling to the surface. And it all focused on one target. Jordan.

"Why did I do that? Because of you! It's always about you!" I hollered, fisting my hands at my side. Jordan leaned down to the floor and grabbed his jeans, putting them back on.

"So the fact that you tried to take out Olivia is my fault? Am I hearing that right?" he asked. I recognized a dangerous edge to his voice but I was way passed caring.

"Well, every single crappy thing that has happened in the past four months has somehow circled around good ol' Jordan Levitt. So you do the fucking math!" I threw at him. Jordan's lips thinned and his face started to flush. His eyes glinted angrily.

"Is that how you really feel?" he asked quietly.

Right then, it was exactly how I felt. None of this would have happened to me if he hadn't decided to chase after me. I was so angry. And damned if in my overly emotional state, it was all his fault. "Sometimes, Jordan, I wish you had never bothered with me at all," I whispered. I realized what I had said as the words hit him. He sucked in a breath and the anger faded from his face. Replaced with something so much worse.

"Maysie. You can't mean that," he choked out. He looked stricken and part of me hated what I was saying. No, I didn't mean it. Well, not entirely. But there was a part of me that was seriously angry and bitter and I was taking all of it...every single bad thing, out on him. It was wrong. It was hateful and cruel. But I was feeling hateful and cruel. I just wanted to stop feeling so shitty all the time.

At whatever the cost.

I looked away, my shoulders sagging. Jordan's fingers curled around my chin as he pulled my face back towards his. His other hand came up to roughly clasp the back of my neck. His fingers were hot against my skin and his breathing was ragged. He wore only his jeans and his fantastic chest gleamed in the darkness. He was so damn beautiful.

"Look at me!" he pleaded and I raised my eyes to meet his. The deep blue of his irises were wet and I realized he was holding back tears. "I'm so sorry you feel that you've had to deal with the fall out alone. I made some shitty choices. I should have handled things better. I hate that you've borne the brunt of that. It kills me." His hand tightened at the back of my neck and I was helpless in his grasp.

"I've gotten my fair share of grief too, you know. The guys at the house won't lay off and that's why I rarely go there anymore," he admitted and I blinked in surprise.

Though that's nothing like what I've had to deal with. The hateful, bitter voice in my head taunted. God I wished it would just shut up. I tried to pull out of his hold but he moved his hands to capture my face.

"Maysie, please. Don't let all of that other crap get in the way of you and me," he begged, his thumbs caressing my cheeks. I closed my eyes against the warring emotions doing battle inside me.

"But it already has, Jordan," I said softly. Jordan yanked me forward and pressed his forehead to mine. His breath came quick and harsh against my lips and I couldn't look at him, so I kept my eyes closed.

"I love you, Maysie," he said in a strangled whisper. I squeezed my eyes tight. No! He could not be choosing this moment to tell me something so important! What the hell?

"Maysie! Look at me! I love you!" His voice was gutted and I refused to open my eyes. Then his mouth was on mine. His lips were persistent and demanding, his tongue running along the seam of my mouth begging for entry. But I wouldn't give it to him.

"Maysie! You promised me you wouldn't run!" he pleaded again, his mouth crushing against me, trying desperately to illicit a response. But I felt dead inside. I was tired and sick of it all. I loved Jordan. I wished I could tell him that. But right then, it just didn't matter. I felt like I had to get control of my life back. And I didn't think I could do that with him near me.

"I need you to leave," I said against his mouth. Jordan stilled, his fingers digging into the sides of my face almost painfully.

"No, I'm not going anywhere," he said stubbornly. I reached up and pulled his hands away from me. I finally opened my eyes and coldly regarded him.

315

"I told you to leave. I can't do this right now. I'm a mess. I need some space," I bit out.

Jordan tried to grab a hold of me again but I was able to move away before he did so. "I *can't* leave. Why the fuck are you doing this?" he asked in a tortured voice. I shook my head. My mind was made up. Sure, I'd probably wake up in the morning, regretting this decision. But right now, it seemed to make perfect sense.

"Because, my life is in shambles and somehow it all seems to come back to you! I just need a breather!" my voice rose and I saw Jordan flinch. Then his eyes shuttered and his teeth clenched. The desperate tenderness was replaced by something colder. Harder.

He picked his shirt off the floor and yanked it over his head. My heart caught in my throat as I watched him shove his feet into his shoes. He grabbed his bike key off of the coffee table and walked to the door with angry steps. Before opening it, he turned to face me one last time.

"I meant what I said, Mays. I love you. So damn much. And you'll wake up in the morning and realize you threw away something fucking perfect for NOTHING!" he yelled. I winced as though his words were a physical blow. He took a deep breath and calmed down.

"I thought you were worth everything. That *we* were worth all the drama and bullshit. I am willing to fight to the death for what we have. But I can only do that if you're willing to fight with me." His eyes drilled into mine, lost and disappointed. My stomach dropped to the floor. He turned his back to me and opened the door. "But obviously you can't do that. Or won't. And I'm a damn fool," he said with a sad resignation that hurt worse than his anger.

I opened my mouth to say something. Anything. I had no idea what I could do to make this better. Whether I wanted to make this better. But I knew with absolute certainty that I was making the biggest mistake of my life. What the hell? My decision had seemed so crystal clear five minutes ago. What was wrong with me? Riley was right, I was sabotaging everything.

But before I could do anything, Jordan walked out and slammed the door behind him. And I was left standing there in the carnage I had created. With my heart in pieces, I dropped to the floor and cried.

CHAPTER
27

To say I was depressed was a massive understatement. The week after Jordan and I broke up found me barely getting out of bed, blowing off classes, only eating when Riley forced me to. I hadn't seen a shower in three days but I was way passed caring.

I had fucked up. Why had I fucked up? Because I was angry. And scared. And I had allowed other people to influence how I felt about the one person who mattered most to me. I was a complete and total idiot.

Jordan hadn't called. I checked my phone obsessively. Even going so far as to sleep with it in my hand. Every morning I checked to see if he had called or sent me a text. Every day began with the same gripping disappointment because he never did.

But why would he? I had thrown him out of my apartment after he had given me some of the most amazing sex of my life. I was an ass. And now I was a lonely ass.

I started skipping my classes and my grades were taking a nosedive. I avoided all calls from my parents. I purposefully ignored Gracie and Vivian's efforts to reach me. I locked myself in my room and wallowed. One thing was for certain. I was a world-class moper.

The hours felt like weeks. The days felt like years. I missed him. I ached for him. But I was scared to do anything about it. Because I had shattered what was between us into tiny, itty-bitty slivers. My parents were right and I *was* a grade 'A' screw up.

"It smells like misery in here," Riley remarked, poking her head around the door of my bedroom. I was curled on my side, staring at my blank phone, willing it to ring. I mumbled something unintelligible. Riley sighed and ventured inside. She sat down on the edge of my bed and took my phone, placing it on my nightstand.

"When was the last time you showered?" she asked, scrunching up her nose. I gave myself a whiff. Man, I was ripe. Riley made a face. "I think it's time you start bathing again. Do society a favor," she said. I sat up and ran my fingers through my greasy hair.

"Fine," I huffed, getting up.

"And shave, Mays. You're growing a forest on your legs," Riley called after me as I went into the bathroom. The shower didn't make me feel better. But, Riley was right, I was bordering on gross.

I wrapped up in my robe and went into the kitchen where Riley handed me a turkey sandwich. "Eat," she commanded, leveling me a look that brooked no argument. I took the plate and held it limply in my hands. Riley rolled her eyes. "You lift the food and put it in your mouth. Like this." Riley took a bite of her own sandwich and chewed with exaggerated slowness.

Normally I would have snarked back at her. This time I just did as I was told and ate a few bites of the sandwich. My stomach rebelled after being empty for so long. "Jeesh, Maysie. You're a wreck." Riley said after watching me struggle to keep down the food.

"Thanks," I said sarcastically, putting the plate down on the counter.

Riley slammed her dishes into the sink and turned to give me a hard-core glare. "Why do you do this?" she asked angrily.

"What?" I asked indifferently.

"You know what. This." She waved her hand in my direction.

I shrugged, not bothering to answer. Riley groaned. "You're forcing me to use tough love," she muttered. She grabbed me by my shoulders and gave me a less than gentle shake. "Snap out of this. Stop turning into a zombie every time your life gets a little fucked up. It's sad and more than a little pathetic. First with that Chi Delta shit, now with Jordan. Enough!" she yelled in my face.

I didn't flinch. My face was impassive as I took her frustration and chucked it away. What did I care that she was angry? Everyone was angry with me. What else was new? Then Riley slapped me. I gasped in shock and lifted my hand to cover my stinging skin. "What the hell?" I snapped, my blood pressure rising.

"There it is! There's the Maysie Ardin I know." She pointed in my face. Crap, my cheek hurt.

"There is no reason to hit me," I bit out, feeling the first signs of emotion wash through me. After a week of being dead to all feeling but grief, it felt kind of good to be pissed.

Riley reached up and took a handful of my hair and gave it a yank. "Ow!" I yelped, pulling away from my psychotic roommate.

"What are you going to do about it? Huh?" Riley pulled my hair again and this time I shoved her.

"Stop it! Leave my fucking hair alone!" I yelled. Oh yeah, I was mad.

Instead of backing away, Riley threw her arms around me and gave me a big hug. She stepped back, grinning. "Nice to see you again. I've missed you," she said proudly, clearly pleased that she was able to get a response out of me. I couldn't help but smile at my whacked out friend.

"That was dirty. Even for you," I admitted gruffly, rubbing my throbbing scalp. The girl was a scrappy fighter.

"Desperate times call for desperate measures. I did the same thing to Jordan yesterday," she told me, smirking. My stomach flip-flopped at the mention of Jordan but I struggled to smile anyway.

"Oh yeah?" I had to ask. I longed for news of him. Just hearing his name was enough to give my heart a lift.

Riley pulled out a sleeve of chocolate chip cookies and crammed one in her mouth. "He's been moping around almost worse than you. His tips have been shit because all he does is bark at everyone. Hell, he almost took Damien's head off the other day for asking what time it was," Riley said, clearly irritated with the whole thing.

Well, that made me feel like crap warmed over. "I'm not sure what to say about that," I said miserably. Riley shook me again.

"You don't have to say anything. Just deal with it. Grow up and grow a pair. You and Jordan want to be together. I'm not sure what happened because you refuse to talk about it. But whatever it was, it's bull. Stop letting your stupid pride and whatever else it is, stop you from being with the person you want to be with," Riley practically shouted at me.

"It's not that simple," I started but Riley cut me off.

"It is that simple." She went back into my bedroom and came out with my cell phone. She shoved it in my hands. "Call him. Now!" she demanded, pointing at the phone.

"I can't. He won't want to talk to me!" I whined. Riley grabbed the phone from me and started scrolling down through my contacts.

"Did you not just hear me say he is as miserable as you are? He'll want to talk to you." She jabbed a few buttons and handed the phone to me. I could hear it ringing.

"Talk to him!" she said, gesturing for me to put the phone to my ear. I sighed; my heart pounding and I lifted it to my ear. What was I going to say? Dear god, what if he hated me?

Turns out it didn't matter because I got his voice mail. I hung up instead of leaving a message. "He didn't answer," I said gloomily, tossing the phone onto the counter.

"And you didn't leave him a message? Maysie!" she chastised.

"I am NOT leaving him some pathetic message. If he wants to talk to me, he'll see that I called and call me back. Case closed." My voice was hard and allowed no argument.

I sat chain smoking out on the balcony. The sun was just setting and the air had turned cool. My feet were propped up on the railing and I rocked backward in my chair on two legs. "Can I bum one?" a voice called from below.

I slammed my chair back down on the floor and leaned over the railing. Eli stood there, smiling up at me in that lazy way of his. He always looked like he had just rolled out of bed. I gave him a small wave of my fingers. "Hey," I called back.

"So, seriously, can I come up and have a smoke?" he asked, scratching the back of his neck. Um. "Come on, I'm nicking out down here," he pleaded.

"Then go buy your own," I replied. Eli laughed.

"Never givin' a guy a break. I promise to be good." His tone communicated that he wanted to be anything but good.

"Get up here," I sighed, before I could think longer about it. Eli grinned and disappeared. A few minutes later there was a light knock at my door. I let Eli in and he followed me back out to the balcony. I handed him my pack of cigarettes and he shook one out and balanced it between his lips before lighting it.

I tapped another smoke out and held it between my fingers. I glanced at Eli. He wasn't saying anything, only staring off into the darkening sky. It had been awhile since I had seen him. Things had always been so uncomplicated with him. None of the crazy drama that came with loving Jordan.

For a brief second, I sort of missed Eli and how simple my relationship had been with him. Even if it was lacking in any real depth and passion, it never made me feel like I was losing my mind. I was torn as to whether that was a good thing or not.

"You don't look so hot, Mays," Eli said after a while, watching me as I finally lit my cigarette. I took a long drag and slowly exhaled.

"Thanks," I said blandly. Eli grimaced.

"I didn't mean you're not still hot, because babe, you'll always be smokin.' It's just you seem different. I don't know... sad, maybe." When had Eli become so perceptive?

"Yeah, things have been a little chaotic lately," I admitted, flicking ash onto the concrete floor. Eli nodded.

"I understand chaos," he said shortly, not elaborating. I could tell there was a story there.

"Oh yeah?" I asked, probing a bit.

Eli took another drag from his cigarette. "Oh, yeah. Life is nothing but mess and fucking chaos. It wouldn't be life it wasn't," he said, the words hanging in the air. I cleared my throat. Not used to this deep side of Eli. I wasn't sure what to say.

His mouth quirked up on one side in the shadow of a smile.

"You and me, Mays. We don't know shit about each other. We started that thing between us without finding out what we were each made of. What made us tick. I thought you were a pretty, rich college chick just looking for a good time. And you saw me as some townie who you could fuck around with until something better came along." I was shocked at how bitter he sounded. Had I really hurt him when I called things off? I had no clue he actually cared about me as more than a piece of ass.

"Eli..." I started but he cut me off with a laugh.

"Sorry, babe. I don't mean to get all serious on you. What I'm trying to say is there's more to each of us than the other thought." He turned to face me and I had a hard time reading his expression in the newly descended darkness. The streetlights had come on and the world was still.

I looked at Eli. I mean, really looked at him. He was right, I knew nothing about him. I had judged him early on and hadn't changed my opinion in all the months since I had met him. But seeing him sitting there, with the cigarette dangling loosely from his fingers with their chewed down nails and callouses from playing the guitar, I knew that I had been extremely unfair to him. Because there was so much more to this good looking guy sitting beside me. And I felt a little disappointed that I wasn't going to be the girl to find out exactly what that *more* was.

"I'm sorry," I said simply, only able to say the basic truth. Eli's face was unreadable.

"You don't have to apologize, Mays. I knew all along that you could do a lot better than townie trash. No hard feelings," he said those words without an ounce of self-pity. He voiced them as stone cold fact. He believed them. Deeply.

"Eli. You *are not* townie trash. You are one of the most down to earth, laid back guys I know. And you deserved a hell of a lot more than to be tugged around by some selfish college girl who doesn't know her ass from her elbow," I told him truthfully.

Eli and I stared at each other for the length of a heartbeat and then he grinned. "Thanks, babe. But you don't need to blow smoke up my ass. But I appreciate it all the same." And just like that our moment of seriousness was at an end. I was sort of glad because I didn't know what to make of this new Eli. It had thrown me for a loop.

"So, where's your new man? I should probably head out if he's comin' by. I don't need him making good on all those threats he's thrown my way," Eli said, stubbing out his cigarette. I followed suit and put my butt in the ashtray. I rested my hands on my knees and closed my eyes.

"You don't have to worry about that. He won't be coming by. We broke up," I said a little breathlessly. It was hard to get those words out. The gaping wound, wrenched wide open. Eli frowned.

"You broke up? Why? I've got to say I'm surprised. With the way that dude threatened to rip my nut sack off, I know he's into you." Guys were so black and white sometimes.

"Yeah, well I broke up with him. There's been a bunch of stuff going on and, I don't know. I guess I let it get to me," I said, surprised I was talking about this with Eli of all people. But after our little moment earlier, I felt like there was a chance he may understand.

Or maybe not.

"Well that's fucking stupid, Mays," he said, short and to the point.

"Gee, thanks, Eli," I bit out sarcastically. He tapped his finger on the back of my hand to get me to look at him. So I turned my head and met his eyes.

"Seriously, Maysie. That's dumb. When you're into someone. I mean, really into them, who gives a flying fuck if there's shit going on? You man up, or woman up, and deal with it. You deal with it and then move on. You put your shit behind you and you stick together," he said emphatically. Wow, I had never seen Eli so passionate about something. And I knew he was speaking about something I didn't understand. Something that rang true for him, deep down.

But I was obstinate. "You don't know what was going on," I mumbled.

Eli snorted. "I don't need to know what's going on to see you've got your head so far up your ass you can't see straight."

My mouth dropped open and I didn't know if I should laugh or be insulted.

"You like the guy?" he asked me. I nodded.

"I think I love him," I said softly. How weird was this? Admitting I loved Jordan to my ex-boyfriend. My ex-boyfriend who as it turns out was way cooler than I thought.

"Well, shit, Mays. Then you need to fight for him. Don't give up on something like that. It doesn't come along very often. And when you find it, you hold on tight. You lock that shit down with an iron fist and you never, ever let go. Even when life tries to take it from you, you smack life upside its head like a little bitch and you keep on fighting for it. You hear me?" I couldn't help but laugh. That was some supremely strange advice. But I got what he was saying. It made sense.

"Thanks, Eli," I said, smiling at him and happy when I saw him dimpling back at me. Eli Bray, truth teller. I liked it.

"Sure thing, babe. You ever need a swift kick in the pants. Or need someone to take them off, then I'm your guy," He smirked and I smacked his arm.

"Why did we never talk like this when we were dating?" I had to ask him. Eli shrugged.

"I was more interested in getting you naked. Didn't feel the need to talk about anything," he said honestly. Okay, well there was that.

"I've got to get going. There's a party I'm heading out to," Eli said, ending our conversation. I followed him to my feet and we went inside. "Thanks for the smoke, Mays," he said, as we made our way to the door.

"Anytime, Eli. And thanks. For the talk," I replied, reaching out to squeeze his hand. Eli leaned in and put his arms around me, hugging me tightly to his chest. I relaxed into him and felt more at peace than I had in days. I wrapped my arms around him.

"Fight for it, babe," he whispered in my ear before placing a soft kiss to my forehead.

I should have known my feel good mood was short lived. And it was unfortunate that Jordan and Riley had to choose that exact moment to open the front door. But there you have it. Eli and I were hugging, saying our goodbyes and then the door swung open. Whatever Riley had been saying died on her lips as she looked from Eli and me to Jordan.

"Oh shit," she muttered.

I stepped back from Eli as though I had been shocked and stared, open mouthed at Jordan. He looked like he hadn't slept in days and hadn't shaved in just as long. He looked tired but he also looked ready to kill or maim, whichever he could do first.

"What the fuck?" Jordan growled, staring at Eli, the vein on the side of his neck starting to pop.

"Oh shit," Riley muttered again as she tried to back Jordan out of the apartment.

"Jordan," I whispered, scared by the look on his face. I peeked up at Eli and his jaw had tensed but he didn't move away from me. This looked bad. Really, really bad. Jordan clenched his jaw.

"I told you to keep your townie fucking ass away from my girl," Jordan told him in a scary voice.

"We were just talking," I said, but Jordan wasn't listening. Because he was too busy moving passed Riley and landing a punch straight on Eli's face.

I heard a sickening crunch before Eli went to the floor. "Jordan!" I screamed, trying to pull his arm. Jordan wrenched his arm from my fingers and leaned down and punched Eli in the face again. Eli twisted to the right and came up onto his feet, blood flowing from his nose. It looked crooked and I worried Jordan had broken it.

Eli's fist shot out and connected with Jordan's jaw, causing his head to whip around. "Stop it!" I screamed. Jordan launched at Eli again and all I could see was a flurry of fists and feet and blood.

"Riley, help me stop them!" I cried out as I moved to try and grab one of them. But I couldn't get close to them. I heard the sound of fists against skin and blood sprayed across the carpet.

"Stop it, or I'll call the cops!" Riley yelled. Eli and Jordan didn't stop. I started sobbing. What the hell were we going to do? They knocked over the coffee table, sent glasses shattering to the floor. Pictures were banged off the walls.

Riley pulled her phone out and was getting ready to dial 911, when Eli's cousin and girlfriend appeared in the doorway. "What the hell is going on in here?" Cicely asked, taking in the sight of Eli and Jordan hammering it out to the death.

"Is that fucking Eli?" Raymond demanded. I nodded.

Then Raymond was in there, pulling Jordan off of his cousin. Raymond was a big guy. He out-weighed Jordan by at least thirty pounds. He yanked on Jordan's arms and hauled him up to his feet. "Fucking stop it!" Raymond roared. For such a chilled out stoner, he was kind of intimidating.

Eli got to his feet, blood running down his face. I jumped in front of him and held my hands up. "Please, just stop," I begged, my eyes pleading with him. I looked over my shoulder at Jordan, who was shaking in his fury. Jordan had busted his lip and there was a nasty cut above his eye. His cheek was swollen and he watched me calm Eli down with a look that made me tremble.

"Get out of here, Eli," Raymond ordered. Eli hesitated, looking at me.

"I'm not sure I should leave Maysie with this fucking lunatic," he said, shooting a murderous look in Jordan's direction.

"Get the hell away from her, or I'll break your fucking arms!" Jordan yelled, struggling against Raymond's hold. Riley stood in the corner with Cicely, her face pale. Our eyes met and my friend mouthed, "I'm sorry."

I shook my head and turned back to Eli. "Just get out of here. I'm fine. I'm so sorry this happened." My shoulders slumped. Eli looked as though he wanted to put an arm around me but shooting a look at Jordan, he must have thought better of it.

"Okay, but you know how to find me if you need me," he told me.

"Thanks," I murmured. Eli started out the door and turned around before leaving.

"And that fighting thing...uh, yeah, maybe we should re-think that." He glared at Jordan and then with a final smile to me, he left.

"Now, can I let you go? Are you done?" Raymond asked Jordan, giving him a little shake. Jordan's shoulders were tense but he nodded. Raymond loosened his grip and Jordan yanked free, breathing heavily.

"We okay here?" Raymond asked me.

"Yeah, we're fine. Thank you so much," I whispered, my voice failing me. Raymond looked at me for a minute then he collected Cicely and left, closing the door on his way out.

Jordan stood in the middle of my trashed living room, taking deep breaths. I was in absolute shock with what had just happened. Why the hell was he even here? But his lip was bleeding pretty badly, so I took a hesitant step toward him.

"Jordan, let me clean you up," I suggested softly, not sure what he would do. I could see the fine tremors going through his body.

He wouldn't look at me. "I can do it," he said shortly and turned toward the bathroom without another word.

Once we heard the click of the bathroom door closing, I whipped around to look at Riley. "What is he doing here?" I hissed. Riley winced.

"I'm so sorry, I should have called. But he was at Barton's. And he had been drinking since early afternoon. He was a freaking mess. I just thought if I could get you guys to talk, then you could figure your shit out." Riley looked over her shoulder, to make sure the bathroom door was still closed.

Then she looked back at me. "I had no idea Eli would be here," she said in accusation.

I glared at her. "Eli was up here bumming a smoke. Then we got to talking. NOTHING happened," I said through gritted teeth. Riley sighed and pressed her fingers to her temples.

"That was crazy, Mays. Remind me in the future that drunk Jordan isn't a happy Jordan."

I groaned. "Great, now I have to go deal with angry, drunk Jordan. Thanks. Next time, *call,* before you stick your nose into my business," I said angrily. I knew Riley was just trying to help, but dear god, what a mess.

"I should go talk to him." I sighed. Riley nodded.

"I'll try and get the blood out of the carpet," she offered dryly. I left Riley to clean up the living room and I knocked softly on the bathroom door.

"Jordan, can I come in?" I said through the wood. I didn't get a response. So I just went on in. Jordan was standing at the sink, wiping his lip and jaw with a wet washcloth. He didn't look my way when I came in. In fact he didn't acknowledge me at all.

Not saying a word, I went to his side and gently took the cloth from his hand. I put my fingers on his face and carefully pulled him around to face me. Jordan's eyes went over my head, still not looking at me. I slowly put the cloth up to his lip and dabbed.

We were completely silent. My heart was beating so fast I thought it would break out of my chest. My hand shook as I rinsed the dried blood from Jordan's skin. His upper lip was starting to puff out and his cheek was red and swollen. I put the washcloth back under the tap and wet it with the cold water. Then I folded it into a small square and held it to Jordan's cheek.

We stood there for a while. Me holding the cloth to his face and Jordan refusing to look at me. "Jordan," I said quietly. He closed his eyes and then slowly reached up and pulled my hand away from his skin.

"Why, Maysie? Why the hell are you fucking with my head like this?" he asked in an agonized whisper. I opened my mouth to defend myself but he kept going, his eyes still closed, a frown marring his brow.

"I've been miserable. I can't sleep. I can't eat. I've wanted to pound down your door a million times. But I kept telling myself you just needed your space. That you'd sort your shit out. So I give you space. Then Riley tells me you're as miserable as I am. So I agree to come here. I had it all worked out in my head, Mays. I was going to come in here and beg you to take me back. Hell, I was going to get on my knees if I had to. Because all I know is that I can't be without you." I think I had stopped breathing.

Jordan finally opened his eyes and he leaned in close to me. His eyes were glassy and I could smell the alcohol on his breath. We were so close, our lips almost touching. I ached for him to put his mouth to mine. I've longed to be this close to him for a week now. But Jordan was angry. And it was clear; kissing was the last thing on his mind.

"And what do I find when I get here? My girl, with her fucking ex. And here I thought what we had was something special. When the first thing you do after kicking me to the curb is crawl back in bed with that douche bag." He snarled and I backed away.

"I *AM NOT* sleeping with Eli. He came up here to bum a cigarette. We started talking. He told me to stop being a stubborn ass and to win *you* back," I yelled, my voice ringing in the tiny room. Jordan flinched but I wasn't through. "I know I fucked up. I pushed you away because I'm a coward. I know that. But you know what you did tonight?" I asked him. Jordan looked confused.

"You made me feel like the slut everyone else has accused me of being. You came here and immediately assumed I was fucking Eli. You didn't ask me what was going on. Your mind went straight to that conclusion." Jordan's eyes cleared a bit and he looked contrite.

"Maysie..." He breathed out but I wouldn't let him finish his thought.

"This thing we have is ridiculous. Why in the world did we think we could start a relationship built on lies? Trust, which is so fundamental, is something we never had a chance to really build with each other. And I think it might be too late."

The anger left Jordan's face entirely. I watched as two tears slid down his face. Oh god, I didn't know if I could handle Jordan crying. His hands were clenched at his side, as though he were fighting with himself to not touch me.

"You're right, baby. We began out of something ugly. But what we became was something beautiful. I just wish I could make you see that." His voice broke and he took a deep breath. My throat closed up and I had to rein in my own tears otherwise I'd be sobbing like a child.

"But you only want to see the ugly, Maysie. And I can't change that. I wish just for once you would care more about what *you* think than what *everyone* else thinks. Why does the opinion of every other jackass on campus matter more than how you and I feel?" He reached up and wiped away his tears with the heel of his palm. Then he scrubbed his hand over his face. "This was a mistake. I've got to get out of here." He stumbled backwards and wrenched open the bathroom door.

I followed him out of the bathroom. "Wait, Jordan. Please," I begged, hurrying after him. Jordan came up short and turned to face me again.

"No, Maysie. You were right. We can't save this. This is broken and it can't be fixed. We've spent way too much time making each other feel like shit. This has to end now," he said sadly.

I saw Riley get up off of her knees, where she had been scrubbing the blood from the carpet. Damn it, the tears were streaming down my face now. "I'm so sorry, Jordan. I never meant to hurt you. I..."I trailed off, not sure what else I could say. Because this had become something so messed up that I didn't know what I could do to change it.

Jordan's face crumpled and he reached for me, crushing me against his chest and burying his face in my neck. "My God, Maysie. I just wish I didn't love you damn much," he cried brokenly, his face pressed against my skin. I had brought him to this. How could I have done this to someone I love? Here he was despairing over the fact that he loved me. That his love was in fact destroying him.

He should have stayed with Olivia. He would have been better off.

Then he pulled himself backwards, almost violently, and stumbled away from me. "Goodbye, Maysie," he said softly, his eyes clinging to my face. Then he turned to Riley. "I'm sorry about the mess," he said. Riley waved off his comment, clearly uncomfortable with what she had just witnessed.

And then he turned and walked out the door and out of my life. For good this time. Because I knew without a doubt that Jordan Levitt was done. There would be no begging or pleading for me to come back to him. What we had was over.

I stood there, stock still, unable to move. "You stupid, stupid, idiot," Riley muttered before resuming her task. I had nothing to say. So I ran back down the hall to my bedroom and slammed the door. Throwing myself on my bed, I burrowed under the covers, never wanting to get up again.

CHAPTER
28

icking yourself up after hitting rock bottom is a daunting task. One that I wasn't entirely sure I was capable of. After my relationship with Jordan tanked so miserably, I was stuck in this strange holding pattern. Caught in the vicious cycle of avoidance and denial, I tried to sleep my life away, refusing to get up for class and only rarely to eat.

After two weeks of this, Gracie, Vivian and Riley held an intervention. They each informed me that if I didn't snap out of it, they would personally call my parents and send me home with a one-way bus ticket.

That had done it. I may have been clinically depressed but hell if I'd be depressed at home. Heck, I'd probably off myself just to get out of seeing my parent's wonderful disapproval. So I sucked it up for my friends' sake and slowly rejoined the land of the living.

It was rough. It took time. But gradually I started reintegrating myself back into society. It was early November already. School would be breaking for Thanksgiving soon and then after that our month long winter holiday. I was planning to go home with Riley for Thanksgiving, not that my parents seemed to be bothered that I wouldn't be heading to South Carolina for the holidays.

I started to find things to look forward to again. I got my act together and started working my tail off in my classes. I think I spent more time in the library than anywhere else for the next few weeks. I stopped hiding out in my apartment. I stopped hiding altogether.

Sure, the looks hadn't stopped. I still heard the whispers but I was working really hard on not letting them drive me any more insane than they already had. Living in a fish bowl was uncomfortable but that was the price you pay for notoriety.

The Chi Delta girls continued to treat me as though I had the plague. And I knew for a fact that they were the biggest culprits in keeping the rumors circulating. I would have thought that after being disgracefully kicked out of my sorority and ending things with the resident heartthrob himself, it would have cooled things a bit. But Olivia and Milla still threw daggers whenever they could.

Trying to be the bigger person was quickly getting on my nerves. Whiny, pathetic Maysie had to take a hike. Because badass, low bullshit tolerance, Maysie was back in force.

I was taking my life back. One nasty look at a time.

Up first, the pretentious duo in my Shakespeare and Chaucer class, aka Cyndy and Aimee. We continued to have to work in our assigned groups for class assignments and they still treated me like I was something they scrapped off the bottom of their shoes. Their looks of disgust and pointed glares, while before would have made me want to curl into a ball, now just pissed me off.

Charlie had at least stopped his outright leering. But it did little to alleviate the awkwardness within the group. One afternoon we were working on a group essay that had to be completed by the end of class. I was writing down ideas the others were tossing around when Cyndy clicked her tongue in annoyance.

I looked up and raised my eyebrows. "Yes?" I asked less than patiently. Cyndy slid a look to Aimee who smirked.

"I didn't say anything about using the theme of time and seasons in the Knight's Tale. I think that's a little obvious for this class. You know, something you'd find in Sparks Notes." Aimee snickered at Cyndy's dig.

Charlie looked uncomfortable but didn't say anything. I gritted my teeth and held out my pen. "Would you prefer to write this stuff down? I mean since your ideas are so superior to mine," I said with sarcastic politeness.

334

Cyndy widened her eyes in mock surprise. "I'm not trying to be rude or anything, Maysie. I mean, I know that's probably the best you can come up with. But some of us take this class seriously and would like a passing grade." She gave me a patronizing smile.

I slowly put the pen down on my desk and folded my hands over the paper. I leveled both Cyndy and Aimee with a hard look. "Okay. It's no big mystery that you don't like me," I began.

Cyndy peered down her nose at me. "Yeah, no mystery there," she said condescendingly.

I cleared my throat. "Okay, let me try this again. I really don't give a fuck what you think about me. Sorry that I actually have a life that involves a bit more than sitting on my couch, eating ice cream and watching PBS while pontificating to my only friend about how morally superior I think I am. See, some of us live our lives and enjoy them. If you spent as much time actually getting to know people instead of judging them, you'd find that you're no better than anyone else. So you tell me why in the hell would I waste one second of my time worrying if two sad and lonely bitches liked me? And, let me make myself crystal clear. If you have nothing more to offer this group than your bad attitudes, then you can do Charlie and me a favor and keep your mouths shut. Because some of us would like to do our work and spend less time listening to your condescending bullshit." I gave them both a bright smile before turning to Charlie, who sat there with his mouth hanging open.

"What are your thoughts on the themes of season and time in the Knight's Tale?" I asked him batting my eyelashes. Charlie coughed and looked over at our fellow group members who seemed taken aback. I had to suppress the urge to laugh. But that would ruin the moment, so I pretended they weren't even there.

Charlie and I opened our books to the Canterbury Tales and started going through the text as I wrote down our ideas. And after a few minutes, Cyndy and Aimee joined in. They were still cool but their scathing comments were noticeably absent. We were able to finish up the essay in record time and when we were done Aimee tapped her pencil on my desk.

I looked up at her and she gave me a small smile. "Good job," she told me. It was on the tip of my tongue to reply with some sort of sarcastic comment, but I figured that would completely undo our tentative truce.

So I had smiled back and said "thanks."

After that, there were no more hateful comments during the Shakespeare/Chaucer class and I felt I had won a small victory. I started walking with my head just a little bit higher. Sure it did nothing to erase the gaping hole in my chest, but I stopped feeling like such a victim. Taking a proactive stance in my life was long overdue.

"Check out the grin on your face! What's the occasion?" Vivian asked as we sat down for lunch one day in the commons.

"Nothin'. Just feeling kinda good," I replied, sliding into my seat and opening my bottle of juice.

"Well that's a nice change," Gracie said, stirring ranch dressing into her salad.

"You know, there's really no point in eating a salad if you're going to dump 2,000 calories on top of it," I told her dryly.

Gracie took a huge mouth full and daintily dabbed her mouth. "Mmm. Delish," she said after swallowing. I rolled my eyes and returned to my lunch.

"So how are things at Chi Delta?" I asked, trying to ignore the accompanying knot in my stomach.

Vivian looked at me pointedly. "Do you really care?" she asked.

I laughed. "Not really, but thought I'd ask." I took a bite of my hamburger, ketchup oozing out of the sides, just the way I liked it. Gracie swirled her salad around in the bowl.

"Do you miss it at all?" she asked me quietly.

I took in a sharp breath. Did I miss it? Of course I did. I missed feeling like I was a part of something. I loved the community and the sisterhood. I missed having the belief that there were forty-five other girls who would have my back. Even if that had turned out to be a lie, I missed the illusion of it.

But I sure as hell didn't miss the cattiness and the backstabbing. And the hatred disguised as friendship. When I thought about it like that, the negatives far outweighed the positives. "Can't say that I do, ladies," I answered truthfully. Gracie sighed.

"Yeah, I figured you'd say that. You know, I'm thinking about withdrawing," she said, shocking the hell out of me. Gracie was Miss Sorority. She loved it. I couldn't imagine her *not* being in Chi Delta. It had come to define so much of who she was, that I worried about her should she no longer have it.

"Why would you do that?" I asked in confusion. Vivian made a noise.

"Oh please. Since you were kicked out, Gracie and I have become Chi Delta's Most Wanted. Sure, they're still nice to our faces, but Milla has made it a point to make us feel very unwelcome." I hated this for them and it stirred up all those guilty feelings.

"I'm so sorry guys," I told them softly. Gracie and Vivian each reached out and took one of my hands.

"Don't you dare be sorry, Mays. This whole thing has just shown me who my true friends are. I don't think I can stomach paying dues to be a part of a group that will attack and humiliate one of their own the way they did you. It doesn't sit well." I squeezed her hand. "Plus, you're my girl. If you jump, I jump." I laughed, a deep, from the belly laugh. Damn Gracie and her ridiculous Titanic obsession.

Vivian looked over my shoulder and froze. I looked behind me and my heart leapt up into my throat. Jordan walked in with a few of his Pi Sig brothers and got in line for his lunch.

It had been a few weeks since our messy break up and this was the first time I had seen him. It was like a fist to the gut. He looked amazing. Gone was the tired, miserable looking guy who had shown up at my apartment drunk and desperate to win me back. The man across the room looked like his old, confident and charming self.

I couldn't look away. Where he went, my eyes followed. After getting his lunch he headed toward the Pi Sig table, which was beside the normal Chi Delta table. I noticed with irritation, that Olivia and Milla were there.

Jordan sat on the end, Olivia on the other side of the aisle. She waved and smiled at him in that sickeningly sweet way of hers. Jordan nodded but otherwise didn't acknowledge her. Much to my sadistic delight.

"Hmmm, I'm surprised he's eating over there," Vivian said, more to herself. I turned back around to look at her.

"Why?" I asked, curious. Vivian tore apart her brownie and placed it into tiny piles.

"Well, it's rumored that he's quitting Pi Sig. He hasn't been staying in the house for weeks and hasn't been to a mixer since the one when school started," Vivian answered.

"Hmm, well I don't take a whole lot of stock in rumors, Viv," I said, stabbing my hamburger with my fork. Gracie made a face at my lunch.

"Do you have to mutilate it?" she asked, pulling my fork out of my sandwich.

"But what Vivian said is true. A bunch of the Pi Sigs were bitching about it last week. Talking about how Jordan came into their chapter meeting, saying he would pay his rent up until the end of the month and then he was out. Said something about moving in with Garrett. And that he would be withdrawing from the fraternity. It's caused quite an upset," Gracie reported, bunching up her napkin and dropping it in her empty salad bowl.

He was dropping out of Pi Sig? I wasn't entirely surprised by that. He had been disenfranchised with the whole thing for a while. But still. It seemed kind of sudden.

I looked over my shoulder again and watched Jordan as he engaged in conversation with his soon to be ex-brothers. As if feeling my eyes on him, he looked up and met my gaze from across the room. I wanted to look away, but I couldn't.

One heartbeat.

Two heartbeats.

Three.

Then he looked away.

That hurt. So damn much. Vivian and Gracie were looking at me knowingly but politely didn't comment. When it was time to leave, we unfortunately had to pass behind the Chi Delta and Pi Sig's table. So much for riding under the radar.

One minute I was walking with my tray, the next I was falling forward, my tray flying from my hands as I ended up sprawled out on the floor, my face having made painful contact with the hard linoleum. "Maysie!" Gracie gasped as she and Vivian helped me to my feet.

I heard riotous laughter and realized both the Pi Sig and Chi Delta tables were laughing their asses off. All of them, except for Jordan. His eyes simmered with heat but he was otherwise unreadable. I brushed off my pants and picked up my tray.

"Oops. You okay?" Milla asked, snickering. Stupid bitch had tripped me. Oh, that was it. I took a deep breath, the laughter ringing in my ears. Then I looked right at Milla.

"Oh, I'm just fine. Wish I could say the same for you," I said sweetly.

Milla frowned, her lips screwed up in a hateful smirk. "And what is that supposed to mean? Is this more whore talk that the rest of us can't even begin to understand?" she mocked and the group laughed even louder.

I dropped my tray onto the Chi Delta table. Milla laughed again. "What are you going to do? Jump me like you did Olivia? Because sweetie, you'll find *I* fight back. To the death," she dropped her voice, her eyes hard.

"I have no desire to fight you, Milla. In fact, I think leaving you alone is the best punishment there is." Milla snorted and Olivia frowned. I leaned in over the table and smiled at the girl who had made it her mission to destroy me. I knew without a doubt that the rumors began and ended with her. She was the one who had those posters hung up all over campus. And her entire motivation was jealousy. She was really one of the saddest people I had ever met.

"God, it must be so exhausting pretending that you like her. That you're her friend." I said quietly, never dropping my eyes from Milla's.

"What?" she scoffed, though her eyes darted sideways to Olivia, who was particularly quiet.

"I know you've been trying to get in Jordan's pants for years. And he has rejected you each and every time. I've also heard how you would go to all of his shows, going to Garrett's parties. Even going so far as to fuck every single one of his band mates, hoping he would pay you some attention. That you liked to call out his name while screwing their brains out. And you have the gall to call me a slut?" I asked in disbelief. Milla's jaw clenched and she started breathing heavily. Her neck flushed a bright red.

I leaned in closer, my comments for Milla and Milla alone. "But the problem with that Milla is he never wanted you. After all of your efforts, he never looked your way. You've always hated Olivia for having the guy you've wanted for years. And then you hated me for the same reasons." I saw Olivia pull in a sharp breath out of the corner of my eye but I didn't move my focus from Milla, who was fuming.

"No, bitch. I hate you because you are a backstabbing whore," Milla spat out. I laughed. A real and true laugh.

"At least I don't pretend to be someone's best friend the entire time I'm scheming to steal their boyfriend. You are a sad and pathetic person. Starting false rumors about me and Jordan, hanging those posters all over campus. Doing whatever you could to get me booted from Chi Delta. And it worked. You got to me. I know you're proud about that." Milla's chest puffed out.

"Damn straight I'm proud. You were a cancer. You needed to be taken out," she sneered.

"Milla!" Olivia said sharply but Milla didn't hear her, her eyes glued to mine.

"But the thing is. None of that made a bit of difference because Jordan still doesn't want you. He will never want you. And that eats you up inside. Olivia is more popular. People love her. And Jordan loves me. She and I have everything you have always wanted. But Milla, people like you will never win. Because in order to win, you have to get something in the end. And you have nothing. No guy, no real friends, no self-respect. And I don't give a fuck if you like me. Or if the Chi Delts think I'm the biggest whore this side of the Appalachian Mountains. I am done worrying about what everyone thinks about me. Because all that counts is that *I* like me. So the rest of you can go to hell." I straightened and picked up my tray. Damn, that felt good.

I was just about to make my grand exit when Jordan got to his feet. "Maysie, wait!" he called out, stopping me. Then he turned back to the table full of Pi Sigs and Chi Delts.

"The bunch of you make me sick. You've been torturing Maysie for months. Making her life miserable. And no one. Not a one of you did a thing to stop it. All because some stupid bitch filled your head with a bunch of lies," Jordan said loudly.

I realized the commons had become quiet. We were the focus of every pair of eyes in the room. Jordan looked down at Milla and Olivia. "Maysie's right, I would never touch you. You disgust me," he sneered at Milla and for the first time her face started to crumble. I almost felt bad for her. Almost.

Then Jordan turned to Olivia. "And you. How could I be so wrong about someone? I thought you were better than this," he said with obvious disappointment and Olivia's eyes brimmed with tears. But Jordan wasn't done. Finally he turned to the table full of his brothers.

"And the bunch of you can seriously fuck off. I told you I was done with Pi Sig. Well I'm done as of right now. Fuck the lot of you and your hypocritical bullshit. You sit around spouting brotherhood. You don't know the first thing about being a brother. Or being a man. Because a real man sure as hell would never have disrespected a woman the way each and every one of you has disrespected Maysie."

Jordan climbed up onto his chair and addressed the rest of the room. "And if the rest of you can't do more with your lives than talk shit about someone you don't even know; then maybe you need to look a little closer at yourselves and ask what kind of person does that make you? And if I hear of one more person saying something derogatory about Maysie Ardin, you'll need to take it up with me."

You could have heard a pin drop, the room was that quiet. My eyes widened as Jordan climbed down and looked at me. "I'm sorry Maysie. I should have done that a hell of a lot sooner." And with that he picked up his bag and tray and left.

I looked back down at the table where my former sisters were sat, looking shell shocked. Well, damn. "Okay then, have a nice day," I said and turned on my heel and left. Gracie and Vivian followed me outside.

"That was the most amazing thing I have ever seen!" Vivian shrieked, hugging me. Gracie was grinning from ear to ear.

"You freaking rocked! I wish I had half your courage! And, god, the way Jordan stood up for you in front of everyone? That was the most romantic thing I have ever seen," Gracie gushed.

I smiled wanly, scanning the quad, looking for him. But he was gone. And I knew he may have stood up for me, but that didn't change the way things were between us. Not a damn thing.

CHAPTER
29

"*I know* he's off tonight. It's safe to go to Barton's. Not that you should be avoiding him like you're in middle school or something," Riley snarked, pulling me by the arm up to the front door of Barton's. I hadn't been inside my former place of employment for months. Not since my first, magical date with Jordan. I should have known this place was the beginning of the end for us.

Too much bad mojo. Maybe I should suggest to Moore to let me smudge the place with some sage or something. "So the place is Jordan Levitt free. Meaning we can commence in getting ridiculously drunk," Riley singsonged, shoving me through the door.

Walking inside was like a bad case of deja vu. My eyes drifted over to the bar out of sheer habit. Lyla and some other guy were slinging drinks to the customers. My eyes caught sight of Gracie and Vivian, who were waving us down. Jaz hurried up and gave her normal squeally greeting. After being embraced far too tightly, she let me know she'd join us as soon as she got off.

I looked at Riley who shrugged. "I thought you could use a good old fashioned girls' night," she said, seeming a little embarrassed at being caught doing something thoughtful. I grinned and wrapped an arm around her shoulders.

"You're good people Riley Walker," I told her.

"Shh. Don't tell anyone please," she threw back but smiled anyway.

We made our way to the bar and I was stopped every few feet by the other employees who acted genuinely happy to see me. I felt a distinct pang in my stomach and realized I missed working here. When we got to the bar, Gracie got up and gave me a big hug. "Hey girl. Guess what?" she asked, bouncing up and down.

"I don't know. What?" I asked, laughing at her excitement.

"Viv and I withdrew from Chi Delta today. We went apartment hunting earlier in the week and found a place a few streets over from you. Vivian's staying around next year, wanted to take a year off, so I won't have to search for a new roommate when she graduates. Isn't that awesome?" Gracie asked jovially.

"Wow. Um, I can't believe you did that. But if you're happy, I'm happy," I told her and Gracie nodded.

"Oh yeah, we were so done. The tension is even worse now that Olivia and Milla are on the outs," Gracie said, picking up her beer from the bar and taking a swig. Gracie had told me that Olivia and Milla hadn't really spoken since my outburst last week. I wasn't sure what went down between the two of them, but they were keeping their distance from each other. But I really didn't care.

I looked over at Vivian and noticed she was sitting super close to a guy with shaggy, dark hair. His back was to me but I could tell by Vivian's body language that she liked him. I leaned against the bar and waved to Lyla who came over. She reached over the counter and gave me a hug. Wow, I was getting hugged all over the place tonight. Good times.

"Maysie, girl! We've missed you around here!" Her eyes sparkled at me and I knew she was referring to one particular person missing me. I waved my hand in dismissal.

"Oh, I think you guys have survived just fine without me."

"Don't be so sure," she said wiggling her eyebrows as she slid a Sam Adams toward me. I didn't say anything, and instead drank half of my beer in one gulp. Damien was still on shift but he came down periodically to give Riley a kiss or to say hello. They had morphed into one of those toothache couples. So sweet, it was borderline nauseating.

Vivian and her mystery guy had yet to acknowledge our

presence so Gracie, Riley and I proceeded to drink our weight in beer. We were laughing with Lyla and the new bartender Jay, who had just started a few weeks ago, when Vivian jumped out of her seat and finally came over to us.

"Hey chicas!" she giggled. I patted the hand that she had thrown over my shoulder.

"Hey yourself. Having fun I see." I teased.

"Yeah." She let out with a self-satisfied grin. The guy had turned around and my stomach dropped. It was Cole. Generation Rejects' lead singer. Oh, just freaking fantastic.

"Hey, Maysie," Cole said, tipping his drink in my direction. I inclined my head in his direction.

"Nice to see you again, Cole," I said, though less than happily. Cole smiled in a way that said he knew exactly what I was thinking.

"We've missed seeing you around. Don't be a stranger." Cole said sincerely as Vivian came back around to sit beside him again. He put a hand on her thigh and she lit up.

"Yep." I responded, letting my mouth pop around the word.

Gracie looked confused. "Cole's the lead singer for Generation Rejects," I explained and her eyes brightened with understanding. We fell into an awkward silence. What was there to say? Oh, hey sorry I fucked over your friend royally...wanna be best buddies?

"So, you girls coming to our show next weekend?" Cole asked, tossing his hair out of his eyes.

I frowned. "I thought you guys weren't playing any gigs for a while." I stated.

Cole shook his head. "Yeah, that was the plan, but Moore is relentless. So we finally caved. Plus he pays out the ass," Cole said, tossing the rest of his drink back.

"Oh, that sounds like fun. We'll be there," Vivian said, a little too enthusiastically. I swallowed my groan.

"Uh, yeah. I don't know," I said noncommittally. Cole gave me a sweet smile. He really was good looking. I could understand why Vivian was having a hard time keeping her hands to herself.

"Oh, come on Maysie. You need to be there. We've been working on some new material that I bet you'd love," Cole said, his eyes saying something else. I just didn't know what.

"Come on, Mays. It'll be fun," Gracie pleaded. My eyes rolled to the ceiling.

"*Yeah*, sure. Sounds great." My friends squealed and I tried not to mutter something rude under my breath.

And that's how I found myself a week later, sitting in the exact same seat, with Riley on one side and Gracie on the other. Waiting for Generation Rejects to start their set. Vivian was off with Cole. They had apparently started dating and had been together every day the past week. I have to say I was pretty shocked by that turn of events. Given what a male slut Cole had a reputation for being. But they seemed pretty into each other, so I reserved judgment.

My eyes darted around the restaurant; looking for the one person I dreaded seeing most. So far, I hadn't found him. Riley squeezed my knee. "Settle down. It'll be cool," she reassured me.

I took a deep breath. "Yeah, sure it will," I said less than convincingly.

Jaz and Damien had just gotten off of their shifts and crowded around us, waiting for their drinks. "I love hearing these guys play! I'm so excited!" Jaz chirped, her good mood doing nothing to dispel my bad one.

"Yeah, they put on a good show," I responded, staring into my whiskey sour.

I was going for the harder stuff this evening. Figured I'd need it.

The crowd was thick and the noise in Barton's was deafening. I could see Garrett and Mitch setting up their amps. Vivian sat on top of one of the rigs, talking to Cole, who was pressed against her, his hands on her upper thighs. Still no Jordan.

I tried not to fixate about it. But it was impossible when I knew any moment he'd show up and shred my heart to bits all over again. "Oh, Maysie! I forgot to tell you. We move into our apartment next weekend. I'd really appreciate it if you could help," Gracie pleaded, batting her eyelashes. I laughed at her.

"Of course I'll help. No need to waste your flirting skills on me. You know I'll do it without all the cuteness," I joked.

"Awesome. Vivian wants to have a housewarming party that night. Just a few people. Nothing crazy. But it should be fun." Gracie started telling Riley and me about the new couch they had just purchased and the green and gold color scheme they had planned for the living room.

I tried to pay attention. I really did. But suddenly the air seemed to leave the room and I knew *he* had arrived. The skin on my back prickled and I discreetly looked over my shoulder. And there he was. His hair was growing out and for the first time I could tell that his dark hair was sort of wavy. It looked good on him. Too good.

He was lugging his drum kit through the door, his arm muscles bulging under his t-shirt. Riley handed me a napkin. "Wipe the drool," she muttered and I swatted her hand away.

"I am not drooling. Shut up," I hissed, looking away, even though it was almost physically painful to do so.

Why was I here? This had to be some form of masochism. I was inflicting unnecessary torture on myself. I was finally in a semi-decent place. It wasn't like Jordan had made any effort to talk to me. That part of my life was over.

So why was I sitting there, in Barton's waiting for him to reach into my chest and rip my heart out all over again?

"Breathe, Mays. It's all good," Gracie whispered, tapping her fingernails on my glass.

"Yeah. All good," I murmured.

The lights went down; Vivian rejoined our group and Cole introduced them. The crowd went wild and my body pulsated with the first beats of Jordan's drums. His draw was intense and instinctual. He literally called out to my body and every inch of me answered.

It seriously sucked.

"We are so happy to be back here at Barton's!" Cole yelled into the mic, after playing a Tool cover. Jordan continued to keep up a steady beat. Cole grinned into the teaming crowd. "I wanted to announce our plans to go on tour next year. Our man Piper has agreed to saddle up with us full time after he graduates! We're gonna hit up places up and down the east coast! You'll be able to find the full tour schedule on our website!" Jordan twirled his drumsticks in his hands and hit out a quick successive beat.

Wow. So Jordan had decided to do it. I was proud of him. Really proud of him. He had stuck to his guns and gone after what he wanted. I didn't think I could love him any more than I did just then.

"And now it's time to unveil a new song our drummer has been working on for a while now. Take it away, man!" Cole flourished his arm out in Jordan's direction and the crowd went quiet. I watched as Jordan closed his eyes. His face was dripping with sweat and he seemed to be steeling himself. I knew that look of concentration on his face. It was the same look he wore whenever he was about to say something important.

I think my heart stopped in that moment. Riley reached down and grabbed my hand, squeezing tightly. Jordan finally opened his eyes and looked out into the crowd of people. He seemed to be looking for something. Or someone.

And I knew when he found it. Because it was the moment his eyes found mine. He leaned into the microphone by his side. "This is for the girl who always runs away," he said softly, his eyes never leaving me. The crowd went wild.

What do I have to do to make you stay?
What should I say to make you mine?
When will you stop running, girl?
I'm watching for the sign.
You build me up and break me down
Over and over again
I crave your seductive destruction
Even as I long for your pain.
But it wasn't all bad was it?
Things weren't always this way.
You filled the space in my empty heart,
Your eyes told me things your lips would never say.
So here I am, watching you run.
I wish you'd stop trying to leave.

How easy you forget
that you're my reason to breathe.
Stop running, girl
It won't always feel like this,
Stop running, girl
Stop running.
We could have our tomorrow
We could have our dreams,
My future is wrapped up in you,
Even as my heart bleeds.
Stop running, girl.
I've got nowhere to go.
I'll wait until forever
I promise to take this slow.
How easily we tore each other down
It's hard to take it all back
Feeding those fears and regrets,
I'm all alone in the black.
Stop running, girl.
It won't always feel like this.
Stop running, girl.
Stop running, girl!
Stop running away!

Jordan's voice rose in a scream as the tears ran uninhibited down my face. My hand throbbed from the vice grip Riley had on it. Jordan's voice trailed off as he slammed a frantic beat on his drums. The song seemed to tear his heart out and I felt my own being ripped free and flopping on the floor.

My fucking god! He'd written me a song. And what a song! All of his heartache and grief rolled through the lyrics and I was at a complete loss. When it was over, the crowd voiced their approval. Then the band launched quickly into another song.

I was breathing heavily and I wiped at the drying tears on my face. "Shit, Mays. That was incredible," Gracie yelled into my ear. I nodded, rubbing my nose with a napkin. Riley let go of my hand and I felt the pins and needles as circulation resumed.

"You need to talk to him. You can't leave things the way they are," Riley urged. I didn't say anything. I couldn't argue, I couldn't agree. I couldn't freaking do anything. So I watched the rest of Generation Rejects' set and I knew my future hung in the balance.

When they were finished, the bar started to settle down. Most people left and those still there were either drunk off of their asses and waiting for a ride, or Barton employees. The band had broken down their equipment and loaded it up in Garrett's van.

They joined the group at the bar. Cole went straight to Vivian, though he stopped by me first. "Did you like the new stuff, Maysie?" he asked, winking at me. I was way too sober for this. I wished I possessed some serious liquid courage right then. But honesty was all I could give.

So, I nodded. "Yeah, it was beautiful." Cole patted me on the back.

"It sure was," he agreed and moved on to Vivian.

Jordan came up to the other side of the bar. There were at least a dozen people separating us. He gave Lyla a hug as she handed him a beer. His co-workers congratulating him on the upcoming Rejects tour quickly surrounded him and telling him how great the show was. Moore came out from the back and locked the front door, turning the little get together into a full-blown party. The kitchen crew was trying to make a beer bong out of a colander and plastic tubing. Jaz and Evian were climbing up on the bar to dance to a bad cover of Britney Spears' Hit Me Baby One More Time.

Moore and Jordan were talking off to the side. The manager had clasped Jordan's shoulder and I could see Jordan smiling. God how I had missed that smile.

I was coerced into playing a rowdy game of beer pong with Rozzi, Tito and Cal. I ended up knocking over more cups of beer than actually drinking. Dina tried to talk me into going out back and sharing a joint with her but I passed.

Then the night started coming to a close. Not once did Jordan approach me. After unloading his heart in that mind-blowing song, he stayed as far away from me as he could. I watched him way more than I wanted to. He had spent the rest of the night talking to his friends as well as laughing with Riley and Damien. I had no idea he had become so friendly with my best friend. She had never mentioned it. But I could see that they had become good friends. And that made me jealous. Because he and I had nothing. Not even a friendship to show for all of it.

Around two in the morning, Moore kicked everyone out. There were more than a few grumbles but everyone filed out good-naturedly, some more drunk than others. Gracie and Vivian were wasted and Cole offered to see them back to campus. Riley was heading over to Damien's place so she handed me her car keys and said she'd see me in the morning.

"Be smart, Mays. For once," she told me shortly, her eyes darting to Jordan, who was helping Cole get Vivian in the car. I nodded and she smiled encouragingly before heading off with her boyfriend.

Garrett was trying to get Gracie to the band's van. She kept falling down, laughing and I could see he was getting annoyed. I hurried over and helped him get her up. "There you are, Maysie!" she squealed, kissing me loudly on the cheek.

"Yep, here I am," I said, trying to haul her up to her feet.

"Jordan loves you, Maysie! No one has ever written me a song before. You are soooo lucky!" she slurred. My face flamed with embarrassment and I quickly looked over at Jordan, but he was still struggling to get Vivian situated. She was making things pretty difficult because she kept grabbing Cole around the neck and trying to pull him into the back seat with her.

Gracie rolled her head onto Garrett's shoulder. "Will you write me a song, Grady? Pretty please?" Gracie hiccupped and I grimaced. Garrett finally gave up and lifted Gracie in his arms, carrying her to the van.

"It's Garrett, sweetheart. As for the song, we'll have to see if you puke in my car first." Gracie giggled as he got her in the back of the vehicle. He threw me a quick smile before attending to my friend.

Finally, everyone was situated and ready to go. "You coming, Jordan?" Mitch yelled from the back. Jordan hadn't looked at me once. Hell, he acted as though I wasn't even there. So I was surprised when he shook his head.

"Nah. Maysie'll give me a ride." I will? Cole leaned out of the open window.

"Is that cool with you, Maysie?" he asked.

My eyes darted to Jordan, but his back was still to me. "Uh, yeah. That's fine. I'll see he gets home," I said.

Cole winked at me again. "Be good you two," he called as he drove away.

We stood silently in Barton's parking lot, watching the lights flicker out as Moore closed up. Jordan started walking toward Riley's car. "Well, let's get going," he said indifferently.

What the hell?

I had to jog to catch up with him. He waited patiently while I unlocked the doors and he got into the passenger seat. I went around to the other side and got in. "You okay to drive?" he asked, still not freaking looking at me.

"Yeah, I'm fine," I shot back.

"Good. I'm staying at Garrett's," he responded shortly.

I flushed with the beginnings of my anger. What was he playing at? I hated that I couldn't read him. Not like I used to be able to. He stared resolutely out of the windshield. I put the keys in the ignition and turned the car on. I was about to put the car into reverse when his voice stopped me.

"Did you like the song?" he asked, his voice sounding sort of funny. I breathed in through my nose.

"It was beautiful, Jordan. I loved it," I told him truthfully. Some of the tension seemed to melt away from his body.

"I'm glad," he murmured. I stared at his profile, willing him to say something else. When it was obvious he wasn't going to, I figured I'd give starting a conversation a shot.

"Congrats on the tour. I'm glad you decided to do it," I offered. The corner of Jordan's mouth twitched upwards in a smile.

"Thanks," he said. And then the silence again.

Okay, this was getting beyond ridiculous. "Was there a particular reason you wanted me to take you home?" I asked, sick of the song and dance we were playing around each other.

Jordan's hand came up and I watched him rub his hand through his much longer hair.

"I don't know, Mays," he let out in a rush.

"You don't know?" I asked incredulously. And then he finally turned his head and looked at me. His eyes crackled with a fire that threatened to melt me on the spot.

"No, I *do* know. I just don't know that you're ready for it," he said gruffly, not loosening his gaze. I swallowed.

"Tell me, Jordan. Please," I pleaded quietly. Jordan was breathing heavily in and out through his nose. His neck was tense and he started clicking his tongue ring on his teeth.

"Why, Maysie? What more do you need me to tell you? Haven't I already handed my fucking guts to you on a platter? What else do you need to hear?" he asked me angrily. Jordan reached out and gripped my chin in his strong fingers.

"Do you need to hear that I haven't stopped missing you for one single minute since we broke up? Do I have to tell you that my heart hurts with how much I love you?" He leaned in close to my face and both of us began to breathe erratically as the air heated up between us. My skin pulsated beneath his fingers and I wanted so desperately to dive into this heady feeling he unleashed inside of me.

"I could tell you how much I want to kiss you. That I want your taste in my mouth, on my tongue. That I want to plunge so deep inside you that it will take me a lifetime to climb back out." OH. MY. GOD!

Jordan leaned in further until his lips brushed against mine. "You have taken my heart, every inch of me and you crushed it, Maysie. I don't know that I have anything else to give you that you don't already have." I blinked back the tears that threatened to spill over. In that moment, I seized what was in front of me. No more hiding what I was feeling. No more worrying about anything but this beautiful man with his heart in his eyes. I had learned since we were apart that life was too short to live with so much regret. And if I let him go now, I knew the rest of my days would be spent knee deep in the worst regret I could imagine.

"I'm so sorry, Jordan. I've been such an idiot. I love you. So much." I let out in a liquid gush. Jordan's face stilled and his eyes roved over my face.

"What?" he whispered, his breath dancing across my lips.

Then I realized he had been waiting to hear me say those words to him. He had told me he loved me before but I had never said it back. "I love you, Jordan. With everything that I am. And I'm sick of wasting time until we can be together. I don't give a shit about anything or anyone but you and me." And just like that, Jordan's face relaxed and contentment spread across his face.

He rubbed his nose against mine. "What the hell took you so long?" he asked before crushing his mouth to mine. At the first touch of his tongue I knew I had come home. Jordan cupped my face in his hands and pulled away. "Promise me, Maysie. No more running. Even when things get rough. Even when we get scared, we'll talk it out. We'll go to each other before fucking it all up. Promise me!" he demanded.

I brought my hands up and held his face as he was holding mine. "I promise to stop being a coward and deal with life as it comes. As long as we're together, I think I can handle anything. You are my life, Jordan. And I'm ready to start living it." Jordan grinned and plundered my mouth again, tasting me, teasing me, leaving me panting for more.

"You're not going to Garrett's. You're coming home with me," I murmured against his lips. Jordan's fingers combed through my hair before gripping the back of my neck in his warm, possessive hold. A gesture that let me know I was his. For always.

"Take me home, woman. We have some catching up to do," Jordan said with a grin and that's exactly what we did.

EPILOGUE
Six Months Later

"**B**aby, I think a small village could survive off the shit you've packed in here." Jordan mused, staring into my bulging suitcase. It lay open on my bed as I added dresses, shorts and shoes to the mix.

"We're going to be gone for two weeks, Jordan. I have to be prepared," I reasoned, throwing in another pair of flip-flops. Now it was on to accessories.

"You know, they have stores in Mexico. If you need something you could always get it there." Jordan put his hands behind his head and smirked as I started sifting through my earrings. I looked over my shoulder at my too sexy for his own good boyfriend and rolled my eyes.

"Don't mess with the Maysie Ardin system," I warned. Jordan chuckled, but left me to it.

It was three days after Jordan's graduation and we were heading to Cancun for two weeks, a graduation gift from his parents. They had been majorly pissed when Jordan explained to them his plans to take a year off and tour with the Rejects. His father had threatened to disown him. But after taking some time to cool down, they had reached a truce. I knew this surprised the hell out of Jordan. He had expected more of a fight.

But his parents weren't as bad as he made them out to be. He had taken me home with him for spring break. I had fallen in love with his mother, who was the exact opposite of my own mom in every way that counted. His dad, while a bit more reserved, clearly loved his son and wanted what was best for him. Jordan was pretty damn lucky.

My parents on the other hand maintained their staunch disapproval of all my life choices. But I had learned that I didn't really care what they thought anymore. That I was officially living my life for me. And that was hugely liberating.

So, we were gearing up for our vacation. I was looking forward to enjoying some sun and cocktails before coming back to work two jobs for the rest of the summer. I had been hired back at Barton's and I would be starting an internship at the local newspaper in July. So I would be pretty busy.

Jordan hooked his finger around the string of my bikini top and held it up. "Oh, please tell me you're bringing this," he pleaded. I walked over to him and grabbed it from his hand while kissing him soundly on the mouth.

"Don't you worry, baby, I have plenty of surprises for you." My eyebrows rose and Jordan groaned.

Then his arms were around me and he had yanked me on top of him. "Jordan! I have to pack!" I squealed as he started to kiss the skin on the side of my neck.

"You need a Levitt break," he murmured, tracing his tongue along the curve of my ear and grabbing my ass with his hands. I shuddered as he pressed me against his hard erection and I couldn't help but wiggle against it, trying to feel the friction between my legs. My fingers went up into his hair. His lush dark hair now fell in messy waves around his forehead. He had changed the barbell in his eyebrow to a hoop and last month and gotten his lip pierced. That was new and took some getting used to. I had stressed when he had first gotten it about getting it caught when we kissed. But I had quickly learned that I loved it. The combination of lip and tongue ring was particularly delicious when we were engaged in certain activities.

I sank into his body, ready to forget about packing for a while, when his foot kicked my suitcase off the bed, sending my stuff sprawling all over the floor. "Jordan!" I yelped, pushing myself off of him. "Now I have to pack the damn thing over again," I complained, picking up my clothes off of the floor.

Jordan joined me, going straight for my panties. "I'll take care of these for you," he teased, holding up a black thong. I grabbed my underwear.

"Just stay out of the way, please," I said nicely, batting my eyelashes. Jordan laughed and returned to the bed.

It still sort of blew my mind that things were so great with Jordan and me. Particularly after the way we started, we drifted into this fantastic relationship. Sure, we still had our bumps. Each of us was still learning to deal with our jealousy issues. Jordan had a tendency to be a bit overbearing in that regard, but he was trying. Just as I was trying to not let any outside bullshit interfere with this great thing we had going.

After Jordan and I got back together, it wasn't immediate sunshine and roses. I still had to suffer through the nasty looks and whispers. But the longer we were together; the less and less I noticed it. I never spoke to any of the Chi Delta girls, particularly since Vivian and Gracie had left. I occasionally saw Olivia around campus, but she was staying pretty quiet. I realized quickly that Milla was nowhere around.

Then came the news, via Vivian, who still spoke to some of her former sisters that Milla had taken a semester off. Hmm, I guess there was such thing as karma after all.

Now that I was no longer in Chi Delta, I found that I was able to fill all that extra time very easily. I started going out with Riley a lot more. Our relationship bouncing back to our pre-sorority closeness. Gracie and Vivian were permanent fixtures at our apartment and we started having Wednesday night dinners that quickly morphed into an excuse to chill out and cook lots of food. Jordan's band mates usually came over as well, particularly since Cole and Vivian were still going strong. Damien and a few of his friends sometimes joined and it was amazing to see how I had developed this great group of friends that I didn't have to pay for.

Jordan had spent a lot of time with his band mates, figuring out their tour dates. They were working with Mitch's cousin, Josh, who helped them book thirty shows in Virginia, Maryland and Pennsylvania. They would be playing in bars and small venues.

The guys were excited to try and make a go at living their dream. And I was stoked for them.

I would miss Jordan terribly and I still had those moments of insecurity when I thought girls throwing themselves at him. But I just had to look into my boyfriend's eyes and know that I had nothing to worry about it. You see, Jordan and I were in it for life.

"I have to sell back a few books, do you mind heading over to campus with me? We can grab something to eat at the Canteen," I suggested, putting the last of my clothes in the suitcase and snapping it shut.

"Sure, baby, I just have to text Mitch. We're supposed to have practice at 2:30. You coming with?" he asked me, putting his arm around my waist and pulling me close. He kissed the back of my neck and my body hummed.

"Sure. I haven't seen Viv this week, so we can hang out and talk girlie stuff while our boyfriends play rock gods." I grinned. Jordan rubbed his nose against mine, an affectionate gesture that never failed to make my toes curl.

"You'll make a great rock star wife. I can see it already," he said. My heart sputtered to a stop. Wife? Was he serious? Jordan's smile widened and I knew he could read me like a book. He had always been able to. He kissed me on the lips this time. "One day I'll get a ring on your finger. You just wait and see," he vowed and my heart soared.

We got in Jordan's truck and headed toward Rinard College. Jordan was talking about some new Generation Rejects merchandise that had come in yesterday. I loved seeing him so excited.

"Is it weird knowing you won't be here next year?" I asked him after we pulled up to the campus. I gathered my books off the floor. Jordan took them from me as we got out of the truck.

"Yeah. I mean I'm really excited for the tour. But I have to admit, I'll miss being here with you every day." He tucked a piece of my hair behind my ear. "I'll miss you, Mays. So much," he said softly, his eyes tender as he looked at me.

I cupped his cheek and rubbed my thumb along the rough hair at his jawline. "Me too. But we'll make it work," I promised.

Jordan grabbed my hand and kissed the palm.

"No more running," he stated, grinning at me. I nodded.

"I'm all run out, baby. You caught me fair and square," I replied. Jordan laced his hand with mine and we walked to the bookstore.

I was able to sell my last three books for a whopping $22. Pocketing the money I pulled Jordan by the hand toward the Canteen. "Come on, babe. This wad of money is burning a hole in my pocket. Let me wine and dine you," I joked. Jordan pulled me up against his front and nuzzled into my hair.

"You sure do know how to treat a guy," he teased.

We laughed all the way until we got to the Canteen. We were about to go inside when were stopped by a voice. "Jordan. Maysie. Hey." I saw Jordan's shoulders tense slightly but his face was relaxed. I looked toward the door and saw Olivia coming down the steps.

She looked beautiful as always. But I no longer felt the burning jealousy I used to when we were around each other. Because I had seen the less than perfect girl underneath it all and I sort of felt sad for her. Olivia had flown under the radar the rest of the school year and I had heard through the grapevine that she was moving back home to the state of Washington where she was from, now that she had graduated.

"Hey," I said back politely. Jordan nodded in her direction but didn't say anything. Olivia looked up at him.

"Congrats on the upcoming tour. You'll be great," she said sincerely, giving him a tentative smile.

"Thanks, Liv," he responded, smiling a bit in return.

Seeing the way she stared up at him, I truly did feel bad for her. Because it was painfully obvious that she was still in love with him. Her eyes became soft and her face held a sad sort of wistfulness. It was hard to stay bitter toward someone who had lost the one thing she had wanted most. Lost it and would never get it back.

Olivia looked over at me. "So, how are you doing, Maysie?" she asked. She seemed to struggle with what to say and I knew this was extremely awkward for her.

"Good. How about you? When do you leave?" I asked. Olivia pulled the strap of her purse higher on her shoulder.

"I'm heading out tomorrow. My older brother is coming in tonight with a U-Haul," she explained.

"Oh, well that's great," I said lamely and then we fell into an uncomfortable silence.

"I uh, guess we should be going," I said finally as Jordan and I started to walk around her.

"Wait!" Olivia called out before we were able to go inside. Jordan and I turned back around. Olivia ran back up the steps until she stood in front of us again.

"I just wanted to say...that I'm really, really sorry with everything that happened this year. I had no idea Milla was doing that stuff to you, Maysie. But it's not like I didn't contribute to it all. I was a bitch. A jealous, spiteful bitch." Her eyes glistened with tears as she looked at Jordan again.

"I'm sorry, Jordan. For never treating you the way you deserved to be treated. I'm sincerely glad you've found someone who makes you happy. I really am." She was being genuine and I knew this was hard for her to say. But I really appreciated her saying it all the same.

Jordan squeezed her shoulder. "Thanks, Liv. I'm sorry too. I handled things really badly and I hate myself for hurting you. You're a good person." They looked at each other for a long minute. I stepped back a bit, knowing they needed this closure.

I was surprised to see that I didn't feel jealous or worried. I was just glad to see that these two people, who had been such a huge part of each other's lives, were ending things in a positive way.

Olivia reached out and took Jordan's hand. "Good luck, Jordan. With everything." Jordan let her hold his hand and I saw him smile down at her.

"You too, Liv. I know you'll be conquering the world in no time." Olivia laughed. Not in a flirty, come hither way, but in a way shared by two friends with a long history.

Olivia dropped his hand and stepped back. "Well, you know, one thing at a time." I watched as she discreetly wiped at her eyes and I knew she had teared up at this final goodbye with the boy she had loved for so long.

Looking back over at me, she smiled. "Take care of him, Mays," she said. Jordan had come back to my side and looped his arm around my waist.

"I plan on it," I responded, giving her a wave as she walked away.

Jordan let out a breath and seemed deep in thought. "How are you feeling?" I asked him as we walked inside.

"Good actually. I'm really glad we were finally able to leave things in a way that didn't hurt either of us." He kissed the top of my head. "I'll always care about Olivia. But it's nice to be able to finally leave that in the past so I can focus on my future." His eyes twinkled and I smiled as he leaned down to kiss me.

I thought I'd be rattled after our conversation with Olivia, but instead I felt only a sense of closure. As though the horridness of the last year was finally behind us.

"Let me get lunch, you go grab us a table," Jordan said. I gave him my order and headed over to a small table by the window. I couldn't help but watch the way he moved through the crowd toward the counter. It still blew my mind that this amazingly wonderful guy was mine. That he loved *me*. After everything we went through to get to this place, I knew I wouldn't have changed a thing. Because it all brought me here. To him.

Ten minutes later, Jordan came over with our food and sat down beside me. He pulled his chair as close to mine as he could get, putting his arm across the back. I leaned into him, never able to get enough of his nearness.

Jordan and I ate our lunches while we planned our vacation. Most of it involved lots of time spent in our room. Though sand and surf were on the agenda as well. Jordan pulled out his cell phone and started searching for a scuba school he had read about. He had it in his head that we were going to learn to scuba dive while we were in Mexico. I was less confident about it than he was. You know with the whole sharks could eat you thing. But Jordan was excited, so I guess I could suck it up. For him. I was learning that that wasn't such a bad thing to do.

He clacked his tongue ring against his teeth as he scrolled through a webpage trying to find the information he wanted me to read. He held my hand in his, our fingers intertwined as if they would never be anywhere else.

I became suddenly aware of a group of four girls a few tables away. I looked up and saw them watching us. One girl leaned over to her friend and whispered something and then looked at Jordan and me again. I recognized the looks on their faces. I knew what they thought of me. I had seen it enough times in the last year. And while the gossip and rumors that swirled around campus about me had died off considerably, it was still there.

In that moment, I knew that it didn't matter that Jordan and I loved each other. That we both felt horrible for how things went down. That it was never my intention to hurt Olivia, to hurt her in any way.

All that mattered to those four girls is that I was the slut that broke them up. That I had something that they all not so secretly wanted. The love and devotion of Jordan Levitt. But I was long passed the point when I would have been eaten up with misery at their disdain. Now, I felt empowered.

Looking each girl straight in the eye I slowly lifted my hand and gave them the middle finger. I heard them gasp. They glared at me and continued to whisper even louder. I tried to hide my smile but failed.

Jordan chuckled beside me. I looked over at him and realized he had seen the whole exchange. "What?" I lifted my shoulders in innocence. Jordan just shook his head and lifted our joined hands, kissing the back of my knuckles.

"That's my girl," he said, giving me a look that erased every bad and negative thing that ever had or ever could happen in my life.

Yeah. I was Jordan Levitt's girl. And as I thought about the nasty looks, bad reputation and the way people thought about me, I knew.... that I just didn't give a damn.

ACKNOWLEDGEMENTS

This journey has been incredible and amazing. And there is absolutely no way I could have done it without the love and support of some very special people.

Particularly my wonderful husband, who is the true inspiration for Jordan and all of his kick ass, rock god ways. We met in a bar. He was the sexy, guitar playing Brit and I couldn't resist. Thank you for just being you.

To my gorgeous daughter who is on her way to being such a fantastic human being. You make me proud to be a mom.

To my amazing beta girls, Claire, Michele, Jennie and Julie. Your feedback was essential and you are beyond awesome!

To my supremely talented and so fast it makes my head spin, editor, Tanya Keech. I'm so glad I stumbled across you on Facebook. Your support for this book has been amazing!!!

And finally to the people who read the stuff I write. I'm still a little blown away that you guys want to read my stories. I'm humbled and in awe of your kind words and heartfelt support. Thank you so much for taking a chance on this unknown indie writer and I hope you continue to enjoy the tales I have to tell.

ABOUT THE AUTHOR

A. Meredith Walters has been writing since childhood. She is also the author of the contemporary romance Find You in the Dark as well as Cloud Walking and the sequel Light in the Shadows. She is currently working on the sequel to Bad Rep, Perfect Regret.

Before that she spent over a decade as a children's counselor at both a Domestic/Sexual violence shelter and later an outpatient program for at risk children with severe mental health and behavioral issues. Her clients and their stories continue to influence every aspect of her writing.

Meredith would love to hear from her fans! Follow her on Facebook, Goodreads or Twitter. Or you can email her at ameredithwalters@gmail.com

If you liked this book, please take the time to leave a review where you purchased it. Thank you so much!

This paperback interior was designed and formatted by

www.emtippettsbookdesigns.blogspot.com

Artisan interiors for discerning authors and publishers.

0794

34464337R00211

Made in the USA
Lexington, KY
07 August 2014